The
Baron
AND THE
Enchantress

THE ENCHANTRESSES BOOK THREE

PAULLETT GOLDEN

Cover Design by Fiona Jayde Media
Interior Design by The Deliberate Page

This book contains an excerpt from the forthcoming novel *The Colonel and The Enchantress* by Paullett Golden. This excerpt has been set for this edition only and may not reflect final content of the forthcoming edition.

Also by Paullett Golden

The Enchantresses Series
The Earl and The Enchantress
The Duke and The Enchantress
The Baron and The Enchantress
The Colonel and The Enchantress
The Heir and The Enchantress

The Sirens Series
A Counterfeit Wife

Romantic Encounters
A Dash of Romance
A Touch of Romance

Romantic Flights of Fancy
Hourglass Romance

This book is dedicated to the readers. With you, happy ever after is always possible.

Praise for The Enchantresses

"The author adds a few extra ingredients to the romantic formula, with pleasing results. An engaging and unconventional love story."

— *Kirkus Reviews*

"It is an extremely well written novel with some subplots that add to the already intense main plot. The author Paullett Golden has a gift for creating memorable characters that have depth."

— Paige Lovitt of *Reader Views*

"Paullett Golden specializes in creating charmingly flawed characters and she did not disappoint in this latest enchantress novel."

— *Dream Come Review*

"...a modern sensibility about the theme of self-realization, and a fresh take on romance make the foundation of Golden's latest Georgian-era romance."

— *The Prairies Book Review*

"What a wonderful story! I have read a number of historical fiction romance stories and this is the best one so far! Paullett does a masterful job of weaving so many historical details into her story...."

—*Word Refiner Reviews*

"The novel is everything you could ever want from a story in this genre while also providing surprising and gratifying thematic depth."

—*Author Esquire*

THE ENCHANTRESS FAMILY TREE

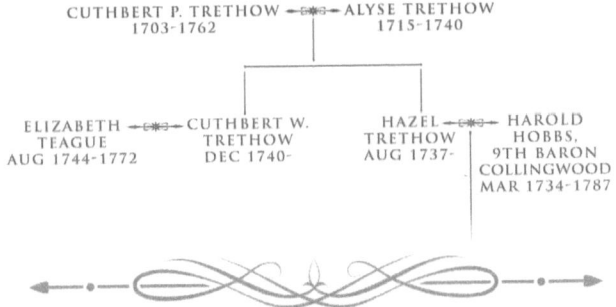

CUTHBERT P. TRETHOW — ✳ — ALYSE TRETHOW
1703-1762   1715-1740

ELIZABETH — ✳ — CUTHBERT W.   HAZEL — ✳ — HAROLD
TEAGUE   TRETHOW   TRETHOW   HOBBS,
AUG 1744-1772   DEC 1740-   AUG 1737-   9TH BARON
                                          COLLINGWOOD
                                          MAR 1734-1787

Visit www.paullettgolden.com/the-enchantresses
to view the complete Enchantress Family Tree

Newly Revised Edition

This book is a clean historical romance. There are references to kissing and innuendos to intimacy, but this is a closed-door romance.

The Baron and The Enchantress was originally published in 2019 as a steamy historical romance but has been fully revised in this new edition as a clean read.

While the original version is still available in audiobook format and by request to the author, all digital and print versions available for purchase have been replaced by this new, clean edition.

If you enjoy reading this book and wish to share it with friends and family, refer with confidence that the version they purchase will be the clean edition. If in doubt, ensure this revision note appears before Chapter 1. I hope you'll enjoy reading the new edition, as this edit has been a labor of love and one I'm proud to share with all readers!

Chapter 1

Miss Lilith Chambers stepped onto the stone bridge, determined. She swallowed against her brewing anxiety.

They would not best her today, she resolved, nor best her again.

She strode across the bridge that separated the village from Sir Eugene's estate, chin held high, spine rigid, bag braced against her chest, and marched more confidently than she felt.

And then she saw them approach.

They saw her.

Her grip tightened around the bag.

Two ladies on horseback cantered down the path ahead. Their bobbing plumes would be comical in any other situation, but Lilith did not laugh. One of the ladies sneered and flicked her reins, urging the mount to pick up the pace.

Lilith hastened her steps. Her quickening stride spurred the ladies to match theirs.

Just as she reached the dirt path at the end of the bridge, the two riders veered towards her. One woman with bouncing blonde ringlets tittered as her mare darted forward, nearly knocking Lilith off her feet. Lilith wobbled backwards onto the muddy riverbank to avoid being trampled.

"I can't imagine what could have startled my horse," said the woman, laughing to her companion.

"Must have been a horsefly," the other woman added.

The ladies continued towards the manor without a backward glance.

Lilith stepped back onto the dirt path, wiping her muddy boots against the stones of the bridge and surveying the damage to her dress. Could be worse, she concluded. Only her dress and shoes were muddied. At least she hadn't careened into the river like last time; and best yet, her bag of midwifery herbs and tools remained clean and safe.

A smile tugged at the corners of her mouth.

She had not given them a wide berth, rather stood her ground. Though they had pushed her off the path when challenged, she smiled that only the concern of being trampled had forced her movement, not the ladies. Orphan or not, Lilith would bow to no one, least of all those leeches who called themselves aristocrats.

She resumed her trek into town with a confident spring in her step, despite the mud-drenched hem of her dress clinging to her half-boots. All in all, a successful morning with the quiet victory at the bridge and before that, the visit to Arbor House, home of Lady Graham.

That morning, Lilith had seen to the health of the twins, not yet one year of age, and to Lady Graham's growing belly, ripe with her third child. Lady Graham was the only blueblood in Allshire who did not treat Lilith as a pariah. Despite Lady Graham's lineage, she respected Lilith, and Lilith esteemed her in return. Since Lilith succeeded where several doctors had previously failed — aiding Lady Graham in carrying a child to term — the woman showed Lilith the utmost deference as the parish's midwife.

The remaining ramble through town could only be described as pleasant with the sun drying the previous three days' worth of rain. The milliner and her husband waved from their shop window as she passed. Other familiar faces smiled their greetings. Even a group of farmers walking out of the Black Bull Inn nodded to her.

Through a lifetime of effort, she had earned her place in the parish as a trusted member of the community.

Just past the church, her cottage stood, a welcoming sight for tired eyes. She loved the cottage with its walled courtyard and herb garden in front, hilly paddock in the back, and wisteria climbing the stone façade of the one-and-a-half-story building. True, it was small with only a single parlor and kitchen, and a set of curved, wooden stairs from the kitchen leading to the bedchamber upstairs, but it was all she needed.

It was home.

Her first order of business was to change into a fresh dress and wash the caked mud before it hardened. At least that was her plan until she saw her visitor.

The Reverend Harold Sands, fourteenth rector of Allshire, paced in the garden. She knew from his agitated state he had waited for some time, as he always did. His brows furrowed over a frown twitching with impatience.

With a sigh, she approached.

"Miss Chambers!" exclaimed the rector, wiping away all evidence of agitation. "What a lucky coincidence you should arrive at the precise moment I decide to call on you." He hurried to greet her at the gate, his youthful face lighting with exaggerated, and feigned, exuberance.

"Yes, a lucky coincidence, I'm sure," Lilith replied, shifting her bag under one arm so she could accept his outstretched hand. "How are you, Harry? Would you like a cup of tea?"

"Your kindness knows no bounds." He released her hand and tugged at his forelock before following her to the stable-door of her cottage.

Lilith opened the door and invited the rector inside, feeling more obligated than cordial. Closing only the bottom half of the stable-door, she left the top open for the breeze and the welcome view of the deep purple wisteria trailing up the terrace wall, not to mention propriety, although no one would question a call from the rector. Setting her bag next to the door, she invited the Reverend Sands to sit at the table while she went to the kitchen to set up a tray.

With a hearty stoking of the dying embers in the kitchen grate, she managed to rouse the remnants enough to heat the kettle. A quick glance to the parlor won her the view of Harold's expectant and watchful visage.

Harold's visits were not daily occurrences, but they felt that way, especially when Lilith had her own plans and little time for his flirtations. While he appeared to believe their union inevitable, she resented his determination to wed her, a determination not based on affection.

"Packed for your adventure?" He raised his voice more than necessary given the short distance from the parlor to the kitchen.

Her eyes trained on the kettle, she said, "I will pack this evening. I leave at first light, so I can no longer procrastinate."

Stealing a handful of currant cakes from the basket she had made for the orphans, she set up the tray.

"I do wish you would reconsider my offer before parting. Think how grand to arrive at your brother's home an engaged woman."

Lilith inhaled through her nose and exhaled through her teeth as she poured the boiling water into the teapot. The tea leaves steeped while she gripped the edge of the counter, answering him with silence.

He did not act the least perturbed by her failure to respond. On the contrary, his eyes twinkled malevolently when she carried the tray to the table. After a dash of milk in his cup, she poured the tea, focusing her eyes on her task rather than his stare.

He had always been her spiritual advisor, the single person to whom she confessed her troubles, but her confessions over the past year had been twisted from spiritual to personal confidences, which was never how she intended them to be taken. Everything she had told him about the recent discoveries of her identity had led to persistent presses for marriage on his part, all in the guise of helping her.

While he might turn out to be a devoted husband, and while she might become content as his wife, she resented his pity and questioned his motives.

"Now, Harry," she admonished lightheartedly. "Let's not revisit that now." Sitting across from him, she hid her displeasure behind a steaming cup.

"You can't possibly be happy at the prospect of spending time with *him*. I know how you feel about aristocracy." He cast her a knowing glance. "And I cannot imagine his wife's family being kind to you." His hand slid across the table to take hers.

She ignored the outstretched hand. "I'm afraid I can't see that," she said, returning her cup to its saucer with a clink. "I'm positive they'll welcome me. I believe they want me there as a family member, not a servant."

At least that was what she hoped.

It had been a shock last year to learn she had a half-brother, the legitimate heir of her father. While she had had the privilege of learning her family identity, which she knew most orphans did not, that privilege had come with the rude discovery that not only had her father been an earl, she had been the by-blow of a premarital affair with a groom's daughter. The only person unperturbed by the details was her half-brother, who was determined to treat her as a legitimate sister regardless of the facts.

"But what of *her* family?" Harold huffed, pulling his hand back to his side of the table. "They're members of the peerage! Has your brother been truthful with them? I cannot believe they would accept an invitation to stay in the same house with you if they knew. Your visit will be a lie, and that is hardly Christian behavior."

Leaning forward in his chair, he tapped his cup with a dirty fingernail.

With another huff, he altered his plea. "Be sensible, Miss Chambers, Lilith, oh, my dearest Lilith," he implored. "Be sensible and marry me so we can remove the impediments to your happiness. If you delayed your departure, we could marry before your visit. You would go as a respectable woman."

"Stop pressing me," she snapped, exasperated. "You're my closest confidante, so I appreciate your offer, but *no*."

He shook his head. "You're not being sensible. Who will offer you what I'm willing to provide? There is not an honorable soul who would offer you marriage, not once they find out you've spent your life in an orphanage." Lowering his voice, he said, "Not once they learn you're illegitimate."

She turned from him, tipping her cup to her lips, a taste of comfort.

He continued unabated, "Your age is no great attribute, either. Three and thirty is not an attractive age, Lilith. Men marry for breeding, and you're past your bloom."

Ire heated her cheeks in what might have been mistaken as a blush if not accompanied by her pursed lips. Although she knew the truth of his words, she hated that he held her past over her head like the sword of Damocles. Could he not admit undying love, woo her like a proper suitor? No, he would not feel the need to woo an aging spinster of questionable birth. From his perspective, he offered her an irresistible proposition.

She traded her teacup for a currant cake but only tasted her frustration.

"Can't you see what I'm offering?" The rector laid a clammy hand on her arm. "I only wish to help. Let me care for you. I will not hold these facts of your life against you as other men will."

No, he would never woo her like a proper suitor. He wanted her to believe the offer an honor, for he, a respected man of God, was willing to look past her faults and provide her security and a home. Had he not already proven his willingness by letting the cottage to her? Oh, but she could not live daily with the look of pity in his eyes. Then, it was not pity that motivated his offer.

Glaring at his hand with its spindly fingers tightening around her forearm, she suspected she knew his motive. She swallowed against the suspicion, such an unchristian notion to have of a man of the cloth, but she could not help using it as a shield against his so-called honorable intentions.

Lilith remembered vividly her confessions to the clergyman of her brother's wealth and the sizable donation he gave to the orphanage earlier that year. There had been little doubt of the rector's intentions when persistent offers of marriage began within days of her confessions about a promised inheritance, a dowry, even an estate to do with as she pleased. Such generosity of coin could not be ignored by a rector.

Her stomach lurched at the thought of her spiritual advisor and the pillar of the community being so conniving. He wanted her for the titled affiliation and for the promise of wealth beyond measure at the behest of her brother.

Straightening her spine and freeing her arm from his grasp, she looked into his beady eyes. "Your offer is kindness itself, Mr. Sands, but I must decline. If your offer is sincere, you will give me time to accustom myself to my family."

She wanted to throw the tea in his face.

Her better judgement won. Unless she truly wished to anger the parish rector, an act that would ostracize her from the community, she was obligated to show kindness and consideration.

They sat in lingering silence, the rector tracing a finger around the edge of his cup, steam encircling his hand. All sounds were magnified in the silence, even the clomping of a horse moving past the cottage, wafting in the scent of sweaty horseflesh. Lilith wrinkled her nose, finding it an appropriate aroma for the conversation. After all, his offer reeked.

Finally, he broke the silence with a cheerful smile and change of subject. "Who is covering your position at the orphanage while you're away?"

Lilith favored his question with a return smile to reassure him of her good spirits and friendship. "Miss Tolkey will serve as both the orphanage's teacher and the parish's midwife in my absence. I believe she's looking forward to both tasks. She even pressed me to extend my stay." Lilith forced a chuckle.

"Good. Miss Tolkey is a perfect substitute." He paused before adding, "If they treat you with disdain, send me word, and I will renew my offer."

"Thank you. You are too kind, Harry." She emphasized his name, hoping to smooth over any earlier displays of irritation. Her livelihood in Allshire depended on him. "My brother has made ample effort to get to know me. I look forward to this opportunity to be part of a family and piece together the memories of my childhood." She spoke truthfully albeit understatedly.

"Well, then, there is nothing more to be said." The Reverend Sands stood to leave, his tea untasted and his currant cake untouched. "I wish you all the best and will count the days until your return. I promise to mind the orphanage in your absence."

He took her hand between both of his before turning to the door and departing, leaving Lilith to wonder which would be more unpleasant — spending time with Harold Sands or spending over a month in a house with aristocrats, who, despite her brother's best efforts, may refuse to acknowledge the presence of an illegitimate.

Even this far inland, the two gentlemen could hear the cries of the kittiwakes along the coast. The site for the new coal mine was busy with construction, the laborers taking advantage of the good weather after several days of hard rain, which fortunately left the earth soggy for easy digging. Soon, this area would teem with the bustle of mining.

It was astounding how much his cousin's husband had accomplished. Granted, the man had a good decade's head start in terms of running an estate and lands, but if Walter were to be fully honest, even with a decade's practice, he could not possibly live up to the standard this man set.

Walter's companion broke his reverie with a single raised eyebrow of inquisition when the two reached the horses on the outskirts of the mine site.

"I think you've made a fine decision," said Walter Hobbs, Baron Collingwood, as if he knew anything about mining.

He mounted his horse for the ride back to his cousin's home.

Sebastian Lancaster, Earl of Roddam, nodded, mounting his own horse. "Thank you for coming to see the site, Collingwood. I'm convinced that with the brewing trouble in France and the threat of war, a coal mine will prove a profitable investment."

"I envy your head for business, Roddam. I hope to learn a thing or two from you this summer," Walter admitted, indeed envious of everything he had seen of Lord Roddam's properties.

He did not so much envy what Roddam had as his savvy and dedication, neither trait Walter could claim for himself.

Roddam led his horse onto the path for home. "My struggle is with the air circulation. After all the research I've conducted in the drift mine method, I'm positive a deep pit is the best choice, but I refuse to send men down until I've resolved the problem. My father-in-law promises to offer advice on safety measures from his tin mining experience."

For the opening stretch back to the castle, Walter listened to Roddam explain his plans for the mine, responding with questions that showed an appropriate amount of curiosity, despite his ignorance on the topic.

The time he spent with the Earl of Roddam could not have come at a more opportune moment, for

Walter admired the man, learning from him what should have been learned years prior from his father, if he had bothered to listen instead of being wayward. That Roddam was younger than Walter did not bother him. The man was a genius in Walter's opinion.

Walter, his mother Hazel, and his uncle Cuthbert had all been in Northumberland for the past month visiting Cuthbert's two daughters, Lizbeth and Charlotte. The family could not be prouder of the marriages of the two sisters, Charlotte to the Duke of Annick and Lizbeth to the duke's cousin, the Earl of Roddam. After spending a month with the duke and duchess, Walter and his family relocated fifteen miles to stay with Lizbeth and her husband.

It had taken Walter the past year to accustom himself to his cousins being wives of peers instead of the Cornish country girls he knew and loved, and now he had to accustom himself to Lizbeth's upcoming motherhood.

While the trip had been planned the previous year for only the summer months, they all agreed to extend their stay through Lizbeth's confinement and the first few months after baby's arrival, at least until late autumn when they would head home to Devonshire, or in Uncle Cuthbert's case, to Cornwall. Walter knew Uncle Cuthbert would be in no hurry to leave since all he could talk about was becoming a grandpapa.

The visit, thus far, had proved a hearty family reunion full of joy and happiness. Walter could not remember a time when he had been happier, at least not since his father died. There had been so much emptiness, so much restlessness since his father died that Walter relished having the family together.

His companion turned to him, their horses trotting side-by-side. "Given any more consideration to the Sierra Leon Company or the slave abolition bill since our conversation?" Roddam enquired.

Walter's smile faltered. He had. He did not want to turn down an opportunity to work closely with his uncle or Roddam, but Walter did not think these endeavors were for him. These were projects close to his uncle's heart, not his own.

"Don't think me ungrateful for the offer or disinterested in helping. You know I'm a philanthropist at heart, but I don't see either as my legacy," Walter said.

"I understand. Say no more. Our invitation stands, as we could use your insight." Roddam paused to consider him. "Only you can decide where your heart lies, but have you thought on the satisfaction to be had in running your estate? The people need you."

Walter slumped in his saddle.

When he made no reply, Roddam continued, "You're not wrong in wanting to enterprise outside the home. Never base your stability on agrarian and tenant management alone. I've seen firsthand how a poor season can destroy lives. Personally, I've invested the profits of my lands in industry. Our peers may thumb their nose at new money while living off their family coffers, but they're fools. I don't wish to overstep my bounds, Collingwood, but have you studied your ledgers to see how the money is being spent?"

"It's not about the money. I know I need to understand the accounts, but I've never been good with figures. I'd prefer to let the steward run the estate so I can funnel my efforts into making my mark. I simply haven't decided how. Build a shipping company? Patron a hospital? Create a pleasure garden? The ideas are plentiful. The logistics, however, are daunting."

"Ah, I see," Roddam replied. "And you don't find the people dependent on you for their livelihood a worthy enough cause?"

Walter grimaced. "I can't fill my father's shoes, but I do want to make a difference." How could he explain himself without sounding listless? "I never wanted this title, at least not until my fiftieth birthday. I'm not ready, no readier than I was last year or the year before. Mama isn't helping matters with her determination to get me leg-shackled. It is her belief that with the right woman, I will stop dreaming of causes and settle into taking over estate business."

"I take that to mean no marriage prospects on the horizon."

"I told myself after Papa died that once I felt secure enough with the barony, I'd search for a bride, but it's dashed unpleasant. I'm getting to be an embarrassing age for a bachelor. And now, Mama is bent on finding me a bride. She has thrown me at every eligible lady, or more to the point every able-bodied woman with a matchmaking mama on friendly terms with her. All the girls are addlebrained, simpering, and attached at the hip to their mothers."

Roddam nodded sympathetically but failed to suppress his mirth. "And now you understand why, for years, I declined all invitations until my cousin had to take a bride. If you hadn't introduced us to your cousins, I suspect we'd both still be bachelors, or at least I know I would."

"Well, I'm not getting any younger, as Mama points out." Walter harrumphed. "Each year it is more awkward, for while I get older, the girls stay the same age. It's unsettling trying to carry on conversations with them, all fresh out of the schoolroom. Bleak, I tell you. Maybe if I wait another ten years, I'll change my tune and find their youth refreshing."

"No sense in rushing marriage, Collingwood." Roddam led his horse around a long and muddy rut in the road. "If you've no pressing reason to marry, wait for the right woman. I can tell you from experience, she is worth the wait."

"You're fortunate to have found her. And now you'll have an heir on top of matrimonial bliss."

Roddam laughed. "You assume baby will be a boy, I see."

"Don't you hope for a boy?"

"I couldn't give two snaps if the children are all girls, all boys, or wild urchins. Lizbeth and I only hope to fill the nursery." Pressing his tricorn more firmly to shield against the strong gusts of wind, Roddam added, "I have never known happiness, Collingwood, not until I met Lizbeth. I want to give our children all the love I never had. And I most assuredly want to give our firstborn a sibling, something I was robbed of at an early age. The more siblings the better, I say."

They lapsed into momentary silence. Walter took in the rolling hills of browning heather and the sparse copse of trees in the dale, leaves rustling in the gusty breeze.

His cousin could not have made a more perfect match, Walter knew. They were both untamed, both too intelligent for their own good, and both full of enough love to make a herd of children very happy indeed. He wondered what his own perfect match would be like.

Roddam leaned towards Walter and said *sotto voce*, "I'll be honest, and don't you dare tell my son if baby is a boy, but I'm secretly hoping our first is a girl." He righted himself in the saddle, smiling conspiratorially.

"If your wish comes true, and she even remotely resembles Lizbeth as a baby, she'll have her papa wrapped around her fingers," Walter ribbed.

"I hope all our girls take after their mother. Heaven forbid they inherit my nose." Roddam bellowed a hearty laugh, his Roman nose prominent above a wide smile.

The pair continued their ride to the castle, the terrain flattening, transforming the hilly country-side into moors and then marshland as they reached the coast. A fierce wind whipped around the riders, pushing against them before circling back to tug them forward. Walter burrowed into his coat. Although the air was warm with no signs of autumn, the wind off the North Sea stung with a sharp chill.

The stone curtain of Dunstanburgh Castle came into sight. Much of the castle was still in rubble from a bygone age, but the earl had restored the keep into a home, a combination of its former glory and his own personal preferences. While Walter preferred his own humble estate in Exeter to this formidable castle, he was awed at Roddam's devotion to rebuilding the ruins.

As the horses followed the path around the meres and to the outer gatehouse, Roddam announced without preamble, "Lilith should arrive tomorrow."

"I look forward to learning more about your sister."

And indeed, he did. Who would not want to learn about a long-lost sister who had only recently been reunited with her brother? The estrangement and reunion were enough to make anyone insatiably curious, but what truly piqued curiosity were the stories Roddam had regaled the family with since their arrival.

Although Lord Roddam had not seen his sister since he was a child, he clearly cherished those memories. For over two decades, Roddam had thought his sister dead, he had told them, only to discover that his father had lied to cover up sending the child to an orphanage around the same time as their mother's death. The cruelty was astonishing.

"Lizbeth has been practicing her argument for why Lilith should move in with us permanently," Roddam said, laughter in his voice. "You'll love her, Collingwood. Everyone will."

"Lizbeth says your sister is a midwife?"

"Yes, she's quite adept it would seem. Have I mentioned she also teaches at the orphanage? Earlier this year, before the London Season, we made a week's trip for the talent show and concert, all arranged by the orphanage. Nothing makes Liz feel maternal like a room full of children singing, I tell you."

"She also directs the choir, then?" he asked.

"Oh, no, actually, she teaches mathematics, but I believe since there are so few teachers, she may teach additional classes. You'll have to ask her when she arrives. Don't laugh, but she's promised to look over my figures for the coal mine. Not what you'd expect to see two siblings doing, is it?" Roddam dismounted at the front gate.

A groom jogged to them to take the horses back to the stable.

"Nothing about you surprises me anymore, Roddam, so I imagine not much will surprise me about your sister," Walter confessed before dismounting and handing the reins to the groom.

"I'll take that as a compliment, my good man." He patted Walter's back and headed for the wicket door his butler held open.

Walter found it humbling that he was three years older than Lord Roddam, he five and thirty and the other man two and thirty, yet he felt at least a decade younger in experience.

Roddam had lived a hard life before gaining his title at a relatively young age. He had then spent much of his adulthood rebuilding the depleted coffers of his estates and repairing the poverty-stricken lands he had inherited from a tyrannical father. Walter, on the other hand, had only ever known a happy family with a small, but prosperous barony.

He wondered what it must be like to find happiness after so much pain. Even Roddam's sister had suffered gravely. At least, he assumed she had, for being raised in an orphanage apart from one's family and station in life sounded like misery to Walter. Nothing could be more life changing than discovering one was not a homeless orphan, but a Lady Lilith, daughter of the deceased Earl and Countess of Roddam, sister to the sixteenth Earl of Roddam. It must be quite a relief for her, he mused, to have a relation to support her at last. No lady should be forced into employment.

All his own troubles diminished in comparison. Perhaps it really was time to take responsibility for his barony instead of whiling away the days dreaming up lost causes. But he could worry about that another day.

Chapter 2

The air crackled with anticipation. To pass the morning before Lady Lilith's arrival, the family gathered in the gazebo on the cliffside of the castle grounds, picnicking in the shade.

Walter sat on a stone bench with his mother Hazel. He wore his finest tailored walking attire, aiming to make a welcoming impression on Lady Lilith. His mother wore a silk day dress with matching parasol and bonnet. They were both dressed to impress. Normally, he would not have noticed what his mother was wearing, but today the two of them could not have stood out more if they tried.

Roddam, Lizbeth, and Uncle Cuthbert were not dressed to impress, to say the least.

Although Walter had accustomed himself to the unusual ways of Roddam and Lizbeth, their daily nose-thumbing at decorum never ceased to amaze him. The two had situated themselves on the floor of the gazebo to enjoy the picnic and were in various stages of undress.

Lord Roddam wore breeches, shirt, waistcoat, cravat, and stockings, noticeably devoid of coat and shoes. Lizbeth was not much better dressed in a simple cotton dress and stockings but without shoes or adornments. Uncle Cuthbert, at least, was fully dressed but in an outmoded country fashion that had not seen London streets in over a decade, if indeed such country fare had ever seen the likes of London.

Their state of dress, or undress rather, was enough to cause a scandal. Walter should not be the least bit surprised since Liz had always been a bit wild and had married a man as wild, if not wilder, but it still made for a strange sight. Yet here the family gathered, incongruous in dress and behavior.

Not that he was a stickler for decorum, but he was embarrassed to think Lady Lilith would be greeted thusly by her own brother and sister-in-law.

He rubbed the back of his neck.

He had never actually seen a woman's feet before. And Lizbeth's stockinged feet with ankles bared below the hem of her dress, as if they had a mind of their own, discomfited him.

To make the day more peculiar, Roddam had not arranged any sort of fanfare for his sister's arrival. Walter would have expected a servant to be watching for the coach so they could welcome her in a receiving line, but when he mentioned this, he earned a laugh, a pat on the back, and a reply that instructed him to go back to the Duke of Annick's estate if he wished for ceremony.

And so instead they all picnicked, enjoying the salty air, the song of the kittiwakes, and the view of the ocean which rolled a deep shade of emerald with pearly froth.

"I will be heard," his mother was saying. "Ignore me if you wish, but I will be heard. You must not remain in the open air any longer. I'll escort you to the castle, Lizbeth." Hazel frowned at her niece.

"When I had my lie-in, I was confined to the bed without the intrusion of light for a full month. The accoucheur visited weekly for bloodletting. And look how healthy Walter turned out." She patted her son's hand.

Lizbeth smiled, her hands stroking her round belly. "I've agreed to follow my midwife's instructions. Lilith knows her business. I'm under strict orders to walk in the sun every day, and I wouldn't dare anger her with disobedience."

Hazel clucked. "Just what you need — more freckles. You shouldn't be walking in the sun at all. I can't think any of this is healthy for your condition. Sister-in-law or not, are you positive of her credentials?"

Cuthbert replied to his sister Hazel in a Cornish accent, "Our Lizzie needs no excuse for a day in the sun. It strikes me she would have interviewed a dozen midwives until she found the one to give her permission to do what she willed."

The family bickered playfully, unaware for some time that the butler was escorting a woman from the castle. Walter saw the pair first and would have announced their approach had he not been struck dumb.

Nothing seemed out of the ordinary, simply a woman walking down the slope between keep and cliffside, bracing against the wind, a hand held to her bonnet. But then she drew closer and looked up, her eyes meeting his for the briefest of seconds.

At first, he felt her more than saw her. His body tingled; his stomach somersaulted; his thoughts fled.

Walking towards him strode the most breathtakingly handsome woman he had ever seen. She towered above the butler in height, likely only a few inches shorter than himself, or at least he suspected from this distance. This was no simpering girl who approached the picnic, rather a confidently poised woman with ample hips and a lithe form.

She was undoubtedly Roddam's sister, for she bore his features, but she did wondrous magic to the shared likeness. Beneath the unadorned straw bonnet, her hair, black as night and plaited down her back, slipped free from the braid a strand at a time to whirl about her in the wind. Brushing the wisps from her face, she revealed a slender visage with an aquiline nose over full, naturally red lips.

She was not the least bit pretty, to be honest. In fact, she was unfashionably the opposite of pretty. Yet, instead of being homely, she was remarkably, austerely…handsome. Regal was the word that came to Walter's mind. In place of her sprigged dress, he imagined her bedecked with crown, jewels, and furs, for never had he witnessed a more noble brow.

Before he could stop himself, he stood and walked towards her, drawn to her as though bewitched. Her eyes lit on his once more, captivating him. They were as dark as her hair, full of wisdom and silent humor, laughing at the world, and likely at him. A swirl of breeze brought her scent to his nostrils, intoxicating him with a mixture of sweat and earth, a heady aroma of *woman* rather than perfume. Who was this enchantress?

A figure raced past him then, breaking the sorcery. Lord Roddam flew at his sister in a laughter-filled roar, embracing her indelicately by lifting her in the air and spinning her in circles. Her laughter mingled with her brother's. Walter stared, transfixed.

The greeting was alarming, hardly appropriate between a lady and a gentleman, even if they were siblings. He supposed their behavior made sense in this strange world in which he found himself, a world of barefoot earls and dark-eyed sirens.

With a nod of appreciation to the butler, Roddam escorted her the remaining steps, one arm wrapped around her shoulders.

"Collingwood, my good man. Allow me the great honor of introducing my sister Lilith," Roddam said, his voice proud. "And may I present to you Walter, Lord Collingwood?"

Walter stepped forward, taking her outstretched hand. He bowed over it as deeply as he would if she were a queen or, more aptly, Circe herself. He touched his lips to the air above her knuckles.

"Lady Lilith. It is an honor," Walter said, hoping the howling of the wind drowned out the pounding of his heart.

Their eyes met.

With a straight spine, she held his gaze steady. He could not read her eyes. He could not read anything about her.

She curtsied. "Miss Chambers, my lord, or Lilith, if you prefer."

His knees weakened.

Had she truly given him permission to use her Christian name? And with such a voice? Her voice was a sultry, husky velvet. Dear Lord in Heaven.

The pair moved past him so that Roddam could introduce her to the rest of the family. Walter remained planted, growing roots while facing the wrong direction. The warmth from her hand lingered in his. With eyes closed, he memorized her aroma, her touch, her voice, her face.

Could this be it? Could this be love at first sight? Fleetingly, he wondered if it was too soon to propose.

Lilith sat next to her sister-in-law, listening attentively to Lizbeth's full report of her dutifully followed regimen of walks, naps, and herbal teas. Only half an hour had passed since her arrival, but already Lilith felt she belonged. Lizbeth treated her as a sister, and Sebastian could not stop smiling at her.

The whole scene felt wonderful.

In fact, the only impediment to her present happiness was the pair of stuffed shirts sitting on the bench gawking at her. The young man was everything she despised. A refined gentleman, an aristocrat through and through, not precisely dandified, but undeniably impeccable in manner and dress.

As Lizbeth chattered to her, Lilith found her eyes flitting back to the man. Lord Collingwood.

He hailed from *that* world, a world full of hate and pride, a world where ladies ran over commoners with their horses without a backward glance and men abandoned their unwanted daughters.

If he had been a Mr. Collingwood, and if he had been dressed in as casual attire as the other men in the party, she would have found him attractive. Green eyes the shade of jade surrounded by long eyelashes, a gracefully lean physique with the faint scent of cologne, and cherubic curls a becoming russet color, red more than brown in the bright sun.

Long sideburns framed an angelic face with smooth cheeks and alabaster complexion. He was, in a word, beautiful.

If he did not wear his peerage on his sleeve, she would find him unquestionably attractive, kissably attractive, in fact; but, alas, she disliked both him and his mother on sight.

She straightened her posture in response to their stares. They would not ruffle her feathers. They would not discompose her. This holiday was for her to help Lizbeth during her confinement and to spend more time with her brother. Nothing could wreck that for her. If they did not like her, *they* could leave.

Lady Collingwood, wearing a haughty expression and fashionable attire wholly out of place for a picnic, pointed a gloved finger at Lilith. "I've a bone to pick with you, young lady."

Lilith bristled.

"My niece says you've been encouraging this reckless behavior of being in the open air in her current condition." The woman scoffed.

"You are not wrong, my lady. I stand by my advice, however archaic it may seem to you. The physician's way, if you'll pardon my saying, is as slippery as a cod walloper."

"Archaic," Lady Collingwood muttered with a harrumph. "Well, I've never heard of this sunshine prescription."

Lilith clenched her jaw but forced a smile. "Trust me to take care of your niece. I know what I'm about."

Lizbeth chimed in, "With or without permission, I would refuse to waste a perfectly lovely day indoors. Have you ever seen a more beautiful day?"

A deep voice answered, "She's the most beautiful I've seen."

All eyes turned to the speaker — Lord Collingwood. He was staring at Lilith.

When he realized they were all looking at him, the tips of his ears reddened. "The day, that is," he stammered. "She's a beautiful day. That is to say, if the day were personified —"

Lady Collingwood interrupted, "It's perfectly understandable to be tongue-tied, my boy. We shouldn't be speaking so openly of delicate conditions."

He rubbed the back of his neck, the redness of his ears spreading to his cheeks.

What a peculiar young man, Lilith thought.

She looked to her sister-in-law, ready to defend herself further if needed, but behind Liz's cheery disposition, Lilith could see her fatigue. As much as she dared not admit it aloud, Lady Collingwood was right. Not entirely, but in so far as Liz's being outside too long.

Holding Lizbeth's hand in hers, she said to the group, "I am thankful for the warm welcome, but I fear I am worn from the trip. Would you all mind excusing me for a brief repose? I do believe I shall take our hostess with me for a private word about herbs."

Rising, Sebastian said, "Rest as long as you would like, Lilith. We won't expect you until dinner." He leaned in and whispered for her ears only, "See that my wife rests. She listens to your sage advice more than she listens to my nattering."

As Sebastian helped his wife to her feet, Lord Collingwood rose from the bench and rushed over to assist.

Looking at Lilith rather than his cousin, he said, "Allow me to escort you both."

Lizbeth patted his cheek. "Aren't you gallant! Thank you, but we'll manage."

The remaining party members joined them at the edge of the gazebo, all agreeing to return to the castle anyway, following shortly behind Lilith and her charge.

Leaving the troupe downstairs, Lilith saw Lizbeth to the bedchamber.

Having visited on numerous occasions through-out Liz's pregnancy, Lilith slipped into the routine of caretaker, seeing to the comfort and health of her sister-in-law before her own. This role gave her a sense of purpose. She could not imagine the discomfort that may come from being only a guest, waited on by servants, pampered by the host and hostess, treated like the lady she was not.

After settling Liz into bed and adding her own herbs to the tea the countess' lady's maid brought, Lilith turned to leave.

"Wait," Liz called out. "I'll have a maid sent to help you refresh and change for dinner. You'll find a few dresses in the armoire. Whatever doesn't fit, we can have altered, but I thought you may like them. You'd look especially lovely in the green, I think."

"Thank you, but no," Lilith countered. "I've never had a maid and don't intend to make a habit of one. I brought enough dresses for the visit."

With a smile, she departed for her own guest room.

The dresses were tempting, as she only owned four, all sewn by herself. Giving into such a temptation, however, would inspire ideas above her station.

Her own dresses might be well-worn, but she would rather wear them than play dress-up in silks and satins designed for a member of the peerage.

The guest rooms were on the second floor of the south wing. Lilith made her way to the second floor of the north wing, instead. Sebastian and Lizbeth had once insisted she stay in the guest wing, but since Lilith visited for the purpose of serving as midwife, it made more sense for her to reside in the nursery. In this way, she would be on hand after baby's arrival to care for both baby and mother.

The nursery stretched across the entire second floor of the north wing, consisting of a playroom, nurse's quarters, sleeping quarters, and several empty rooms still awaiting designation, all intended for future children. Windows lined the north and south walls of the wing, one side looking out to the beach and the other down to the inner courtyard. Before making her way to the nurse's quarters, Lilith admired the changes they had made since her previous visit.

The playroom's décor was sea themed with a gilded frieze of mermaids bordering the room and an underwater mural with the top half depicting the horizon at dawn and the bottom half a seascape with sea castles, sea creatures, and Poseidon with his trident. She imagined a child being happy here, for the love and attention that went into designing this wing shown evidently in each detail.

Walking to the mural, she touched the image of Aphrodite born on the sea foam at the horizon of the painting. She trailed her fingers along the textured waves until she reached seahorses swimming with nymphs. Lilith stopped at one of the underwater sandcastles, a memory tugging at the edges of her mind.

The longer she stared at the sandcastles, the stronger images from her childhood superimposed on the painting, slipping her into a poignant memory as vivid as though she were present in that scene rather than in a nursery.

The woman she believed at the time to be her mother pinned a new bonnet to young Lilith's hair. Lilith couldn't have been more than five years old in this memory. The woman who raised her, Sebastian's mother, beamed at her, adjusting the bonnet.

"Dance for me, my love," she instructed. "Let us see how becoming you look in your bonnet."

Eager to please, young Lilith twirled in place, curtsying, then filling the room with giggles.

"You look like a little princess," the woman said, her smile faltering when the door to the lady's dressing room opened and hit the wall with a *thud*.

Young Lilith looked up, tentatively stepping forward to the scowling man. "Papa? Do you like my new bonnet?"

The man crossed the room with heavy steps, reached out to Lilith, and ripped off the bonnet, yanking out the hair that had been pinned to the silk. Before he said a word, Lilith ran from the room, tears blurring her vision, her scalp burning from the pulled hair.

She ran blindly back to the nursery to find Sebastian riding a rocking horse, a boy intent on riding across the great plains of the nursery to rescue the dolls in distress.

Lilith tugged at her brother's sleeve, and without her having to say a word, he understood. His youthful eyes met her own red-rimmed ones, and he knew exactly what to do. He took her hand in his, slipped past the dozing nurse, and together they sneaked out of the estate to enjoy an afternoon at the beach, their private oasis from the wicked hand of their father.

That day, they built a grand sandcastle, so tall it reached the sky with rooms large enough to fit three countries' worth of toys. They lived in the sandcastle for the rest of the day, each taking turns to describe what they would do in every room and who would be invited to call. In Sebastian's favorite room, lived an elephant, visited daily by monkeys. Lilith's favorite room housed a troupe of acrobats who danced on her command.

They lived in the sandcastle until the tide lapped at its walls. Lilith transformed into a mermaid, forsaking her human form to join the creatures of the sea. Sebastian pledged allegiance to Poseidon, desirous to serve as the guardian of mermaids. Lilith put in a good word for him. They played in harmony until their sandcastle became ammunition for a mud fight. Not once before they returned home, a muddy and wet sight, did they think of their father, but they certainly did after the footprints in the entry hall gave them away.

Lilith let the memory wash over her, one of the few she still carried from before the orphanage, one of the many combining torment with happiness. Her fingers still touching the sandcastle on the mural in the nursery, she shook her mind free of the past.

At dinner that evening, Lilith straightened her spine at finding herself the center of attention. All at the table were curious about her.

"You say you *teach*?" Lady Collingwood asked with derision, or at least her question sounded derisive to Lilith, who knew to expect little else from aristocrats.

"Yes, I teach mathematics. Although, since there are so few willing to teach at an orphanage, we take turns instructing those subjects in which we do not naturally excel. Miss Tolkey and I, for instance, alternate the weeks we teach dancing, she instructing on the first and third week of the month, and I on the second and fourth." Lilith stared at Lady Collingwood as she tasted the soup, daring Her Ladyship to speak derogatorily.

"Instructing orphans in *dancing*? This is quite a progressive orphanage, I daresay. Do orphans dance often when they mature?" Lady Collingwood laughed as she asked her nosy questions, but Lilith could not decide if she laughed at the prospect of orphans dancing or laughed with good will that orphans were trained for more than the workhouse.

The lines around the lady's mouth and the crinkles around her eyes indicated she laughed often, a merry woman, yet Lilith doubted the *haut ton* did more than laugh *at* people, so she found the woman difficult to read.

Lilith pursed her lips and set down her soup spoon. She prepared to defend her home against this woman if need be.

"Mrs. Brighton, God rest her soul, opened the orphanage some fifty years ago with the fiscal aid of the parish church," Lilith explained. "She used church facilities at the time. After a generous bene-factor donated a sizable enough amount, a two-story building was erected next to the church to both house and teach the children. There is talk from the current headmistress, Mrs. Copeland, of expanding with a foundling hospital. Our rector, the Reverend Harold Sands, is most supportive of the expansion."

Lilith paused to taste her wine, hoping it would strengthen her resolve to defend what she held dear against potential naysayers, namely the Lady Colling-wood, who was asking most of the questions. Though, she might need to defend against her son, as well, for while he had yet to say a word during dinner, he had not stopped staring at her.

She continued, "Mrs. Brighton believed in a God-loving orphanage rather than a God-fearing one. She wanted a place where children, ranging from those discarded from illegitimate births to those left behind after their parents' death, could be educated in much the same manner had they tutors and gov-ernesses. In addition, children were apprenticed to work in positions within Allshire and surrounding parishes. We are unlike most facilities which either rule with an iron fist or ship off the children, even as young as seven years old, to cotton mills or other horrid places for slave labor."

Footmen brought in the second course, inadver-tently interrupting her. Instead of placing the dishes at the table, the footmen set up various plates and bowls along a sideboard at the side of the dining room.

Sebastian stood and said, "Help yourselves. As you all know, we don't stand on ceremony here. Fill your plate with as little or as much as you would like but do please save room. Cook has arranged a cornucopia of delectable desserts."

They each rose and explored the table of delights. To Lilith's surprise, Lord Collingwood stepped next to her and held out his hand. She stared at it.

"May I plate for you, Miss Chambers?" he asked.

Caught off guard, she could not think of an excuse fast enough. She nodded, setting her lips in a line of displeasure. Did he think her incapable of filling her own plate, or was this some sort of gentlemanly act?

She stood for a moment, unsure of what to do while he filled her plate. This close, his eyelashes seemed longer and darker, especially in contrast to his alabaster skin. Such a beautiful man, even if he was an aristocrat. When he inclined his head to her chair, she hastened to sit, if for no other reason than to avert her eyes from his eyelashes.

Not long did she wait until he set the plate before her chair and smiled, his eyes twinkling in the candlelight. *Oh my*, she thought, arrested by the genuineness of the smile. Her heart caught in her throat. No aristocrat had the right to be this charming, not when she hated the lot of them — with the exception of her brother and his wife, of course.

Once they were all seated and enjoying the meat dishes, Lizbeth said, "Continue, Lilith. You were telling us about the education at the orphanage."

Lilith sampled the fish before answering. "Yes, well, for much of their education, we teach them what ladies and gentlemen would be taught from tutors and governesses — embroidery, comportment, elocution, dancing, French, Italian, and Latin for languages, geography, mathematics, and so forth. They do not want for accomplishments, I assure you."

"But to what end?" asked Lady Collingwood.

"Much depends on the circumstances of their enrollment. Some arrive with their stay paid by a benefactor, usually anonymous in the cases of illegitimate children," Lilith began.

She said these words without a hint of bitterness, regardless of the circumstances that brought her to Allshire. Unlike many of the children whose stay was only minimally paid, her father had funded her admission to the orphanage beyond room and board, even including the sizable donation that had allowed the extension of the building and several years' worth of supplies. If he had not been the ruthless man she knew he was, one might mistake him for generous, caring even.

She continued, "Some children, however, arrive without support and are thus dependent on the church's funding until they can be apprenticed for work. In the case of the legitimate children who lost parents, their futures still hold promise, as they could, with the right training, go into a respectable business or secure advantageous marriages."

Defense of the orphanage against a nosy peer had become pride in her home and identity. For a reason she could not say, she wanted her dinner companions to understand how rare and wonderful was the place she grew up and now resided.

"We want to afford them all the best opportunities, so we train for every eventuality." Lilith admitted,

"I will say, most of the children are apprenticed for work, such as farming, blacksmithing, millinery, and so forth. It is a rarity they marry well, are adopted by relatives, or find lucrative prospects, but we can boast of a few cases. Jerome, for instance, has recently written to inform us he is now a solicitor in London. Isn't that grand?"

The din assented in his good fortune. She wondered if any of them saw the irony of rejoicing in a workingman's employment when no one at the table aside from her had worked a day in their life.

Lord Collingwood spoke, then, his green eyes trained on her with inquisitiveness. "Do the children ever meet their parents or learn about them? You mentioned some are adopted by relatives."

Lilith remembered the evening dreamscapes. The children exchanged stories of what life might be like should their parents come back for them, should they discover they were really princes and princesses in hiding, should a long-lost relation search high and low for them to reunite the family. Those stories were the dreams of hopeful and lonely souls sharing a single room with dozens of other hopeful and lonely souls.

Those dreams were not reality.

"Only rarely, my lord," Lilith answered. "Orphans wonder about their parents more than they ever learn about them. And even if they should learn, who is to say they would like what they hear? Imagine a child who dreams of being a lost prince only to learn he's the son of a ravished woman turned out by her family from shame, who then discarded him to seek employment at a house of ill repute."

When she saw him flinch, she realized she over-stepped the boundaries of genteel conversation.

"Pardon my bluntness. I hope not to put off anyone from their dinner, but there is little delicacy when speaking of the lives of orphans. If you ask, you should be prepared for the answer."

After a moment of silence, Lord Collingwood spoke again. "And you? How has the newfound knowledge of your parentage affected you?"

Her cutlery paused midair. A remarkable question. But how to answer?

Not only was he the first to ask that question, but it was the very question she struggled with and hoped to answer with this visit. She stared back at him, holding his gaze steady, unsure how to respond.

To delay her answer, she finished the last bite of fish and washed it down, swallowing the lump in her throat in the process.

"It has certainly improved my dinner plans," she declared with a smile. "If this is to be our evening fare for the entirety of my stay, I believe you will have to roll me back to Allshire. Once they see how corpu-lent I've become, every one of my pupils will beg to accompany me on my next visit."

They all joined in her laughter, none the wiser that she had not honestly answered the question, none save the man with the angelic face and curls, who smiled politely but did not laugh with the others.

Chapter 3

S etting the letters on her brother's desk, Lilith looked up to find Sebastian studying her. He expected her to say something, she suspected, but what was there to say? She gleaned nothing new from their father's correspondences, letters she had read many times since reuniting with her brother. There was no point in reading them again.

The letters might paint a picture of her past, but it was not the past that coincided with her memories. She cherished her few memories, clung to them as a lifeline, yet each reading of the letters frayed those memories little bit by little bit.

The bleakest days at the orphanage, the most hopeless of nights, all were manageable with the memories of her mother, even the few memories tainted by the presence of her father. These letters told a different tale. They told the tale of a stranger being her birth mother rather than the loving woman from her memories. A birth mother who did not want her, who abandoned her, just as her father did years later.

She glanced back to the letters on the edge of the desk, avoiding her brother's eyes.

One letter expressed love, hinted at an elopement, and implied being in the family way, a letter written by Lily Chambers, nothing more than a servant's daughter at the Roddam estate. That letter had been written to the earl's son and heir, Tobias Lancaster. Another letter, also written by Lily, a year after the first, briefly introduced Tobias to his daughter, a baby she had abandoned on the doorstep of the home he now shared with his new wife, Jane. The last of the three letters, written by Mrs. Brighton of the orphanage to Tobias seven years after the second, confirmed the removal of Lilith from the Roddam estate to be brought to the orphanage forthwith.

Her whole sordid existence lay on her brother's desk.

"It's a wonder you didn't end up in a workhouse," Sebastian said, reaching for the letters.

Lilith looked out of the window, losing herself for a moment in the view of waves licking black rocks on the beach below.

As much as she had always loved the water, it was a wonder she found any solace in Allshire with it being a landlocked parish nearly a hundred miles from the coast. How could she ever call a place so far from the sea her home? But then, how could she ever call any place home? She did not belong anywhere. Not really.

"Surely," she said, turning to face Sebastian, "he felt some affection for this Lily Chambers, for my — my mother. It could have been guilt, but I believe he was more compassionate than we give him credit. Of all the orphanages, he chose one that educated the orphans rather than prepared them for the workhouse. How else can we explain his securing my position at that particular orphanage if he didn't care? And why donate enough money not only for my livelihood but for renovations of the facilities? To be accepted at the orphanage, orphans must be financially sponsored, but nothing more is required or expected aside from their livelihood for the extent of their stay. Yet he paid so much more than that."

Sebastian tapped his fingers against the desk, scowling. "Our father didn't have a compassionate bone in his body. No man with compassion lies to his son by telling the boy his sibling is dead. No man with compassion blames his son for the death of that sibling and then beats a mere child within an inch of his life as punishment for that death. No, that man was not compassionate. He was pure evil."

"I'm sorry you suffered, 'Bastian," she said, her heart aching for all he endured.

"You have nothing for which to feel sorry. He abused us both, even if the abuse took different forms." Sebastian stood and walked to the window, leaning himself against the stone wall. "I don't know his motive for sending you away when you had been raised as his and our mother's daughter. He could very well have continued to raise you as his legitimate daughter after Mother died since no one knew the truth. I don't know his motive, and I don't care to know. Frankly, I don't see the point in trying to rationalize his behavior. Forget about the woman who birthed you and forget about our father. We both shared a mother who loved us until her death. Shall we be content to be together again and stop digging up the past?"

The tension in the room chilled Lilith. She knew how much Sebastian had suffered at the hand of their father, but was it so wrong for Lilith to want to learn more about her past? She only wanted to make sense of who she was.

"Can you so easily let go of the past?" Lilith queried tentatively.

"Not easily, no," Sebastian admitted. "Lizbeth has been instrumental in helping me let go. You cannot imagine how the past tortured me, Lil. I felt responsible for your death. I accepted our father's abuse as my own deserved punishment." He beat his shoulder against the stone wall and growled. "Devil take it, Lil. I spent my life thinking you drowned because I left you to play alone, never realizing you were safely tucked away in an orphanage." He turned back to her, crossing his arms over his chest, his eyes black and inscrutable. "I spent a lifetime clinging to the past. I'm only now learning to let go. I suggest you do the same."

"Very well, then. Burn the letters," Lilith challenged, not at all sure she wanted him to act on the gauntlet she had thrown down.

"Pardon?" He stared at her with incredulously wide eyes.

"Burn them. Right now. Toss them into the fire. Keeping them does neither of us any good." Picking up the letters, she thrust them in his direction, her lips pursed and her hand steady.

Sebastian said nothing. Instead, he reached across her for the tea tray and filled their cups before taking his seat. His eyes flicked to the letters in her outstretched hand but otherwise paid no heed to her request.

"My steward at Roddam Hall has been shipping one crate at a time from Father's office. Lizbeth and I have been cleaning out his possessions. Most of what we find is discarded. A few items have been kept and may be put to some use. He had, for example, a collection of travel journals that we're planning to publish. I tell you this, Lilith, because this is how at peace I am with the past. I can look through his possessions and not feel raw fury. At least, not anymore. I now see everything of his as objects, not as representations of the man." He looked at the letters again then back to Lilith. "These letters are not items to be hated. They led us to you, after all. There is no need to mull over them every time you visit nor is there a need to destroy them. They are only letters."

"Only letters," she repeated with a scoff.

"I don't need to understand the past. I refuse to be hurt by inanimate objects, letters included. I only want to move forward." Softly, almost under his breath, he added, "As should you."

He was right. There was nothing more to be learned about her past, and there was no way to second-guess a dead man's motives for cruelty or kindness. Even if she could learn more, what would it prove?

Knowing the uselessness of such enquiry did not stop Lilith from wondering if their father had loved her birth mother or if he resented a youthful mistake that resulted in a consequence. She could not stop from wondering why her mother had chosen to leave her on her father's doorstep. She could not stop wondering why her father's new wife had taken her in and raised her as her own.

The letters told a cold story, one of facts without emotion or motive. They were inanimate objects, as Sebastian said, incapable of causing pain.

The feel of the paper burned her fingertips all the same.

Her arm still stretched, she flicked the letters towards him, willing him to take them away, at least, to hide them in a drawer where she could not find them. They were nothing more than reminders of abandonment by people who should have loved her and reminders that the memories of her mother were not of her *real* mother.

"Devil take it, Lil." He growled.

In one swift motion, Sebastian snatched the papers out of her hand and launched himself across the room to the hearth, tossing the letters into hungry flames.

She heard a gasp when the fire devoured the paper, startled to realize it had been she who gasped. Her body perspired as if she, too, were being devoured by fire. Her hands gripped the armrests to restrain herself from rushing over to save the remnants of her birth mother.

After the ashes settled, Sebastian turned to her. "Drink your tea. You're as pale as death," he rumbled.

Her fingers, stiff, unfurled one by one from the wood. She flexed against the ache from clenching too tightly.

Nothing would bring back the letters. It was done.

"The tea, Lilith," her brother repeated, his voice softer and closer.

Blinking rapidly against tears that had not formed, she obeyed. The tea was hot and sweet on her tongue, just as comforting as he knew it would be.

"Have you given any thought to moving in with us?" Sebastian asked, returning to his seat behind his desk. "I've spoken with my solicitor about setting up an account for you. You needn't ever worry about money."

"I thank you for both offers, but I'm much happier at home," she said with as much pride as she could muster, trying not to choke on the word home.

"Help me convince you. You know we want you here," he said, tasting his own tea. "Move forward, Lilith. Let's move forward together."

"No. Thank you, but no. I'm settled there, 'Bastian. I've made a home for myself. People see me for what I am and accept me," she replied, silencing the memory of how poorly the local gentry treated her.

A crease appeared between his black eyebrows. "And what are you that they so willingly accept?"

"An orphan. A spinster. And let's not forget a bastard," she said bluntly. "While no one except the rector knows the truth, it is assumed that most orphans are illegitimate."

He drew his brows closer together, the crease deepening, making him look quite ferocious. "Is that how you see yourself, Lil?"

"It's not how I see myself. It's who I am. I see no point in giving myself airs. I belong in Allshire where my identity is known. I need not hide any part of my past or feel shame for who I am."

Sebastian cleared his throat. He opened his mouth to speak then closed it. After swirling the dregs of his cup for several long minutes, he let the cup clatter against its saucer.

"Look deeper. Your place may not be here in my home, but I don't believe it is in Allshire. The parish isn't even by the ocean, and don't for one second tell me you don't long to live by the ocean." He paused, as if daring her to contradict him.

She did not.

"I don't presume to tell you where you do or do not belong, Lilith, but if your only reason for staying at the parish is to embrace that dismal excuse for an identity, then it's not a good enough reason. You are none of those things. You are my sister. At one time, you knew a home with a doting mother. She was your *real* mother. I don't care two snaps if she didn't birth you. She was your mother just as she was mine. You would have never known any differently if that devil of a man hadn't displaced you. But look at what you have now. You have a loving family who wants you to be part of their lives. You are beautiful and confident with the world at your fingertips. Look deeper, Lil."

As heartfelt as his words were, they did not describe her. They described how she ought to be, perhaps how she once saw herself, but these words did not describe her as she was now. They told an incongruous tale from that of the letters. He was her *half*-brother. The woman she thought had been her mother was *his* mother. Lilith was *illegitimate*.

Before she could reply, he slapped his open palm against the desk. "I wish I had never shown you the letters. Curse me for the mistake. I wish I had only told you we were siblings and that our father sent you away after the death of our mother. I was a fool to tell you the truth. You only remembered me as a brother and only remembered our parents as being your own. I regret my short sightedness."

She clenched her dress in tight fists. "No, Sebastian. You did the right thing. Lies accomplish nothing.

How cruel would it have been for you to tell me I'm legitimate, and after accepting the new life, have a stranger learn the truth and expose me as a fraud? I'm much happier knowing I'm not a member of your world. I don't want that burden. I don't want anything to do with the aristocratic life. I'm happier living the life I have built with people who know me for what I am," Lilith argued.

Sebastian heaved a sigh, clearly frustrated, but Lilith could not help his reaction. If he wanted a polite response or a sentimental answer, he needed to look elsewhere, for she would answer only in truth.

"If I had burned the letters from the start, a stranger would have never learned the truth. Even now, you're the only one holding you back from the future that should have been yours." He rested his elbows on the desk and tugged at his hair. "I don't want us to argue," he said to the top of the desk, fistfuls of his hair clenched between fingers. "I've spent too much of my life missing you for us to argue."

"I didn't come here to fight about the letters. Could we please not fight?"

He meant nothing but goodwill, so why did she insist on contradicting his every word? It was this feeling of limbo, not knowing where she stood in life or how to move forward. Moving forward meant accepting his financial support instead of earning her own way as an independent woman and, more pointedly, accepting his version of her identity. It would be so much easier to move backwards or not to move at all. Forward held nothing but foreboding.

Releasing his hair from the stranglehold, he steepled his hands under his chin, staring at her in silence.

Had she not felt so tense, so emotionally drained from the conversation, she would have laughed at the tufts of hair sticking out from his head. She wanted to laugh. A laugh would be just the thing to put an end to the disagreement. Try as she might to laugh, she only succeeded in grimacing.

"Do you find Lizbeth in good health?" Sebastian asked.

The sudden change of subject startled Lilith. She stared at him, not sure how to respond when her mind was otherwise engaged.

"I confess, as the time draws near, I worry," he continued. "Her mother died in childbed with her sister, you know. Be honest. Is there cause for worry?"

Closing her eyes, she forced herself to focus on his question and disengage from the letters, from their brief quarrel, from her own inner turmoil.

"Lilith?" His voice nudged her, a pleading whisper. "Lizbeth's health. Is it sound? Is she safe?"

When she opened her eyes, she saw a nervous twitch in his jaw, a tick of clenched teeth. Lilith shook her mind free and focused on his questions. The longer she took to answer, the more he would assume her hesitancy was in regard to Liz rather than herself.

She nodded, assuring him. "She's sublime. If it isn't tooting my own horn to say, she's in good hands. I have yet to lose a mother or a babe."

"There are no chances of complications?"

"Complicated births aren't uncommon, but I have worked with her throughout her confinement to ensure a healthy progression. You need not worry. I will be with her through the final steps." Lilith tried to reflect confidence in her expression.

"And what if there is a complication? Should I summon a physician to be safe?" he asked, looking at her helplessly.

She straightened her posture by reflex, taken aback by his insinuation. He meant no insult, she reminded herself. He was simply worried for his wife and child. She allowed herself to relax before answering.

"No. No need for a physician," she reassured. "My quick thinking, skill, and prayers are far superior to the abilities of any leech, I assure you."

"I trust you, Lilith. I do. Truly. I trust you with my life, for that's what Lizbeth is to me. She's my life." His steepled fingers scratched his chin before he twisted his mouth into a strained smile, trying to appear light-hearted, but clearly still thinking about his wife's condition. "Now, let's talk about how you're enjoying meeting my in-laws."

With thinned lips, she said, "While I want to enjoy my time here, I —" A knock at the library door interrupted her.

They both turned to the opposite side of the room to see a crown of russet curls appear from around the door. Lord Collingwood.

Ignoring the hitch in her breath at seeing the handsome face, Lilith jerked to her feet. She was not the least interested in conversing with him or with his handsome face.

Curtsying to Collingwood and Sebastian both, she excused herself.

Once outside the study, she felt a tinge of guilt at leaving so abruptly. He would think her rude. Thus far in her visit, Lord Collingwood had been the epitome of politeness and did not deserve rudeness.

But…well, it was simply too late now to regret her hasty departure. Truth be told, she did not know the first thing about conversing with people of his ilk. And besides, he was only predisposed to kindness on the pretense she was a lady and Sebastian's legitimate sister. He would not be so kind if he knew the truth. Defusing her guilt thusly, she made her way to the first floor in search of Lizbeth.

Walter wondered again if it was too soon to propose.

Throughout the second day of Lady Lilith's visit, or rather Miss Chambers' visit, Walter bumped into her everywhere he went. From her expression, one would think he encountered her intentionally.

He had not meant to find himself in the same room as her nearly every hour of the day, but he certainly did not mind when it happened, except every time it did happen, she straightened her spine like a schoolmistress, narrowed a steely gaze at him, and avoided conversation.

Despite the lack of verbal exchange and the accusatory looks she cast his way, he took each of the opportunities to admire her. She wore the same sprigged dress as the day before, and her hair was again worn straight and braided, not curled or styled.

He admired her simplicity, an elegant and natural beauty that needed no augmentation, least of all by ringlets, baubles, and perfume. Visions flashed in his mind's eye of her in a ballroom, unadorned by jewels in a plain gown, shaming all the women of the *beau monde* in their layers of gaudy fabric, gold, and diamonds.

His valet Kory slipped the bug in his ear that Miss Chambers had denied the use of a lady's maid. Walter could not imagine dressing without the aid of his valet. How would he shave without nicking his skin? How would he don the tailor-fitted coat without Kory's help? How would he tie the neck-cloth evenly? How would he know which stockings matched which waistcoat?

One look at Miss Chambers explained why she did not feel the need for a lady's maid, but Walter wondered if she was too proud or simply unaccustomed to such luxuries. Surely, once she saw the rationale for a lady's maid, she would never be without. As silly as he felt thinking of lady's maids, he could not help himself. He absorbed every piece of information he heard about her.

Initiating conversation was the next goal. He could not very well offer marriage if they had never conversed. Well, technically, he could. Engagements happened frequently enough without the couple exchanging words beyond the offer and acceptance, but Walter refused to be one of those couples, and he suspected Lady — er, Miss Chambers would, as well.

He could see it now. She would be sitting in the parlor alone, embroidering. Wait, no, she did not seem like the embroidering type. She would be sitting in the parlor alone, painting. Dash it all. That did not seem right either. Had she said at dinner that she painted? Would she even paint in a parlor? No, that would not do.

She would be sitting in the parlor alone, reading. Yes, that seemed a realistic fantasy. He would accidentally catch her in the parlor, apologize for the intrusion, but upon seeing her smile, he would proceed into the room, encouraged.

With quick strides, he would cross the room, drop to the floor before her, clasp her hands in his, well, after she politely set aside the book she had been reading, and then he would say, "Lilith, beautiful siren of my heart, will you do me the honor—"

"Practicing, I see?"

Aghast, Walter spun towards the parlor door to see his mother observing him with her quizzing glass.

With hand to heart, he laughed a single *ha*.

"Thank the Lord, it's you, Mama," he breathed in relief. "I thought for a minute it might be—"

"Lady Lilith, the siren of your heart?" she finished for him.

"Precisely." He laughed again, his pulse still racing, and crossed the room to offer an arm to his mother.

After seeing her comfortably seated, he took the chair next to her.

"Shall I ring for a tray?" he asked.

"Heavens no. I'm going to float home at the end of the visit. I've never seen a family drink so much tea. I could use a sherry, or better yet, a brandy, to be honest," Hazel said, looking around the room, her quizzing glass still in hand. "Do you know, I haven't seen a single strong drink since we arrived. Found it in abundance at the ducal estate—you know how the duke favors brandy—but not a drop here. Do you think the butler has it hidden from guests, or does the early simply not imbibe? Well, no matter. Let us return to your proposal. One day and already Lady Lilith has caught your eye?"

"She prefers Miss Chambers, Mama. I suppose after a lifetime of being one name, it is difficult to get used to another."

"Nonsense. She's being obstinate. Although she needn't get too used to Lady Lilith, either, if you're planning to offer for her." She patted his hand. "Walter, my boy, I'm pleased someone has finally caught your eye, but I hope you realize she may not give you a second glance."

Startled, Walter stammered, "Why on earth would you say that?"

"She's the daughter of an earl, dear boy. Without doubt, her brother will set up an impressive dowry for her. While her age won't do her any favors, her lineage and inheritance will curry favor. A duke would be more fitting for an earl's daughter. If you want her, you'll need to woo her with more than your title, I'm afraid. Although, and I say this as both your mother and a woman, I cannot imagine any lady of sense not being taken by you. You take after your father. So handsome." She tittered.

Walter cringed with embarrassment and shook his head. "You think Trelowen would be too quaint of a home? You think she would prefer to be a duchess in some ostentatious palace like Cousin Charlotte?"

"After growing up in an orphanage and having to work for a living, I wouldn't doubt that she would set her sights on just such a life. She has the means and money now. Can you imagine her settling for Exeter when she could have a dukedom? And what of your plans to spend summers on the Cornwall coast with your Uncle Cuthbert? I can't see her following you to a seaside cottage to take in the views or visit tin mines. No, if you have your eye on her, you'll need to do far more wooing to make any of that sound remotely attractive."

Walter slumped his shoulders. "I hardly slept last night from convincing myself she would prefer the simple life of a baroness. With her experience at the orphanage, I even convinced myself she might be interested in helping me with my philanthropic endeavors, whatever they end up being. I know, I know, I've already dreamt of a life with a woman to whom I've never spoken, but I know she's the one, Mama. I know it. I can feel it."

"I don't doubt you, my boy," Hazel said. "But heed my words; you will need to work for her. Her life has changed in the past year. She's a lady now. No doubt, she will move here with Sebastian and Lizbeth, for no lady would continue to work when she has relations to care for her; it's ungenteel. With the help of Lizbeth, she'll enter Society. Once she tastes the life she was meant to live, she'll not return to a simpler life. You must woo her, so if some foppish duke happens by, she'll have eyes only for you. Yes?"

He nodded, remedying his posture with renewed confidence. The ladies during the London Season had certainly been taken by his charms, so if he could win them over with a smile, surely, he could win over Miss Chambers, as well—she could not be immune to smiles, could she?

"And you don't mind, Mama, that her background is less than perfect?"

Hazel swatted his arm. "You forget my own humble origins, young man. She may have grown up in an orphanage, but she's still a lady. Her background

adds to her charm, I think. She'll be quite the curiosity when she enters Society, the long-lost daughter
of the fourteenth Earl of Roddam. Oh, I think she's
remarkable."

Walter strengthened his resolve to pursue her. He
need only engage her in conversation. Mix charm
with compliments, and she would be his before the
end of their visit.

A new vision formed in his imagination of the two
of them waving to their family from inside a carriage.
Wedding guests threw rose petals into the air as the
couple rolled their way from the church to his estate
to live happily ever after.

Chapter 4

One week passed before Walter found an appropriate opportunity to converse with Miss Chambers. Try as he might, she excused herself each time he approached, or she made a point to include others in the conversation so they could not talk exclusively. Earning a woman's attention had never proven more difficult.

In sheer desperation, he had even accompanied Lizbeth and Miss Chambers for their daily walk about the castle grounds, but the topic of discourse during each of those outings focused on Lizbeth's health and the approaching arrival of the baby. On one such walk, he had been forced to excuse himself when the conversation turned embarrassingly to the physical reasons Lizbeth must walk while in the family way.

Such words were not for mixed company.

After turning varying shades of crimson, Walter wished them both a good day and bowed out, vowing not to make the same mistake again. In hindsight, he suspected Miss Chambers chose the topics to discourage him from joining them. But why?

Fleetingly, he wondered if his mother had guessed accurately. Perhaps Miss Chambers noted his design and meant to discourage him because she had set her cap higher.

Dash it all.

Perseverance, he told himself. He must persevere. If he could get her alone long enough, she would see his charm, and from that point forward seek his company rather than avoid it.

Today, luck found him.

Roddam and Uncle Cuthbert were tucked in the library working on the slavery abolition bill, which had bored Walter to tears in under an hour. Lizbeth and Mama were huddled in the parlor, clucking like hens. And Miss Chambers was nowhere to be found, at least not without scavenging on the part of Walter. He at last spotted her sitting in the gazebo outside.

Armed with a shawl, he set out for the headland, planning all the way his excuse for disturbing her, and what better excuse than a gentlemanly display of offering her a shawl against the sun and briny wind? Of course, if she had wanted a shawl, she would have brought one, but he could not very well go up there without a proper excuse, so the shawl would have to suffice.

A warm wind welcomed him to the cliffside. Miss Chambers did not. In fact, she did not bother to look up when he approached.

He stepped into the gazebo and stopped next to her bench. Strands of her hair escaped the braid and whipped about her face, but she did not seem the least bothered. She looked out to the ocean, her hands folded in her lap, framed handsomely by the floral embroidery on a dress that had seen too many summers.

The only visible indication she noticed his presence was the slight stiffening of her posture.

He held out the fabric. "Would you care for a shawl to shield against the wind, Miss Chambers?" he asked, feeling like an imbecile.

Looking up, she stared at him as though he had sprouted two heads. "You brought me a shawl?"

"I thought you could use a shield against the wind."

"You thought of *me*?"

Her surprise made him self-conscious. Why should he not think of her? He was a gentleman, never mind his attraction to her.

With a suspicious glance at the shawl, she took it with a quiet "Thank you" and wrapped it around her shoulders, returning her gaze to the sea.

Dash it all. He had not planned for what to do after bringing the shawl. Should he sit? Should he leave? He shifted his stance to one foot and stared at her awkwardly, hoping for inspiration. Not the best start to a tête-à-tête.

"Are you planning to stand there for eternity or join me?" she asked, her eyes still trained on the sea.

"If you wouldn't mind the company, I would be honored to join you. I shall fetch Liz or my mother to serve as chaperone," he said, delighted for the chance to talk with her at last.

To his surprise and chagrin, she laughed heartily, turning her eyes his way. The dark brown irises pinned him in place, filled with reproachful merriment.

"A chaperone? I hope you're jesting," she said, the deep tones of her voice caused his stomach to somersault.

When he did not respond quickly enough, she said, "Don't be foolish, Lord Collingwood. I hardly need a keeper. At my age and with my background, my reputation is not at stake, not to mention we're safely housed at my brother's estate away from the prying eyes of your polite society."

Walter stammered. "But I care for your reputation, Miss Chambers. You're a lady, and I am a gentleman, and it does neither of us favors to be seen talking privately without the presence of a chaperone, even among family."

Laughter still in her words, she asked, "And what do you expect would happen if we were caught talking privately? Do you expect my brother to call you out? A duel on the castle lawn, perhaps? Do you suppose he would force us to marry for the sake of propriety? Oh, heavens. We do come from different worlds, don't we?"

Unsure how to react, Walter shifted from one foot to the other, glancing back at the castle before returning his stare to Miss Chambers. In some respect, it did seem foolish to worry about propriety when they were both in their thirties and in the company of family. But he was a gentleman through and through. Respect was ingrained in him.

"Look around you, my lord. We're in my brother's own private world where decorum is neither here nor there. I appreciate your concern, truly, but there is no impropriety with which to worry yourself. Go back to the castle if you prefer. Or sit here with me. The choice is yours."

Before he talked himself out of this rare occasion, he sat next to her on the bench. The cold stone, shaded by the gazebo roof, contrasted with the warm day. He shivered at the touch.

They sat in silence, her eyes returning to watch the waves, his flitting back and forth between the side of her face and the water. When had flirting become so difficult? Never in his life had he needed to initiate conversation, for typically the girls did all the talking while he smiled politely and listened or smiled politely and daydreamed.

At a loss, he tried to think of what to say.

Will you marry me?

He choked at the thought of fumbling those words as a conversation opener.

You're the most beautiful woman I've ever met.

He cleared his throat against the temptation of saying such a line.

You're a goddess.

That would not do either. He smoothed his hand over his knee, becoming ever so tense.

I don't even know you, but I'm hopelessly infatuated with you.

Instead, he blurted, "Lovely weather we're having. Don't you agree?"

She turned, an eyebrow arched and a mocking smile tugging at the corners of her mouth.

He ventured to add, "I've never been this far north before. It's unexpectedly warm. Do you find it this warm every year?"

The amused smile lingered as she turned back to the sea without a reply.

He cleared his throat again. "The bonnet you wore yesterday was most fetching. Is it your favorite color?"

A mirthless laugh startled him.

When she did not follow the laugh with an explanation, he asked, "Have I said something to deserve derision?"

The pair of dark eyes turned his way. "The weather? Bonnet colors? I've never heard such ridiculous conversation in my life."

Walter's throat tightened. He did not think it possible to feel annoyance towards a goddess, but his ire rose as she continued to laugh. At him.

"It's called polite conversation," he defended.

"If that is polite conversation, then I've no wish for it."

Through gritted teeth, he explained, "This is what gentlemen and ladies do—they carry on polite conversation."

"What a waste of breath," she said. "How does anyone get to know anyone else if everyone is talking of the weather and bonnet colors?"

A retort at the ready, he paused in order to study her expression. If he read her expression correctly, it was not one of ridicule but curiosity. He did not want to be laughed at again. Was she being rude or inviting discussion? Examining his choices, he narrowed his decision to three possible actions. He could excuse himself and return to the castle. He could snap back a harsh reply. Or he could answer her question candidly.

"They don't get to know each other," he answered at length. "There's no need. The only purpose for a gentleman and a lady to converse is in the hope of a betrothal, which is secured for advancement, status, and money. A proper courting period is expected before linking family names, so to avoid silence during courtship, the individuals fill the space with an endless stream of polite conversation. Given most conversations are chaperoned, there isn't much else to talk about, to be perfectly honest."

"How dreadful. Marrying a perfect stranger, then. Why anyone would want to be part of polite society is beyond my understanding," she said, her lips lifting at the corners into a teasing smile.

"Polite conversation has its virtues, Miss Chambers. It is an art we're trained in from birth. We engage in impersonal conversation to ensure others feel at ease. Few *want* to discuss personal matters, and not everyone is confident in company, and so polite conversation allows for the easy flow of dialogue. It's called good manners."

"Sounds dull, if you were to ask me. What do friends talk about?"

"Hmm. Well, the ladies gossip with each other, and the men talk about horses and gaming. Mixed company talks about the weather and fashion."

"Aren't you glad, then, you're not in the company of polite society? I say we dispense with all that silliness. Silence is underappreciated, in my humble opinion. It is rare to find someone with whom to share companionable silence." After a heart-stopping smile, Miss Chambers turned back to the water, initiating silence.

At first, he wanted to say something. He wanted to cut the silence. How awkward sitting with another person without saying a word. How was he to get to know her? How was he to charm her if nary a word was spoken?

Minutes passed, and he sensed her relax next to him. In the distance, kittiwakes dipped towards the waves, calling above the howl of the wind and the roar of the waves.

As a quarter of an hour passed of the two listening to the world around them, he realized with a startling awareness that this was perhaps the best conversation he had ever shared with a woman. He chuckled to himself.

"The ocean has no expectations, no judgment, no prejudice," she whispered throatily, ending the silence. "I would love nothing more than to find a cottage by the sea to live out my days."

Walter continued to practice companionable silence.

"No words about the weather, my lord?" she jested. "*This* is what real people talk about. They talk about life, dreams, plans, fears, anything of substance. Do you have any substance to add?"

He racked his mind for something of substance. Here, at last, he sat with the woman of his dreams, and yet his mind was blank of anything meaningful to say. In truth, he'd never exchanged meaningful conversation with anyone but family. Where to begin with a stranger, and more pointedly, a stranger with whom he desperately wanted to make a good and memorable impression?

"I want to do more with my life," he blurted, though he knew not from whence the words came.

"More than be a baron?" she enquired.

"I don't know if you believe in someone having a calling, but I'm sure I have one. Only, I don't know what it is. I happened into my title, a consequence of birth and death, nothing more. I don't begrudge it, but it's not who I am. I want to make a difference, you see, do something with meaning. Dash it all — I'm babbling."

Miss Chambers angled herself on the bench to see him more fully, her eyebrows raised, warmth in her eyes. "Ah. So, there *is* more to you. I had wondered."

She did not explain her meaning.

Instead, she asked, "What have you done to answer this calling?"

He gave a short *ha*. "Nothing. Nothing of note, anyway."

"Why not? Seems to,me, if I had money, influence, and charm, I'd allow nothing to stop me from achieving my dreams."

"Well, I don't know how. I know not how to see any of my ideas to fruition. It takes more than money, influence, and charm to achieve goals. I can't simply throw money at fantasies."

"My, my, Lord Collingwood. Who knew you would be the type to make excuses to keep you from your dreams? Nothing stops me, I'll have you know. If I have a plan, I see it to the end."

Her words may be true, but he did not consider himself an excuse maker. Never had he intentionally devised an excuse. He would like nothing more than to see his plans to fruition, but nothing was so simple.

"Yes, well, then, what are your dreams?" he said, turning the table to avoid talking about himself further. This whole conversation of substance was not nearly so fun when the focus was on him.

She looked away, brushing the strands of hair out of her eyes with an irritated swat of her hand. "I was speaking hypothetically, of course," she said in a tense, tight voice.

Walter would have felt smug that she did not like having the attention on her any more than he did, though she had been the one to wish for a more substantive conversation, except he did want her to feel at ease with him and did want a genuine conversation to get to know her.

Giving her his most charming smile, he asked, "If you could have any dream in the world, what would it be? Anything. Don't hold back."

Her shoulders rounding, she folded her hands in her lap and stared at them, lost in thought. "My dreams are simple. I want that cottage by the sea. It would be large enough to have a parlor for guests, for I do enjoy entertaining friends, but nothing ostentatious or grand. It would have a garden, a place for me to grow my own herbs. When not knee-deep in the soil, I would spend my time usefully, purposefully, doing something to help people."

"That's a beautiful dream, Miss Chambers."

"There's no need to mock me. I know peers of the realm would find a quaint cottage humble, gardening beneath their dignity, and being useful ungenteel."

"Did I mock you?" He pressed a hand to his heart. "No, indeed, Miss Chambers. You heard my own confession. I, too, want to help others and be of some use to this world. And while my home is not precisely a cottage by the sea, it is modest, no more than ten miles from the Jurassic Coast. We are not so different, you see."

As if he had said something to offend, she stood, tightening the knot of the shawl. Walter rose, surprised by her sudden movement.

"We are from different worlds, Lord Collingwood, different worlds entirely. Now, if you'll excuse me, I must return before it rains."

He watched her retreat, unsure what he said to offend. A bright sun shone above, mocking him.

Three days later, the family walked along the Embleton coast in two-by-two formation with Lizbeth and her father Mr. Trethow leading the troupe. Lord Collingwood and his mother walked in the middle. Sebastian and Lilith took up the rear.

The sun beat against bonnets and tricorns, the wind wrapping them in a warm embrace, the wet sand a fine *chambré*, all in contrast to the frigid ocean lapping at their soles.

Aside from Lord Collingwood and his mother, all pairs carried shoes and stockings in hand, the wet sand squishing between their toes in a warm and grainy squelch. Lilith welcomed the sensation of tugging her feet against the quicksand of the wet beach. It reminded her of life before the orphanage, those memories she clung to and dug for, hoping to pull the variations of her life together into a single narrative.

"And how are you finding your welcome?" Sebastian asked his sister, his arm under hers in gentlemanly support, though she did not need his aid. "I hope my in-laws are increasing the pleasure of your stay. I believe you'll like Hazel's company once you get to know her."

Lilith delayed answering, casting him a polite smile from under her straw bonnet. She need not look up into the sun to see his face, as they were nearly the same height.

How could she answer such a question when none of his in-laws had given her a reason to dislike them except their status in society? Even as she thought this, she knew it was unfair to dislike someone on status alone, just as the ladies in Allshire disliked her on status alone. But she knew their type well enough to warrant the distaste.

Yet, how could she say she did not like them because they were aristocrats when her own brother was an aristocrat? She did not see him in the same way, though, for he was simply her brother. His birthright could not be helped any more than could his in-laws; nevertheless, they were different. Their clothes, their manners, even their accents were all so different, so…austere.

Her brother's eyebrows raised in anticipation of her answer.

"They are perfectly amiable," she replied politely albeit curtly.

"Ah. I see. Yes, that tells me everything I need to know. I can read you like a book, you know, dear sister. Promise you will give them a chance?"

She nodded without looking at him. It was not about her giving them a chance but the other way around. If they but knew what she really was.

"And what of Collingwood?" he hedged. "I note a distinctive twinkle in his eyes when he looks at you."

Clenching a fist about her shoes, she said with clipped words, "And what of him? Lord Collingwood is a peer of the realm who would no sooner look at me than he would a beggar in the street. Have you already forgotten what I am?"

Sebastian exhaled his exasperation. "I meant no offense, Lil. I only thought you might find in him a friend. He has a desire to do some good in this world, just as I believe you do."

As if his ears burned from Sebastian's words, Lord Collingwood looked back to Lilith and cast a soft smile.

"I'll beg you not to meddle. He and I have nothing in common."

"At least give him a chance before you judge too harshly. Give them all a chance. If I can love them, you can. And before you say the fondness is because I'm of the same blueblood, let me remind you of two points. The same blood flows through your veins, though you're loath to admit it. And, more importantly, they saw past my boorish reputation with which I first made their acquaintance. They saw me for who I am, not for who others believed me to be. For my final defense, lest you forget, my father-in-law is *not* an aristocrat, nor was Hazel before her marriage. Before you judge them, get to know them. They may surprise you."

"It's not my judgement of them that's the problem," she defended. "It's what they would think of me if they knew the truth. Do you think Lord Collingwood would speak to me if he knew of my illegitimacy? I think not."

Her brother chuckled. "Has it ever occurred to you that he speaks to you because he wants to? Because he finds you charming and attractive?"

Lilith scoffed. "Don't be silly. He speaks to me because he thinks I'm of his ilk. It was wrong of you not to warn them, and it's dishonest not to correct them."

"Lilith. Stop. Your birth does not define you. You had a loving mother and still have a loving brother. You belong in this life, in my life, as Lady Lilith, just as *our* mother intended."

Lilith scoffed again but said nothing. Her heart was torn asunder, one part belonging to the mother who had loved and raised her as her own, the other part trapped with the stranger who birthed her and abandoned her.

To her dismay, Lord Collingwood dragged his feet, allowing his mother to continue ahead of him. Within seconds, she and Sebastian had caught up to him. Her brother winked when she cast him an accusatory glare.

"If the two of you wouldn't mind," her brother said, "I'm going to catch up to my wife."

Sebastian offered Lord Collingwood his place at Lilith's side. Inwardly groaning, she allowed the man to take her arm in her brother's stead. Leaving them alone and very much distanced from the group, Sebastian trotted ahead.

"May I carry your shoes, Miss Chambers?" Lord Collingwood said in way of a greeting.

Did he suppose they were too heavy for her feeble arm? What a toff.

"No, thank you, my lord."

"Yes, I suppose you've been independent for a long time," he said cryptically.

They walked in silence for a time, a companionable silence, to her surprise, much like when he brought her the shawl on the cliff side. She liked that he did not attempt conversation about the weather or bonnets this time, instead falling into the rhythm of their footsteps slapping wet sand. Against her better judgment, she relaxed, feeling comforted by his presence.

"If I may be so bold," he said when the others ahead of them stopped to pick up seashells, "I would like to say, you look most fetching. The sun and exercise have flushed your cheeks becomingly."

If it hadn't been an aristocrat to say such words, words she was sure he doled out to every lady he met...she pursed her lips to keep from smiling, a blush undoubtedly pinkening her cheeks further.

"Thank you," she murmured.

"I've been thinking since our last conversation."

He said it with such novelty, she almost laughed aloud. Should she commend him for thinking? The pesky smile threatened to escape her lips.

"I may like to open an orphanage," he declared. "I've been in search for how I can help others, but nothing has felt right, not to mention I've no idea how to start a business venture. But this feels right. And with your help, I shan't fail! I'm sure this is my path, my calling. Fate has brought us together, you see."

She did laugh aloud this time. "Aristocrats don't own orphanages, my lord."

"Why not? And here I thought you would like my idea."

His tone was pouty enough that she could not stifle her smile any longer.

"If you'll pardon my bluntness," she said, "aristocrats do not acknowledge *that* side of the bed from which most orphans are sired. They certainly don't associate with such riffraff by owning establishments for housing them."

"What an inane generalization. I hope you don't think me one of those sorts. I see nothing remotely wrong with my wanting to open an orphanage. And with your experience, I could open one that resembles what your Mrs. Brighton accomplished, with a school, refinements, apprenticeships, the like."

As he rambled on about his idea, she realized he was quite serious. Not knowing what to make of it, she listened without interrupting.

"I could coin it Colling Orphanage. See the pun? Colling meaning to embrace, as in taking the unwanted children into a welcoming embrace, this being my calling, and me being Collingwood. Brilliant, yes? Well, let's not dwell on my poor humor. I was thinking, what if Colling Orphanage kept detailed records on parentage? Then, if the orphans wished to know the truth of their parentage, we would have those records. Wouldn't you have liked to have known sooner?"

Her mirth over the orphanage name lessened at his question. Good heavens. Would she have wished to know? She was not sure she liked knowing even now, aside from it giving her a brother she dearly loved.

"And what if the parents don't wish to be found?" she asked, avoiding his direct question. "You do realize, my lord, that most orphans are the by-blows of aristocrats. They're not acknowledged and never would be. What records would there be to keep? And should there be such records, as I mentioned at dinner on my first night, not all children would like the truth. Truth is a heavy burden to bear. How might it change a promising young pupil to learn his father was a murderer hanged for his crimes? Some truths are better left unknown."

"But it should be their right to know, if they chose. Wouldn't you have asked Mrs. Brighton about it if you knew she kept records?"

"Ah. But she did. My father corresponded with her himself. But that wasn't your question. Would I have asked her? I'm not sure. For so long, I wanted an answer to the mystery of my memories, but how might I have taken the truth if I found out at a younger age? For that matter, how would my brother have taken it? Not until our father died did he piece together his life. And what if I had found out while my father still lived? No, I would not have wanted to know sooner."

"But you *are* happy to know, yes? What a wonderfully life-changing moment that must have been to discover the truth!"

She felt strangely compelled to answer his question, but with what? The truth? A half-truth? A deeper truth than she was prepared to admit even to herself?

She took her time answering. Disclosing the dirty truth seemed an easy way out of the conversation, especially when he had a right to know he was conversing with an illegitimate, but something in her stopped those words from tumbling out.

As much as she disliked his type, she decided she rather liked his company and conversation. There was something genuine about him, unlike anyone she had met, a desire to humor and an eagerness to befriend. Of course, when one's usual company was the likes of the Reverend Sands, it was no wonder she found Lord Collingwood pleasant company, even if there was an aristocratic rogue hiding behind the angelic handsomeness.

Lilith and the baron stood apart from the others, watching as Sebastian brought seashells to Lizbeth to inspect. Lady Collingwood pointed at various areas of the beach, shouting instructions to her brother who ambled about to do her bidding, guffawing when he shocked her with a handful of water instead of shells as she expected. Lilith's good humor returned at the sight of Mr. Trethow splashing his sister.

Turning to her expectant and patient companion, she allowed herself to return his smile. Good heavens, he was beautiful. Why did he have to be titled and out of her reach? And there was a silly thought. She was much too old to be thinking of romance and much too distracted by all life had brought her over the past year.

"Yes, of course, I'm happy to know my brother and make sense of my past," she said, finally answering his question. "But it's more complicated than that, more complicated than a single emotion of happiness. You couldn't possibly understand what it's like to learn who you are, who you *really* are. The truth would alter your perception of yourself and of those around you."

He rubbed the back of his neck and adjusted his stance, his boots having steadily sunk into the sand. "Not all of us who know our parents know who we really are, but I suppose that's not what you mean. I've been searching for my purpose in life since the moment of my father's death. No, I've never been orphaned, but I also didn't know who I was. I'm still sorting it, to be honest. But this conversation isn't about me, is it? I want to know more about you. Your perception must have altered for the better. You learned you're a lady with a family to care for you. That must be a monumental relief."

"That's the complicated part, Lord Collingwood. The thing is, I'm not a lady. Not in my heart of hearts. I've built my life from the ground up to be the way I like it. I cannot so easily accept the role of *lady*, which comes with it a new world full of the very people I've learned to dislike. I don't see myself in that world, among those people. I cannot accept a world in which I would be pampered by maids, idle for days on end, looked at as a source of gossip. I much prefer the world I've built for myself, a world where I know my place and am useful, full of purpose. People respect me. Not for my bloodline but for what I give to the community. I earned that respect."

Would she feel differently if she were not illegitimate? She wondered. No, she would stand proud of all she had accomplished. No, she did not want to be part of his world, even if she woke up tomorrow to discover Jane Lancaster, the Countess of Roddam had birthed her rather than Miss Lily Chambers.

His carefree smile was broad when he said, "Then we really aren't so different. Haven't you been listening? I want the same. I've always been idle. I was a right proper hellion before my father's death, the worst of the lot really, but I want to be useful and earn my place in the world outside my title. You and I are so much alike, Miss Chambers!"

There he stood in his perfectly tailored attire, at ease in his smile, while her own was strained and her dress was the same one she'd worn three times that week, and instead of being appalled, he saw them as being similar. How could he not see the insurmountable differences between them? He who dreamed but never accomplished, she who accomplished and avoided dreaming. He who had nary a worry in the world, she who could not imagine living in a worry-free world.

A stir to her left caught her attention just as Sebastian howled her name against the cry of the wind. "Lilith!"

All in the group turned to see Lizbeth clutching her abdomen with one hand, the other hand gripping Sebastian's arm.

Before Lilith reached them, Sebastian had scooped his wife into his arms, holding her like a babe. Panting from the dash across the beach, Lilith assessed her sister-in-law, who appeared fatigued and flushed but otherwise well.

"What is it?" Lilith asked gently, despite being winded.

"Has it started?" asked Sebastian. "Is it time?"

Lilith ignored him and stared at Lizbeth, nodding encouragement.

Lizbeth nestled her head against her husband's chest, her hand cradling her belly. "I—I felt a pain, then—then swooned. Never swooned in my—my life," she stuttered, clearly upset by the incident. Closing her eyes, she winced from what Lilith assumed was another contraction.

Her sister-in-law was in far worse pain than she let on in front of Sebastian, but Lilith knew it was a good pain, the pain of new life.

Looking to her brother, Lilith said in the same calm voice she had used to address Lizbeth, "It isn't time, not yet, but we're close. Take her to the castle and to her bedchamber. Have the maid bring her tea. I will attend as soon as I retrieve my bag."

With a curt nod, her brother jogged back towards the castle, Lizbeth in his arms, carried as though she were weightless. Lilith smiled to his retreating back. She would be an aunt before the evening ended.

Chapter 5

A clock in the armory, one floor down, struck midnight.

No one was abed. Lord Collingwood, Sebastian, and Mr. Trethow were in the parlor waiting. Lady Collingwood perched on the edge of a chair in Lizbeth's bedchamber, nodding off to sleep between head-bobs of wakefulness.

Lilith took the spiced wine from Lizbeth, set it on a table, and helped her sister-in-law to lie on her side on the pallet. The warmth of the fireplace protected them from the chill of the evening, the pallet setup in front of the hearth. Pains had plagued Lizbeth for over fourteen hours, pains that were coming with increased frequency and intensity, but labor had not begun.

What Lilith had not voiced, but knew with certainty, was the unexpected complication. It was not a complication she had considered but neither was it one that overly concerned her. At least not yet. Although the situation could quickly turn dire if her ward became stressed, Lilith remained confident that her skills and prayers would not abandon her.

The complication was babe's position. He was breech with no signs of turning. Lilith needed both Lady Collingwood and Lizbeth to remain calm as she did all in her power to help baby turn naturally of his own volition. If the pain increased, Lilith would be forced to turn him by hand before the sac ruptured. And if the baby refused to turn…well, fortunately, they still had time.

With Lizbeth curled on her side, Lilith rubbed her sister-in-law's back and said, "Slowly, bring your knees to your chest. This will help relieve the pain." What she did not say was it would help coax baby to turn.

They stayed like that, Lizbeth breathing deeply and Lilith rubbing her patient's lower back soothingly, for an uncountable length of time until Lizbeth's scream of pain woke Lady Collingwood with a start.

It was not the first scream of the past fourteen hours, nor would it be the last. Lilith murmured encouraging words, continuing to massage the lower back. Lizbeth moaned and clutched for Lilith's arm, her breathing becoming shallow and ragged.

"You need to relax, Lizbeth. Focus on the sound of my voice and relax."

"Something is wrong. I can feel it." Lizbeth wailed between words. "Tell me. Tell me what's wrong."

"This too shall pass," Lilith said gently, flinching as Lizbeth's nails bit into her arm. "The pain will pass, as it has before. When it does, we will have some caudle. That will help."

"No, no, no." Lizbeth shook her head in agitation, tears wetting her cheeks, sweat beading her brow. Strands of auburn hair clung to her face. "Don't placate me. Something is wrong. This feels wrong."

Lady Collingwood stood and approached them, her voice higher pitched than usual, words tight. "I demand to know what you are doing to my niece. I demand to know now."

Lilith gritted her teeth. The last thing she needed was either of them panicking. For the baby to turn, Lizbeth needed to relax. There was already little room for babe to move, but if Lizbeth tightened her muscles, a flip would be hopeless.

"All is well," Lilith reassured. "I am helping baby move into position. It seems this little one is as stubborn as his father. If you must know, he is facing the wrong direction."

"What is that supposed to mean?" Lady Collingwood asked over Lizbeth's sobbing. "I demand an explanation. This is my niece and grand nephew's life you have in your hands."

"It means baby is bottom first, Lady Collingwood. Shall I pause to sketch you a drawing?" She bit her tongue, not intending her words to be rude. But really, she was trying to work and did not appreciate the questioning. "Please, forgive me. I need this willful babe to turn before the sac ruptures. If you'll kindly step away, I can focus."

The lady did not step away.

"And what happens if the, you know, what you said, occurs?"

Lilith affected calm, despite mounting annoyance. She knew Lady Collingwood meant well, but it was important everyone remained calm. "I don't speak in what-ifs. Now, if you please, I know my profession."

Lady Collingwood continued to rattle on, protesting and demanding to be heard. Lilith ignored her.

Unraveling her fingers from Lilith's arm, Lizbeth's crying settled as she attempted a smile, mumbling that the pain was subsiding. The look of worry mingled with fear in Lizbeth's eyes was not lost on Lilith. Her sister-in-law was thinking of her own mother dying in childbed. Lilith knew it.

Lilith also knew they were running out of time. The last bout of contractions had occurred not long enough ago to maintain Lilith's earlier confidence. Though she had wanted to avoid this, she realized she would need to turn baby by hand, sooner rather than later.

In theory, it would be safe and relatively easy since this was only pre-labor. At least, that was what her training and studies assured her, not that she knew from experience. She was nowhere near as confident about turning babe by hand as she wanted them to believe, for she had never seen a breech in person and knew if the turning were not successful, this could be fatal for mother and babe.

Bolstering her will, she decided she had given him enough time to turn on his own. Stubborn to the end. Auntie Lilith would have to do it. She ground her teeth, determined. Never had she lost a patient, and she certainly was not going to start with her sister-in-law.

The calmer she appeared, the calmer Lizbeth and Lady Collingwood would remain, and she desperately needed Lizbeth to be as relaxed as possible. Helping her sister-in-law move from her side to her back, Lilith embraced the rounded abdomen with her palms to feel the positioning. Once she completed the flip, she would have Lizbeth walk about the room to promote labor in hopes of a swift delivery in case Lord Stubborn decided to turn back to breech between the successful flip and the delivery. Once labor began, she would move Liz to the birthing chair.

"What are you doing? What is happening?" Lady Collingwood demanded, her voice strained in pre-hysteria.

Lilith ignored her again, reaching for a blanket to cover Lizbeth for modesty. Casually, slowly, with a loving smile and feigned placidity, she draped the cloth about Lizbeth, tucking the edges beneath the makeshift pallet. After she rubbed her hands together to ensure her touch would be warm, she reached under the blanket and lifted Liz's dressing gown over her belly to expose her abdomen to touch.

Lilith pressed firmly against Lizbeth's belly to locate baby's feet and head. Leaning closer to Lizbeth to be heard over Lady Collingwood's continued rants, she said, "This may feel rather unusual. Please, remain relaxed. The more relaxed you are, the easier and less painful this will be. Think of a warm, summer day with a good book. I'm going to turn baby now."

Lizbeth nodded, looking down to watch Lilith's hands move beneath the covering.

With each press against the abdomen, Lilith's efforts were rewarded with breathy moans and ragged cries. To make matters worse, for every centimeter she moved the babe, he moved back two. She swore an oath under her breath. Obstinate child. If he refused to flip, she would have to wait for Lizbeth to relax and try again. She would have to continue to try until labor began. At that point, she would have no choice but to attempt to birth him in breech. She prayed that would not happen.

"Tell me what you're doing?" Lizbeth's voice trembled, her hair damp from sweat, her face flushed from discomfort. "It will help me focus."

Lilith talked Lizbeth through each press of her hand. Surprisingly, she felt her sister-in-law relax the more she talked. Such a strong woman, Lilith thought. She admired Lizbeth's strength, a strength she was not sure she possessed herself.

As she explained her attempts to shift baby by hand, Lady Collingwood's agitation increased, clearly horrified by Lilith's maneuvers. The woman was making it difficult for Lilith to concentrate. While she could understand being concerned, could the lady not trust in Lilith to do what was best? Not only did Lilith know her profession, but she loved her sister-in-law and would let nothing bad happen.

Yes, she was terrified. No, she was not as confident as she had been an hour ago. But she would do all in her power to see this a success. A bit of trust, please.

Lizbeth relaxed against Lilith's hands, and the baby began to turn under her persuasion, ever so slightly. Slow and steady would win this race and avoid other complications like a twisted cord. With deep breaths, feeling the babe in her hands, her whole concentration on the sensation of his movements, she stared unseeing at Lizbeth, willing all her strength, perseverance, and love to channel from her to her sister-in-law.

And then the baby gave a swift kick to move back into breech. Lizbeth cried out for Sebastian, grabbing for Lilith's arm. Exhaling, Lilith leaned back on her haunches. They would need to begin again after Liz settled and relaxed.

Lady Collingwood's shrieks were bordering on hysteria. "We need a physician! My niece is going to die if we don't have a physician!" the woman howled.

What Lilith needed was Sebastian to remove this banshee from the room. Liz would be calmer with him by her side, and he could help Lilith in the process.

Aggravated, Lilith replied, "Physicians have nought to do with birthing babes, Lady Collingwood. All they are good for is opening veins or applying leeches."

"But we're aristocrats! Physicians have *all* to do with birthing our babies. My niece needs to be bled, not this, this *mad*wifery. You'll be the death of my niece!"

Closing her eyes, she gave a silent prayer, then looked back to the woman. "Bring Sebastian."

As if Lilith's request translated to "all is lost," Lady Collingwood ran shrieking from the room. "Lord Roddam! Sebastian!" she cried down the spiral castle stairs. "Come! Quickly! Your sister will be the death of our Lizzie! Send for a physician!"

Lilith closed her eyes again, willing herself to remain calm and in control. Fear and reason never made good bedfellows.

Turning back to Lizbeth, she smiled and asked, "Now that we have a bit of quiet, shall we continue?"

Walter stared at his hands, his forearms resting on his thighs. Despite it being after midnight, he was wide awake, his mind circling the events of the day and the anticipated arrival of his cousin's baby.

The three men waiting in the parlor had lapsed into silence some time ago. Lord Roddam took turns pacing about the room and sitting while fidgeting. From time to time, he cursed under his breath. He had gone to the bedchamber at least twice per hour to check the progress but came back each time to say Hazel had shooed him away.

Uncle Cuthbert fought his exhaustion by intermittently describing all the ways he would spoil his first grandchild. After having repeated himself a number of times, he took to clawing his sideburns anxiously. Walter wondered if his uncle was thinking of his own wife dying in childbed during his second daughter's birth, an event that nearly had been the destruction of the man, as he had loved his wife beyond measure. Walter had been sixteen at the time and all too aware of the devastation.

As eager as he was for all to be resolved upstairs, his thoughts selfishly shifted to Miss Chambers more than to the two men with him or to his cousin.

He had been mulling over her words from that morning, her words about not being a lady. At first, such words had not made sense to him, but after fourteen hours of sitting in a parlor over analyzing their conversations and interactions, he felt he understood her meaning perfectly.

How different life was between lords and ladies. His inheritance of the barony had been a catalyst, a moment when his world tilted, charging him with a need to search for the meaning of his life. And then there was Miss Chambers, or Lady Lilith rather, who had already found the meaning of her life and been living it happily until her inheritance of a ladyship, a catalyst in reconsidering her role. Yet her role had not, in her eyes, changed for the better.

Initially, he could see no qualms with realizing one was a person of importance, but when her definition of importance was so different, then yes, he could see all the reason in the world to find distaste in the alteration of status. Her love was in midwifery, or at least he assumed it was, and lest he forget, her work at the orphanage. Ladies could not be seen teaching in an orphanage and certainly not assisting in a birth. Society would not allow it. She would be shunned and ridiculed. For her to accept her new role, she would have to give up all she loved.

What an imbecile he had been to think she would set her sights on a duke when she most likely would never even consider a baron, not if she had no intention of taking up her mantle as Lady Lilith. Her continued use of Miss Chambers rather than Lady Lilith was proof enough of that decision. At first, he assumed it was from familiarity of name, a name Mrs. Brighton had likely given her upon admittance. Now, he saw it was a resistance to all her true name entailed.

He vowed to find a way into her heart. There must be a way in. He would have to prove he was not some toff bent on turning her into a parlor-sitting wife, but rather a supportive, fellow humanitarian who would encourage her every dream. Colling Orphanage was surely the way. If they managed it together, a joint effort, the censure would be less. And besides, she would have his protection. He would challenge anyone who said she was anything but the perfect lady.

"Lord Roddam!" His mother screeched from the gallery. "Oh, Sebastian! You must come! Your sister is killing my niece with her bare hands!"

Startled, all three men stood, staring at the open door of the parlor as his mother burst inside, a line of curious servants gathering behind her.

"You must come." She heaved, leaning heavily on the doorframe. Gulping in air after a hearty run down two flights of stairs, she gasped and choked and cried, "Lizzie. Lizzie needs a physician. Oh, do come."

Roddam sprinted to action, bolting past her, and taking the stairs two at a time. His mother did not spare him or her brother a glance before turning to follow Liz's husband.

Uncle Cuthbert turned to Walter, his brows furrowed, his hands clawing at his sideburns again.

"*An Jowl,*" Cuthbert swore quietly in Cornish.

Walter walked over and laid a hand on his uncle's shoulder. "You know Mama is prone to exaggeration. All will be well. Lizzie's the strongest woman I know."

Signaling to the butler, who stood not far from the parlor door, he requested drinks, something strong but palatable for his uncle. Cuthbert rarely imbibed, but Walter suspected this may be a moment when a strong drink was in order, anything to steady the man's nerves.

And the waiting continued.

There was nothing to be done except sit. Cuthbert adopted Roddam's role of fidgeting and cursing under his breath. Another hour passed, maybe longer, maybe not quite. Walter was too lost to the rhythmic tick of the mantel clock to notice.

A movement at the door stirred the men.

Miss Chambers stepped in, solemn. Her features were drawn from exhaustion, her lips turned at the corners in a frown, her hair in wild disarray. What gave Walter pause was the blood-covered apron she wore. When he tore his eyes from the stains to look into her face, he was startled to realize she was staring at him. In the silent moment when their eyes met, Cuthbert took the scene to mean the worst and started to weep.

Mama rushed into the room, shrieking again, the pitch lower at least. "She's *beautiful*, Cuthbert! Oh, she's beautiful!" She ran to her brother and embraced him, her shrill laughter joining his stuttering confusion.

Walter's eyes had not left Miss Chambers. Only when all heads turned to her did she speak, her voice low and hoarse, but commanding the room to silence.

"The Earl and Countess of Roddam are proud to announce the birth of Lady Freya Elizabeth Jane Lancaster. Both mother and baby are well."

At her words, Cuthbert wept anew, tears of joy.

Her frown twitched into a gentle smile, but Walter noticed the effort was taxing. She looked on the verge of collapse.

"I must excuse myself to settle mother and babe for the evening," she said. "I know you all long to see them, but please, do not disturb them 'til the morrow. They will be ready to receive you all after a good night's sleep."

With a nod, she swept from the room.

After a tiresome trudge up the grand staircase from the gallery to the great hall, and then up the slender spiral of stone stairs leading to the bedchamber, Lilith knocked twice then let herself into the room.

Sebastian and Lizbeth did not look up. Liz had been moved to the bed where she sat against a fortress of pillows, Lady Freya cradled in her arms. Sebastian sat with her, his body molded against hers, one arm draped around her shoulders, the other palming his daughter's head.

Lilith paused at the door, embarrassed to have intruded on such a tender scene.

With a glance down, she groaned, only now realizing in her exhaustion she had forgotten to remove the apron. No wonder Mr. Trethow and Lord Collingwood had looked so alarmed. She removed the offending garment, folded it, and set it on the linens soon to be removed.

"You were right," Lizbeth said from the bed, eyeing Lilith drowsily. "She had quite the appetite." Since her sister-in-law refused to use a wet nurse, Lilith had encouraged her to feed the newborn while she announced the arrival of the newest Lancaster to the family.

Having been acknowledged, Lilith made her way to the bed. If Lilith thought she felt tired, she need only look at Lizbeth to know her own exhaustion was insignificant.

Sebastian kissed his wife's temple, rose from the bed, and exchanged Liz's supporting arms with his own to hold the bundle.

"Thank you," he said to Lilith in nought but a whisper. "The two great loves of my life are here because of you."

With a worn heart and a weary smile, Lilith held out her arms for the babe. The exchange was brief but gentle. A kiss to his daughter's head and one to Lilith's cheek, he returned to his wife's side, the two watching her sleepily.

Never had she seen a more perfect child. A full head of black hair, inquisitive slate-grey eyes, and a rosebud mouth. Freya's tiny fist squeezed Lilith's finger as she carried the baby to the crib for swaddling.

"So, you're the one who gave me so much trouble," Lilith said with a breathy laugh. "I apologize for thinking you were Lord Stubborn when it should have been clear to me from the first sign of obstinance that this sort of headstrong behavior could only come from a Lancaster lady."

In reply, Freya yawned and fluttered her eyes closed.

Less than half an hour later, with Lizbeth and Freya settled for the night, Lilith made her way to her own room. Soon, she would share the space with the baby until a full-time nurse could be hired, but for now, she was relieved Freya would stay with her mother. Lilith's exhaustion knew no bounds.

When she reached her bedchamber, she closed the door silently behind her and leaned against the wood, shutting her eyes against the pounding in her head.

Never had she witnessed such love between two people. Of all the births she had attended, never had the husband been so helpful or so clearly infatuated by his family, a family bonded by love alone. She wanted what they had. She wanted it so much she ached. How many births had she attended, yet none of them had inspired such a desire for a family of her own? Perhaps it was Sebastian's whispers to Lizbeth that she was a warrior, whispers calm but infused with courage. Or perhaps it was how he held her to him during delivery, his arms empowering.

"My lady." A tentative voice startled Lilith. "I've readied a bath."

Staring in wide-eyed confusion, she saw a maid standing at the door of the dressing room. She had thought herself alone.

With a curtsy, the girl said, "Lord Roddam ordered me to attend you this evening." Staring at the ground and blushing, she added, "He said not to take no for an answer. Your bath awaits."

As irritated as she normally would have felt, a hot bath sounded divine.

Sighing, she approached the girl. "Call me Lilith. And you are?"

Glancing up, the girl said, "Hannah."

"Well met, Hannah."

Lilith followed Hannah into the dressing room and allowed herself to be undressed and bathed, a luxury she had not experienced since a child. It seemed foolish to have someone help her do things she had done on her own for the entirety of her adult life.

Oh, but it did feel good to be pampered this evening. Although, it was not evening, was it? Good heavens. She had no idea what time it was. Two in the morning? Three? Maybe not so late?

"I hope you won't think me impertinent, but I've set out a lovely nightgown from the bureau. And I took the liberty to choose the green dress for tomorrow."

She did not open her eyes as she submerged to her chin in the water. From the bureau? Ah. The dresses Lizbeth gave her. Too tired to protest and thinking green sounded a heavenly color, she nodded.

When Hannah prompted her to rise, Lilith begged to be left alone for the night. Her tone was warm, her words grateful. She hoped not to offend the girl by sending her away.

As she headed for the door, Lilith called out, startling them both. "Wait. Hannah."

"Yes, my l—Lilith?"

"Will you assist me in the morning? I do warn you I will wake quite early, so if you would rather—"

"Oh, yes! Ring as soon as you wake. I shall bring you a hot chocolate."

If it were possible for anything to be more divine than a bath, it would be a cup of hot chocolate to greet the morning. She sighed and nodded a dismissal to the lady's maid.

The pleasure she felt at seeing the girl's happiness to satisfy her mistress surprised Lilith. She had thought it an abuse of station having someone wait on her when she could do it herself. The hypocritical nature of being illegitimate yet acting the part of a lady had bothered her, as well, giving her pause to accept any help. But it felt shockingly good to acknowledge the hard work of someone else and know that acknowledgment meant the world to another person's esteem.

She smiled to herself at this unexpected pleasure as Hannah left her alone to soak in the warm water. She smiled until she felt wetness on her cheeks, wetness not from the water but from tears.

How foolish to be crying in a tub!

The clinical, logical Lilith was not prone to such an outpouring of emotion. And yet, she cried. Her tears turned to sobs and her sobs to heaving and convulsing gasps. For the first time in a year, she cried, purging herself of every emotion she had felt but not given into.

She cried over meeting her brother for the first time since childhood. Over discovering her parentage. Over being manipulated by the Reverend Sands. She cried at the fear she felt when nearly losing her sister-in-law in childbed, at the unconditional love she felt when first seeing her niece, at the longing when witnessing the affection between her brother and his wife. Most unexpectedly, she cried at the yearning she felt when staring across the parlor into Lord Collingwood's green eyes. But above all, she cried because she wanted what she could never have.

Chapter 6

A shrill cry woke Walter.

He blinked, trying to focus his eyes in the darkness. Straining, he listened for the sound. Dream or reality? He had been dreaming of sirens, enchanting sirens, all with long, raven hair.

The shrill sound whistled this time, a long, hollow whistle. Burying his head in the pillow, he realized it was the wind wheezing into the stone walls of the castle. A storm raged outside with a symphony of sounds: whining, whipping, whistling, howling. Turning onto his back, he stared up at the wooden canopy of the four-poster bed, too caught up in the crescendo to sleep.

With a grunt, he pushed back the covers and swung his legs over the bed. Bare feet against cold stone elicited a curse as he walked to one of the windows and parted the curtains. Sheets of fog rolled towards the castle, masking the rain that moved sideways in one direction, then with a gust of wind turned the opposite direction. Pre-dawn light filtered through the fog, enough for him to make out angry ocean waves beyond the outer wall.

Another grunt later, he shuffled back to bed and tucked himself under the layers of bedding, covering his head with the pillow to drown the sound of the storm. His last thoughts before he drifted back to sleep were that his father would never know the joy his Uncle Cuthbert experienced of having a grandchild.

After what felt like only minutes, Walter woke again to a bright light streaming across his eyes. Dash it all — he had forgotten to close the curtains. Groaning, he threw his arm over his eyes to settle back to sleep.

Tic toc. Tic toc. Tic toc.

For pity's sake! He peeked beneath his arm to glare at the longcase clock in the corner of the chamber. Blasted, noisy devil. Who put a clock in a bedchamber? Someone who did not want guests, apparently.

Quarter until seven in the morning, the beast of a timekeeper displayed. Tossing off the covers as he had done nigh minutes ago, well, perhaps hours ago, but it felt like minutes, he rose and headed for the dressing room. With a splash of icy water from the basin, he cleansed his face of sleep.

There was nothing for it. He needed a run.

Nothing beat being home where he could go for his morning row on the Trelowen lake. His visit to Dunstanburgh had been sedentary, shamefully sedentary. And if he was not mistaken, his waistcoats were feeling decidedly snugger each morning. While staying at Lyonn Manor with the Duke of Annick, he at least had the opportunity to fence with his old Oxford mates. But here at the castle? No such luck. It was his own fault for not taking initiative. He had slept in every morning and done nothing of worth.

Seven o'clock. He would have time for a run before calling for Kory, his valet, for a wash, shave, and dress. His favorite coat and set were at the ready in the dressing room. He smirked. Kory knew him well. The man knew Walter would want to celebrate Freya's arrival in one of his old favorites.

Yes, plenty of time before anyone would be awake for breakfast.

A sweep of his hand across his face proved he needed that shave, but it would wait. Donning the worn pair of breeches he used for fencing and an unadorned pair of stockings and boots, he pulled a shirt over his head and headed out of the bedchamber, tucking the ends of his shirt into his breeches as he made his way down the corridor.

The castle was silent, all still abed after the summer's longest night. He made his way out of the guest wing, down a flight of stairs, through the gallery, and outside to the courtyard in quick and silent strides, hoping not to disturb anyone from their well-deserved slumber. Following the slope of the headland, he left the castle grounds through the back gate by the stables and jogged down the northern slant to the beach. His plan was to first tackle the beach for the challenge of running against sand, and then circle through the dunes, back around the meres, and up through the front gatehouse.

The sky was bright but sunless, a heavy fog with wet air hovering over the area. The rain, thankfully, had abated before dawn. His boots hitting sand as he jogged, he glanced over his shoulder at the imposing curtain wall receding in the distance. The castle disappeared behind a haze of grey.

Crisp air bit his cheeks as his legs pumped him forward. The storm had brought with it a sharp chill. The waves to his right gently rolled, wetting the hard, packed sand. He ran against the soft sand near the dunes, his calves burning from the exertion.

Why he had not been running every morning, he could not say. Just laziness, he supposed. As with so many aspects of his life, it was time to stop dreaming and take action. He wanted to put quill to parchment this week regarding his plans for the orphanage. Did he want a foundling hospital as part of it, just as Miss Chambers had said the Allshire orphanage was planning? A list of necessary staff would be important, facilities, costs, oh, so much to plan. He must pen a missive to his secretary to ask if the man could do some digging on what it took to make this dream a reality.

There was no denying his motivation for taking action: Miss Chambers. She inspired him. If he could put together a solid enough plan, she would believe he was in earnest. Would his dedication and vision tempt her to be a partner in the plan? Entice her to think of him as more than her sister-in-law's cousin? Charm her even?

Veering to the left, he jogged for the sediment stream flowing between the two largest of dunes. A perfect cut-through to circle back towards the castle via the gatehouse. He could, of course, run over the dunes, but they were quite steep with some unpleasant looking grasses and brambles. Not laziness, but unsafe, he justified.

He kept to the sandy edge of the stream since the stream looked deceptively deep. As he rounded the dune, he stopped short, nearly tripping headlong into the water.

"Oh, ho ho!" he exclaimed.

Skittering to one side, he only just avoided trampling Miss Chambers.

Walter struggled for a moment to catch his balance and his breath.

Miss Chambers sat on the edge of the dune, her bare feet dipping into the stream. She looked as shocked as he felt, drawing her shawl about her shoulders and hugging her arms across her chest as though self-conscious. She had no reason to be. She looked breathtakingly gorgeous, her cheeks rosy from the wind, her hair loose about her shoulders and down to her waist.

He was the one who should feel self-conscious, caught unawares in nothing but a shirt, sweat, and his shabbiest of breeches and boots.

Dash it all! He cursed silently as he combed his fingers through his wet curls.

"Good morning, Lord Collingwood," she said, her shock turning to amusement as she took in his dishabille.

Her eyes roamed over him from head to foot and back up, taking in every inch of his dishevelment. His ears burned in mortification.

"Yes, yes, it is, yes a good morning indeed," he stammered. "I, uh, I mean, that is to say, good morning, Miss Chambers." What a bumbling clod she must think him! "Do forgive me, Miss Chambers. I, uh, I didn't expect anyone to be about at this hour. I do apologize."

"No apology needed. It seems we have caught each other in a rare and unguarded moment."

"Yes, I suppose. If you'll excuse me, I'll return to the castle and not disturb your peace."

"No!" Miss Chambers raised a staying hand, fleetingly looking both frantic and vulnerable.

When he made no move to leave, she dried her feet with the hem of her dress before slipping a pair of scuffed half-boots over bare toes. Standing, she secured her shawl with a knot to keep it from flying away, then looked steadily at him with bewitching eyes.

"Shall we walk together, my lord? I would like the company."

A quick look around showed she had not brought a maid. But of course, she would not.

Feeling sheepish and more than a little in love, he grinned and held his arm for her to take. His only hope was that he did not smell like a horse.

She nudged him back to the beach rather than following the dunes. Though they walked a good distance at a casual pace, she made no attempt at conversation. Walter found it difficult not to admire her profile. The top of her head came level with his eyes—a kissable height. She wore a placid smile, as one at peace with the day and her surroundings, though her eyelids drooped from weariness. The wind caught her hair and whipped it about. More than once, she swept a hand across her face to tuck the strands behind her ears.

"You must be exhausted," he said.

"Aren't you a perceptively posh pickle this morning, Lord Collingwood. Is it the dark circles under my eyes that gave me away?"

With an awkward *ha*, he said, "I meant no slight, only that it was a long night, and I didn't expect to see anyone awake this early, least of all you who worked so hard to bring new life into the world. And for that matter, I don't see dark circles. You look beautiful in the morning light."

She bowed her head, preventing him from seeing if she blushed and smiled or scowled with annoyance. The compliment was too bold, he feared. But why should he not let his feelings be known? This woman was not wooed by innuendo.

"Morning is my favorite time of day," she replied, ignoring his compliment. "A time before the world wakes. When everything is private, quiet. It's a time to reflect. I'm more surprised to see you this early. I was under the impression peers of the realm prefer to laze all morning since they have nothing better to do than sleep."

Her words were not accusatory, rather whimsical. She was teasing him.

"Ah, guilty as charged, my lady. At least since I've been here. When home, that is not the case. I may be a dreamer, but I'm not lazy."

Giving him a long, assessing look, she said, "You look different this morning. I hardly recognize you."

Embarrassed, he cleared his throat. He could not recall a time when a woman had seen him in only a shirt, much less such shabby attire. The sweat and sand did not do him any service either. He must look appalling.

"I do apologize. Again, I didn't expect to see anyone. Had there been a chance—"

"Now you mistake *my* meaning," she interrupted. "I like this version of you. You look—how should I say this?—human."

"Human?" he echoed.

"Quite. You are always so polished, and yet here you are, *raw*. Even your cheeks are rough with stubble. Yes, you look human, and I very much prefer this version. You don't look titled."

Frowning, he said, "But I am titled."

"Yes, so you are."

They lapsed into silence.

A light drizzle sprinkled, but she did not seem to mind.

"I would rather have my father than a title, Miss Chambers."

She directed him to the black rocks at the base of the hill leading up to the curtain wall and signaled for them to sit. He chose the smoothest and largest rock for them to share, holding her hand only long enough to guide her safely until seated.

Miss Chambers leaned back, her arms behind her, her palms flat against the rockface, her face tilted to the sky to feel the drizzling rain.

Leaning forward, he rested his forearms against his thighs, snagging a small rock to roll in his hands. Anything to occupy him from staring at her.

"How did he die?" she asked, breaking the silence.

"Carriage accident. It was a blind bend. He ran head-on into a curricle racer. He was thrown from the carriage. Died on impact."

The rock in his hand was smooth, weathered by the sea.

"You were close to him," she said.

"Yes and no. Yes, we were close. He was my hero. But those few years after Oxford, I was a hellion. He wanted to teach me estate business and make it a real father-son venture, but all I wanted to do was be with my mates, stay out late, get foxed every night. You know, all those things you think spoiled children of aristocrats do. Only, I was a grown man with no excuse for such behavior. I regret every minute. Those were minutes I could have spent with him."

He could not believe he was rambling and to a woman he wanted to impress. How could she ever be impressed with him after admitting such foul things about himself? She would think him the very type of man she would want to avoid.

Much to his surprise, he felt a featherlight touch against his cheek. He flinched and glanced at his companion. Her hand stilled in the air, inches from his face.

"It's softer than I expected," she whispered, tentatively reaching her fingers to his cheek again, running the tips against his stubble. "I thought it might be rough to the touch."

Feeling daring but not brave enough to break the spell with a kiss, he tossed the rock aside and caught her wrist. She made no motion to pull away, simply stared at him with unreadable brown eyes. He leaned his cheek into her palm, pressing her hand hard against his skin, raking it against the soft bristles until her palm met his lips. Pressing his lips to her skin, he kissed the ungloved, satin flesh.

She closed her eyes, allowing him to press a kiss to the heel of her palm, and then against the inside of her slender wrist. Only when he began to lean ever so slightly closer did her eyelids flutter open. She tugged her hand free and looked away.

He burned for her, the memory of her skin still on his lips. He wanted nothing more than to kiss her. Yet, the moment had passed. Her gaze was on the castle wall, not him, discouraging him from doing what he desperately desired.

Filtered sunrays found a thinness in the fog through which to peek.

"Would you like to return to the castle, Miss Chambers?" he asked hoarsely.

"No, but I do suppose it would be sensible to head that direction."

Willing his ardor to cool, he stood first before helping her down from the rocks. She took his arm, and they walked towards the slope that would take them around to the servant's entrance.

"It's not that I dislike you because you're titled," she said abruptly. "It's only — Well, we're from different worlds. I can't relate to the polished version of you. You're always formal and stuffy."

He could not help but laugh at that assessment. Not quite the image he had of himself. No one had ever accused him of being formal or stuffy.

"But I like this version of you. Very much."

Her tone was matter of fact, as though providing a diagnosis after an examination. Her words, however, flip-flopped his heart.

Opening the wooden door in the curtain wall, he held it for her to enter the castle grounds. Halfway through the doorway, she paused. She stared at him as though she had more to say. But then, she did something he never would have expected.

Placing two warm hands against his chest, she leaned in and kissed his cheek.

It was not a quick peck. It was a slow kiss wherein she brushed her mouth against his skin, tickling her lips with his stubble before pursing her lips. She held the kiss, as though memorizing the feel of him.

Just as slowly, she retreated, her hands still against his chest.

He knew he was blushing. He could feel his ears growing hot and his neck flushing. Before he could make a move of his own, she patted his chest, turned away from him, and walked with quickened steps towards the castle, leaving him standing alone in the doorway.

Walter stepped into the morning room, ravenous.

The space flooded with sunlight. Two walls of windowed, double doors afforded an uninterrupted view of the ocean to the east and the inner courtyard to the west. Two sideboards of food stood to either side of an inglenook fireplace, lit to combat the chill from the evening's rain.

Disobedient eyes searched the room for a glimpse of Miss Chambers.

No signs of the enchantress.

Only Mama and Uncle Cuthbert were at the table, not that he expected Roddam or Lizbeth to join them when they had a new babe to coddle. Ignoring his grumbling stomach, he joined the siblings, greeting his mother with a kiss to her cheek and his uncle with a pat on the back. Cuthbert was bright eyed and jovial, laughing at whatever Mama had been saying.

"Do join us, Walter," she said. "I'm regaling Cuthbert with how unceremoniously Sebastian tossed me from the room last night."

Walter chuckled. "And yet you're laughing about it. I suspect you weren't at the time."

"Oh, heavens no! I was most put out." Even as she said it, she chortled, all forgiveness in light of the happy outcome.

As his mother rattled on, he made his way to the sideboard to snatch the remaining soft-boiled eggs and toast. Not for a moment did he pay any real attention to what else he put on the plate; his mind was too fixed on if Miss Chambers would join them for breakfast. Would she act differently around him now? Would she be disappointed that he had changed? His cheeks were smooth from Kory's shave, his hair styled with a light touch of cologne, his attire an older set but one of his favorites, worn in honor of Lady Freya's arrival.

Never was his look frippish or toffish, at least not in his opinion, nothing to his old Oxford mates who bordered on dandyism. He liked a neat look, clean lines, simple embroidery, no foppish lace or frills, never too starched, but always a tidy cravat that showed good taste. He typically favored the *trone d'amour* knot.

Try as he might, he could not see himself how Miss Chambers described. What had she meant by preferring him *raw*?

He had stared at himself in the mirror long enough for Kory to ask if all was well. The reflection revealed only himself, no insight to what she liked or did not like about him. While he could appreciate her desire for a man of humble origins, he disliked that she saw his title rather than him. He was who he was. He was born an heir, and now he was a baron. There was no pride or shame in holding a title, merely a fact of life. He was who he was.

His plate a mountain of delights, he strode back to the table and took the seat next to his mother. She was still chattering, entertaining her brother with some tale about toddlers she had seen in Hyde Park during the Season.

Walter did not listen. Instead, he eyed the door between bites, eagerly awaiting Miss Chambers' arrival. After their encounter this morning, he was encouraged to court her. Seeking out permission had seemed rash when they had spoken so little, but now that she showed clear interest, it was the logical next step. Until that morning, he had suspected her pride regarding her life as Miss Chambers was holding her back. And perhaps it still was. Somehow, he would need to combat that to show her life with him was worth the leap.

The door to the morning room opened. Walter's pulse raced. Swallowing his bite of toast whole, he looked to the door, ready to rise to his feet.

Lord Roddam stood in the place Walter had expected to see Miss Chambers. His heart sank. His eyes also watered from the too-large piece of toast he gulped.

"Liz and I would be honored if you would all join us in our private sitting room. Freya is awake and ready to meet her family, though I suspect she will not be awake for long." Roddam awarded them a tired but soft-hearted smile.

It took less than a second for Mama to screech with excitement and abandon her breakfast, Uncle Cuthbert at her heels. Walter shoved an egg-coated piece of toast in his mouth, whole. Then he grabbed another piece to go. It would not do to meet the newest member of the family with a growling stomach.

The troupe followed Roddam through the downstairs corridor, into the gallery, and up the grand staircase. When they reached the great hall, which now served as the armory, Miss Chambers stood waiting.

No, not Miss Chambers. Lady Lilith. Very much Lady Lilith.

Walter's breath caught. Just as it had the first day. Nay, not like the first day. Different. He physically could not breathe.

Miss Chambers had transformed since he last saw her only a few hours before. She wore a *robe à l'anglaise* of silk taffeta woven with alternating green and gold vertical stripes. The green was striking on her. The sleeves were elbow-length with turned-back cuffs. Around her bosom was a delicate silk fichu with lace ribbons.

Her dress was so decidedly different from her usual choices, he did not know what to make of it. It was an older dress, to be sure, one Walter suspected had been Liz's during a previous Season, but it looked stunning on Miss Chambers, though the hem was a good bit too short, made up for by a lengthier petticoat.

Her hair was braided, but instead of hanging down the length of her back, it was coiled in a wreath around a top knot. Of everything about her to see, he was most taken by the slope of her neck, elongated by the coiffure. What he would not do to kiss the skin just there.

She seemed unsure of herself with a grim expression and clenched hands, but as he approached, her demeanor softened. She thrust out a determined chin and smiled ever so coyly, looking at him rather than the others.

"Brava! Brava! Our heroine in the flesh!" Mama cried out, startling him from his admiration.

Miss Chambers looked far more startled. Her eyes widened, and her brows knit. She stared at his mother as though the woman were quite mad.

Mama was undaunted. She flurried to Miss Chambers with arms outstretched and embraced her in what had to be the century's most awkward hug, as one party stood rigid while the other tittered.

"Without your cunning," his mother said, "my niece and great niece might not be here today. I may have been a tad unjust last evening, but I'm sure you'll forgive me. Now, show me the way. Onward!"

Roddam and Uncle Cuthbert were already halfway up the spiral, stone steps to the library before Miss Chambers guided his mother and him behind them. At the far end of the library, they went through a pocket door leading to the couple's private sitting room, a descriptor wholly understated given the room was the length and width of the great hall below. Walter's own humble home could not compare to the grandeur of a castle, and he preferred it that way, just as he knew Miss Chambers would, as well.

A sizeable breakfast tray perched on a table in the middle of a circle of chairs. All too clearly, Liz, Roddam, and Miss Chambers had eaten here instead of the morning room but had requested a fresh tray in case the others were still peckish after being interrupted at table.

Lizbeth and Lady Freya sat waiting.

Liz looked drawn but glowed with happiness, her cheeks flushed and her eyes bright, signs of weariness showing in her rounded shoulders and sleepy smile. She cradled a swaddled bundle making gurgling sounds.

Walter stayed back, watching his family coo over both the new mother and new babe.

It was not that he did not want to see or hold Freya, but that he was merely the cousin, the bachelor cousin with no experience around babies. This moment was for his Uncle Cuthbert and his Mama. Mama fussed over Liz while Cuthbert exclaimed over the baby, taking the infant into his arms to cosset.

When he glanced at Miss Chambers, he was surprised to catch her looking back at him. Had she been assessing him? Disapproving his clean and tidy appearance? With a lilt at the corner of her lips, she returned her attention to the family, exchanging words with Cuthbert as he rocked the newborn.

Walter lost himself for a moment in admiring the arch of her neck and the curve of her waist, her movements nothing less than graceful. Not until she came towards him did he realize she had taken the baby into her arms to bring to him. Miss Chambers' head bent close to the bundle to whisper soft words.

He rubbed the back of his neck and shifted his weight to his other foot. Walter felt notably awkward.

"Would you like to hold Lady Freya, Lord Collingwood?"

Not especially, he thought. What was he supposed to do with a baby?

"Mimic me," she said. "Hold up your arms like this."

He obeyed, mimicking the positioning of her arms with a bend of his elbows, creating a hammock with his forearms.

"You're a natural, my lord."

Before he could dissuade her, she placed her own arms into his, standing so close he could feel her breath on his cheek. And then a baby was nestled in his arms. To his dismay, she withdrew once Freya was settled safely.

He swallowed against the lump in his throat. What if he held her too tightly? What if he dropped her? What if he made her cry? Walter was terrified and overwhelmed.

Nestling the baby's head into the crook of his elbow, he swallowed again and looked down. Freya *oohed* up at him, appearing for all the world as fascinated as a newborn could, a tiny bundle of happiness, her slate-grey eyes gazing at him in wonder, her eyebrows wiggling. It was love at first sight all over again.

"Welcome to the family, little one," he said.

She gurgled.

Though Lizbeth had auburn hair and greenish brown eyes, both lighter shades than his own, the baby notably took after her father's dark features.

Looking up, he realized Miss Chambers watched him intently. Was it too far-fetched for him to wonder what a baby might be like between her and himself? Would the child have reddish-brown curls or black? How absurd to question a nonexistent child's likeness when the woman of his dreams was determined they were opposites never to attract. Never mind that up until this point, he had had no interest in a family of his own.

But he knew she was the one.

Reaching into the cradle of his arms, Miss Chambers took Freya into her own to return to Lizbeth. Walter remained standing apart from the others, watching, yearning.

"Lilith will be helping me interview nurses," Lizbeth was explaining to Mama as she took Freya.

"It will be so much easier, my dear, having your sister-in-law living here," Mama said to her niece. "She will be an excellent mediator between you and the nurse, and we cannot deny her experience with children. I'm relieved I will be leaving you in capable hands."

"Oh, but I won't be living here," Miss Chambers interjected. "I return to Allshire in a little over a fortnight."

Gasping, Mama placed her hand to her bosom. "Preposterous! There's nothing for you there. Your home is with your family where you can be cared for. No more of that nonsense about returning. I'll not have it."

"Your concern is appreciated, my lady, but I do have a life in Allshire and am content as I am."

"Sebastian!" his mother cried. "Talk sense into your sister!"

Lord Roddam, standing behind Lizbeth with his hands on the back of her chair, questioned, "You think I haven't tried, Hazel? I've been hoping to wear down her will during this visit, but she'll not listen to reason.

She's set in her ways, a stubborn Lancaster through and through."

"I'll not hear of it," Mama insisted. "You are a member of this family, Lady Lilith, and simply cannot return to old ways. You are a *lady* now, don't you see? Your home is here where you can be supported."

Walter could see Miss Chambers bristle, her posture rigid, her lips pursed.

Mama was not finished. "Enough of that nonsense. I know just the thing to convince you. Let us, you and I, venture into town this week for shopping. I do love shopping, and I've quite the eye for fashion, if I do say so myself. It will mark your embarkment on a new adventure!"

He held his breath, waiting for a sharp set down from Miss Chambers.

Her eyes fixed on his before she addressed his mother. "I should like that, Lady Collingwood. I accept because you offer out of kindness, and I am overdue in making your better acquaintance. But do not think it will dissuade me from my present course. On one thing, though, we must be in agreement. I insist you call me Lilith."

Mama cast a more-than-obvious glance at Walter before taking Miss Chambers' measure, a mischievous grin on her lips. "Only if you call me Hazel."

As though sensing she were no longer the center of attention, Lady Freya began to cry, a breathy wail.

Mama and Uncle Cuthbert took their leave of the family with warm words and high spirits. Walter followed them out of the sitting room with a quick glance to Miss Chambers who watched their departure.

A few hours later, Lilith sat in the conservatory, read-ing a book from Sebastian's library. Which book, she could not honestly say, as she had re-read the first page repeatedly for the past hour without absorbing a single word. Lord Collingwood was not the only object of her attention, though he did dominate her thoughts more than anything else.

She had been unguarded in the morning hours, still exposed from an emotional evening. That did not change the fact that she knew she was in trouble. As much as she had denied it before, she knew for cer-tain he was taken with her, and now she had given him reason to think she felt the same.

The trouble was, she did feel the same. Only, there was a difference between his attraction for her and hers for him. He saw her as an eligible match. She, however, knew they could never be, for it took far more than attraction to live happily ever after, espe-cially when illegitimate girls did not marry titled boys.

All morning she had tried to convince herself she only liked him because he was the first handsome and decent man to pay her any mind. When that course of thought did not hold water, she then tried to per-suade herself into believing she saw him as a means to an end — a way to have a family in her desperate and advancing years. It, too, was all hogwash, of course. She liked him because she was attracted to him and had been from the first moment she laid eyes on him.

And now his mother was in on it. Lady Colling-wood, Hazel rather, wanted to take her *shopping* of all the silliness.

What was she supposed to do? The simplest course of action was to tell the truth and be done with it, tell him she was illegitimate and watch him run the opposite direction. And yet, it was not so easy. He was so different from other aristocrats, different even from the landed gentry in Allshire.

Though they had not spoken many times, the few times they had spoken showed her a man of warmth, a gentle spirit with a soul of gold. Having seen him in full dishevelment hours ago, she could not unsee *him*, the lover behind the blushing glances, the masculine physique beneath the pomp, the reddish curls dusting the hollow of his throat usually hidden by his cravat, the tender longing in the emerald eyes.

Before that morning, she had held his title as a shield against his charm, for he could never be a real suitor if their stations were so far removed. Seeing *him* behind the title had been her undoing. She wanted to give in to her desires, allow herself to be Lady Lilith, courted by Walter Hobbs, Baron Collingwood, and trussed by his mother. Did it all have to be so complicated? Could she not have a bit of sunshine in her life?

A knock at the far end of the conservatory disrupted her reading of the forgotten book. A charming head of russet curls poked around the door. Her heart skipped a beat. Setting aside the book, she smiled an invitation for him to join her.

Lord Collingwood bowed. When she indicated for him to sit, he chose the chair closest to her and leaned in her direction, his elbow resting on the upholstered armrest, one of his legs crossing over the other.

"*Evelina*?" Lord Collingwood asked, looking at the book she had tossed aside.

"Oh, is that what it's called? I hadn't noticed. Sebastian insists I'll enjoy it, but I can't get beyond the first page. Have you read it?"

"Never heard of it." He shrugged. "Is the first page so terrible?"

"No. I'm distracted. I'm certain I will enjoy it if Sebastian recommended it."

"He's a man of good opinion. And I say that for no other reason than he married my cousin. Clear signs of intelligence and good taste."

Lilith laughed at his jest.

"Yes, well, without beating about the bush, I'm here to apologize for my mother," he said unexpectedly.

"Your mother? Whatever for?"

"For prodding you about moving to the castle. I could tell it bothered you. My mother doesn't mince words, as you've probably gathered by now. She is blunt but caring. She wants everyone in the world to be happy, and if she can have a hand in that happiness, she'll stop at nothing to do her part. I hope you took no offense, for she meant none."

"Rest assured, I took no offense, not once I realized she meant well."

His next words caught her unprepared.

"I hope you won't find me impertinent for saying this. I suspect I know why you'd prefer to stay in Allshire, Miss Chambers."

Lilith stared at him, aghast. Did he know she was illegitimate?

When she made no response, he continued, "From what I've learned about you, I gather you're fiercely independent, proud of all you've accomplished, and are determined to resume your work helping women and children in the parish. Am I warm?"

Not until her fingers ached did she realize she had been clenching her hands, afraid he would speak the words that would sever their chance for something more than friendship. Looking at him now, his eyes hopeful, his brows raised in question, she knew she did not want him to discover the truth. She did not want to see his admiration turn to scorn.

"You are not wrong, Lord Collingwood. It is difficult for me to imagine a life without my patients."

"Walter," he said, a bashful smile on his lips. "I would be deeply honored if you would call me Walter. We are, after all, among family."

"Only if you promise to call me Lilith."

Her heart beat erratically at the sight of his shy smile broadening, a man victorious in securing the given name of a woman he fancied. Oh, yes, she was in trouble.

Chapter 7

T he hearth fire crackled, warm flames licking hungrily, hissing at the cool air seeping through stone. The parlor inhabitants, ensconced in a game of cards, sat indifferent to the fire's efforts to keep them warm.

Every day for the past several days had been the same—a warm and sunny morning with an afternoon of leaden skies and cold rain.

Walter took advantage of the mornings to repeat his run from earlier in the week. His body thanked him, as did his waistcoats. More to the point, it gave him time to think and plan, to envision the orphanage he hoped to build, to envision life with Lilith. A great many details were yet undecided, but at least he had a sense of direction.

Lord Roddam drummed his fingers against the table.

Walter looked up to find an arched brow mocking him over a fan of cards. So lost in his daydreams, he had missed his turn.

"Distracted?" Roddam enquired, his other brow arching to mirror the first. A telltale grin teased the corners of his mouth as he lowered his cards.

"What makes you ask? I'm merely plotting my next move."

Roddam grunted. "I'm winning."

"Now, now, no need to rub it in."

"Nay. The fact that I'm winning tells me you're distracted."

Before he had a chance to answer, the parlor door opened, catching the attention of the two gents.

Lilith stepped into the room.

Her cheeks were flushed and her smile wide, the coiled coiffure ever so slightly windswept, strands of black escaping about her shoulders. Her dress, he noticed, must be new, for it was not one of the usual dresses, nor was it ill-fitting, indicative of Lizbeth's old dresses offered in gift. No, this dress framed Lilith's figure in collar-heating ways. His eyes caressed her, noting with interest the pale, sapphire blue. The style was understated, simple in design, but of the latest fashion. It emphasized her natural vivaciousness.

Both gentlemen rose from their chairs and bowed, Walter's bow deeper and more reverent, his heart beating a tattoo to see her looking so spirited.

"Did you lose Hazel at the modiste?" Roddam asked, as Lilith approached their table.

"Almost. She didn't exaggerate about loving to shop. Alas, I dragged her away before she purchased the lot, but only just."

Walter eyed the door. "I suspect we'll hear about fans and bonnets for the remainder of the day. Did you have to lock her in her suite? It's unlike her to delay bragging of her latest conquests."

"You've been granted a brief reprieve," said Lilith. "Your saving grace is our visit to the nursery. She couldn't tear herself away from the fun Mr. Trethow and Lizbeth were having with Freya." With a laugh, she added, "Never underestimate the charm of peep-boo to entertain adults more than babies, especially a newborn who would much rather be sleeping."

His hand on her shoulder, Roddam offered his seat to Lilith. "Sit. Warm yourself. I'll ring for tea while you tell Collingwood about your shopping adventure." He did not wait for a response but walked away to the bell rope.

Without further invitation, Lilith took the seat across from Walter.

Wearing his ardor on his sleeve, his smile broad and his eyes admiring, he asked, "Am I to look forward to a conversation on bonnet colors?"

Her laugh, deep and throaty, was genuine. "You should be so lucky."

"I wouldn't have assumed you a lover of shopping; yet here you sit, glowing with happiness and showing a new dress to its advantage."

The blush tinging her cheeks warmed his soul. His smile broadened.

"You noticed the dress?"

Her hands smoothed the jaconet muslin, fanned fingers running the length of her midsection from waist to hip. Although the motion revealed her to be self-conscious of the dress, his mouth went dry.

Swallowing against his parched throat, he said, "How could I not notice? You're radiant."

Her blush deepened. Avoiding eye contact, she glanced to Roddam, who remained conspicuously on the other side of the room.

"Yes, well, you do know how to flatter a girl. I must admit to feeling silly—whenever will I wear this in Allshire?"

He held his tongue. If he had anything to say about it, she would not be returning to Allshire.

Tracing the inside of his collar with a finger, he redirected the conversation. "Did you find a dozen treasures you couldn't live without?"

Her eyes met his beneath sooty eyelashes. "It wasn't so much the shopping I enjoyed as the company. The apple has not fallen far from the tree. Your mother is as much the charmer as you, my good sir."

Oh, how his heart did pound. "Your resilience to survive the day does you credit."

"It was not so difficult. In fact, I owe you an apology," she said, looking sheepish, if such a woman could look sheepish.

"An apology?"

"A confession, more like. I should not have been so quick to judge you or your mother." She traced the embroidery encircling her sleeve. "Considering my own brother has been an exception to the rule, I should have suspected you might be different."

"Different? How so?"

"You know. Not a toff."

"Good heavens, Lilith," Walter said with undisguised surprise, his smile faltering. "Have my mother and I ever given you the impression we're snots?"

He would not describe himself as annoyed, not precisely, but his thoughts of her midriff slipped to the farthest cubbyhole of his mind. After so many weeks in each other's company, she still obsessed over their difference in station, or should he say, his current status compared to her former status. It was as though she could not see herself as anything but an orphan, never mind she was now Lady Lilith.

"No, neither of you has given me such an impression. At least, not exactly. It was my experiences that tainted my perceptions. You have both proven yourselves of different quality, and so, I apologize for ever thinking less of you."

"I'm relieved we haven't lived up to your negative expectations."

She folded her hands in her lap and stared down at them.

There was something so vulnerable about her at times, something he could not put a name or explanation to, but as strong willed and mature as she was, she seemed decidedly vulnerable in her unguarded moments. One day, he would be in a position where he could reach over and take one of her hands in his, be her shield when she felt exposed.

As though reading his thoughts, she unfolded her hands and began tucking loose strands of hair into the untidy coiffure.

Almost under her breath, she said, "I do wonder if your mother, or even you, would be so kind to me if I weren't the sister of your host. If you both saw me in the street, would you be so kind?"

Eyeing Roddam, who remained across the room busying himself with absolutely nothing, Walter said, "You can answer that question better than I can. How did my mother treat the shopkeepers and villagers today?"

"Oh, well, she was nothing but amiable. That's not the same, though."

"I quite think it is. Thus, you've answered your own concern. Any airs you think we put on are residual of our lifestyle, not from any assumption of being better than anyone else. You know my dreams, Lilith. Are my dreams those of an arrogant man? I do hope I have never given that impression."

Shaking her head, she said, "No. Not as such. And yet, you are both polite; the kind of politeness that is all proper and reserved. Austere, really."

This was not the first time she had implied thinking him being formal or stiff. Walter laughed, a shaky and humorless sound to his ears.

Misconstruing the sound, hearing only Walter's laugh, not the cause, Roddam looked over at him and winked.

"Lilith, I'm not austere. I'm me. I am who I am. I've never perfected the *beau monde's* ennui and have no intentions of doing so, but I do practice politeness. Is there something more, something from today? Did Mama say something that concerned you?"

"Of course not. She was wonderful, despite convincing me to buy frivolously. It is a good thing she doesn't live close, or I'd spend a year's pocket money in a single week."

Her shift in conversation was not lost on Walter. With a half-smile, he reached absently for the cards and began to shuffle them.

"Come now, Lilith. Tell me you didn't spend your own money. Have the shopkeepers send the bills to Roddam. Or, if it wouldn't be so bold of me to say, I'd be honored if you'd send the bills to me. I'd like to think I had a hand in bringing you happiness."

"I could never!" Her eyes widened.

Had he overstepped his boundaries? It was a bold offer, perhaps too bold. Her frown said as much. Dash it all.

A maid arrived with tea, then. Roddam rejoined the table, but not before waggling his eyebrows at his sister, a silent tease. Walter did not for a minute miss that the entire family was, at this point, aware of his intentions and, dare he say, as hopeful as he.

After Lilith prepared and poured the tea, Roddam said, "Grab the chips, Lil. Shall we play loo? 'Ev'n mighty Pam, that Kings and Queens o'erthrew / And mow'd down armies in the fights of Lu.'"

"What the deuce are you on about, Roddam?" Walter asked, chuckling at the absurdity.

"Not a fan of Alexander Pope, Collingwood? Pope puts me in the mood to lose at loo."

Shaking his head, Walter dealt the cards until Lilith had the Jack. Her deal. She tossed in three chips, and the game began.

They played without conversation until Roddam made mention of Walter's estate, all too clearly goading the pair to resume discourse.

"Is it grand?" she asked, taking the bait.

He studied his hand, then exchanged a card before answering.

"Trelowen is far from grand. Modest. Elizabethan. Sixteenth century. Built by the fifth Baron Collingwood, my great-great-great-grandfather."

Walter waited for Roddam to pass his turn before adding, "Funnily enough, before he inherited, Godfrey Hobbs was from Cornwall, not Devonshire. And so, he named the manor a Cornish word meaning 'happy home.' And it is. A happy home, that is. Trelowen isn't as quaint as your cottage by the sea, but it is modest, as far as manors go. You'd like the garden, I daresay. Daffodils, snowdrops, a

smallish knot garden, just to name a few horticul-
tural pleasures."

"Lovely," she said with a smirk as she won the hand.

New cards dealt, new chips added to the pool,
Lilith said, "I want to picture you at home in your
element. Tell me your favorite part of Trelowen."

"Ah, that's easy. The yew tree. I haven't the foggiest
how old it is. Old. Sprawling branches as wide as turrets
and a trunk nearly as tall as the house. I would spend
hours climbing it, hiding in it, playing pirate games."

"Behavior of late?"

"Cheeky." He chuckled.

"So, when you say modest, what do you mean?
How many rooms?" Lilith asked.

"Twenty-two. A far cry from the Duke of Annick's
Lyonn Manor, I know."

"Twenty-two?" She exclaimed more than questioned. "Hardly modest! What a terrible waste of
space for only one man."

He rubbed the back of his neck. "Well, it is modest,
and it's not for one man. It's for my family when I
have one, not to mention extended family should they
need a place to live, future generations, and even
guests. The rooms rarely go unused since Mama
enjoys parties. It's a cozy home, Lilith, one filled with
happy memories of my father."

They lapsed into silence until the next round.

At length, Roddam chimed in as he tossed chips
on the table. "Tell her about the cottage. The cottage
by the sea."

Grimacing, Walter paused his play to hide behind
his teacup. He wanted to woo Lilith, not press his
advantage so ardently she ran.

Lilith eyed him from over her cards. "What's this about a cottage? Have you been holding out on me?"

Taking another sip of his tea, he swallowed and said, "It's not mine. It's Uncle Cuthbert's. It belonged to my Aunt Elizabeth's family, her childhood home from before she married Uncle Cuthbert. Before her father died, Uncle Cuthbert purchased it to ensure his mother-in-law would be well provided for after her husband's death. Now that she, too, has died, the cottage sits empty. Uncle and I have talked at length of my purchasing it from him. I stay there from time to time to escape. It's nothing, though. It's not even mine." He eyed Roddam askance.

Lilith exchanged a card, deep in thought.

In hushed tones, she said, "All my talk of a cottage by the sea, and you never thought to mention your own enjoyment of such a setting."

"I, well, it's not even mine," he repeated, tugging at his ear in discomfort.

What was he supposed to say? That he had access to her dream cottage? That she should marry him for a cottage that was not his? That he would purchase the cottage of her dreams on the condition she married him? No, no, no.

"You *have* been holding out on me," she said, her lips curving into a smile.

By Jove, that smile flirted with him. Here he was growing increasingly uncomfortable with the conversation since he had not mentioned the cottage before, as though hiding it from her, and only mentioned it now as if it were a bartering chip for her hand in marriage, and yet, she smiled at him.

He returned the smile, the corners of his mouth inching upwards until he grinned like a Cheshire cat. Their gazes held, two smiling fools sharing a secret he did not understand.

And then Lilith won the pool. Again.

The door opened as Walter reached for the deck to reshuffle. Mama flitted into the room, a bubbling brook of chatter.

Lilith tightened the ribbons of her bonnet as the family ascended the steep path to Bamburgh Castle. All in the family were present except Hazel, who wished to stay with Lady Freya and avoid the excessive walking planned for the outing.

Lilith was delighted to see her sister-in-law looking bright-eyed and vigorous. Lizbeth's decision to join them was a marked turning point in her healing over the past week and a half, not to mention an improvement in her sleeping schedule since Freya required feeding every few hours throughout the night.

Today, Sebastian promised them a treat. His grand scheme was while he and Mr. Trethow met with Mr. Granville Sharp about the slavery abolition bill, she, Lizbeth, and Walter would meet with Dr. John Sharp for a tour. Her brother had made the acquaintance of the Sharp brothers some time ago, the castle being only thirteen miles from his home at Dunstanburgh Castle, a shorter distance even from their cousin's estate at Lyonn Manor.

Walter made his excitement known, insisting this would be inspirational for his orphanage should he wish to have a foundling hospital attached. Lilith was more curious than excited.

Dr. Sharp, archdeacon of Northumberland, ran a rather unique infirmary and dispensary at Bamburgh Castle. Unlike the usual infirmaries and dispensaries in the country, his was free to the poor, funded exclusively by a charitable trust, and thus no arrogant or prejudicial board or group of subscribers to determine those worthy of being treated and those not. While not a lying-in hospital, such as many foundling hospitals, it was mostly an outpatient facility that did have a few rooms for those needing a brief repose.

How could Lilith *not* be curious?

She held a strong dislike for physicians since so much of her work was correcting what they had done wrong, not to mention their treatment methods always involved bleeding a patient, applying leeches, or sawing off limbs, hardly the treatments of those concerned with healing. And yet, from what all she had heard, Dr. Sharp was of a different ilk.

While not as windy as the headland of Dunstanburgh Castle, there was undeniably an ambitious gust, chilly at that.

As though it were the most natural of actions, she stepped closer to Walter. He offered his arm. Placing hers over his, she leaned even closer, absorbing his warmth, strength, and good humor.

Before them, the keep loomed, an imposingly tall square.

Dr. Sharp waited for them outside, hunched with age, crow's feet around his eyes, and a hearty, but tired smile on his lips.

"Welcome to my little hospital, lords and ladies!" he said, waving them forward.

They made short work of the introductions before proceeding inside. The tour began in the lower rooms of the castle where surgery was held, followed by a showing of the dispensary, the infirmary, and the apothecary.

Dr. Sharp ambled, a cane in one hand, the cold stone walls against his other as he used them to propel himself forward. Everything about the man aside from his stooped stature, aged cough, and slow progress revealed a keen figure. His mind was sharp, his wit sharper, and his heart full. He was kindness itself.

He admitted to staying at the castle with friends and family in the tower apartments during the summer and returning home to Durham during the winter, but he was uncertain he could make the trip for much longer.

"These stones are as much part of me as I am of them," Dr. Sharp said. "Every renovation of this pile of rubble was conducted under my command. I was a determined lad, eager to see my dream to fruition. Nearly twenty years, we've been together. I grow old, though. I grow old and worry what will become of it when I'm gone."

He spoke more to himself than to the group, and so no one thought to answer. When they rounded a corner, he opened a wooden door that led to a schoolroom.

Walter stopped in his tracks. "A schoolroom, Dr. Sharp?" he voiced incredulously.

"Yes, my lord. It is humble, but the children of the poor have nowhere else to go."

"And it has not been too much of an undertaking to run both a school and a hospital?" Walter asked.

"Not with the right staff, though our patient needs of late have overwhelmed our number of hands. We used to see no more than two hundred patients per year. Now, it exceeds one thousand. As I age, the more useful I become in a schoolroom than by a hospital bed."

"You may as well know, Dr. Sharp," Walter said, "I hope to open an orphanage in Devonshire. It will serve as a school, as well, and I'm entertaining the idea of a foundling hospital in connection. Your work is an inspiration, as I would be doing this purely out of charity to help the poor."

"Ah, you're a good lad. Don't spread yourself too thin or overwork your staff. I nearly lost my surgeon from overwork. Start small. Build from there." Dr. Sharp patted Walter's shoulder, then led them to another room. "Here, the children receive their small-pox inoculations on their first visit to the schoolroom."

"Smallpox inoculations?" Lilith echoed. "And you haven't encountered criticism?"

"Oh, indeed, I have. A great deal of criticism. I am invested in supporting the use of inoculations, nonetheless. Other physicians may not laud my efforts and instead call me a quack, but I have saved lives. I'll have you know, I've been inoculating since 1777. Ask me how many of my patients have contracted smallpox. Ask me, and I'll tell you none."

"You're surprisingly progressive," Lilith said more to herself than to the doctor who was ingratiating himself to her with each step of the tour.

She was eager to have a chat with him about herbs. The apothecary reminded her more of her

own storehouse at home than any doctor's surgery
ever had. The more he spoke, the more chagrined
she felt of her dislike of physicians. Just as with her
initial prejudice against Walter and his mother, she
had nearly allowed her past experiences to blind her
to the good will of Dr. Sharp and all he had accomplished at Bamburgh Castle.

They proceeded through the hallway to view more
rooms, and along the way met other staff, including a
kindly Dr. Cockayne, resident surgeon, who stopped
to make pleasantries for as long as he was able.

After the surgeon moved on, Dr. Sharp said, "I
am most fortunate to have Dr. Cockayne. I received
applications from across the country, but none so
impressive as his."

The next area they entered consisted of impressive bathing facilities, boasting a seawater bath, a hot
bath with thermometer, and a cold bath with a deep
well pump. Everything about the hospital signified
to Lilith a place of healing not sickness. No leeches.
No sawbones. No scarificators or lancets.

"Given this is an outpatient facility, doctor, what
ailments do you treat?" Lizbeth enquired.

"Everything, my lady. From cough to hemiple-
gia. We do have rooms for those who need a lying-in,
but we are not staffed to keep them for long. I must
gloat, however, that we have the finest medical tech-
nologies of any hospital in the country, including an
electrical machine for therapies and a bellow appara-
tus for respiration. Many of our patients suffer from
water inhalation after near drowning or shipwreck. My
brother, William — a surgeon, you know — offered us
several items, including a carriage and a sedan chair.

When the infirm cannot otherwise come to us, we fetch them."

The tour at an end, they followed the good doctor to his study where they were to meet his brother, Mr. Granville Sharp. The study was tidy, the décor mostly architectural plans of the castle and renovation diagrams. A window looked out to the ocean, but the desk faced the door.

Anyone could see this hospital was to be the man's legacy. Lilith wondered if seeing this would spur Walter into action with his own plans.

"What makes us successful," Dr. Sharp explained, "is we have married science with religion. The medical science we practice is nothing more than a tool for His healing, a way for us to act on His behalf."

Sebastian leaned to Lizbeth and whispered words all in the room could hear. "I'll place my wager on science."

Dr. Sharp's grey brows rose, his forehead a rippling wave of wrinkles. "I wouldn't have taken you for a doubter, Lord Roddam."

Crossing his arms over his chest, Sebastian said, "Try non-believer, Dr. Sharp."

Instead of taking offense, the doctor nodded. Scratching his chin, he said, "You have walked through the trial of fire, then. Only those who have felt the flames speak as you do. You're young. In time, you'll learn your survival is due to grace and faith."

Sebastian grunted. "With all due respect, you're mistaken. I saved myself from the fire. If you'd seen what I've seen, you'd put your faith in the hands of man, not an unseen entity who leaves children to cruel fates and mothers to die." Turning to Lilith, his eyes black and penetrating, he said, "It was skill, not God, that brought my daughter into this world and saved my wife from her own mother's fate."

Lilith swallowed against the lump in her throat. Smiling thinly at her brother, she asked, "Do you not think it was prayer that guided my hand?"

Sebastian stared at her, his expression unreadable. With a hand to his arm, Lizbeth leaned in to whisper to him.

Dr. Sharp turned his attention to the door. Mr. Granville Sharp entered, a man who looked to be in his fifties. His hair was heavily powdered, and his collar starched. His eyes lit on Lilith as he bowed to her first before turning to the others. Despite his age, he was a handsome man, narrow of face with an angular nose and warm eyes. She glanced at Walter to find him looking curiously at her. Casting him a smile, she wondered at how well Walter would age—would he be as handsome as he was now when he reached fifty? Would he age as well as Mr. Sharp?

For a heartbreaking moment, she worried she would never find out.

After Sebastian and Mr. Trethow joined Mr. Sharp for a private meeting, and Dr. Sharp returned to his work, Lizbeth, Walter, and Lilith explored the grounds. Lizbeth admitted to wanting fresh air, finding the hospital impressive but oppressive. They walked together in relative silence, each admiring all within the curtain wall, Lilith on one of Walter's arms and Lizbeth on the other.

The eastern edge of the castle grounds featured a low wall overlooking the beach. Squinting, Lilith tried to spy Dunstanburgh Castle to the south. Though she could not make it out, she could spy Lindisfarne to the north.

Freeing herself from Walter's arm, Lilith walked a short distance away from her companions to take in the sights and sounds of the castle. She leaned her hip against the stone wall and closed her eyes, feeling the wind tickle her exposed neck.

All about her, nature reached out to embrace her. She inhaled the salty scent of the air as it kissed her skin. Gooseflesh covered her arms beneath the wooly warmth of her cloak.

A short distance away, Walter and Lizbeth talked, two cousins at ease with each other. He was telling her a joke, but Lilith could not make out the words above the roar of the wind, only the laughter. Lilith stared at him, admiring. Not for a moment did she understand his interest in her, but it was unmistakable. The whole family knew. The whole family found ways to encourage their solitude, even if that only meant busying themselves on the other side of a room. Why her brother should encourage the match, she was unsure, for he knew as well as she that a union would not be possible, no matter how ardent Walter was.

And yet she could not bring herself to tell him the truth. Instead, she hoarded their moments together. No matter the topic, she cherished the time with him. During dinners, the family would turn to each other to talk, leaving the two of them with no one to speak but to each other. And she loved every minute.

His smile tickled her stomach. His laugh fluttered her heart. How could she ever tell him the truth?

How could she not? There was no doubt of his intentions or where his flirtations would lead if she did not stop this silliness soon. He would accuse her of toying with his sensibilities. It was only a matter of time when he would turn from her without acknowledging her existence. People like him did not acknowledge people like her.

He turned to her, then, as though feeling her eyes admiring the slope of his shoulders, the tapered waist, the lithe but strong thighs molded with tailored breeches. With a brief word to Lizbeth, he distanced from her and closed the space to Lilith, a twinkle in his eyes.

"Shall I shield you from the wind?" he jested.

"You assume I need a knight in shining armor?" she teased.

"I hope you want one rather than need one. Alas, we're short on knights today. Would a baron in walking attire do?"

She threw her head back and laughed. When she returned her gaze to his, her heart skipped a beat to see those long eyelashes framing green orbs. His eyes reflected the sunlight, full of hope and promise.

"What do you make of the facilities?" Walter asked, leaning against the half-wall, a gloved hand resting on the stone.

"Curious. Illuminating. I would have liked to spend more time with Dr. Sharp, but I can see he is a busy man and easily fatigued. I may ask my brother to bring me here again should the archdeacon have the time."

Walter nodded. "Now that you've seen what all you can accomplish, you must have a plethora of ideas churning in your mind."

Lilith furrowed her brows, confused. "All I can accomplish? I'm afraid I don't follow."

"No? I was certain you were planning during the whole of the tour. Would it not be fulfilling to manage a place such as this?" Walter asked.

"Manage it? Walter, I'm a parish midwife," she said with an incredulous laugh. "I'm not in a position to manage anything, much less a place of this size. Fulfilling, yes, but for someone like Dr. Sharp, not for me."

"You're only seeing the now. Think of the future. Think bigger, Lilith!" he exclaimed, his eyes glowing with an inner light, his smile eager. "You could make a more significant influence with a facility such as this than you can as a parish midwife."

"I'm afraid you don't understand. I haven't the means or connections to do more than what I do now."

"You have a family who supports you, and with that, there is no limit to what you can accomplish. I know you want to be useful, and I know you don't want to sit idle. But you must realize you cannot continue as a midwife." He paused, as though waiting for her to confirm.

When she made no reply, he removed his tricorn to run a hand through his curls and said, "Ladies are not midwives. It's unseemly. You don't have to lose the joy of helping others if you think on a larger scale. Instead of being the midwife, you could establish an entire school for midwives, a hospital that uses your techniques. Don't you see?"

"I'm afraid I don't."

That was not true. She did see what he was saying, and it frightened her.

It frightened her because of how much she wanted it. Not a hospital or school, exactly, but something. It would be a monumental undertaking. But oh, how fulfilling indeed, just as Walter said. It was not so simple, though. She could not snap her fingers and be what she was not.

With the sunlight brightening the red in his curls in most attractive ways, Walter continued, "There would be some talk regarding your direct involvement, but it would be entirely within the realm of possibility for a lady of your station to patronize such an establishment and visit regularly. Your reach would be much farther than the women and children of a single parish."

Her smile faltered.

He was right. As Lady Lilith, she could accomplish so much more. He saw what she had been unable to see, so focused as she was on the past and her immediate reality. But what was she supposed to do? Announce to the world she was Lady Lilith? Be trained this late in life as to how to conduct herself in polite society? It was preposterous! Aside from the fact that it would be a lie since she was *not* a lady, too many people knew the truth to make it feasible.

Sebastian and Lizbeth could claim as the day was long that she was legitimate, but it would only take one word of doubt. Too many people knew. What if her mother showed up after all these years? What if the Reverend Sands said something? And there were her and Sebastian's aunt and cousin, the Dowager

Duchess of Annick and her son the Duke of Annick, not to mention the duke's wife. They knew, and they wielded a great deal of power.

Yes, Sebastian's mother had raised Lilith as her own. Yes, she had presented Lilith to the world as the legitimate daughter of the Earl and Countess of Roddam. But then life changed. Now, she and others knew the truth. She could not turn back the clock and be what she was not.

If she could, would she?

If Walter accepted her as she was, would she, in turn, accept him?

His words were beyond tempting. *He* was beyond tempting. With a cause greater than she at her fingertips, if only she had the courage to grasp it, it seemed selfish not to try.

Looking back to him, his body leaning forward in anticipation of her response, she returned the smile and said, "I believe that with your vision and my planning, we could take the world by storm."

The tips of his ears turned red. "You said *we*."

Chapter 8

L ady Freya flailed her fists, a spontaneous smile with spittle on her lips. Lilith rocked her, wiping the drool with deft hands.

Alas, this was a losing battle. Sleep was the furthest activity from babe's mind. Given Freya's antics with the loose strands of Lilith's hair and a few awkward attempts to suckle Lilith's dress, the transfer from Auntie Lilith to Mama would need to be soon. Wanting to give Lizbeth and Sebastian a bit more time together since their private moments were few and far between these days, Lilith made her best attempts to distract the increasingly fussy babe, who was showing her usual signs of disinterest in all but the search for her mother's teat.

In as lyrical a voice as Lilith could manage, considering she was anything but musically inclined, she sang.

> *Bobby Shafto's looking out,*
> *All his ribbons fly about,*
> *All the ladies gave a shout,*
> *Horray for Boy Shafto!*

For her efforts, she received a jab to the chin. Chuckling, she kissed Freya's nose. This time, she was awarded tiny fingers with sharp nails pulling at her bottom lip. Oh, the joys of being an auntie, she thought with warmth, love, and a touch of sarcastic humor.

Offering her finger for Freya to grip, Lilith leaned back in the chair and gazed out the window to the meres beyond. The slender drive winding its way between the meres to the first gatehouse could just be made out from this distance. In fragmented memory, she could recall the view from her own nursery at Roddam Hall.

It had looked out to a weedy garden, one that might have been glorious a generation or two earlier but had been left to ruin. Though Lilith searched through her memories, she could not recall if her mother, or should she say Sebastian's mother, had ever visited the nursery. She did not think so. A nurse lived there full-time, a new nurse nearly every year. If her father dismissed them, or if they refused to work for him, she could not say, but she distinctly remembered a rotation of nurses over the years.

No, she could not recall her mother ever visiting the nursery. Jane Lancaster had rarely left her private sitting room. At the time, being only a child, Lilith had thought little of it. She always knew where to find her mama, and that suited her quite well. Together, they would play-act in fancy dress, she pretending to be a princess and Mama pretending to be a visitor from another kingdom. Such memories had kept her lying awake at night when living at the orphanage. As the years passed, the memories faded, becoming more mysterious, for she convinced herself the woman at the tea table must have been a figment of her imagination since mothers did not abandon their daughters to orphanages.

As an adult who better understood some of the situation and who knew Jane had died around the same time Lilith had been sent to the orphanage, she knew the woman, her mother for a time, was most certainly real and not a figment. But why had she rarely left her sitting room? Had she been avoiding encounters with Lord Roddam? Had she been ill?

A strange wetness startled Lilith. Looking down, she found Freya trying to suckle the dress. There was no denying this little one a minute longer. She rose from the chair just as Freya scrunched her face in a silent wail, the stuttering cry delayed by at least a full minute.

This would teach her to wear a nice dress while caring for her niece.

Soothing Freya with coos, she trekked her way from the north wing to the west and up to the lord's bedchamber, by which time, Freya had stopped crying but was displaying her displeasure by kicking Lilith's arm. The door was ajar. If it had been closed, she would have knocked, but ajar it stood.

Without pausing, she pushed against the wood and entered the chamber, stopping short when she caught sight of the couple.

Sebastian and Lizbeth stood in the middle of the room, not far from the bed. The fact they were standing was a blessing. The two were caught in an embrace to end all embraces, one of his arms wrapping around Lizbeth's waist, the other palming the back of her head. Lizbeth's own arms snaked up her husband's back. They shared a kiss far from chaste.

Lilith's eyes widened, her heart pounded, and her face flamed with the horror of having interrupted them.

For a moment, she could not move to absent herself. She could not tear her eyes from them. All she could do was stare with a near painful longing, a hunger to be kissed like that, loved like that, part of a whole, desired passionately without reservation.

She gave herself a mental shake. With one silent step backwards, and then another, she inched her way to the door, fully intending on hiding behind it before knocking firmly. They need never know what she witnessed. Freya had other ideas. With a masterful cry, she let out an ear-splitting squall. Lilith squeezed her eyes shut and cringed, not at Freya's rhythmic wail, but at having been discovered.

Peeking her eyes open, she saw her brother coming towards her wearing a sardonic grin. Lizbeth, she noticed, stayed put, pressing her palms to her cheeks.

Sebastian relieved her of the bundle of screeching joy. "Care for a change of scenery?" he asked as he hoisted Freya against his shoulder, his hand holding the back of baby's head.

"Are you trying to get rid of me, 'Bastian? Think you'll replace me as midwife with yourself?" she teased with a solitary tut, still feeling self-conscious.

"You're not off the hook so easily. Hazel has been pestering me all morning about lawn bowls. After Freya's down for a nap, fancy a game?"

"Ah, I see. Yes, that does sound lovely."

With a wink, he said, "Change into something more comfortable, eh?"

She suspected she need not point out a change of attire would be necessary, lawn bowls or not. The front of her dress was quite wet from Freya's determined efforts to find food.

Sebastian presented his daughter to Lizbeth with a courtly bow before leaving the room.

With Lilith's help, Liz situated herself on the bed. Once settled, a contented babe nestled in the crook of her mother's arm, Liz said, "You must play on my behalf today. I do believe Freya and I will take a very long nap."

Lilith busied herself by ringing Liz's lady's maid for tea, mixing in her herbs to speed Liz's recovery, and setting up a chair by the bed.

Once seated with her own teacup, Lilith questioned, "Are you feeling less fatigued?" She had noted how much livelier her sister-in-law was looking with each passing day.

"Oh, yes. I've been sleeping better, as well. We all have. Your schedule is genius, I'm sure," Liz said. "I do have a question, though. I—"

When her sister-in-law stopped, Lilith reached over to touch her shoulder. "Yes? What is it? Don't hold back, especially if it's about your health."

"It is. In a way. But it's delicate, and I'm not altogether certain it's something I should ask you. Only, you're my midwife. How horribly complicated I'm making this." Liz combed Freya's silken hair with her fingers.

"Come now. You can ask me and tell me anything. I can't help if you don't disclose all."

"You're right. But if this makes you uncomfortable, or if I should not share, please, stop me. I've made too big of a deal of it now, of course, so it'll be more embarrassing than it should. Alas. I had better be out with it." Liz took a deep breath. "It's not that I'm ready, yet, but I was wondering when I might, you know, feel ready again and how I will know I'm ready," She said the last few words in barely a whisper.

Lilith nearly choked on her tea. "You mean *sex*?" Lilith asked dumbly. How foolish. Of course, she meant sex. "Lizbeth, you had a baby less than two weeks ago. You need time to heal. It could be months before you feel ready again. It will take time for your body to adjust. I say this next bit as your midwife, not as your sister-in-law. If he's pressuring you, I advise pushing him off for at least another week."

"Oh, no, it's nothing like that. You mustn't think that of him. He is a saint of support, patience, and love. It's just, well…"

Liz trailed off, looking as embarrassed as Lilith felt, though Lilith tried as she might to wear her clinical expression. It seemed silly to be embarrassed over such a topic when she had these conversations with patients often, usually since their husbands refused to wait, especially when the babe was a girl rather than the desired heir. She knew her brother was not that type of man, but she was embarrassed because this topic did involve her brother. There were some things she would rather not know about her sibling.

Liz sighed and said, "It's only, well, for a moment, it was getting close to Freya's feeding time, and I felt inexplicably, shall we say, sensitive to touch. He barely touched me, yet I was overcome with the need to be held, to be kissed, almost frenzied. It was not so much the need for marital intimacy as simply *need*.

Does that make sense? Only it's more complicated. I needed him to hold me…but then…oh, I'm humiliated to admit it. How should I say this? I don't know if something is wrong or….I, um, *leaked*, and then I was so terribly embarrassed for him to see…well, I knew I should speak with you about it. I'm not making much sense, am I? Two questions in one, really, or is it three? But the leaking first. *The milk*, you know. Is that normal? *Leaking milk*?" Liz had reverted to whispering.

With a reassuring smile, Lilith said, "Perfectly normal. Your body and your baby are on the same schedule, remember. Both knew what time it was. It's not uncommon to feel tender or emotional at the approach of feeding time. Don't discount weeping, either. I suggest, however, delaying marital intimacy, if possible, no matter how, er, sensitive you feel."

"Oh." Liz shifted Freya, who had already fallen asleep mid-suckle. "Thank you. I mean it. Thank you."

With a cloth on her lap, Lilith took the sleeping Freya into her arms, nestling the baby's chest against her palm. She rubbed baby's back then patted gently. Freya stirred from her slumber, groggy and grumpy. Only after the little lady cleared the air from her stomach did her Auntie Lilith rock her back to sleep and settle her in her baby bed, snug as a bug.

Lilith returned to her seat beside Lizbeth so they might finish their tea before she left Liz in peace. Though their conversations were always punctuated with baby care and medical questions, Lilith valued their time together. She had never had a friend, much less a sister. Over the past year, Liz had become both, and she cherished their conversation time.

"While we're being blunt," Liz said after a taste of her tea, "I was curious if you've developed a *tèndre* for Walter."

The question was such a non sequitur, Lilith rattled her teacup against its saucer.

"I do beg your pardon," Liz said after seeing how shaken Lilith was. "It is none of my business and rude of me to ask."

Lilith could feel Lizbeth's eyes trained on her, though she did not look up from her teacup to meet those eyes. She would not ordinarily feel bashful, and certainly not with Lizbeth, who never spoke in innuendos or polite euphemisms, but given Lilith had only a short time ago witnessed a kiss of the likes she had never before seen, all while thinking of what it might be like to kiss Walter in such a way, she felt beyond bashful.

The tea licked the sides of the cup as Lilith tipped the saucer this way and that.

"Now that I have asked," Liz said, "I shan't retract it. You can't deny he shows a marked interest in you. Are his advances welcome?"

With a sigh, Lilith met Lizbeth's eyes. "They are. But to what end?"

Liz tilted her head to one side and studied Lilith. "Do you think him insincere?"

"Oh, no, nothing of the sort. I believe his intentions are honorable. But I question my own. It seems dishonest to encourage his attentions when the only answer I can ever give him is no."

Liz pushed herself against the wooden headboard of the four-poster bed, sitting up straighter though her eyelids were beginning to droop. "If you're interested, and if he's interested, why would you say no?"

"Come now, Lizbeth. We may be in our own corner of the world at the moment, but the real world is out there, and at some point, we must face the reality of that world. I would never be accepted."

"Nonsense," Liz said. "You've always been and always will be Sebastian's sister. Society would meet you as such, the daughter and sister of an earl. There are only a handful of people who know Jane wasn't your birth mother, but she was your mother in every other sense. There's nothing to stop you from living the life she intended for you. No one who knows would dare say a word against you. As to becoming accustomed to manners and rules and the like, we can guide you. Have you told Walter?"

Lilith shook her head, setting her teacup and saucer on the bedside table. "I will. I must." With a half-smile, she rose from her chair. "For now, you must rest. You can barely stay awake."

Her sister-in-law did not argue, merely nodded sleepily. Lilith leaned over and kissed her cheek before settling her into a comfortable slumber.

When Lilith returned to her room, she called for Hannah to help her change. She had not worn one of her old dresses in a week. To be quite honest, she did not want to wear one now. She had only a short time remaining before she returned to Allshire, to her old life. Though she was not fond of the stays, she had grown accustomed to the new dresses. Well, only one was new, the others being Lizbeth's old dresses, but they had been worn so rarely, they were practically new, and certainly new to Lilith. She liked them all the same.

Walter looked at her differently when she wore them.

No, that was not right. He looked at her the same no matter what she wore, but there was a certain brightness in his eyes, an appreciation, perhaps, when she stepped into the parlor with a new dress and coiffure. She enjoyed seeing his face brighten at her appearance.

How silly of her. Never in her life had she been vain or given to fripperies.

Hannah helped her out of the dirtied dress and into a worn, sprigged dress of dandelion yellow. Lilith's hair was simply styled, up, but not as fanciful as Hannah was wont to do. Much like the dresses, Lilith would miss the upswept coiffures when she returned home. At first, she had felt bald without hair against her neck, but once she realized how much lighter, how much cooler, she really did prefer the coiled styles, though she would never be able to replicate them on her own.

The family was not in the parlor when she ventured downstairs. The obliging butler met her in the hallway and escorted her through the morning room to the east side of the castle grounds.

A table had been set up outside with sweets, savories, and tea. Hazel and Mr. Trethow sat with their backs to the morning room doors and their chairs facing the lawn. Sebastian and Walter were already in play.

As Lilith stepped out, Hazel heckled Walter about his bowl rolling a good two feet beyond Sebastian's. Walter paid no mind. He had spotted Lilith. Though he wore a tricorn, his hand met his brow to shield against the glare of the sun. With that bright and contagious smile of his, he abandoned the green to approach her.

All heads turned her way.

As soon as Hazel spotted her, she stood and clapped her hands, "At last! I daren't challenge these men without you present. Together, we shall show them never to wager against a woman. You do play, my dear?"

Lilith returned Walter's smile as he came to her with a bow, an enticing whiff of cologne, and a proffered arm. Taking his arm, she looked to Hazel, "I do indeed. However, you may regret having me on your team when you realize how poorly I play."

"Fiddlesticks. We shall make these men weak in the knees." Hazel led the way to the green, waving over her brother.

Mr. Trethow and Walter paired against Lilith and Hazel. Sebastian served as umpire.

Bowls at the ready, the game commenced.

Walter's skill exceeded everyone present. He did not boast, rather danced a jig and flexed when each of his bowls stopped close to the jack. Mr. Trethow was a fair player, but he made a showing of faking his sneezes every time his sister released her bowl. Hazel sought revenge by poking him with the tip of her shoe each time he lined up his shot. With such fierce competition, Lilith had no choice other than to strike their bowls with her own to give Hazel a chance to win for their team.

Never could she recall having this delightful of a time. If this was what having a family was like, she wanted one. She wanted this family. However much of an impossibility it was, she wanted it.

If only they never had to face the real world.

She watched Walter throughout the game. He, in turn, watched her. The first time he caught her gaze, he appeared surprised — his eyebrows raising, posture straightening, body turning to her as though expecting to hear her speak. The second time, he flushed. The third time, his eyelids drooped, slumberous, as he eyed her with a half-smile. The next time he waggled his eyebrows.

Before long, it became a game, each outdoing the other with silly expressions. Perhaps she should have been more genteel about her admiration of him, turning her head away as though denying she had been looking at him. Perhaps she ought to have cast him a quick, polite, and tight-lipped smile before turning her attention to the game. Perhaps she saw no point in doing either since she was neither genteel nor polite. And why should she not openly admire him?

It would all come to an end when she confessed the true nature of her birth anyway, so she may as well enjoy herself.

They played for nearly two hours, by which time the gentlemen had made a showing not only of their skill but also of their chivalry to let the women win. Between Hazel and Mr. Trethow's antics, and her and Walter's unusual flirtations, it would have come as a shock to her to learn anyone had concentrated on the game.

Before offering his arm to Lilith for the return to the table, Walter removed his tricorn to sweep a hand through his curls. Such a simple movement, but

Lilith's breath caught. She wanted to run her own hand through those curls. She wagered they were soft. Ah, how could she tell him what she was when there was so much she still wanted to do and talk about with him? The longer she delayed, the more deceitful her omission would seem, but she could not bring herself to do it quite yet.

Once back at the table, they sat to enjoy the fresh brew a footman brought. Walter polished off three sandwiches in the time it took Lilith to pour the tea.

Mr. Trethow accepted his cuppa from Lilith and said to Walter in his Cornish inflection, "If ye keep eatin' like a horse, me boy, ye'll be as round in the middle as yer uncle." He patted his girth for emphasis, causing Hazel to titter before hitting his arm with her fan.

"I say, you'd better hide the sandwiches, then," Walter jested. "If I prove myself a glutton in front of Lilith, she'll never have me!" He laughed heartily until the realization of his words dawned.

All at the table stilled.

Good heavens.

An awkward silence ensued. Walter rubbed the back of his neck, his smile now a grimace. Lilith smoothed her dress, avoiding eye contact.

Sebastian finally spoke, his chair scraping against stone as he stood. "Anyone fancy a walk along the beach?"

Following a collective sigh at having the silence broken, Hazel said, "If I spend another minute in the open air, I shall melt."

"Ye owe me a game of piquet anyway," Mr. Trethow said to his sister. "Don't think I'll let ye win this round."

Hazel tutted.

"I'll join you, Roddam," Walter said.

Although no one looked at her, she knew their ears were perked, listening intently for her response.

Lifting her chin, she turned to her brother. "A walk would be divine."

Chagrined from the verbal slip, Walter followed behind Roddam and Lilith down to the beach.

Dash it all. There would have been no finer way to make an arse of himself. The whole family would now expect a declaration. They all knew he fancied her, but he had never spoken so presumptuously, much less in front of her or to her.

If she was embarrassed by his words, she gave no indication, thankfully.

He ought to take her aside, if given the opportunity, and apologize, but he was not certain he wanted to. If she was not aware of his intentions at this point, she was not very perceptive. Had she not been subtly encouraging him, he would feel far more embarrassed than he did. The point was, though, she had been encouraging him.

Over the three weeks and odd days since her first arrival, he had had the chance to observe her, really get to know her, far and beyond the prim façade she donned. Not that he would admit this even under interrogation, but he had wondered if they would suit. Love at first sight because of handsome features and a certain depth to one's eyes did not mean two people would suit. In the beginning, he had so desperately wanted them to suit that he searched for every sign, every indication that they were right for each other, to the point of ignoring her harsher characteristics, namely her blunt dismissiveness of his initial advances. Had he not been attracted to her, he never would have pursued her beyond such harsh behavior. He would have found her brusque, rude even, and certainly uninterested in him. But he had been attracted. And so, he had looked further. He was glad he did.

Walter suspected not many saw beyond her somewhat prickly exterior or proud chin to meet the soft-hearted and good-natured woman beneath. She had a sense of humor he did not expect, and no one, after seeing her with Freya, could say she did not possess a depth of love rare in polite society. Never did she disguise the love she felt for her niece or her family. Undoubtedly, she was a rare bird. Whether it was because she grew up in an orphanage away from the strict training of ladylike behaviors, or because this was who she was in her core, he could not say. He only knew she was a rarity in a world of deceptive ennui.

He was not so naïve to believe she shared his views in all things. He knew they saw the world differently, but that did not make them opposites. They complemented each other. He was sure she realized that as well. He might be an idealist, but that did not mean he was blind to reality, merely willing to find a way to make his dreams reality. With her at his side, no dream was beyond reach.

As the trio walked the beach, the gap between Walter and the siblings widened, Lilith and Roddam deep in conversation.

They should have thought to bring a shawl or cloak, for surely, she was chilled by the wind. Should he see so much as a single shiver, he would run back to the castle to fetch her wrap. He watched for indications of her feeling cold. Of their own accord, his eyes roamed her figure in the nearly thread-bare dress. He felt roguish to eye her outline when he only meant to ascertain her health, and so looked away. With a will of their own, his eyes returned, admiring the cut of the dress, accentuating her slim waist and supple hips.

As he made to tear his eyes away again, she glanced back to him and stuck out her tongue before turning back to her brother. By Jupiter, she was flirting! Had she known the direction of his thoughts, she might not have felt it wise to flirt.

He hastened his steps to catch up to them, searching his mind for something witty to say, something that would have her in peals of laughter. Oh, he did love her laugh. And how its velvet huskiness sent warm shivers up his spine.

Just as he reached them, she did laugh, but not as he expected. A shriek pierced the air as Roddam lunged and tackled his sister, lifting Lilith off her feet and slinging her unceremoniously over his shoulder.

Walter stood slack jawed.

"Help!" Lilith cried between laughs, her fists pummeling her brother's back. "Walter! Save me from this brute!"

Roddam jogged to the water, Lilith struggling against his shoulder. Before Walter had taken so much as a step forward, Roddam waded into the ocean and tossed his sister into an incoming wave.

Walter panicked. He stripped off his boots and coat with haste and set off to rescue her. But then she surfaced, sputtering with a bark of laughter, and steadied herself in barely waist-deep water. Wet hair clumped to her face and shoulders, her coiffure undone. She splashed her brother and set off on a mission to pull Roddam into the water with her.

Walter stood rooted, dumbfounded.

Realizing his heroics were unnecessary, he circled back for his boots, which were now doused in sand. Instead of dressing, he carried his coat to one of the dunes and sat, one leg stretched, one bent, an arm hooked over his knee. What else was he to do? Join them? He was not so — what had she called him? *Raw*? Yes, that was it. He was not so *raw* he could leap headfirst into an ocean fully clothed. Call him stiff and formal, but that was not his style.

From this vantage point, however, he could enjoy the show of Lilith and Roddam taking turns dunking each other into the waves. Had someone told him on the first day he met her that he would witness so carefree of a scene, he would have called them out as a fibber. Her guard had noticeably lowered as she had stripped so many metaphoric layers since that first day.

Removing his hat, he shook the sweat from his hair. Aside from the coastal winds, the day was warm. The sun shone high in the sky, deceptive to the rain likely to come in the afternoon. But what of the water? It must be freezing. He dared not find out for himself.

Lilith shrieked, rising from the sea foam as Aphrodite. The pair had drifted farther up the beach, the currents leading them adrift. In a moment of lucidity, they looked back to Walter and waved. He raised his hat.

They were both a hideous sight of clinging clothes and sopping hair. Roddam's hair ribbon had come undone, and his unfashionably long mane whipped about him, making him look ferocious and feral. Lilith looked a fright. Part of her hair still clung to her head from resolute hair pins, but the rest splayed about her body like black seaweed, her straw bonnet sodden and limp, hanging sideways, held only by a deter-mined and knotted ribbon. She wiped the locks from her eyes, pushing strands behind her ears.

And then she was wading towards Walter, a smile stretched across her features.

Tearing his eyes from her, he donned his hat, struggled to wedge his feet back into the sandy boots, and then hastened to stand, tossing his coat over his forearm.

By Jove. His eyes widened. He cleared his throat.

Her dress might as well have been transparent for how it clung. As much as he wanted to gape, he averted his eyes, holding fast to her own steady gaze as she came towards him, oblivious to the irresistible temptation she presented. What he would not give to take her in his arms and kiss her. He hardly cared that her brother looked on from afar, the heathen still splashing about in the water.

"Only a stiff toff would look on without joining us!" she called as she approached, her eyes twinkling with merriment.

He nearly choked on her choice of words, hug-ging his coat closer.

"Good heavens," she said. "I was only poking fun. You look positively morose."

He cleared his throat and strained a smile. "I thought for a moment I might have to save you."

"From what? Sebastian or the water?"

"Both."

She chuckled, wrapping her arms around her torso. What a daft fool he was! Her teeth were practically chattering! Here he was worried she might notice his admiration when she was freezing to death in nothing but a soaked bit of fabric.

Without another moment's hesitation, he held out his coat for her. Her smile slid as she studied his expression, as though questioning his kindness, and then she held out her arms so he could wrap the coat about her shoulders.

"Thank you," she said, her voice soft, no longer jovial.

"Planning more sea bathing, or shall I escort you to the castle?" he asked.

"Yes, do. My shoes are ruined, and my toes are cold. My brother is mad, don't you think, to swim in that ocean? How he doesn't catch his death is anyone's guess." She slipped her arm through his and leaned against him. "I hope I don't ruin your coat."

"Nonsense. It is honored to serve you."

"Silly. Do you know what sounds perfect right now? A warm fire and a good book. Will you join me after I've dried and changed?" She looked sidelong at him, those wet strands of hair clinging in enticing ways to her cheeks.

"I would be honored," he said.

"As honored as your coat? What a pair the two of you make."

He laughed, wishing he *were* the coat at that moment, embracing and warming her.

"Walter," she said in nigh a whisper. "I have a confession to make."

He looked over at her in surprise.

"Before I make it, I want you to know I value your kindness. You have proven to me not all aristocrats are heartless. However, I'm afraid once I make this confession, our friendship will change. We are friends, are we not?"

His heart thudded against his ribcage. He had never thought of her making declarations of affection before he did, but this seemed to him a prelude to just such a declaration.

"Yes, I hope you consider me a friend, Lilith. You must know I esteem you."

She walked quietly for a moment, then looked at him askance again, her eyes darkening and her expression more maudlin than he would have expected from someone about to confess attraction or love.

"Let's stop here, please." She tugged at his arm, pulling him to a halt.

He only then noticed they had reached the doorway to the curtain wall where she had kissed his cheek that early morning nearly two weeks ago. Was the door a sign? Were they about to cross a threshold wherein the rest of their lives awaited on the other side?

Walter braced his heart for her confession, relaxing his features to reveal his hope and adoration.

When she released his arm and turned to face him, her expression somber, he reached out to take her hand in his. It was cold to the touch, ice cold. He rubbed it between his own to warm her, hoping his liberties with her person were welcome in light of her coming confession. She did not pull her hand free, only stared at him, frowning.

"Walter, I — " She paused, her brows furrowing.

Her expression was not what he would expect from someone about to confess undying love. In fact, her expression worried him. His smile slipped, his own brows furrowing.

"What is it? You can tell me anything, Lilith."

"Yes, well, this isn't anything. This is something quite specific. It will change how you see me." She squeezed his hand, then pulled hers free, wrapping her arms about her shoulders, tugging his coat tightly around her. "Oh, bother. I haven't the words. Yes, I do, but I don't know how to say them."

He waited.

She stared at him, her eyes dark and unreadable.

The hopeless bonnet remained askew, hanging from her neck by the trusty ribbon. Her skin glistened where the sun caught water droplets. She smelled of the salty sea. His eyes, those treacherous, roaming eyes, dropped to her lips. Full, scarlet, kissable. Unwittingly, he licked his own lips, his tongue dry.

"I like you, Walter. I want you to know that before I — " She stopped mid-sentence again.

Taking her bottom lip between her teeth, she reached out a hand to touch his arm. A light touch, her palm resting on his upper arm.

"I'm afraid you won't look at me the same way after I say this."

He breathed a *ha*. "Nothing you could say would change how I feel about you. If we're being honest, I'm fond of you, Lilith. More than fond. The truth is—"

"Shh." She touched a finger to his lips. "Don't say another word. Please."

He chewed the inside of his cheek, not at all sure he understood the direction of the conversation.

And then he did not need to understand. As she had done the last time they stood in the threshold, she placed both hands on his chest and leaned against him. Instead of kissing his cheek this time, she kissed his mouth.

Her lips puckered against his, warm and yielding, salty from the ocean. He inhaled sharply through his nose and parted his lips. Her hands moved up his chest to wrap around his neck, threading her fingers through his hair, knocking the tricorn from his head as she pulled him closer. Invitation offered, he accepted by wrapping his hands around her waist and pulling her against him, a shock of cold wetness to his warmth.

With an eager tilt of his head, he slanted his mouth over hers to deepen the kiss, his world plunging into fathomless depths of soul-deep affection. She was no submissive party. Clinging to his neck as though she might fall, she lengthened their kiss each time he made to retreat.

He was a man bewitched.

Moving his hands up to her shoulders, he awarded them both a tender end to an unexpectedly passionate kiss before relinquishing her mouth and pushing her gently away. As much as he would love to continue to whatever end that might have led, this was not the time, place, or way. She deserved more than frenzied madness.

His hands on her shoulders, hers around his neck, they stared at each other. Her pupils were so dilated, her eyes appeared black, a stark contrast to her reddened lips and flushed cheeks. Though she looked outwardly like a woman who had been thoroughly kissed, her eyes told a story of a woman distracted, worried, heartbroken. Why the devil would she look heartbroken? Did she fear rejection? She need not for his heart was full! He was ready to go down on bended knee!

Touching the backs of his fingers to her cheek, he asked, "Was that what you wanted to tell me, or was there more?" This certainly would change their friendship, and it certainly would affect how he looked at her.

She opened her mouth to speak, then shook her head. "Kiss me again."

He shuddered a chuckle, a man invited to kiss a goddess. Walter leaned in to press his lips to hers in a slower, gentler kiss, a chaste display of his affection as he brushed his mouth against hers.

When he pulled away, she banished her doleful expression with a smile. Without a word, she bent down to retrieve his hat and positioned it back on his head, pushing it down snugger than it needed be. Her smile growing broader with each passing moment, she reached up to fix her bonnet.

"Good heavens!" Her hands explored the mess of tresses frizzing a halo around her head. "I must look frightful."

"Indeed, you do," he said.

"That was *not* the least gentlemanly of you to say. You should have said nothing could mar my beauty. Don't they teach you compliments when you learn to converse politely?" she teased.

"But you see, I know you well enough not to be daft enough to lie. Let me try again. How about this? You are stunning even when bedraggled. I suspect there is no condition in which you would look anything but extraordinary. No, make that breathtaking."

"Oh. Yes, that will do nicely." Slipping her arm through his again, she tugged him onward.

They made it as far as the conservatory doors before Roddam caught up to them, jogging past them in a wet, sloshing state.

Shaking his head, he showered them in a rain of droplets. "Imagine Liz's surprise when I wake her," he said with a wink before dashing ahead of them to torment his wife.

Chapter 9

"**A**nd then — brace yourself," Lilith said with a dramatic pause, "he tied their braids together." Walter's mother hooted with laughter.

"When they stood, the poor girls were knotted together until Miss Tolkey could untangle the mess."

Though Lilith was turned to face his mother, her eyes flicked his way. However brief the glance, Walter felt himself emotionally undressed beneath her gaze. If this continued, he may rethink the wisdom of leaping headfirst into the frigid ocean.

"I daresay, if he had been a child of mine, I would have strung him by his toes," Mama said, touching Lilith's arm. "Go on! Go on! Tell me more."

The family gathered in the parlor several days after Walter and Lilith's private moment. Roddam and Lizbeth played cards at the table — Liz clapped and preened enough to appear to be winning. Uncle Cuthbert walked his granddaughter around the room, singing quietly. Mama and Lilith exchanged anecdotes of naughty children. Walter sat with them, relaxed against the chair back, one leg crossed over the other, hoping his mother would not share another when-Walter-was-young tale. She had already shared enough to turn his ears pink for a week.

He was not the only one wooing Lilith. His mother was doing her part with impressive skill.

Neither Lilith nor Walter had spoken about the kiss. They remained, however, well aware of their shared intimacy. She could not look at him without blushing, and he could concentrate on little else. Each day, she sought him out for conversation. The times she did not, he sought her. In the back of his mind, he wondered if she had wanted to tell him something else that day, but she made no mention of there being more, and so, he assumed she had only wished to tell him, and show him, how much she cared for him. Her nerves and melancholy before the kiss were attributed to fear of rejection. Courtship, thus, progressed.

Had she been a young girl, he would have proposed by now. Lilith, though, was a grown woman who knew her own mind. He wanted to give her ample time to know him and to accept him, to assure them both that this was a good match into which they willingly entered without reservation, especially given that he suspected her time at the orphanage had left her more vulnerable than she would admit. Intentional delay or not, he knew he needed to speak with Roddam soon.

To everyone's surprise, the butler stepped into the room and announced with a formality Walter had not yet heard from the man, "His Grace the Duke of Annick and Her Grace the Duchess of Annick."

Heads swiveled to the door with more than a few excited exclamations.

The immaculately dressed duke, laced and frilled in a gold and peacock-blue ensemble, swaggered into the room. Behind him sauntered Walter's prissy cousin, Charlotte, wearing an exquisite dress that shimmered as though gilded, her chin held high in hauteur, a smile of condescension on her lips.

"I say, old chap, where is my reception? Where is my grand entrée? I expect fanfare, pomp, *something* after traveling the length of some fifteen miles," Annick announced, his stare fixed on his cousin Roddam.

Lord Roddam rose from the table, his features brightening in greeting. "Well, well, look who has finally graced us with his presence. You do realize our daughter was born over two *weeks* ago, not two *days* ago?"

Annick waved his hand, the rings lining each finger clinking together. "Being a duke is hard work."

Lizbeth approached Annick, her arms outstretched to take his hands in hers. Everyone rose to greet the duke and duchess with exchanges of hugs, cheek kisses, or handshakes.

Annick bowed deeply to Walter's mother and kissed the air above her knuckles before kissing both her cheeks. "Has it only been since June that I last saw you?" Annick said to her. "It feels a lifetime that I've been deprived of your company."

She made a showing of blushing and tittering.

Walter grasped Annick's hand in a hearty shake, happy to see his old Oxford mate. The family had stayed at the ducal estate for the first part of the summer, but that did not lessen his pleasure at seeing a friend.

Annick turned to Lilith, who stared at him with pursed lips. "Ah, cousin. I had hoped you would be here. I warned Charlotte, if we delayed so much as a single day more, you might have returned home. I am charmed you stayed. A certain lady will have two doting aunts to spoil her."

Charlotte joined him, smiling to Walter, kissing her aunt's cheek, and touching Lilith's arm. "I had hoped I wouldn't miss you," Charlotte said to Lilith. "We've not had the best of luck crossing paths this year to become better acquainted, but I hope to remedy that. You *are*, after all, my sister's most favorite person in the world. Well, next to me that is." She giggled at her own jest.

The duke turned back to Roddam "Now, if you would be so good as to introduce us to the new arrival."

However much Walter would have liked to strike up a conversation with Annick, the visit was for his hosts, the center of attention being the new baby, and so he sat ever so slightly apart from the others.

Uncle Cuthbert, cradling Freya, who had miraculously slept through the hubbub, introduced his granddaughter to her aunt and uncle. They cooed and exclaimed over her, as expected. Before long, everyone grouped off, Cuthbert, Roddam, and Annick sitting together with Freya, and Lizbeth, Charlotte, and Mama squealing over whatever ladies squealed about.

Lilith, too, sat apart, discomfited. She picked at the embroidery on her dress before smoothing out non-existent wrinkles.

They were in a similar position, Walter discerned. They were both family but not of immediate relation. He was a mere cousin to Charlotte and friend to Annick. She was likewise a mere cousin to Annick and near stranger to Charlotte. And so, they sat apart, both looking in, neither feeling the need to interject.

"We're off to Vienna until the new year," Charlotte was explaining to Lizbeth and his mother. "His newest opera debuts, you know. And yes, before you say a word, we've considered all you've said about the turmoil in France, but Drake assures me Vienna is perfectly safe. We'll return before you know it and shan't miss a moment of the Season. Will Freya come with you?"

"Yes, of course. Lilith is helping me interview nurses. With a nurse present, Freya will have full-time care in London," Lizbeth said. "But April is forever away! You will hardly know her by then."

"Don't be a silly goose." Charlotte tittered. "I promise to visit every other day until we leave. Or maybe every three days. Let's see, shall we? And we'll be back at least a month before Parliament resumes to travel together to London. I would have been here sooner, only, well, we needn't bore you with family drama. It's Mary, you know. She and Mama Catherine haven't been getting on lately."

Walter drummed his fingers on the arm of the chair, not hearing much else of the conversation. Lizbeth, Charlotte, and Mama chattered on about Annick's sister, Mary. Roddam, Annick, and Uncle Cuthbert carried on their own conversation with occasional attentions to Freya when she stirred.

He looked to Lilith again. She looked back at him. He waggled his eyebrows. She looked down at her hands.

Well, dash it all.

With everyone focused on their own group's conversation, no one would notice Walter changing chairs. He walked over to Lilith. Taking the seat next to her, he leaned towards her with an elbow on the armrest.

"You appear delighted. Are they not your two most favorite people in the world?" He grinned devilishly.

"Sebastian always has a kind word about our cousin, and Lizbeth says her sister and I will become fast friends once we've become better acquainted. Would you find me rude if I said I doubt their judgment?" She swept a hand over her ear to tuck her hair back, though no strands had fallen.

Walter laughed. "They take some getting to know, but I believe you can trust your brother and sister-in-law's assessment. Annick is all show with a heart of gold, and Charlotte is naïve but caring. Give them a chance."

"Funny. That's the command my brother gave regarding you and your mother."

He raised his eyebrows. "And the verdict?"

"He was right. And you know it. But I can't see how *those* two can be anything but arrogant. The few times we've interacted, they've been nothing less than pompous."

"You won't believe me when I tell you, but neither is arrogant. They put on airs, yes, but you couldn't have better people on your side."

She scowled. Her demeanor reminded him of when they had first met. She held her spine just as straight, her hands just as clenched, and her lips just as pursed.

"Once, when Charlotte was maybe ten years old or so, she and Lizbeth came to stay at Trelowen for a couple of weeks, as they often did. There, in my favorite tree — you know, the climbing tree — the girls found a nest with baby birds and, naturally, told everyone at the estate. One of the groom's boys ran out the next day and knocked it out of the tree. Charlotte was so distraught, she made us all play nursemaid to baby birds until they were healed, fat, and feathered enough to fly away. Now, does that sound like an arrogant woman to you?"

Lilith's smile accompanied a soft laugh. "No, but she was only a child. People can change."

"Yes, they can, but not their fundamental core, not who they are inside. As it's said, a leopard can't change its spots."

Before she could respond, Annick approached. So engrossed in their conversation, Walter had not seen Annick move from his seat.

"I say, what a delightful coze the two of you are sharing," Annick drawled.

Walter indicated the nearby chair. "Join us. We were remarking on how men become arrogant when they inherit ducal titles."

Lilith choked on air.

Annick threw back his head and laughed. "Too right you are." With a flourish, he sat next to Lilith. "Ah, Collingwood, my good man. She's a striking beauty, is she not? It will be up to us to ward off the rakehells in eighteen years. I'll keep the sabre sharp."

"I pity the boy who looks at her sideways," Walter said. "He'll have a formidable gang against him. Between us, I wouldn't want Roddam as my enemy."

"The problem is," Lilith said, "no one prepares girls for the world. Parents hide them away until they come of age. The girls are uselessly innocent and uneducated, all in the name of virtue. Rakes and other nasty sorts prey on them, such easy victims, taking no time at all to convince the girls they're in love, if they even bother to do that much. The girls are so ignorant of the world of men, they don't know the signs to watch for, can't tell a soul about the attentions they're receiving, and don't realize until it's too late that they've been outmaneuvered by a skilled seducer."

Annick propped his chin with his palm, and Walter sat back in his chair. Well. Goodness. He had not realized how passionate she felt about the topic. Then, why would she not? She taught children on into adulthood, and he wagered that as a midwife, she saw her fair share of unpleasant situations.

"And you propose what exactly?" Annick asked.

"Educate them. Teach them not only about the marriage bed but how to defend themselves against would-be ravishers and rogues." Lilith's eyes were trained on Freya, the latter blissfully unaware of the evils of the world.

"Revolutionary words, cousin. I can see why you and Lizbeth get along. And what of you, Collingwood? Do you think women should be kept ignorant or taught as schoolgirls about the old Tib and Thomas?"

Walter had not realized until asked a direct question that his jaw was clenched, and his fingers ached from gripping the arm of the chair. This was *not* appropriate conversation for mixed company. He was horribly embarrassed. What was he to do? Excuse himself? After years of knowing Annick, he was not surprised how blasé the man was to be having such a conversation. And after a month of knowing Lilith, he should not be surprised, but it did concern him ever so slightly.

He did not want to change her. He liked her as she was, but for heaven's sake, she was saying these things in front of a *duke*. Yes, Annick was her cousin, but that did not make him any less of a personage in the peerage. Would she know better than to say such things at a dinner table in London during the Season? She could say all she desired to him and to family, and he did appreciate her forthright nature, but polite conversation would be expected with others — could she be polite? Would she? Was it from her own ignorance of polite society or her refusal to conform?

Dash it all. He did not want to change her, but this was inappropriate.

Running a finger between his neck and cravat, which felt too tight, he said, "Such is at the discretion of the governesses and parents, I say."

Lilith scoffed, "And what of those with parents who refuse? It is the girl who pays the price, not the parents. She is blamed for that which she knew nothing about and cast off, an outcast in her own family."

"Out to save the world?" Annick raised a mocking brow. "There's nothing we can do about other people, but we can protect our own families. Stand by them and all that." He stared intently at Lilith who held his gaze.

Walter felt out of his depths.

"Would you?" Lilith questioned her cousin.

"Protect and stand by my family? I'm sitting here, am I not? Don't doubt me. My own sister is an impressionable girl who fancies herself in love. It has taken me precious time to chaperone their encounters after discovering she had been sneaking off to meet her beau—aye, 'tis true. I'll not have some young buck compromise her because he wants a titled connection. If ought were to go awry, I would call out the boy, and then, I would stand by my sister. Or my daughter, should I have one. Or anyone else in my family. Say, a cousin, for instance."

Lilith sat up straighter, the corners of her mouth lifting. "You're a rarity. I'm fortunate to have you for a cousin."

"Bloody right you are," Annick said with a slap of his knee before standing. As he turned to walk away, he pivoted back to Walter and said in a less than discreet whisper, "Don't let that one get away, eh?" With a wink, he walked over to Lizbeth.

The duke and duchess stayed for dinner, though they would not be staying for the night. The evening proceeded as normal with conversations that conveniently excluded Walter and Lilith, encouraging their own private discussion. Neither complained.

Lilith relaxed gradually through the evening, her smile widening, her eyes brightening, her shoulders less rigid. She and Charlotte had even shared a brief conversation before dinner. Not that Walter intentionally eavesdropped, but what little of it he heard, they discussed music. He had a silent laugh since he recalled Lilith confessing herself as less than musically inclined.

Since the talk in the parlor, he had been thinking about Lilith's tendency to say all she ought not. His cousin Lizbeth had always had the same tendency, but even Liz had a limit to her discussions in mixed company. She also found a good match with Roddam, who was as blunt as she. Walter, however, was not blunt; he was polite. He was a gentleman. Several times, Lilith had accused him of being too stiff and proper, too formal, and perhaps she was right. However much he did not see himself that way, he was aware of the differences between him and Annick or him and Roddam. Roddam was blunt to the point of rudeness. Annick was blunt to the point of shocking. Walter was polite.

These were not doubts of their future together; he knew she was the one and that they were well suited. These were merely observations of the gulf separating their social etiquette. Not insurmountable by any stretch, but certainly present and undeniably concerning. Would she prefer someone less inhibited? Would he be embarrassed by her?

The real conundrum was the aspects that might embarrass him in a social situation were what attracted him to her. She was unlike anyone he had met. How could he simultaneously find her behavior attractive and embarrassing?

Filling his fork with food, he leaned in to hear Lilith better over the din. She was telling him the progress of some of her patients, one little boy having taken his first steps earlier in the year. He loved the look in her eyes when she talked about her patients. There was an energy, a contagious passion that sparked to life in her expression. She spoke animatedly, using her hands to help convey her story. The whole of the conversation exemplified the quagmire he faced. No lady of the *beau monde* would speak animatedly, much less of patients or children, and certainly not while using their hands to speak. And yet, he found her tantalizing.

Earlier in the conversation, they had exchanged ideas for his orphanage. His secretary had written regarding property for purchase that might prove an ideal location. Walter could scarcely believe it was all coming together so quickly. Lilith had remarked with a coy grin that she was on the verge of believing him in earnest.

Charlotte spoke then, loud enough to be heard across the table as she addressed her sister. "Mama Catherine sends her best. She wants you to bring Lady Freya as soon as you are able."

Lizbeth said, "I had expected her to accompany you, to be honest. She accepted my invitation and included a lovely message."

Charlotte shook her head. "You know how she is."

"Yes, but why not come with the two of you? I will call on her soon, but it's rather inconvenient. It could be several weeks before I feel comfortable taking Freya in a carriage."

"You know perfectly well she feels it improper," Charlotte said after a taste of her wine.

"I'm offended by that, Charlotte," Liz said, putting down her cutlery. "If it weren't for Catherine, we wouldn't all be together now. She's the one who sent me to Allshire in the first place. And she knows how important family is to me and how much I want us all to be together. I shall return with you tonight and give her a piece of my mind."

After Liz's outburst, all at the table listened to the exchange.

Roddam interjected, "You most certainly will not. Let her stew in her own misery. If she wishes to be alone in the world, so be it. This is our family, not hers."

"It's not right," Liz said. "I'll not have it. She cannot treat people this way. Freya is her great-niece, and Lilith is her niece. They are her family, and they deserve respect."

"Lizbeth," Charlotte said with a laugh, "don't be silly. You know very well she lives by the strict dictates of Society. It doesn't matter that *we* accept Lilith. Mama Catherine will never acknowledge her as a niece."

Knowing it was not his place to defend her given they were not affianced, he felt protective all the same. How dare the woman not accept her own niece! It was not Lilith's fault she had been shipped off to an orphanage, estranged from her family.

"I say," Walter cut in, "this is preposterous. If you'll pardon my language, ladies, the woman can go to the devil if she's going to hold her own niece's time at an orphanage against her."

Roddam trumpeted, "Hear, hear. I propose a toast to Collingwood's wisdom. To the devil with my aunt." He raised his glass.

"Sebastian!" Lizbeth hissed.

Roddam smirked but put down his glass.

"My mother has always been, shall we say, old fashioned," Annick said. "We can't expect Society to be as forward thinking as we are."

With a hand to her heart, Mama said, "I'm surprised to hear this sort of prejudice from the dowager duchess. I've grown fond of her and am shocked beyond words she would turn her back on her niece over a little time at an orphanage. It isn't as though Lilith was an orphan. She was displaced! I'll go with you, Lizzie, dear. I have a few choice words to share with her."

Charlotte tutted, "It's nothing to do with the orphanage, of course. Mama Catherine could not give a fig about that."

"I can't begin to understand that woman," Mama said, huffing. "What in the good Lord's name does she have against our Lilith?"

The table fell silent, everyone looking at everyone else. Lilith caught Walter's gaze and held it. He was fit to be tied but gave her an encouraging smile. He had half a mind to accompany his mother and Lizbeth to say a few words of his own.

In a clear and steady voice, her eyes level with Walter's, though she addressed his mother, Lilith said, "As you know, polite society does not recognize illegitimacy, my lady. And I am illegitimate."

Chapter 10

Walter lunged with long-legged strides from room to room, his mind a jumble of contradictions. He had to find her. He had to speak with her. Determination silenced reason. He had to find her.

After the declaration, Lilith had excused herself from dinner. Walter had been too dumbstruck to respond, to stop her from leaving, or to follow her. They had all known. All except him, his mother, and his uncle. They had all known. Of course, they had known, for they were all her family, all except the three who were Lizbeth's relations. And they had *encouraged* the match!

Only when a maelstrom of voices stormed around him did he come to his senses and excuse himself to go after her.

Room after room, he searched. No sign of her. She would have returned to her bedchamber, he realized through a haze of dim-wittedness. It was the one place he could not follow. As he turned into the gallery from the parlor, heading for the grand staircase, his mother stepped in front of him.

"Walter, we need to talk."

"Can't. Must find her." He sidestepped her to traverse the gallery, a space that appeared to lengthen with each step.

"You will stop and talk to me first," she commanded.

"Must find her," he repeated, one foot on the stairs, then another. "Must tell her it doesn't matter."

"Walter, you stop this minute and talk to me. It does matter. It changes everything. Come with me to the parlor."

"It doesn't matter. I must tell her." Two steps at a time, he ascended.

"Walter Alexander Hobbs!" his mother screeched from below.

He halted, one step away from the top.

"You do neither that girl nor yourself any favors by going to her. Into the parlor. *Now*."

Walter closed his eyes. An onslaught of dizziness had him reaching a hand for the railing to steady himself. Squeezing his eyes tighter, he gripped the banister until his fingers ached. How cruel was life?

The memory of when he had learned of his father's death blindsided him. Of all the things to think of in this moment, he thought of his father. He remembered taking him for granted, assuming he would always be there, assuming they had all the time in the world to be together. He could not equate his father's death to this new blow, but how unfair life was to good people. How cruel of fate.

A warm touch to his upper arm jolted him. His mother stared at him through knowing eyes, eyes of green, the same shade as his own.

"Come," she said, her tone firm, her touch soft.

Nodding, he followed her to the parlor. She directed him to a chair by the hearth. Not until he sat did he realize he was shaking, chilled by the knowledge, angry at life, distraught by his powerlessness.

They had the parlor to themselves. The others, he assumed, remained in the dining room, finishing their meal.

"I can't turn my back on her now," Walter said, wanting to get in the first word before his mother attempted to dissuade him. "She needs me."

"I rather doubt that. She's a grown woman capable of looking after herself."

"You're turning on her? Just like her aunt?" Walter stared at his mother, incredulous.

"I've said no such thing. If you're going to put words in my mouth, we shan't get far. Now is the time to listen, son."

Walter rested an elbow against the arm of the chair, covering his face with his hand. Sweeping the palm over his eyes and down to cover his mouth, he waited for his mother to speak ill of Lilith, to point out all the reasons they could never be together, even to warn him against being duped by a deceitful title huntress.

"Do you love her?" his mother asked instead.

With knitted brow, his eyes focusing somewhere beyond her head, he said, "Yes. No. Not as such. We've not known each other for long enough. But I'm *in* love with her, Mama, and in time, I will love her. Before you say a word against her, know that I've pursued her, not the other way around. Don't think she's tried to trap me. She's not like that."

"Walter," his mother said with a warning tone. "I'm not your enemy. Answer my questions, and then listen."

His eyes met hers. She stared back at him with a fierceness he had not seen since he was a boy. A loving fierceness. A protective mother hen who would shred any soul who crossed her family. He tugged at his sideburns, nodding.

With a determined exhale, Mama said, "If you think this a passing fancy, an attraction based only on beauty, mystique, and proximity, you would do well to let her go. This is not a love story with a happy ending, my boy. A relationship with her, should you pursue it, would only lead to heartache."

He nodded but made no response.

"There are any number of younger eligible ladies awaiting your acquaintance. Come next Season, we can begin in earnest to find your ladylove."

His head, as though fitted with rockers, continued to nod of its own accord. He was not really listening. He had to find Lilith and tell her it did not matter. They could elope and be done with it. Society could go to the devil.

"I do find it surprising you would fall for a girl so independent and bold given your reservations of Lizzie over the years. However, if you are in love with the girl beyond the superficial, we will find a way."

Walter stopped nodding and stared wide-eyed at his mother. Had he misheard?

His mother continued, "I know marrying for love is gauche, but as I've always told you, I married your father for love. I had hoped you would find such a match for yourself one day. What you must understand is love alone is not enough. There's far more to a successful marriage. In this situation, love will never be enough. There will be repercussions. There will be consequences. This is not a decision to take lightly. This affects the *entire* family, and if not handled well, Society will drive you both apart."

He tucked a clenched fist beneath his chin. "With Roddam and Annick supporting her, and with you sponsoring her, they'll have no choice but to accept her. Everyone looks to you. They value your opinion. Even so, Annick's influence alone would be enough."

She gave a sharp laugh. "Thank you for the vote of confidence, but it will take far more than that. You cannot be naïve about this, Walter. Titled men do not marry illegitimate women. There *will* be a scandal, and it will affect everyone, not just you. The girl will receive nothing but censure — do you want to put her in a position where she is ridiculed? It is selfish, for she will suffer, and that tension would strain the marriage. She could grow to resent you. This must be handled carefully, Walter, very carefully. Think of how the scandal would affect your cousins and their children. Think of how it would affect your reputation in the House. You would be shunned. Think of the children you would have. They would be shunned. I'm not saying you must let her go. But I *am* saying this needs to be thought through. If you run to her now, careless and chivalrous, you will destroy many lives in the name of love. If you are willing to face the consequences, I will help you, but this will take planning, strategic planning."

"You're assuming she would say yes. She may not want me," Walter mumbled, staring at the rug, morbidly depressed.

"Well, goodness. Why would she say no? Not only have you been the catch of the Season for years, and I say that because it's true, not because I'm your mother, but lest you forget, she has no other options."

"Not so," he said with a shake of his head. "She has her own life in Allshire, a life with which she's content. I'm uncertain she would want aught to do with Society. It would be narcissistic to take credit, but I do think the changes we've seen in her of late have been her attempts to step a toe into our world to see how it feels, maybe to see if I would be worth the sacrifice."

"You? Worth the sacrifice?" She scoffed. "Good heavens. I'm not sure I like a woman thinking she must make sacrifices to be with you. She should be honored. Not to mention you would be the one making all the sacrifices."

"Mama, please."

She huffed.

"Assuming she would want me, what can we do? This is hopeless, is it not? You've said it yourself. Society would tear us apart through scandal and censure."

His mother leaned against her chairback, something she rarely did, and thought for so long, Walter began to suspect she, too, realized there was nothing to be done. It was a hopeless situation.

"I need to think this through. We all do. Discreetly, of course, for it does no one any good to make plans for a union with a woman who you think might reject you, but then, is there a reason to propose if we do not have a plan? Ah, which one is the cart and which the horse?"

Leaning his head into his hand, he closed his eyes, wanting to shut out the past half hour.

Mama continued talking, "When Lizzie and Sebastian were courting, I had any number of ladies recalling his sister to me. The Earl and Countess of

Roddam brought *both* children to London for the Parliamentary Season each year until Lady Roddam died. After that time, Lord Roddam rarely came to London, and the children were not seen again until Sebastian inherited. He returned to take his seat in the House, but the girl was never seen again. All the ladies who spoke of the family knew the little girl as Lord and Lady Roddam's daughter, not a by-blow of Lord Roddam. If I sponsor her introduction to Society, and we focus attention on her being the long-lost and reunited sister, it would feed the gossips enough not to question her parentage. They already know, or think they know, her parentage."

"So, we lie," Walter said.

"No, not lie. We simply never reveal the truth."

Walter groaned, raking his fingers through his hair. "Someone is bound to find out. They always do. If we can't get the Dowager Duchess of Annick to accept her own niece, we've no hope of succeeding. *She* will say something if no one else does. Who else knows? All North England could know for all we're aware."

"That is something we will need to confer with Sebastian and Lizzie."

"It'll never work. Lilith will never agree to it." He could not speak for Lilith, but from all he knew of her, she was too proud to live a lie.

"If she's in love with you, she might. If she loves you, she will. There will be gossip regardless, but we *can* redirect that scandal to be the discovery of the long-lost daughter rather than the long-lost by-blow. There are factors to consider. Her Grace is one of them. Lilith is another. She would need to be brought up to scratch. Thanks to her Mrs. Brighton, she's not completely rustic, but she is certainly countrified and far too blunt with no awareness of what can and cannot be said in front of company — you must have noticed. With the right fashion and hairstyle, she'll look the part. With lessons on etiquette, deportment, rules of precedence, and so forth, she will be respectable."

Walter's mother sat up in the chair, growing increasingly excited about her impromptu campaign.

"She'll never agree to that, Mama," Walter rebutted. "We would be changing her into someone she's not."

"If she loves you, she will. She'll know she's not being changed and that you do not want to change her. She is merely learning respectability. She can do, say, and wear whatever she likes in private. This is the only way it will work, Walter. You must understand that. You *cannot* marry her as she is and toss her into the lion's den. They would tear her apart and besmirch us all in the process. Need I remind you, titled men do not marry illegitimate women."

Walter pinched his thigh, hoping to wake himself from this nightmare.

That night, Walter lay awake, staring at the wooden canopy of the four-poster bed. The impossibility of the task ahead daunted him. It was not his mother's improvised plan that concerned him so much as Lilith's feelings towards him.

Had she been legitimate, as he previously thought, courtship was relatively simple — build a foundation of mutual attraction and find love along the way. Marriage first, then love. His greatest battle had been to convince her to leave her old life in which she appeared content, independent, and proudly stable. But now, the situation was far more complicated. She would not just be leaving behind her old life. She would be participating in a grand cover-up wherein success depended on her ability to fit into the very world she resisted.

How the devil was he to convince her he was worth it?

He could not walk up to her and offer marriage, not now. She knew better than he the complications that lay ahead. Though she had been receptive to his flirtations, she had resisted them from the start. It all made sense now. She had resisted because she knew he was an impossibility.

That was the first hurdle, the tallest hurdle — Lilith. As his mother pointed out, Lilith would only take on such a monumental task of learning to live in Society, not to mention living a lie, if she loved him. Well, she did not love him. She was not even infatuated. She was...what? Curious? Attracted? Yes, certainly attracted.

Attraction was a far cry from love, and love would have to come before marriage. She had to fall so deeply in love with him that she would feel him worth sacrificing her old life, worth changing to fit Society's expectations, worth living as the legitimate sister of an earl despite the risks of discovery.

How the devil was he going to get her to fall in love with him?

Early the next morning, Walter stood in Lord Roddam's library. He wrung his hands behind his back, far more nervous than he should have been after spending a month in the casual company of the earl. The man himself stood with his shoulder against the stone of the window alcove. His arms were crossed, his ankles crossed, and his head bowed. Not a good reaction, Walter thought.

"It has taken me over two decades to find my sister. Now, you come to me and ask my permission to haul her off to Devonshire?" Roddam asked with a menacing growl.

Walter squeezed his hands so tightly his knuckles popped. Wincing, he said, "That's not quite what I asked. I only ask permission to court her. Officially."

"A man only courts a woman for one reason, marriage. Unless you're planning a long-distance marriage, the inevitable conclusion would be hauling her off to Devonshire. Four hundred miles away from me."

Walter cleared his throat. "Yes. Ultimately. If she'll have me."

Roddam growled again.

They stood in silence, Walter feeling a bead of sweat trickle down his brow. By Jupiter, he was like a schoolboy facing the headmaster.

Then Roddam barked a laugh. Walter nearly jumped out of his shoes. The man turned from the window, a wide smile replacing the formidable scowl, his arms uncrossed and outstretched to embrace his companion. In swift strides, Roddam hugged Walter.

"I'd be honored to have you as a brother-in-law rather than a cousin-in-law. I've no idea why you asked my permission, but I'm happy you did. She's well beyond her majority and needs no one's permission but her own. You do realize she's three and thirty? Only two years younger than you? She's not some green girl you'd meet in London. All the same, I appreciate that you respect me enough to ask." Roddam invited Walter to take a seat by the fire, which burned a low blaze despite the temperate morning. "I suspect my permission isn't the only reason you're here."

"I'm under no illusion she'll accept my advances. I do think, if it's not conceited to say, she has an affection for me. I don't know if affection is enough." Walter crossed a leg over the other and clasped his hands in his lap.

"Have you spoken to her since dinner?"

Walter shook his head. He suspected she was breaking her fast in the morning room at that very moment. As hungry as he was, he had chosen to speak to Roddam instead. It was not that he was avoiding her, or at least that was what he told himself. It was more that he was not ready to face her. He needed a plan to convince her. Dashed if he knew what plan, though.

"I don't know my sister's mind," Roddam said. "She's as much a mystery to me as she is to you. However, I would hazard to guess she will see you in a far better light when she learns you're not bothered by the circumstances of her birth. You aren't, are you?"

"Not in the least. It does complicate the situation, however."

"I don't see why it should. She's my sister. She was raised by my mother as her legitimate daughter. No one outside immediate family knows the truth, and it's my own fault for telling *her* the truth. She would have been none the wiser. As far as I'm concerned, she *is* legitimate, and I'll not listen to any words to the contrary. She's her own worst enemy, for it is only she who cares."

"But what of your aunt, the dowager duchess? So adamant against Lilith, she refused to call on you."

Roddam grunted. "Who gives a rat's tail what she says or thinks."

"Society does."

Roddam clasped his hands behind his head. "For what it's worth, I would call her a liar to the whole of the aristocracy, but I don't suppose that's the answer you're looking for." He stared up at the coved ceiling. "She's a crusty old bat, and I've not the first clue what my wife sees in her. If anyone can talk to her, Liz can."

"Do you think she can be convinced to stay silent? It doesn't mean she has to accept Lilith as her niece, but at least not cut her?"

"No idea. As I said, Liz and her get on. All else fails, to the devil with her," Roddam said.

"And what of Lilith's birth mother? Who was she? Are they in touch? Could she be someone to step forward and call out Lilith as illegitimate?"

"Deuces, Collingwood. Your mind has been calculating since dinner. You're quite determined to marry her, then?"

"If she'll have me."

Roddam nodded. "Never would have thought the two of you would get on. Pardon my saying this, but I had thought you opposites. Pay no mind to me.

I'm just the boorish brother without a romantic bone in my body."

Walter chuckled and waited for his companion to answer his questions. When no answer seemed forthcoming, he nudged, "Her mother?"

"Ah, yes. That. No idea about her either."

Walter slumped in his chair. Roddam was not being as helpful as he had hoped. This was not a problem that could be swept under the rug.

Roddam shrugged and added, "As far as we've pieced together from the letters between her mother and my father, her mother was the coachman's daughter. Lily Chambers was her name. Only a young girl at the time, well under the age of consent but fancied herself in love. Left Lilith in a basket on the doorstep. Somewhere between their tryst and the abandonment, my father married my mother. My mother took Lilith in and raised her as her own. I was born a few months later. Granted, all the servants would have known, but they were loyal, and by now most have died. I've no idea what became of Lily Chambers. Never cared to find out. If the woman cared, she would have sought out Lilith years ago."

"She might have tried but not succeeded."

How had he not thought to question the name? He had never given her name much thought before to be honest. Lilith Chambers. He had assumed it a name the orphanage gave her after being sent by a father who no longer wanted her. The truth had stared him in the face the whole time.

Roddam frowned. "And I suppose you want me to investigate her birth mother's whereabouts? Ensure she won't cause trouble?"

"At least discover her whereabouts." For what purpose, Walter could not say, but it seemed sensible.

"I don't see her as a threat. She abandoned her baby and was never seen again. Should my sister accept you, she wouldn't even be Lilith Chambers anymore. If the woman tried to find her, it would make for a difficult search."

"What evidence is there that she's illegitimate? And for that matter, is there anything that could prove she's legitimate?"

"My word," said Roddam. "Ah, but I know what you mean." He scratched then stroked his chin, lost in thought for a moment. "I don't believe anyone will investigate her past. They'll be satisfied enough with the gossip that my sister is alive, that you're no longer available, and that you thumbed your nose at all the young hopefuls for a mature woman, the long-thought-dead sister of a recluse. Gossip enough for an entire Season. No one will question her legitimacy."

Roddam took a deep breath and crossed his arms over his chest. "If you're this concerned, know that I burned the only evidence of her illegitimacy, namely the letters from her birth mother. I don't know what records my parents might have kept once they took her in, but I'll do some digging. Peace of mind and all that, eh? From my perspective, your only enemy in this situation is Lilith. She's the one determined to see herself as devil's spawn born on the wrong side of the blanket. All I see is my sister. Seems to me it's you who has the proud honor of convincing her of that fact."

Chapter 11

"You can't hide here all day," Lizbeth said in reproach.

"I'm not hiding. I'm spending time with my niece and sister-in-law."

Rocking Freya, Liz said, "And you're hiding."

Lilith busied herself by pouring them a fresh cup of tea and choosing a few delectable breakfast items. Walter would be enjoying his breakfast in the morning room, she supposed unwittingly. It was not that she was avoiding him so much as she was not ready to face him. Guilt, shame, regret, and longing encapsulated her feelings.

As though understanding Lilith's wish to change the subject, Lizbeth said without preamble, "Papa and Sebastian are going to the coal mine site today. Sebastian hasn't seen it in weeks." Kissing Freya's forehead, she added, "He's been the teensiest bit distracted by his new role as a father."

It still amazed Lilith to see Sebastian with Freya. All her memories of him were as a young boy. From the moment she arrived at the orphanage, she had clung to those memories until life and time made her question everything she thought she remembered, including him. By the time she reached her majority, she had all but forgotten him except in dreams.

There were moments over the past year when she would look at him with confusion, as though she expected to see a boy standing before her rather than a grown man with a family of his own. How remarkable was time?

She grimaced to realize Lizbeth had been talking while she reminisced.

"Papa is helping him with mining methods. I love seeing the two of them together. Sebastian never had a father figure, not a good one, that is. Not that I expect him to see my Papa as a father figure, but I do wonder if he might…in time."

"Will your father visit every summer?" Lilith bit into a breakfast roll, savoring the buttery flavor and smooth texture before licking the bits that clung to the corners of her mouth.

When she returned to Allshire, she would miss such decadence. Something so simple had come to mean much to her. The morning hot chocolate would be especially missed. Hannah's company and expertise when dressing, hot baths, abundance at every meal, tea trays she did not have to prepare herself, and, oh, the list went on with the simple pleasures she had enjoyed more than she expected.

"Nothing has been decided," Lizbeth said in answer to Lilith's question, "but Papa is considering a move north."

Lilith looked at her sister-in-law in surprise. "Here? But what of his home? What of his mine?"

"The hall will be Walter's one day, by way of the entailment, but the mine is Papa's to do with as he wishes. He's undecided, but he's considering either selling it or willing it to his grandchildren while a

manager oversees the daily tasks. I believe he's leaning towards the latter, for if he hired an experienced
steward, the man could live at the hall while oversee-
ing the mine, ensuring all was well tended in Papa's
absence."

"There's an entailment?" Lilith stared at Lizbeth,
confused. "I thought they only followed the male line.
I don't mean to pry, but I don't know of any cases
of entailments that go to a *daughter's* son. Then, I've
never left Allshire other than to visit you, so pardon
my country ignorance."

"Don't be silly! You're not prying or ignorant. But
are you prepared to hear family gossip?" Liz said
with a teasing smile.

Lilith leaned forward, nodding, ever curious. She
was not a lover of gossip, on principle, but...Lizbeth's
family embroiled in gossip? How could she resist?

"I don't know the details, but I've pieced together
a thing or two over the years. Apparently," Lizbeth
began, leaning towards her conspiratorially and
reaching a hand to touch Lilith's arm, "my grandfather was quite desperate to wed my Aunt Hazel to
Lord Collingwood's son and heir, Harold Hobbs. He
was willing to make an attractive settlement to help
persuade the match. At first, he only agreed to make
will provisions for any children of the union but there
were promises of continued fortune through the years.
Well, years later—Walter would have already been
born and well into childhood—my parents began to
court. There was some sort of stratagem concerning
my grandfather wanting Papa to secure the Teague's
tin mine, but in the process, Papa fell in love with
the mine owner's daughter. My grandfather was

infuriated by the match and threatened to cast him off without a penny should Papa pursue her—or so says Papa, and he's known to exaggerate."

Lizbeth paused for a taste of her tea, Freya sleeping soundly in the crook of her arm.

"Well, when Papa defied him, Grandpapa sought revenge by arranging with his solicitor an entailment—to be enacted in the event Papa marry Miss Elizabeth Teague—with the settlement being any male descendent of the female line, namely Walter. A fee tail female is all but unheard of, for why would someone want their property to end up in the hands of their daughter's husband? Well, when Papa did marry my mother, the entailment was legally enacted. This strengthened the friendship between Grandpapa and Lord Collingwood while disinheriting my father's children, should they be girls."

Lilith covered her mouth in a silent gasp.

"I do wonder if Grandpapa only meant it as a show of disapproval, never expecting Papa to go through with the marriage, and even if he did, never expecting Papa not to have an heir. But that's me giving Grandpapa more credit than he might deserve. And so, Walter is heir to the Trethow family home and fortune. To make amends, for years, Aunt Hazel pressed a match between Walter and me so that I could keep my family home. You see how much either of us fancied that idea," she said with a laugh.

When Lizbeth stopped talking, leaning back in her chair to reposition Freya who had begun to stir, Lilith realized she had scooted to the edge of her own seat, a half-eaten bread roll forgotten in her hand, so ensconced was she in the tale.

From all Walter had told her during their many conversations, his parents had been deeply infatuated, and thus, he had grown up in a house of love and happiness, but had it not been a love match from the start? Hazel's desire for Walter to marry for love seemed all the more poignant if she had not done so herself, at least not in the beginning.

There was, however, more to a happy marriage than love.

Not that she was thinking of either love or marriage. And certainly not with Walter.

"If you'd be so kind," Lizbeth added, "best not mention any of that to Walter or Hazel. Family gossip and all. And besides, what I know comes from Papa, so I'm not altogether certain how much Hazel knows about Grandpapa's financial courtship of Lord Collingwood and his son, or how much she would want others to know. Aside from there being an entailment, we've never spoken about how it came to be."

Lilith placed her hand over her heart and smiled. "And so," Lilith said, "Mr. Trethow is thinking of moving here to spoil his granddaughter on a full-time basis."

"Yes, he's considering it. There's nothing for him in Cornwall other than the mine and memories. Both Charlotte and I are here. We're not like other families, as I'm sure you've gathered, where the woman is seen as a burden to unload. No, we are quite close. Oh, Lilith, I do hope he'll make the move. I can't stand the thought of him being alone."

They talked afterwards about any number of things that did not involve Walter, but as distracting as the conversation was, Lilith could think of little else.

Most of her thoughts were of regrets. She never should have flirted with him. From the beginning, she had known he was an impossibility. Now, he would be nothing but a sore topic of conversation for her and her family. She should set out for Allshire immediately. The return was already overdue; now, it was imperative. Lizbeth's family would not want her here, not after finding out the truth. And how much more embarrassing that the truth had gone untold for an entire month, as though she had hidden it intentionally.

Oh, what must he think of her?

She pinched the bridge of her nose, feeling the onset of a migraine.

"You can't avoid him forever, you know," Lizbeth said.

Lilith squeezed her eyes closed, willing away the dull ache behind her forehead.

"What am I to do, Lizbeth? I've made a right mess of everything. All I had to do was ignore his advances, tell him from the beginning I wasn't interested. What am I to do?"

"Go to him, accept his proposal, and live happily ever after."

Lilith choked a cynical laugh. What absurdity. "He'll never look at me again now that he knows what I am," Lilith protested.

Lizbeth tutted. "Give him more credit than that. I'm sure he was taken aback at first, but he is the kindest of gentlemen. If he's developed a *tèndre* for you, and we both know he has, he'll let nothing stand in his way, not even an inconvenient fact."

"Hardly inconvenient! It'd be the worst of scandals. You can't deny that."

Liz smiled warmly. "I can. And I will. You are Sebastian's sister, and that's all anyone needs to know. Hang the gossipmongers. They would never dare question the Earl of Roddam's claim to you as his sister."

"And what of my aunt? Or the Reverend Sands? Oh, it doesn't matter. I don't want to be part of that world. I have my own life, a life I treasure. I'm respected in Allshire. The women and children of the parish need me. There's nothing for me in that world except heartache. What would I do all day? Sit around in drawing rooms dressed like a trussed peacock, making conversation about the weather? Pah! There's nothing I want in that world."

"Not even Walter?" Liz asked.

Lilith bit her upper lip.

"He needs you," Liz said when Lilith did not answer. "For three years, he's been lost. Ever since my uncle died. I believe he was lost before then, but it was a different kind of lost. He was a tad wild, gave his parents no end of grief with his reckless ways, curricle races, practical jokes, noisome parties, carousing, nothing at all respectable. He's close friends with your cousin, if that tells you anything. But then my uncle died. He's been listless and searching for meaning ever since. He needs you."

"I don't see what I have to do with anything. I can't help him find meaning."

"Ah, but you already have. I've seen such a visible change in him since you arrived. We all have. For the first time in his life, he's motivated. He has a direction and a passion. Has he not talked nonstop to you about the orphanage he wants to build? He's been searching for a purpose, a legacy, a family of his own to love. And here you are, his driving force."

"I'm flattered to have inspired, but *I'm* not a purpose. If he's taking responsibility for his life that's grand, but he doesn't need me to do it."

It was at that moment Freya chose to fuss. Liz hoisted Freya against her chest, tucking the baby's head between her shoulder and neck. With coos and humming and a caressing hand on Freya's back, Liz settled the babe again.

"Do you feel anything at all for him?" Liz asked. "Are you withdrawing because of your parentage or because you don't care for him?"

Lilith thought for a long while how to respond. She did care for Walter. She did not love him, not exactly. She had not known him long enough to love him, but she most certainly was attracted to him. She was, truth be told, a little *in* love with him. Had life been different, and had she been the Lady Lilith her brother believed her to be, she would rush headlong in love with Walter without question or consequence. Alas, life was cruel. Against her better judgment, she had allowed herself too many liberties. Whatever feelings she had for him needed to be torn asunder. Quickly. Irrevocably. The sooner the better.

"It's hopeless, Liz. My feelings matter not."

"I beg to differ. Love will find a way if you let it."

Lilith strained a half-smile. She could already feel herself slipping back into the familiar, the safe and understood familiar of her parish life. Despite the protests of her heart, she knew her decision.

By early afternoon, Lilith had resigned herself to seek out Walter.

It seemed silly to hide from him when they were not even courting. They were merely house guests who had exchanged light flirtation, and he likely had not spared her a second thought since her declaration at dinner.

He was not difficult to find. With Sebastian and Mr. Trethow off to the coal mine, and Hazel and Liz taking tea with Freya in the parlor, Lilith suspected he would be in the conservatory. Indeed, he was.

The door to the conservatory stood open. As she walked the hall of the ground floor, she spied him lounging in one of the chairs, one leg crossed over the other, one elbow resting against the arm of the chair, half turned to face the sea, only his profile visible from the hall. Though it was only his profile, her heartbeat quickened. His features were soft, but his nose and chin strong. She could almost make out his long eyelashes in the afternoon light.

The double doors were all open to the outside, giving way to a cool breeze and the sound of the gulls and waves.

Lilith steeled herself before stepping into the room and announcing her presence. Would he prove himself the sort of heartless blueblood she had expected all aristocrats to be? Would he claim he did not care, confess undying love, and try to convince her to elope? Would he do what she expected an arrogant toff to do and invite her to become his mistress, enabling him to keep her in some capacity since he could not marry her?

The consolation was she had their kiss to cherish. No matter how he acted in the next few moments, she resolved to remember him how he had been at the curtain wall, his eyes pools of open admiration, his lips reddened with desire. If she had to, she would separate in her mind that man from this man so as not to tarnish her memory, the memory of her first and only kiss.

Spine straight, lips pursed, chin up, she stepped into the conservatory.

He must have heard her steps, for he turned to face her before she made it halfway across the room. Though his eyes swept over her, taking in the simply braided hair and the old dress she had chosen to wear, his expression revealed nothing but a polite smile. But then, the polite smile seemed to reveal everything. He was not going to cut her, but neither was he going to rush to her in an awkward embrace with declarations. Was she disappointed?

Grimacing a polite smile of her own, she approached as he stood, turning fully to her, a breathtaking specimen of manhood. Gosh, when had she become so sentimental?

With her own sweep of a gaze, she spotted a book in his hands. Unusual sight for a man who did little reading. She took the seat diagonal from him and indicated for him to return to his seat.

Resuming his casual posture, the book tucked into the side of his chair next to his thigh, he spoke first. "Did you ever finish reading that book Roddam recommended?"

Well, at least it was not a comment about the weather, she supposed.

"What book?"

"*Evelina*. I caught you reading it one day if you recall." The polite smile had not faltered.

The title sounded vaguely familiar. If memory served, she had not got past the first page, either distracted or bored, maybe both. She was not a fan of sentimental novels and had been confused why her brother would recommend it. Her eyes flitted to the book wedged next to his thigh.

"Unless I misremember, it failed to hold my attention," she said.

"Shame. You should read it."

She raised her eyebrows. "Pray tell, why?"

"I've not finished it, and I don't want to spoil the best parts for you, but I think you'll find it entertaining. You see, it's about a young woman introduced to Society. She has some misadventures because she's, shall we say, a tad rustic, but she catches the attention of an aristocrat."

Lilith narrowed her eyes. "And this would interest me why?"

"Because she's illegitimate."

Oh.

Lilith's breath caught in her throat. That was certainly one way to broach the subject. She knew not how to respond, so she remained silent.

He said, "Well, the thing of it is, she's not *really* illegitimate, but she thinks she is. I won't spoil the plot for you. Instead, I think you should read it for yourself."

Exhaling, she said, "I hardly see the point. I have no intentions of being introduced to Society, so whatever parallels you are implying are a wasted effort."

Walter's polite smile deepened into a genuine smile. "Do you ever dream, Lilith?"

Frowning, she said, "Dream? As in, when I sleep? I suppose everyone does, though I've not given such thought much consequence."

"No, not at night. Do you *dream*? Do you ever imagine the ridiculous—being able to fly, being able to breathe underwater, being able to sing in the opera? What about things you may want to do, places you'd want to travel? Dream a life that isn't yours but could be?"

She laughed. She could not help herself. What absurdity!

"Those are the thoughts of children, not of adults. I see no point in dreaming of what can never happen. I deal with the here and now, the practical," she said.

"But nothing is achieved without first dreaming it." He cocked his head to one side, studying her.

"And yet, if it's not achievable, then there is still no point in dreaming."

"Tell that to men of science, Lilith. They invent the impossible, all because they dreamed of the impossible. I believe that achievement begins with a dream, no matter how ridiculous, and if you want it enough, you'll find a way to make it happen."

Lilith smoothed the invisible creases in her dress. What a perfectly absurd conversation. If she had known he would talk in riddles, she might not have sought him out.

"Be sensible, Walter. Poverty stricken laborers cannot dream themselves into riches or happiness.

Unwed mothers cannot dream themselves into a legitimate marriage or with an accepting family. Ravished women cannot dream themselves back to innocence. You've lived in a fairy tale life and have no awareness of what the real world is like. I live in the real world."

Though he still smiled, a crease had formed between his brows. It was not pity in his eyes, but a sad curiosity.

"I can't dream my father back to life or dream back the time I could have spent with him but didn't. What I can do is live my life to honor his memory, to make him proud of the man I've become. That begins with a dream, a dream of what such a life would look like. Without the dream, I would remain a listless son, forever regretting my father's death. I refuse to live in a shadow. If we get too stuck in the muck of our present situations, we can never see the potential of the future. There are always ways to achieve our goals if only we focus, plan, and *dream*. I never said it would be easy, but it is possible."

She sat in stunned silence. However foolish his words should sound to her, she felt more the fool. And yet what would she dream?

Neither spoke for a long stretch. They both stared at each other, Lilith frowning, Walter assessing.

"A puppy," she said at last.

He coughed a laugh. "A puppy?"

"I always dreamed of having a puppy. My father wouldn't allow it, but I dreamed it all the same. A childhood dream, I know, but I've thought often as an adult that there's not much stopping me from fulfilling the dream now. Only, I never have. It's never seemed practical. I spend my time at the orphanage and making house calls. When would I have time for a puppy?"

Why in the world was she making such absurd confessions to him? A puppy indeed!

"What of the hospital we visited?" he asked. "What of opening a training facility for midwives?"

"Oh, Walter. None of that is practical. I'd end up disappointed and depressed if I spent all my time dreaming of what could never be."

He sighed and rubbed the back of his neck.

Before he distracted her again, she said what she came here to say, "I'm returning to Allshire. I've accomplished what I came here to do. Freya and Lizbeth are healthy, and we've narrowed the possible nurses to three, so Lizbeth can make the final choice. I'm ready to return to my own life."

"You mean you're ready to hide from life," he muttered.

"I do beg your pardon." She straightened her spine and clasped her hands. "I am not hiding from anything. I *like* my life."

He shook his head. "You have it in your power to create any life you could dream. You could live anywhere. Why not be with family? Why not stay here at Dunstanburgh? Or go to Roddam Hall and reclaim your roots? The possibilities are endless, Lilith. Don't hide because you're afraid."

"How absurd. I'm not afraid of anything."

"No?" He arched a brow. "Prove it. Let me court you."

Lilith stuttered a laugh. Staring at her hands, she said, "You don't mean that. You don't even know me."

"I know enough. Lilith, I do not say this with loose words. I want to court you. I beg you to give me a chance, a proper chance. I don't care who your mother was—is that what you need me to say? I mean, I do care, because she was your mother, and I understand fully the consequences, but let's take one step at a time, shall we? Starting with a proper courtship."

She sighed, her eyes still trained on her clenched hands. "It would be better if you forgot you met me. I'll ensure our paths do not cross again. Go home, Walter. During the Season, you'll find a lady of your station, and I'll be but a memory. I'll return to my life and be content, and one day, perhaps, I'll meet someone of my station who doesn't mind I'm long in the tooth. Or perhaps I won't. Either way, we'll be far better off to forget about this month."

She would never forget, but he would.

"You can't even look at me when you say it, so I know you don't mean it." He reached over, brave soul, and covered her hands with his. "All I'm asking is for you to agree to a courtship. If we decide we don't suit, then so be it. And if we do, we'll cross that bridge when the time comes. For now, let's dream the impossible. Go back to Allshire. I'll follow you there in however many weeks you need in which to be alone first. I'll then court you on your terms. I'll court you as Miss Chambers, parish midwife and teacher. Please say yes."

Chapter 12

In a deep and intoxicating inhalation, Lilith breathed the sweet, honey-scented aroma of nirrhe, a late summer bloomer, and admired its white blossoms. She waved to Mr. Turnbow, the owner of the best garden in Allshire. Though he was knee-deep in soil, planting crocus and tulip bulbs that would overwinter for vibrant blooms next year, he waved back with enthusiasm. His garden offered an abundance of grape hyacinths, daffodils, brush bush, and other delights, a rainbow of nearly year-round color and heady scents.

They took tea once a week to talk gardens and sometimes exchange clippings, though their gardening tastes and purposes differed, she being an herbalist and he a gardener. She had seen his wife through six successful births, their most recent having the audacity to arrive during a winter snowstorm earlier in the year. The Turnbow family was among the many acquaintances she had in the parish.

Slowing her pace, she took in all the day had to offer. The sun shone in a cloudless sky, the day warm, much warmer than it had been on the coast, no cool sea breeze or temperamental weather here.

It felt good to be home. All was familiar.

Her daily schedule resumed. She had never been one to sit idly or waste a day. Each hour of each day was carefully planned with teaching at the orphanage, calling on patients, fussing in the garden to weed or harvest herbs, and other comforting and predictable activities.

It had only been a fortnight since she had returned to her little world, but already time at the castle dimmed to a distant memory. She embraced the simplicity of life in the parish, life in her one-room cottage.

Though several people in the parish asked about her visit, none pried. Lilith suspected they all wondered why she did not move to the castle. They knew of her brother given the parade of nobility last year, her family having marched into Allshire searching for her, catching the attention of all and sundry since people of such consequence had never come to the parish. A countess, an earl, a duchess, and a duke had all come in search of her.

Since no one would go to such lengths to find an illegitimate sibling, all in the parish assumed her the legitimate sister. Curious, that, since she had given the excuse to her brother that all in the parish thought her illegitimate, and she had taken comfort from that fact. The curiosity on the part of the parishioners now was that she had not gone with her family, rather had insisted she retain the name given to her at the orphanage and returned to her life as though nothing had happened. Not the actions of a legitimate sister? Or perhaps she was merely stubborn.

They all wondered, yet none were brave enough to ask.

Or so Lilith mused.

Until last year, life had been simple, and everyone knew where the lines were drawn. She was an orphan and treated accordingly. Respect was earned by contributing to the community. Over time, she came into her own as a skilled midwife and trusted teacher.

The visit from the Earl of Roddam had blurred the lines.

No one knew where the lines were now. A few saw her as they always had. Others became nearly obsequious, believing her to be *my lady* rather than Miss Chambers. Some were unsure so avoided her altogether. Strangely, the views of the local gentry had not changed, for she had always been and always would be an orphan. Unless the earl publicly acknowledged her as his legitimate sister, Lilith remained, in their eyes, rubbish. It would serve them right, she thought at times with cynicism and spite, if he did acknowledge her and they were suddenly to court her favor, all for her to give them the cut direct. But such was spiteful, and Lilith was not a spiteful person, neither was she someone who wanted or needed acknowledgment.

She was perfectly content in her current life, even if some of her neighbors gave her sidelong glances they had not given the year before.

When she returned to the cottage, ah, her lovely little cottage with its wisteria and stable door, she stripped off her hat, shawl, and boots, and made for the kitchen, eager for a cuppa. She did not even mind having to tend to the grade or stoke the embers until she had soot on her arm and cheek after wiping a bead of sweat. Maids and butlers were overrated. She was perfectly content making her own tea.

Sometime later, she cradled her cup in a most unladylike manner, leaned lazily back into her chair, and watched the world go by from the comfort of her front garden. She tried to ignore the tug at her heart to be cradling her niece rather than her cup. Freya had resurrected Lilith's dream of having children. Ah, *dreams*.

A memory tugged at the fabric of her mind, peeking at her through the threads. She was but a child in this memory. Her mother's face, *Jane's* face, looked down at her, glowing with happiness, cheeks scarlet from flushed exuberance.

In that breathy way she had of speaking, her mother looked up to someone behind Lilith, and said, "Thank you for saying so, and thank you for calling on us."

Little Lilith pirouetted for the guests, two older ladies and a young woman. As Lilith curtsied, her father entered the room.

With a brusque nod, he turned to his wife, "I told you to keep the children in the nursery. My son is sitting on the portico for all the world to see, poking at bugs. And now I find my daughter displayed like a marionette."

Lilith did not see the visitors' expressions, for her eyes, wide with awe, were only for Papa, a man whose attention she sought yet was afraid to receive.

Behind her, someone exclaimed, "We don't mind her taking tea with us, Your Lordship. Lady Lilith is an angel of gentility and a divine beauty! She looks so much like her mother."

Before Lilith could comprehend the moment, her father grasped her arm and yanked her to him so forcefully she heard a pop and felt a sharp pain.

As he dragged Lilith behind him, he thundered, "She looks nothing like my wife. She looks like the devil's spawn."

Tossing her into the hallway with such ferocity that Lilith slid across the newly polished tiles, he stormed off to his study without taking polite leave of the guests. Lilith saw nothing but a blurred world beyond her tears and felt nothing but a throbbing pain in her shoulder until a warm embrace lifted her from the floor and rocked her.

When the tears had been wiped from her eyes, she saw the face of her mother, the world's most beautiful face to a little girl. She smiled, not because she was happy, but because she loved her mother, and there, staring back at her with doe-eyes, was the love of her life, soothing her aches and pains.

"You are my gift from God, Lilith. He brought you to me Himself. Promise me you'll always remember that."

Little Lilith nodded, her thumb suckled between pouting lips.

"You're God's gift, and no one can take you from me."

The memory faded into its shadowed corner. Lilith wiped away tears she had not noticed until now. What a sight she must look, crying into her teacup in the courtyard!

Oh, Mama, she thought.

Her mother had been mistaken, of course, for Lilith had been taken away, though she did not know that until last year. Instead, she had believed her family abandoned her, even her mother, especially her mother. How could she have known at the time that her mother was dying and Lilith's journey to the orphanage had nothing at all to do with her mother's wishes?

Her ability to forget her family over time had more to do with *wanting* to forget them. She could not bear waking up every day in an orphanage to think of the betrayal and abandonment by her own parents and brother. She set out to forget them. And she had.

Until last year.

Good heavens. When had she become such a watering pot? Wiping more tears, she ducked her head back into the cottage, not wanting to make a spectacle of herself.

With bated breath and pounding heart, Lilith, perched at the cottage window, watching her most ardent suitor approach, his strides long, his shoulders stooped in pursuit, a swell of the first stare with his fashionable Anglican attire.

The Reverend Sands advanced towards the cottage, his double-breasted cassock flowing about his ankles, his white neckband tighter than necessary, and his Canterbury cap secured firmly on his sweaty head.

Teeth bared, she welcomed the rector.

"Harry," she said. "Do come in. Would you like tea?"

"Always a superb hostess. Alas, no time today." He took her unoffered hand into his for a clammy squeeze before seating himself at the table.

Not that she cared for formalities or propriety, but her blood boiled at his audacity to sit before either being offered a seat or waiting for her to take her own seat. His manners had become more appalling in her month's absence.

"I've received a correspondence from the esteemed Earl of Roddam," he said as she took a seat across from him at the table.

She looked at him with undisguised alarm.

"I am deeply honored to be so condescended but, of course, he would feel a kinship to me with my being the humble benefactor of his patronage to the orphanage. I daresay he will consider me a friend before long, if not an altogether closer relation in time."

He paused to give her a long and penetrating stare.

"His Lordship informed me that he will arrive in a fortnight to see for himself the progress of the foundling hospital since it is his patronage that has funded the build. He will be pleased."

Lilith ground her teeth. It was the smugness of his smile as he took full credit for work that was not his own. Mrs. Copeland, headmistress of the orphanage, had the idea for the foundling hospital some months ago. When she appealed to the rector, he was wary, not wanting to use the earl's donations on new buildings or staff, especially if he could not see a quick turn on investment. It had taken nearly six months to convince him. Only when Lilith left Allshire for the castle had construction begun.

Not wanting to appear discourteous, she said, "Yes, he will be surprised by the progress. As will his cousin-in-law. Baron Collingwood hopes to open an orphanage and foundling hospital of his own, you should know, and will be accompanying my brother to survey the facilities and interview Mrs. Copeland."

The rector blustered for a moment. "Welcome tidings! His Lordship failed to mention this in his letter, but I'm happy for the opportunity to impress upon Lord Collingwood all that we do in God's name. He will, no doubt, wish to join the esteemed name of his cousin as a patron."

It took great fortitude not to roll her eyes.

"Alas, I have more calls to make. Should my time allow, I will call on you daily. A woman such as yourself can't receive many callers, and I would be derelict in my duties not to realize that and remedy it. You need not be without company on my watch." He said this last with a pitying expression before leaving.

Lilith clenched her fists, infuriated. He made no mention of wanting her company. Instead, he would offer her his company since she was an aged, illegitimate spinster, pining at the window of her cottage with nothing better to do with her time. It was all a ploy, a transparent ploy. He could try to make her feel inferior and desperate enough to accept his hand, but she would not fall for it.

Clouds loomed. Lilith stood at the gate of Miss Tolkey's home, or rather the quaint cottage of the grandmother with whom she lived. Drumming her fingers against the wooden post, Lilith scowled at the sky. *Don't you dare*, she warned in silence to the leaden ceiling. It would not do to arrive to church as a drowned rat.

Though Lilith's cottage was next to the church, she walked all the way to the outskirts of the village to meet Miss Tolkey and walk back with her to the church. Lilith dared not allow the girl to walk alone. At one time, the grandmother had accompanied her, but now the elderly lady was bedridden. The Reverend Sands typically walked Miss Tolkey home in order to bring the church to her grandmother's bedside.

The corners of Lilith's mouth twitched into a smile when Miss Tolkey ran out, making a meager attempt to tie her bonnet ribbons beneath her chin. The girl, mousy in appearance with coltishly long legs, was barely one and twenty. She had been teaching at the orphanage for two years and learning the midwife trade from Lilith, just as Lilith had learned from Mrs. Brighton. Though a bit unusual for unmarried women to learn a trade almost exclusive to the married or widowed, the parish was remote enough not to be too picky if someone was fervent enough to learn and practice. Miss Tolkey was an eager pupil and apt *protégée*.

And a friend.

The bonnet ribbon tied, the two women linked arms and walked to the church. Miss Tolkey had a spring in her step and a rosy tinge to her cheeks. She looked almost pretty today.

"Have you thought over marriage, Miss Chambers?" the girl asked, turning her face to look up into Lilith's.

Lilith was so surprised, not to mention taken aback, that she faltered in her steps. Catching herself with an embarrassed laugh, she looked with raised eyebrows at her companion.

"Marriage? From where did *that* question arise?"

The girl blushed. "I hope you don't think me impertinent. It's only, Grandmama is encouraging I look about me before I lose my bloom. I thought of you and how advanced you are in age. *Have* you thought of marrying?"

Hmph. Advanced in age indeed. The comment was not said cruelly, and Lilith did not suspect the girl meant offense, but it raised the hair on her arms.

"I have accomplished more than most and known a freedom one cannot know in marriage. Yes, I've thought about it, but I'm not altogether resigned to the idea." Not untrue.

"Are you waiting for the right man or the right offer?"

"Are they mutually exclusive?" Lilith asked. When Miss Tolkey frowned in confusion, Lilith sighed. "I'm not waiting for anything. I'm living my life."

"But should the right man or the right offer happen your way, would you say yes?"

Miss Tolkey's innocence had crossed the border of impertinence. Lilith attempted a tight-lipped smile.

In a soft but severe tone, she said, "All would depend on the circumstances, the situation of my life, the man himself, and what we both had to offer."

Miss Tolkey thought for a stretch of the walk. Lilith embraced the silence and hoped the chatter was at an end. Between the rector's persistent hints and this, she was ready to scream. She already had enough to think of in the way of marriage.

Unfortunately, Miss Tolkey broke the silence before they reached the church. "What do you think of Mr. Sands? Do you believe he would make a good husband?"

Lilith could have choked on air. How did Miss Tolkey know of the rector's pursuits? Ah, but someone would have to be blind not to see his marked attention. House calls were not unusual since he paid them to everyone, but he all too often singled out Lilith, walked with her through the village, and visited the orphanage unnecessarily often.

Lilith bit her tongue before saying, "He's an amiable and honorable man."

What else could she say? That he was a weasel? That he shamed his profession with his greed? That his breath smelled as odious as his intentions? No, she would not speak openly against a man of the cloth, and certainly not a man upon whom her livelihood depended. Her hope was to refuse his suit with kindness enough times that he saw it best to press his advances on someone else.

She reasoned his greed stemmed from his role as rector. Even his decision to enter the church seemed driven by his desire to line his own pockets as rector rather than pay for a vicar, parson, curate, or otherwise. If he had only been a vicar, his heart in the church rather than in tithes. Alas.

Lilith turned the tide of the conversation by asking after the grandmother. The girl chattered for the remainder of the walk.

When they reached the church, it was to find Mrs. Copeland and her sister-in-law waiting with a foxtail of orphans, all in their scruffy Sunday best. The happy queue, punctuated with the fidgety miscreants, greeted the Reverend Sands in his vestments before filing into the pews.

The sermon began with the calling of banns.

"I publish the banns of marriage between Miss Harriette Ains of the Ainses of Allshire and Mr. Isaac Wimple of the Wimples of Boding. This is the second time of asking. If any of you know cause or just impediment why these two persons should not be joined together in Holy Matrimony, ye are to declare it," said Mr. Sands from his pulpit.

The congregation remained silent. She knew Harriette, a sweet-tempered girl, the eldest of eight siblings.

Lilith felt old. Harriette was only sixteen.

The sermon continued with celebratory words on marriage. Nothing struck her as unusual about the rector's words, mostly because she was too busy swatting at Bartholomew's hand as he reached for Minerva's braid. With the children settled, her mind drifted. To say her mind was otherwise engaged would be a pointed turn of phrase, as she could think of little else than the one person she had tried *not* to think about since returning home.

Walter.

In two weeks, he would arrive to pay court to her.

The first week of her return, she had missed him more than she would admit. She had missed every-thing and everyone. Solitude had felt a sort of prison. If he had arrived during that first week, she would have leapt into his arms with a resounding yes.

The second week of her return, she had made a point to remember all she loved about her life and all she would hate about not only being married, but also being part of his world. Even now, the sight of the back of the local gentry's heads from the front padded pews made her stomach knot. There was an air about them of haughty condescension. Why would she want to become one of them?

"'For if they fall, the one will lift up his fellow: but woe to him that is alone when he falleth; for he hath not another to help him up.' Ecclesiastes 4:10."

The Reverend Sands' voice rang out above the congregation, exalted, his figure imposing, however slight. "There are those who choose to remain alone, to offer their body to the Lord, to spend their days married to God. There are those who know the sins of the flesh and choose to marry, joining their spirit in worship of the Lord. But then, there are those who choose to remain alone because they are selfish, greedy, undesirous of worshiping the Lord with their mind, spirit, or body."

Lilith looked up at the rector, her grim study of the front pews interrupted. Was she mistaken, or was he staring directly at her?

"It is those who have partaken in sinful thoughts, who have felt lust, who know the wicked ways of man, seen the fruit born of the seed, yet remain alone who are the dissenters. Their minds are unchaste."

Oh, yes, he was looking at her. Not in an overly obvious way, but his eyes paused at her with every sweep of his gaze. Good heavens!

It was too late now to disguise the flame of her cheeks. It was not his stare that had her flushed, but his words. Guilt for her sinfulness weighed heavily. He must be subtly referencing her work as a midwife, for he could not know her impure thoughts of Walter or the intimacy they had shared at the curtain wall door. He could not know that the memory of Walter's lips kept her awake most nights, as did the vision of his green eyes.

Could anyone blame her? He found her desirable. He did not care that her bloodline was tainted. He did not care that she was in her thirties. He found her desirable. More than desirable. He found her marriable. Was it a sin, then? And was it selfishness or selflessness that gave way to her hesitancy?

"I am reminded of Corinthians, and you know of which I speak. 'But if they cannot contain, let them marry: for it is better to marry than to burn.' Corinthians 7:9. As we learn from Corinthians 7:34, the unmarried woman is devoted to the Lord, devoted in all ways, holy in all ways, but only if her mind remains pure. I look now at my flock, and I see those with sinful thoughts. You know who you are. Those who are not devoted to chastity court temptation and encourage fornication. We must abstain from unholy thoughts and temptation or else marry, for marriage is the honoring of God. I know the sins of your heart. Marry in haste. I say to you, I know you. Get thee to a church and marry or else burn."

The blood drained from Lilith's face. She shook herself free of all guilt, for his words were not of God. His words were of a greedy suitor. He was talking *of* her, *to* her, manipulating God's words to encourage her to marry him, by threat of damnation no less! Oh, he was a vile man.

After a lengthy sermon on the joys of marriage and the sins of fornication and impure thoughts, they joined voices in worship before dismissing.

Mr. Sands saw each person out with a handshake and brief word. Lilith saw it as a steep toll to pay. With lips pursed, an orphan on each hand, she approached him.

His expression lit with open adoration. "My dearest Miss Chambers," he said, reaching a hand to capture hers before checking himself that her hands were otherwise occupied. "I do hope your brother the Earl of Roddam will join us for service," he trumpeted. "How delighted he will be to see all settled and able to wish us happy."

To wish us happy? *All settled*? It took all in her power not to throttle the man. How *dared* he insinuate such things in front of others. What must they think?

In a desperate attempt to twist his words for those eavesdropping, which was everyone, she said, "Yes, I do believe he will be delighted to see all settled with the construction of the hospital. He will, as you say, wish us happy for all we've done to help Mrs. Copeland bring about her vision. A good day to you, Mr. Sands."

Without awaiting a reply, she directed the children to meet a grinning Miss Tolkey.

Chapter 13

The clink of wine glasses echoed in Lilith's ears, cacophonous to the rumble of voices around her. Her mind tumbled away from the present. Only a handful of anticipatory days before Walter would arrive, riding a white stallion, armed with the words of love and devotion needed to whisk her away to his palace in Devonshire.

What a ridiculously romantic vision!

Smiling to herself, she turned her attention to whatever Mrs. Copeland had been saying during the toast. Oh, yes, something heroic her sister-in-law did when they were younger. Lilith looked around the table at the guests, all smiles and bright eyes, their happiness haloed by candlelight.

This evening was Mrs. Elliot's birthday, Mrs. Elliot being Mrs. Copeland's sister-in-law. During the celebration, Mrs. Elliot, middle-aged and slight of frame with anxious eyes too large for her slender face, busied herself with embroidery, her needle moving to and fro. Her house was a cozy but cluttered cottage. Tawdry porcelain figures of shepherds and shepherdesses decorated the house, including the dining table. Mrs. Copeland regaled the guests with stories of Mrs. Elliot's youth, their childhood homes being adjacent farms.

Lilith was having a grand enough time, but her mind wandered through the whole of the evening, even during charades when her failure to guess three turns in a row brought unwanted attention from Mr. Sands.

Her companion for the evening was supposed to have been Miss Tolkey. Lilith learned the grandmother had taken ill only after arriving to their house to meet Miss Tolkey for the walk back across the village to Mrs. Copeland's. She understood; of course, she did. That did not keep her from feeling ever so slightly annoyed that a message of apology had not been sent in advance, for it was not a short walk, and her dinner slippers were not kind to feet after traipsing gravel, dirt, and rocks for miles.

Pained by the memory, she slipped her feet out of the shoes under the discretion of the table and rubbed a sore sole against the top of one foot and then the other.

Mr. Sands turned to her and guffawed at whatever turn in the story had been told. Lilith returned a smile. Tedious. She did not suppose the evening would have been better if she had sat at the table next to Miss Tolkey rather than Harry Sands, but it could not possibly have been worse. How peculiar life was.

She recalled her first dinner this summer at Dunstanburgh Castle with her brother and her sister-in-law's family. The evening had felt much like this. Awkward. She had hardly known what to say or how to act. They had pelted her with questions and been shocked by her honest and vulgar answers. That had changed over the course of a month. With each meal, she felt more comfortable, more open, more at home, especially considering most meals offered an exclusive conversation with Walter. And now she felt out of place with her oldest and dearest friends. They had families and lives and homes, even histories of their own, but she was just a guest who did not quite belong.

That was grossly unfair. She did belong. Except, she did not.

Oh, it was no use making sense of her feelings. She wanted Walter, and that was the truth of the matter. She wanted Walter, but she did not want the life that came with him. At some point, she would need to decide. He had made his intentions clear. Could she live in his world? Conversely, could she live in her world without him?

Ah, the guests were rising. Lilith exhaled in relief. How ungrateful of her. Mrs. Copeland and Mrs. Elliot could not be kinder or gentler souls, and they were so pleased she had accepted the invitation. But she wanted to be home. She wanted to think of Walter in peace.

Mr. Sands stood and offered his arm to Lilith. Announcing to the table rather than to her, he said, "I'll see Miss Chambers safely home."

There was no time to protest, for all exclaimed how chivalrous he was.

Mrs. Turnbow said, "You are the soul of kindness, Mr. Sands." Turning to Lilith, she said, "Did you know he walked Miss Tolkey to and from the orphanage every day during your absence? I daresay, he will make a devoted husband to the young woman lucky enough to ensnare him!"

All at the table laughed, especially the rector.

"I must see to the safety of my flock, Mrs. Turnbow." With a bow to all, he tucked Lilith's arm under his own and led her out of the house and down the lane.

Lilith sighed, a captive.

A bright flash of light streaked across the sky followed by a clap of thunder.

"We had best quicken our pace, Miss Chambers, unless we want to be caught in the rain."

Thank heavens for small favors, she thought. Without the motivation of the coming rain, he may have dawdled at a snail's pace to lengthen the walk. If she had hoped for a silent walk, however, such hopes were to be crushed beneath the rector's heel.

"I couldn't have asked for a better ending to the evening than to have this quiet moment with you. I'll get to the point lest it rain away this opportunity. The Earl of Roddam and his companion arrive within days, Miss Chambers. There is not a moment to lose. Shall we make the announcement as soon as they arrive or host a dinner to celebrate?"

With a hollow laugh, she said, "Your meaning escapes me. *What* announcement?"

He raised her hand to his lips for a thin-lipped kiss before lacing his fingers with hers. Involuntarily, she shuddered. With a determined tug, she tried to free herself.

"Why, the announcement of our betrothal, of course," he said, tightening his hold on her hand. "I've observed you since your return, and I know you're contented with your life here. I know you've come to your senses after seeing where you don't belong. It's time you realized your place. By my side, that is. I can protect you from criticism, Lilith."

Still attempting to pull free of his grasp, she said, "I do beg your pardon, but we are not betrothed."

Another flash of lightning revealed her cottage in the near distance. She could not get there fast enough. Alas, it was not to be. He halted their progress and turned to face her, her hand held hostage.

"You're right, of course. This must be done properly." To her mortification, he went down on one knee, taking her hand with him. "Lilith Chambers, will you do me the honor of making me the happiest of men by uniting in holy matrimony? Before you answer, look to your heart. You know I will protect you from judgment and ridicule. With a man of God at your side, no one would dare criticize your birth, your time in an orphanage, or your rustic ways. No one would dare speak ill of your age or your features, which may not be the prettiest to most men, but do appeal to a man such as myself. Can you not see how I am struck by Cupid's dart?"

She hoped in desperation for lightning to strike her to end the humiliation of this moment. If his words had been ones of adoration…If his proposal had come before she knew of her brother…Well, if circumstances were different, she might have considered his suit, for at one time he had been a devoted friend. Now, greed illuminated his features with each flash of lightning.

"Harry, do stand up."

"Are you not convinced by my ardor? What can I do to prove to you my feelings?"

In a swift movement, he rose to his feet and pulled her against him, pressing his mouth to hers. She shrieked, the sound muffled by his kiss. With closed lips tightly pursed, he held himself to her. The kiss only lasted a moment, but through her panic, she realized she felt nothing from it save revulsion and the sweat on his upper lip. Tensing, she took a step back and pulled herself free.

Wiping her mouth with the back of her hand, she said, "*Harry*. I did *not* give you permission for such familiarity. No, I will not marry you. I appreciate all you have done for me, but I will *not* marry you. Please, do not ask me again."

Try as she might to keep her tone even and courteous, she could hear the shake of her voice, the tremor of fear. Oh, it was not *he* she feared, for he meant well, but she feared her future in Allshire if he found her ungrateful to his kindness.

The thunder clapped only seconds after the lightning, the storm fast approaching. His features shadowed as the moon hid behind shifting clouds. There was a chill to the air, from the wind or the moment, she did not know. She shivered.

"You're conceited," he said, stepping away. "I had hoped staying with your brother would show you your place, but I see it has had the opposite effect. You now think yourself above your station. Might I remind you, Miss Chambers, you are illegitimate. Your birth is a sin. By associating with your brother's in-laws as a single woman of low birth, you bring shame to their family. Only I can bring you respectability. Only I can give you a name. Only I can cleanse your sins. Only I."

Her anger rising, she asked, "If I'm all these terrible things, why do you wish to marry me? Why *me*?"

"Because I'm selfless and wish to help you. I think only of you. I see myself in a position to save you."

"Do you even desire me? Have you ever desired me?" Questions she did not want answered.

He recoiled, a hand to his heart. "How could you speak of such vulgarity? Marital relations is a duty, nothing more."

"And what of children? Wouldn't you be ashamed to have children with an illegitimate woman? A woman born of *desire* that had nothing to do with procreation?" She was going too far, she knew, but she could not stop herself before the words tumbled out.

"A marriage of God's will would absolve you of the sins of your birth."

"In that case, why could I not marry anyone of my choosing?"

"I would keep your secret safe, and I would have God's blessing to do so. To marry another, you would bring scandal to the family. Do not think me chastising you, Miss Chambers, for I'm not a vengeful man, but only I have the ability to make you respectable, for God is on my side. This is your last chance, your *only* chance to absolve yourself. If you don't accept me, you'll not receive another offer, and you'll forever be a lonely spinster, aged, illegitimate, and without family. I offer you this final chance because I'm a giving man devoted to helping others. Accept me."

Lilith did not know until she analyzed her actions much later why she answered as she did. This was not his concern. This was something she did not want known. This was something about which she had not made up her mind.

And yet she blurted out to him, "You're wrong. You are not my only or even my last chance. Baron Collingwood is paying me court."

As soon as the words left her lips, she wished to recall them. It was a wonder her hand did not fly to cover her mouth.

The rector's affect changed.

His spine erect, his lips sliding into scorn, he retorted, "Either you're a fool for thinking his intentions chaste, or he's a fool for thinking you eligible, *if* you speak the truth. Your conceit will be your undoing. I take my leave of you, Miss Chambers." Turning on his heels, his movements stilted, he left her.

On shaky legs, she scurried to her cottage just as a black cloud opened in the heavens and released a downpour to rival the great flood. Once inside the safety of the dry interior, she leaned against the door and shivered in violent tremors, chilled inside and out.

What had she done? Oh, no, oh, no. What had she done?

He was not an enemy she needed. But she now had to face the repercussions of so boldly rejecting him and admitting to the courtship. Perhaps her fears were unwarranted. For years, she had respected and admired him. He had been a good friend. Time and again, she had called on him for advice in dealing with the uncomfortable situations she encountered as a midwife, as well as advice on how to handle some of the more mischievous children at the orphanage. She had liked him as a friend and confidante.

How had she been so naïve not to see through him before? Had he always been this way, or had greed of her brother's wealth, a possible dowry, and a titled connection wheedled at him until it brought forth his baser nature?

Regardless from where his intentions stemmed, his words of bringing shame to the family weighed heavily on her, for she knew them to be true. The scandal of a titled man marrying an illegitimate woman would destroy Walter's family and hers. It was selfish to agree to Walter's courtship. What did she think would happen when he arrived? Did she think they would fall in love, marry, and live happily ever after? The more fool she.

Chapter 14

I f Walter expected a peaceful morning to ready himself, he thought wrong. Kory had only just finished shaving him when Roddam knocked to warn him that a veritable army had arrived at the inn to greet them. With a splash of cologne, a comb through his curls, and a final adjustment to his cravat, Kory sent Walter to meet his fate.

The pair had arrived at the parish before dawn. The timing awarded them a chance to repose and refresh.

Though the sun had barely risen, they had passed their fair share of villagers, some stopping to watch the approach of handsome strangers in riding finery. A few children had stepped out of houses to wave, as dazzled by the luggage coach—wherein their valets rode in the jostling comforts of Walter's well-sprung carriage—as by the gentlemen. Walter and Roddam had waved in return.

Clearly, word had spread of their arrival. Given the size of the parish, Walter supposed everyone knew before breaking their fast.

It was just as well. He could hardly contain the mounting anticipation of seeing her. Would she be part of the welcoming committee? Would she run to him, arms wide, for a scandalously public embrace?

That would not be her style, but it did not stop him from fantasizing.

A month! How had he survived a month without her company? The idea had been genius, though. This would enable him to court her on her terms. There were other benefits, as well. He needed to know what it was like to miss her — interminable. She needed to know if she could leave her home and friends to live a life amongst the *beau monde*. And they both needed to know if they liked each other in a more natural setting, without staying under the same roof with family. Walter could not see himself changing his mind about her, but this would help her come to terms with her affection for him, for he fully intended to propose at the end of the visit.

Roddam waited outside Walter's suite.

"You didn't want to steal center stage by venturing down alone?" Walter jested.

Roddam grimaced. "The only thing I'm steeling is myself for the onslaught of forelock-tugging sycophants. My hope is they'll fawn over you for being better dressed."

Roddam slapped Walter on the shoulder and pushed him forward, as though to use him as a human shield. Dressed with a winning smile, Walter strode downstairs to meet the eager faces.

Standing in the commons were the innkeeper and his wife, a clergyman, a smartly dressed gentleman who looked of Walter's ilk, and a handful of nondescript onlookers who peered over shoulders to see the two newcomers. The smartly dressed gentleman approached first to shake Roddam's hand before turning to Walter. Roddam, who had been here on more than one occasion over the past year, conducted introductions.

"Allow me to introduce to you Sir Eugene Graham. Sir Eugene, this is Lady Roddam's cousin, Baron Collingwood."

"The pleasure is mine," Sir Eugene said with a nod. "But please, I'd rather Gene. Only my mother calls me Eugene, and that's when I've displeased her."

The baronet spoke and dressed with far more polish than Walter would have expected in this remote village. He was a tall and thin man with an ample wave of blond hair. He apologized for his wife's absence. Lady Graham was in a delicate way and feeling indisposed, he explained. Onlookers listened curiously to the light conversation, including an invitation for them to dine at Arbor House the next evening.

Stepping aside, Sir Gene urged the clergyman forward.

The young man, mid-twenties if Walter hazarded a guess, looked as though he would have an unmanly fit of vapors if left ignored for much longer. He was exactly the type Walter knew Roddam could not stand. Ingratiating and obsequious. Walter scolded himself for thinking ill of a man of the cloth, but the fellow was vile. He gave Walter the shudders with his too-wide grin and knee-scraping demeanor.

Granted, if he were not groveling at Roddam's feet, he might have been a decent looking man. Medium build, a tad on the short side, at least compared to Walter and Roddam who were taller than average, angular face with hazel eyes and a well-combed head of black hair. Not that Walter paid attention to such things, but he would assume the man a favorite amongst the ladies, if they could look past the weak chin and light array of pockmarks.

Roddam scowled. "May I introduce the parish rector, the Reverend Harold Sands?"

Walter was sorely tempted to say no.

"How do you do, Mr. Sands? Lord Collingwood" Walter said, extending a hand. "If I may add, my father's name was Harold, as well. Harold Hobbs, the ninth Baron Collingwood."

The man, who had been staring up at Roddam in wide-eyed worship, turned scornful eyes to Walter. "How fortunate I am to share the name of so great a man," said the rector.

Though the man accepted Walter's hand in a limp and clammy grasp and bowed over it, Walter did not fail to notice a slight hesitation. He searched his memory for any mention of a rector in Lilith's tales of Allshire, but he could not immediately recall anything. Before he could analyze further, a flurry of movement by the door caught the attention of all those in the common room.

And there she stood.

Walter was thunderstruck, not for the first time, upon seeing her. She stepped into the room with a radiant smile, flushed cheeks, and a halo of frantic frizzes, her hair windswept as though she raced to the inn from across town. She looked first to Roddam and then to Walter. Her gaze lingered before turning back to her brother.

The rector interrupted the reunion by stepping to Lilith and taking her arm, linking it through his rather than the more respectable placement on top of his sleeve. A rush of liquid jealousy fueled Walter's veins. How ridiculous to be jealous of such a man, but he could not stop the feeling once it started, especially given how familiar the movement seemed to Mr. Sands. He ground his teeth as he watched the two approach Roddam.

"Long at last, Lord Roddam has arrived," said Mr. Sands, talking to Lilith while Roddam looked on. "Now is the moment when he can wish us happy."

Walter's heart skipped a beat. Lilith met his gaze with an arrested expression.

"And I'm wishing you happy on what account, exactly?" Roddam asked, widening his stance and clasping his hands behind his back.

The rector smiled a sly grin at Walter for a fraction of a second before saying to Roddam, "We have toasted this week to a milestone in construction progress. You will wish to see the hospital, of course. Shall we begin the tour immediately?"

Roddam frowned. "Not at present. I came to see my sister and wish to do so posthaste. It was good of you to welcome us, but I fancy a tea. A *family* tea."

The earl glowered at the rector until Mr. Sands slipped his arm from Lilith's and stepped back with a reverent bow. For once in Walter's life, he valued Roddam's ability to speak his mind, though Walter doubted Roddam had said all he was truly thinking.

Not to miss his cue, Walter stepped forward and offered his arm to Lilith, who took it with a smile and blush, her eyes meeting his beneath half-lidded lashes.

The devil! She was flirting with him in front of everyone.

They nodded to all as they left the inn, Roddam lingering only long enough to have a kind word with the innkeeper and his wife before catching up to them to take Lilith's other arm for the walk to her cottage.

The cottage was quaint, if not a tad shabby. Well-cared for, yes, but old and cramped. Coming from this, Walter could see why she might think Trelowen excessive, though why she would not want to stretch her wings after such confinement, he could not say. Breathless with excitement, Lilith prompted them to sit on either side of the fireplace while she readied the tea. She dashed into the kitchen.

Walter sat, crossing one leg over the other, and looked about him. Low ceilings with exposed timber beams, a bare wood floor, and white cob walls adorned the one room ground floor.

Dash it all — where was she to sit? There was nothing in the parlor except the two drab chairs Roddam and he occupied, and the world's smallest wooden table pushed against the wall with a pair of rickety chairs. Thinking swiftly before she returned, he grabbed one of the chairs to move by the fireplace. He would sit in the wooden chair, of course.

A glimpse of her in the kitchen caught him by surprise. He had not realized the kitchen was so close or open to the, well, he supposed it was the dining table, though there was no separation between it and the parlor. Just behind her was a narrow set of steps that wound up and around the corner — to a loft? The whole of the cottage would fit into his dressing room at home.

And she preferred this to a manor? Humbling.

He turned back to observe her as she prepared a tea tray. Good heavens. She was really preparing them a tray. If he had realized *she* would be doing it, he would have declined. They could have had tea in the private parlor at the inn, after all, without her slaving over a kettle. How short-sighted of him.

Rubbing the back of his neck, feeling ever so uncomfortable, he carried the wooden chair three feet across the room to join Roddam. Roddam arched an eyebrow.

"She's making us tea, dash it all," he whispered to the earl.

"Aye, that's why we came, isn't it?" Roddam smirked.

"I suppose, but I didn't expect…well, *she* is making *us* tea, by Jove. No wonder she says we come from different worlds." Walter shook his head.

"And this, old boy, is your competition." Roddam waved his arms about him to indicate the cottage.

"Oh, I say. I don't know how to compete with *this*. I have jewels, money, and servants to offer, but if she wants *this*, I'm a lost cause."

After what felt like half an hour but could not have been that long, Lilith returned with the tray. She set it on a footstool between Roddam's chair and the empty chair before looking about to realize Walter had changed seats.

"No, that will not do. You must sit here," she said, indicating the more comfortable chair.

"I refuse to have the lady of the house sitting on hard wood. Please, take the chair across from your brother." When she frowned, Walter added, "I've always had a fondness for splinters."

She stared at him, confused, and then laughed.

Oh, he had missed that laugh. Low and sultry, a velvet kiss for the ear.

They exchanged pleasantries over tea and cinnamon biscuits for the next half hour. Most of the conversation was about Lizbeth and Freya. Walter spent the time staring at her, admiring her, drinking her in for every day he had been without her. Each time she looked over at him, her cheeks turned the faintest shade of pink.

He wondered if she ever thought about their kiss. Heaven knew he did. Daily. Nightly. Especially now.

"Sir Gene has invited us to dine at Arbor House," Roddam was saying during one of Walter's more distracted moments of gazing at her lips.

"Oh, how kind of him. You shall tell me all about it, of course," she said.

Roddam leaned forward. "I shan't have to tell you because you'll be dining with us."

"Goodness! I most certainly will not," she said in good humor. "I'm positive if you search your memory, you will recall he did not extend the invitation to me. He would never expect me to go. I'm the orphaned midwife here, if you've forgotten. The baronet wants to dine with an earl and a baron, not his wife's physician." She laughed merrily at the prospect.

Roddam did not laugh.

Walter cleared his throat. "Lilith, I've come to pay you court. Unless that is no longer desirable to you, I intend to do just that. This means a public courtship, all in the village aware of my intentions. If I'm invited to dinner, then it goes without saying that I would bring the lady I'm courting, *you*."

She looked down at her hands, then from him to Roddam and back. "Yes, but Sir Eugene didn't know that at the time. If he had known, he might not have offered the invitation. I'm respected here for what I *do*, but you really must understand I am not respected for who I *am*. In everyone's eyes, I am lower than nobody. This is one of the reasons I wanted you to come here, to see me as I am, to see me how others see me."

Though her brother sat across from her, watching, Walter reached over and took her hand in his. "And I'm courting *you*, the orphaned nobody who conveniently happens to be the sister of an earl. Sir Gene *will* accept you at his table. He wouldn't dare not."

Roddam chimed in then to say, "The baronet isn't a representative of Society. Far from it. We may have a steady hill to climb with the higher sticklers, but we must start somewhere, Lilith. I plan to introduce you this coming Season. We don't have to talk about it now, but you can't hide in this godforsaken cottage all your life."

Lilith bristled and scowled but did not remove her hand from Walter's. "I like my cottage. I'm not hiding. And we *will* talk about that later. This is my life, you know, and you can't make decisions for me. But I'll go to dinner with you. You can see for yourself how well I will or will not be received by *your* Society."

Walter squeezed her hand. He wondered if she worried she would embarrass them or if she feared the censure. Which of those had him worried? A little of both, he suspected. This would indeed be a test. He had not expected such a test so soon in the courtship, but perhaps it was best to suffer the trial by fire first.

Chapter 15

Kory brushed invisible lint from Walter's coat and stood back to admire the freshly ironed ensemble and sheen with which the riding boots shone.

"Well? How do I look?" Walter asked, tugging at the edges of his waistcoat.

"Like a man ready for a Hyde Park promenade," said his valet with a swat at Walter's hand to keep him from wrinkling the fabric.

"Splendid."

"Might I advise less bravado for a country parish?" Kory asked.

"No, you may not. Well, I suppose you may advise it, but I'll not listen. I don't care if the walk is around the village center or to one end and back again, I'll look my best."

Walter tapped his heels together and left the dressing room at his inn suite, his destination Lilith's cottage. His valet was right—he was overdressed. But a man could not court a woman dressed sloppily.

Topped with his favorite tricorn, the ensemble for the day was a dark, basil-green waistcoat and matching coat with floral embroidery, a sensible but ornately knotted cravat, buckskin riding breeches tailored on the snug side, and his best riding boots. Indeed, he looked more fitting for a ride down Rotten

Row during the fashionable hour than a walk around a small and dusty parish. For tonight's dinner, he had instructed Kory to ready his satin, to be accentuated by clocked stockings and buckled shoes. There would be nothing for it but Lilith to fall for him.

The cottage was not altogether far from the inn, so Walter footed it. He made a show of touching his hat to all he saw, displaying far more enthusiasm than was necessary, but he wanted it known that Lilith was a respectable lady being courted by an eligible gentleman. No one would accuse her on his watch of being anything less. Walter aimed to turn the tide so all would see her as the very legitimate sister of an earl, a lady who, through unusual circumstances, condescended to live in Allshire. She could undermine his efforts, as well as Roddam's, but it would not be for a lack of trying.

As he passed the church, he spotted a garden overflowing with flowers. Flowers! What a dolt! He had not brought her any flowers. In his defense, he had never courted anyone before. Some leeway for his shortsightedness was in order.

Approaching the gate, he hailed the man stooped over a fragrantly prepared bed, fragrant with manure, that was.

"Good day, my good man! I say, you wouldn't happen to be in a position to aid a fellow gentleman?"

After a brief but satisfying conversation and a bouquet of freshly cut roses, Walter was back on the path to the cottage. He sniffed at the pink and red array. The dear man had prattled on about the types of roses, how he grew them for late blooms, which were the most fragrant, and so forth, but Walter had smiled and not heard a word. He had gardeners for such things.

Lilith liked gardening, though. Hmm. He might need to pay the man another call.

Yes, in fact, he must. Walter recalled distinctly a conversation Lilith and he had shared about her love for gardening. She had been nonplussed by his comments of having his gardener expand the parterres at Trelowen. She had told him he missed the point, which was to get knee-deep in the soil and sink one's hands into the earth, to be one with nature, to find peace in the simplicity while reveling in the magic of planting a seed to have it grow into a living element. She was right. He had missed the point. What different worlds they lived in.

For a few steps, he slowed his gait, self-conscious. What did he have that she could possibly want? Here, she had a one-room cottage, friends she had known for years, and a garden she loved. And he had what to offer? He had everything she did not want — gardeners to do the gardening, maids to dress her in finery, more than one stylish carriage to be seen in by all those worth being seen by, a set of friends who preferred to dance than share silence.

Dash it all. To a woman like Lilith, he had nothing to recommend him other than himself. He would say he was enough, but he came with all those things she did not want.

He paused, his smile faltering.

Though it had grown cool by the coast, cool enough to keep the fires lit, it was still warm in the landlocked village. His neck itched from the starched collar, sweat irritating his skin.

There was nothing for it. He would have to try harder. He would have to prove to her he was worth all the baggage that came with him. Thinking of all that would normally entice a woman — wealth, connections, popularity — as being baggage brought a laugh. Granted, it was a sardonic laugh, but a laugh, nonetheless.

Renewed in spirit, he approached the cottage and greeted it with a resounding knock.

The door opened moments later to a surprised Lilith. She gave him a thorough enough head-to-toe assessment that his ears warmed. He verbalized his nervousness with a chuckle.

When her eyes met the bouquet in his outstretched hand, her surprise turned to a smile. "Ah. I see you've met Mr. Turnbow," she said, taking the roses with a blush that matched.

"Yes, a fine fellow. Do you fancy a walk? I hear from the innkeeper there's an attractive path down to the lake worth exploring." Walter remained outside the threshold, hopeful.

"I'm afraid I can't." Lest he misunderstand, she hastened to add, "Not that I don't wish to, but I have patients to call on today. I was about to begin my rounds, actually. I will see you tonight at dinner?"

Crestfallen, Walter said, "I could accompany you. I can be an unofficial assistant today, an ignorant but earnest man-midwife. Walter, the *accoucheur*, at your service."

Shaking her head, she said, "That won't do. A noble gesture, but I'll be spending half an hour at each house, and my calls will include an examination. These are not social calls, mind."

Walter frowned, his shoulders rounding. Well, dash it all.

"Wait here. Let me put these in water," she said.

Leaving the door open, she took the bouquet to the kitchen, which he could see well from the doorway. Goodness, the cottage was small. In five determined strides, he would be from the doorway into the kitchen.

She fiddled about for a brief time then came out with an old teapot filled to burst with roses. Arranging it in the center of the world's smallest dining table, she beamed at him.

"My first flowers," she said.

Adorning her head with a bonnet and grabbing a largish bag, she shooed him away from the door and shut it behind her. "My first stop is to Mrs. O'Shane on the far side of the village. She's the wife of one of Sir Eugene's laborers, so the house is on his property. It's quite the journey, but I would enjoy your company. That is, if you don't mind the lonely walk back."

With a bow, Walter offered his arm.

Lilith wore one of her old dresses, one that he had seen several times at the castle. Her hair was braided down the back, just as it had been when he first met her.

While he fancied her no matter what she wore, he had grown accustomed to seeing her in finer clothing. He missed seeing the lengthened bit of bare neck that arched swan-like when her hair was styled up. He missed, also, how well the other dresses had enhanced the natural shape of her physique, rather than hiding her beneath limp and slightly wrinkled linen. Did she not like such a look on herself, or was it a necessity of her work that she dressed plainly in drab and tired dresses?

She glanced at him, her lips curving into a smile that reached her eyes, the irises a chocolate brown in the bright sunlight. He had remembered them as being such a dark brown they were almost black. Not today. Not in the rays of the Allshire sun. Good Lord, she took his breath away.

"If your goal was for all in the village to see me on your arm, your wish has been granted," she said with a teasing lilt.

"Am I so transparent? You see straight through me, Lilith. I suppose it was presumptuous of me to assume you would still want to proceed with the courtship. Do you? Tell me you do."

If she had been shorter, she could have hidden her face beneath the straw bonnet, but as she was near his own height, he could see the rose of her cheeks. Try as he might, he could not recall her blushing so much at the castle. Had she missed him? Had she decided she wanted him as a husband?

"I do," she said.

For a moment, he truly was robbed of breath, thinking she had answered the questions in his head rather than in reality.

"I do want to proceed with the courtship, Walter. I warn you, though, I'm not convinced I want to be part of your world, but I do want to know you better and you to know me. This would all be easier, I must say, if you were a simple farmer."

"Alas, I don't know a root from a bulb," he said.

"Oh dear. It's a good thing I have two employments, then, for I would have to support us no matter how meager the earnings." She laughed until she realized what she had implied, then she slipped into a bashful hush.

Walter did not mind. He rather enjoyed having the moment to fantasize them living together in the tiny cottage, two children running about the place while he bobbed a baby on his knee, she arranging flowers on the too-small table.

"That house is home to the haberdasher, Mr. Tilson, and his wife and their children." She pointed to a whitewashed cottage with baskets of flowers propped outside the windows. "And that is the home of the blacksmith, Mr. Brown. He and his wife never did have children, but his younger brother lives with them." This time, she pointed to a stone cottage only slightly bigger than her own.

For the entirety of the walk, she pointed out people, houses, landmarks, dogs, and even a few sheep, all of which had names. She seemed to be enjoying herself, animatedly regaling him with stories of Mrs. Jenkins' two mischievous children, Ralph the sheepdog who had an affinity for Mr. Bilkins' poultry, and other such tales about people Walter would never remember, though he heard the names of every person, child, and pet in the parish, he was certain. He did not think he was impressing her by doing little but listening except the occasional question; yet he enjoyed the listening. This was a glimpse of the real Lilith, unguarded, at home in her surroundings, proud of the life she had made despite muddled origins.

When they reached a pebbled lane, she stopped and turned to him. "This is where I leave you, I'm afraid," she said, pouting playfully.

"I could wait, if you'd like, and walk you to your next appointment."

The prospect of standing about outside for half hour intervals did not sound all that appealing, but if it meant more time with her, he would do it gladly.

"Tempting, but each patient is along the way back to the cottage, so the walks between stops would be too short for real conversation. You would have only enough time to tell me about the weather, and that simply will not do."

She reached out a hand to cup his cheek. Her touch sent waves of longing rippling through him, smooth flesh against his cheek, tender in its caress.

"I will see you and my brother tonight," she said, letting her hand fall to her side.

"Yes, we'll come by way of carriage at dusk. Do you...um...did you...well, should you need a dress for dinner, I could have something delivered from the modiste's shop," he stuttered, hoping he was not overstepping his bounds or insinuating that whatever she might wear would be an embarrassment.

So long as she was by his side, she could wear a tea towel to Sir Gene's if she wished.

Instead of being offended, as he worried she might be, she laughed. "I have something to wear, Walter. No need to worry. I'll see you at dusk."

With that, she hoisted her bag into both arms, turned around, and walked down the lane to an unseen house. Walter watched her until she crested the hill.

"For crying in a teacup!" Lilith cursed, stabbing her hair with a pin.

For what seemed an eternity, she had been trying to style her hair. The pins would not hold with conviction.

"My kingdom for Hannah's help," she said to the mirror.

Of course, it would be simpler if she stayed home. Never had she needed to bother with her hair or dress, but then, neither had she been invited to a dinner such as this.

As bothersome as it was to attempt to don stays, a dress with petticoat, and hair pins without assistance, she was excited about the dinner. Yes, she was nervous she would be ill-received, but above all, she was excited.

It had been Walter's doing. When he had shown up with flowers in hand, dressed in those shockingly tight buckskins — oh my! — looking dazzlingly handsome, she had known herself fallen for his charms. That did not mean she was ready to enter his world, consigning her days to polite conversation with fake-faced toffs and leaving behind her happy home, but it did mean she was tempted. She *wanted* to be convinced. As incongruous as they must have looked on the walk to Mrs. O'Shane's, she drab and he posh, she had felt at home on his arm.

Was that not what she had always wanted? To belong? Through her childhood, she had been made to feel an outsider by her father. Once abandoned to the orphanage, she again did not belong, for she had been raised a lady. Growing up, she had fought to belong in the village, doing all she could to befriend her neighbors, but there was an invisible wall she could never surmount. Though she had carved her place, she knew she did not belong.

And yet, on Walter's arm, she had belonged. There was a feeling of rightness about it.

She hoped he would find a way to convince her. It was such a leap to move from one world to the next and such a risk of censure for them both, but she wanted to make it work somehow.

Angling the hair pin into the sloppily arranged knot, she gave a hearty shove. "There. I've bested you at last," she said to her reflection.

Her dress was nothing new. Had she not wanted to save the dress she purchased with Hazel for a more special occasion, she would have worn it instead. The dresses Lizbeth had given her were still at the castle, waiting for her return. The dress she chose for this evening was one she kept in the back of her bureau, tucked away for christenings and weddings. It was a deep, crepe shade of pink, open in front to reveal a petticoat of a lighter shade. The sleeves were elbow length with a short edging of lace. It had never been particularly fashionable. There were no pleats, no stomacher, no corset, and no pannier. It was a simple close-bodied bodice with matching skirt.

Giving herself a final look in the mirror, she headed downstairs to wait. As luck would have it, she did not have to wait long, for a quarter of an hour later there was a knock.

Walter stood in the courtyard, the carriage waiting behind him past the walled garden. She gawked. He looked ready for a ball. Oh, she wanted to run back upstairs and hide! What must he think of her in this ancient and dreadfully simple dress?

He was breathtaking.

Without a hat, his curls roamed freely. What had she called him when they first met? An angel? He wore a cobalt-blue ensemble, the coat and waistcoat of brocaded indigo silk. It was exquisite. Lilith longed to reach out and feel the threads. His breeches matched, and though they were not as tight as his buckskins, they hugged his frame deliciously. His stockings were clocked, and his shoes were buckled and heeled. *He* was exquisite.

Before she stepped over the threshold, he closed the space between them. She thought, for a second, he was going to embrace her. Her breath caught.

"Turn around," he said.

Not the opening line she expected.

"I beg your pardon."

"A strand of your hair escaped. If you'll allow me…." His eyes laughed when her hands flew to her hair.

"Oh, for crying in a handkerchief! Yes, please by all means. If you can win against these dastardly pins, I'll be forever in your debt." She turned her back to him.

When he responded, he was much closer than she had anticipated. "How shall you repay me when I call in the debt?" His breath grazed her ear, making her shiver, his voice a low caress.

All she could do was laugh. If she spoke now, the tremor in her voice would betray her.

His hands worked at her hair, adjusting more than one pin. As he repaired the damage, she could concentrate on nothing except the awareness he stood inches away.

"I don't claim to be a hairdresser, but hopefully the pins will hold. Not that I would complain if your hair tumbled down before the end of the evening." He said the last line so close to her ear, she could feel the shadow of his lips touching her skin.

And then he was gone. A cool air wafted against her neck, and she felt bereft. She turned back to face him. He was standing a few steps away.

"Shall we conquer the world?" he asked with a mischievous twinkle in his eyes.

"We shall. One dinner party at a time." She laid a gloved hand on his arm.

Sebastian was waiting for them in the carriage, looking devilishly handsome, his long hair swept back by a large, scarlet ribbon, his ensemble matching in wine-red silk. With his dark features, he appeared almost demonic next to the angelic Walter.

They exchanged light conversation as the carriage made its way to Arbor House, a much shorter drive than she was accustomed to since she always trekked it on foot for her appointments with Lady Graham. How unusual that tonight would be to visit as a guest rather than a servant. The only rooms she had seen were the lady's chamber and Sir Eugene's study. Would they feel imposed upon by her presence or welcome her as the sister of an earl? A tiny corner of her mind mulled over if she wanted her brother to announce her as lady or miss.

The carriage halted before a manor with classic columns. A groom set down the steps, opened the door, and helped Lilith out with a regal bow. With Walter at her side awarding her a wink and Sebastian taking the lead, Lilith walked to where the butler waited.

Goodness. She had never entered by way of the front door. There was something otherworldly about this moment, as though she were a different person in Lilith's body, having a glimpse of what life could have been, what life might still be, if she chose to embrace it despite the risks and consequences.

As they were shown in, Lilith's knees knocked. She knew so little about this world and its conventions. She was not completely ignorant of their ways given she did deal with the local gentry from time to time, but she had much to learn if she were to consider becoming part of it. What if she made a grievous faux-pas and embarrassed her brother and Walter?

The butler ushered them upstairs into a drawing room, which was smaller than she had expected, an impressive pianoforte taking up much of the space. Several people were standing at the far end of the room, having risen to greet the guests.

Her heart raced to see it was not only the host and hostess. Three other people stood with them. Three people she did not want to see. A wave of apprehension swept over her.

"Lord Roddam and Lord Collingwood! So glad you've come," Sir Eugene said, approaching the trio. "Ah, and Miss Chambers." As an afterthought, he added, "My wife will enjoy your company."

The group she did not wish to see followed in step with the host. Lilith sucked in a breath.

In jovial spirits, Walter exclaimed, "Oh, I say! I never expected to see you here!"

Dismayed, Lilith gawked. Did he know these beasts?

Two slender women with bouncing blonde ringlets and high-held chins tittered their way to him, followed by a fair-haired gentleman who bore a family resemblance. Though she had only seen the gentleman once before, she knew the women, or knew of them, rather. They were the two ladies she oft passed on the bridge after her appointments with Lady Graham. However silly it would be to think they timed their visits to catch her as she was leaving, she wondered if they did.

With eyes that twinkled, they set their gazes on Walter, ignoring Lilith.

"Miss Carmichael, Miss Lynda, and Mr. Carmichael — what a pleasure!" Walter bowed over the hands of the women and nodded to the gentleman. "How's the viscount? I didn't see him in London this year."

"Father has developed a cough. Nothing to worry about, but his physician recommends bed rest until it clears," said Mr. Carmichael.

Sir Eugene took the initiative to introduce the Carmichaels to Sebastian. Lilith stood to one side, forgotten. It was for the best. She had no wish to socialize with *them*.

Just when she turned to speak with Lady Graham, Walter said, "Allow me to make introductions."

She hoped her groan was not audible.

"May I introduce to you Miss Carmichael, her sister Miss Lynda, and their brother Mr. Carmichael?" Walter looked at her expectantly, his eyebrows raised, his mouth twitching a hidden smile.

It took her far too long to realize what he had done. He had asked her if he could introduce *them* to *her*, as though she were their superior, the daughter of an earl. Good heavens! Her emotions were split between reverence for his genius and annoyance for his presumption. There was not time to think of a suitable response or even to decide if she wanted this.

She nodded ever so imperceptibly.

Turning to the haughty women with their tall plumes and flaxen curls, he opened his mouth to speak, but the eldest interrupted him.

"We know Miss Chambers," the woman said in clipped tones. "No need for introductions."

Well!

Lilith straightened her spine, bringing herself to full height.

Walter's smile deepened. "Ah, then you've not been *properly* introduced. Allow me the privilege of introducing Lady Lilith."

Lilith's heart beat so furiously, she thought it might burst. She cast a scolding glance at Walter for taking away her right to choose. Although, perhaps, it was for the best.

The youngest girl sniffed, her chin raising ever higher.

Without a trace of a smile, Lilith said to the two women and gentleman, "Lilith, please."

They did not reciprocate with their given names.

Instead, the eldest sister looked Lilith from head to toe and said, "I believe I had a dress similar during my second Season, two years ago. It is so difficult to find good fashion this far north."

The veiled insult was not lost on Lilith, nor was the fact that all women present, including Lady Graham, though she was increasing, wore high waisted dresses with short, puffed sleeves. Miss Lynda's dress was exceptionally trendsetting, made of so nearly sheer of gauze that Lilith could make out the outline of her figure in the candlelight. Lilith could not have been more out of place in her long-waisted and long-sleeved dress with petticoat if she tried.

"Yes, some of us are more fortunate than others," Lilith replied humbly. "Some, such as yourself, have held their beauty over the years well enough to wear even the most youthful of fashions and colors, though such are usually reserved for those in their first Season rather than their fourth. I could never be so bold as you, Miss Carmichael."

Lilith smiled, albeit a tense smile. Miss Carmichael sniffed.

Mr. Carmichael stepped forward with a bow, clasping Lilith's hand to kiss the air above it. He was a fine figure of a man, if one liked fair hair and blue eyes, though she suspected he wore padding to accentuate muscles he did not have.

Dinner was not for another hour. They remained in the drawing room, conversing about the weather and how the sunshine could not possibly last for long, certainly not with autumn around the corner. Lilith did not contribute. She sat with knees pressed together, spine straight, and hands folded in her lap.

She relished the moment when the butler announced dinner was served.

Since she was seated next to Mr. Carmichael at the table, dinner was as tedious as the drawing room. She tried to eat silently, not tasting much of the food, though she assumed it was delicious, but Mr. Carmichael was determined to converse. Surely, he was disappointed when she had little to say to his enquiries about the new addition to Arbor House—an expanded conservatory, or so she gathered. She had not known there was a new addition.

After dinner, the men stayed in the dining room for port and cigars while the ladies proceeded to the drawing room. Oh, why could she not stay with the men? She loathed the idea of being in a room alone with the Carmichael sisters. Even Lady Graham was an uncomfortable companion, for all Lilith could think to say to the woman pertained to her health, her condition, or the twins.

Would the evening never end?

She need not have worried about being in a room alone with the women because they ignored her. They spoke of new bonnets, new dresses, and a cornucopia of topics that had Lilith's mind drifting elsewhere. One specific elsewhere, to be precise. A place of belonging. A place of mutual respect. This was not that place.

For so long, she had etched her identity as a fellow parishioner. Now that she wanted to be convinced she could fit in another world, she feared the futility of it.

She had never been opposed to marriage, quite the contrary. Her orphaned mind had dreamed of a gallant knight sweeping her off her feet and the two of them living happily with a fluffle of children. But dreams were not reality. In her waking days, she wanted nothing but to fit in, to find a home for herself. She put down roots in the parish, carving a reliable and secure future, one in which she knew what to expect. There had been too much unknown in her life, and she feared being lost in a sea of unknown, insecurity, and disrespect.

This house full of representatives of so-called polite society was not a place of respect or belonging. She sighed and stared at a flickering candle while the women whinged.

The men did not linger long in the dining room. Sebastian likely had much to do with that, as he was not a social person, not to mention he would be anxious about her trapped alone in the lion's den. With Walter and Sebastian at her side again, she felt easier.

Sebastian opened the conversation. "Collingwood and I had the opportunity to visit the construction site for the foundling hospital this afternoon. The Reverend Sands showed us about."

Their host said, "Yes, dreadful business. Such a facility can only bring rubbish and sin to the village."

"It was my patronage that made it possible," Sebastian said without inflection.

Lifting his quizzing glass to his eye, the baronet studied Sebastian. "Good for you," he said at length. "Someone must stand up for the children. I applaud your efforts. I was saying to Mr. Wimple the other day—wasn't I, Ethel?" He turned to Lady Graham. "That when someone speaks disparagingly against the orphanage or the hospital, he need only look to the Bible."

"Need he?" Sebastian raised a single brow. "And what will he find?"

"Well, you know." Sir Eugene huffed and waved a hand without expounding.

"Do I?" Sebastian asked.

All at the table were quiet.

Raising her voice for the first time all evening, Lilith said, "James 1:27 and Psalm 127:3, for starters, speak to the love we must show to children, all children, especially orphans." She fixed her gaze on her host. When he made no effort to respond, she turned to Walter. "Were you able to speak with Mrs. Copeland, Lord Collingwood?" Glancing back to Sir Eugene, she added, "His Lordship plans to open an orphanage of his own. Did you know?"

Walter, in his wonderful way, beamed with pride. "Yes, and I've toyed with adding on a foundling hospital, though it seems an enormous undertaking."

Miss Carmichael, with a thin-lipped smile, asked in a tone of innocent condescension, "Do you not find it lowering to associate with miscreants?"

Walter frowned. "I think not, Miss Carmichael. I will be honored to have a hand in rearing a future generation. Their futures may seem bleak, but I would know their childhood to have been safe and constructive and their work ethic schooled. We all have a place in this world, a destiny to fulfill. What a privilege it'll be to help them embark on that journey of discovery."

Sebastian glared daggers at Miss Carmichael. "And what do you recommend be done with them? Bar them in a room and slide food under the door?"

Miss Carmichael tittered as though Sebastian had made a joke. Turning to Lilith, she said, "Speaking of the bleak futures of orphans, tell me. What's it like to be *employed*?"

Lilith clenched her teeth. "Enriching. Rather than waste my time, idle until death, I see to a better future."

Miss Lynda joined the conversation, her words acerbic. "What do orphans know of the future when they never leave the confines of their village?"

Flexing her fingers and splaying them against her thighs to keep from wringing her hands, Lilith said, "Traveling does not show the future, Miss Lynda. Traveling shows us history and culture. Dreams are what create the future. Orphans do little but dream of what could be. As a teacher and midwife, I help children and parents realize their dreams, even if such a dream is as simple as to be a blacksmith's apprentice or to have one's first child."

Out of the corner of her eye, she saw Walter lean forward.

She had thought a lot about dreams over their month apart. The trouble was that her dreams were dichotomous, one being her life as a midwife and another as Walter's love, two dreams that could not exist simultaneously. More troubling were the sacrifices she must make to achieve one or the other. Fear kept even the bravest from taking a leap of faith.

Rather than respond, Miss Carmichael rose from her chair and eyed Miss Lynda. "Shall we take a turn about the room?" she asked her sister.

With the two women in private discourse, Mr. Carmichael launched into conversation with Sebastian and Sir Eugene. Lady Graham attempted to make conversation with Lilith, who only half paid attention. Not that she needed to pay attention since the conversation solicited no more than one-word responses.

If she were a betting woman, Lilith would wager the lady was discomfited by her presence. She was, after all, Lady Graham's midwife. To Sir Eugene's credit, he had insisted she call him Sir Gene. She had smiled, called him Sir Gene, and then went right back to thinking of him as Sir Eugene. There was an intimacy with the name she was not ready to share.

As Lady Graham chattered, Lilith watched the Carmichael sisters promenade about the room. Her focus was riveted on their interactions with Walter. With each turn, they called for Walter's attention at the precise moment they walked in front of a candelabra. As thin and sheer as their dresses, little was left to mystery. It could not be Lilith's imagination that the timing was planned to emphasize their figures.

They were flirting with him. Outrageously.

But then, why would they not? He was handsome and titled. Miss Lynda was young, pretty, and eligible. Miss Carmichael was attractive, available, and undoubtedly growing desperate since she was practically on the shelf.

In their eyes, Lilith was no competition, being an uncouth leper who had been raised in an orphanage and was well into her dotage, at least from their perspective. Though she might have felt frumpy, jealous, or any other emotion, she instead suppressed a smile. Her angel of a suitor paid them about as much mind as he would two pigs in sacks. No, that was unfair to the pigs, for she was certain he would have noticed prancing pigs.

Lady Graham tittered breathlessly, interrupting Lilith's train of thought. "Was the wedding between Miss Ains and Mr. Wimple not sumptuous?"

Miss Lynda, who had stepped dangerously close to Walter's chair to fawn over him, responded first. "Mr. Wimple is a true gentleman. She doesn't deserve him by half."

Lilith's ears perked. She wanted no part in gossip, but she knew Harriette and her family well. If they were to speak despairingly of the young girl, Lilith would feel obliged to offer a severe set down. She ought not, for she was a guest.

Miss Carmichael nodded. "I hear he's so honorable that he married her to save her from scandal."

Lady Graham's eyes widened. "Scandal? Why have I not heard this?"

"Rumor has it," said Miss Carmichael in hushed tones, "that she very nearly compromised him, nothing to force the nuptials, but enough to stir the pot. This is conjecture, and you didn't hear it from me, but rumor also has it she trapped him to hide a little secret. Have you not noticed how plump she's become?"

Sir Eugene interrupted with a clearing of his throat. "Ethel, why don't you favor us with a song? My wife has a splendid voice."

Lady Graham blushed and stood.

"You'll need accompaniment on the pianoforte," Miss Carmichael said. "Lady Lilith would be happy to do so, and Lord Collingwood may turn the pages." The woman's smile was all that was wicked and scornful as she looked to Lilith. "Oh, but how thoughtless of me. Having been raised in an orphanage, you aren't accomplished, are you? It's best, then, that my si—"

Lilith stood, her chin raised high, her blood boiling. "On the contrary, Miss Carmichael. I've had music instruction since I was five."

The carriage swayed at a leisurely pace.

"That was a decadent delight of a meal," Walter said. "The only improvement would have been more courses or larger plates."

Sebastian chuckled. "Is food all you think of, Collingwood?"

"No need to envy my discerning palate, old chap. It's a natural affinity."

In the darkness of the carriage, Lilith could feel Walter looking at her. Though she could only make out a shadowy profile, she could feel his eyes on her. She could also feel his foot.

A stockinged foot, free of its shoe, slid over the top of her slipper and rubbed her ankle. She was thankful for the absence of light. If her face reflected the over-warm sensation of the rest of her, she would surely reveal her sentiments to his touch, namely the desire for his embrace.

There was no shame in what she felt. Yes, she was unmarried and ought not to be tempted, but she was also a grown woman. Her lack of personal experience was made up for by her education in midwifery. Lilith was well aware of her desire for Walter. He may be too much of a gentleman to act on it, but she knew he desired her in return. It was something she had given a good deal of thought during their month apart.

"I don't suppose you had a good evening, Lilith. Was it a terrible disappointment?" Walter asked, his foot massaging hers in a sensual caress syncopated by kneading toes.

"On the contrary. I took inexplicable pleasure in seeing Miss Carmichael's expression when I accompanied Lady Graham with all the grace and dignity my ten thumbs could muster."

Sebastian howled with laughter, oblivious in the darkness that Walter slid his foot higher up her leg to rub her calf.

His voice light with laughter, her brother said, "A glorious set down. I wager that bat couldn't have performed with any more finesse, Lil."

"It was not an evening I would have chosen for myself, and I'm not eager to repeat it," she said. "And yet I was entertained by their antics, for they behaved no differently than I expected them to. Would it be cruel to compare them to performing monkeys?"

"Oh, I say, Lilith!" Walter exclaimed with a humored chuckle.

"Come now, you must have noticed their behavior. They insulted everyone and anyone to feel better about themselves," she responded. "I don't blame them. They have nothing to show for their lives. They go to balls to dance, to dinners to eat, and to drawing rooms to gossip. That is the extent of their lives. What have they accomplished? What will they ever accomplish? Their only hope is to make an advantageous marriage so they may go to more balls, more dinners, and more drawing rooms. I feel sorry for them."

Sebastian asked rhetorically, "There's no reason, is there, to mention why I rarely accept invitations?"

"Oh, but 'Bastian, how could you resist? Do not all women dress as the Carmichaels and strategically position themselves in front of candles to tease and tempt with their coltish outlines?"

Lilith heard a *thwack* as Sebastian slapped his leg before roaring with laughter.

Walter coughed a nervous laugh. "I can't say I noticed."

"No, I don't believe you did," Lilith said. "You were being quite wicked to those poor women who were all but prostrating themselves. The least you could have done was pay them a compliment," she teased.

"Ah, but I only have eyes for you, my enchanting siren," he said.

"Oh." She blushed furiously in her shadowed side of the carriage. "Oh, well done."

The trio fell into silence, Walter's foot continuing its exploration of her calf, thankfully, not venturing any higher.

As the carriage neared the inn, Lilith scolded, although her tone was light, "It was naughty of you to introduce me as Lady Lilith."

"I noticed you didn't contradict me," Walter said.

The lanterns hanging from the inn's corner posts slanted a dull glow across Walter's face. He was smiling coyly at her, his eyes half-lidded.

"You knew I wouldn't." Lilith swallowed against the onslaught of yearning those half-lidded eyes caused.

"Not so. I honestly thought you might. You're, shall we say, willful enough to have put me in my place before the entirety of the household."

"I'll never embarrass you, Walter, not intentionally. But do know this is my decision to make. Only mine."

Having properly scolded him, she softened her words by slipping her own foot free of its confines to caress his other leg. Though it might have been the wind, she thought she heard a sharp intake of breath.

"We've learned a valuable lesson this evening," Sebastian said as the carriage came to a halt in front of the cottage's walled garden. "While the doors may bar against you if your illegitimacy were publicly known, acting the legitimate Lady Lilith will incur its own censure. It would seem, dear sister, that you're ridiculed if you do and condemned if you don't. What is your weapon of choice, should you choose to accept this challenge?"

Wedging her foot back into its shoe while a groom set down the steps and opened the carriage door, she considered his question. "Oh, dear brother, you underestimate my cunning. I shall watch them fall on their own swords."

Chapter 16

The following day, Lilith met Sebastian at the inn for tea. Walter joined them only long enough to escort Lilith to the first house on her rounds.

As delightful as it was to be courted, she could not help wondering if he was hurting his reputation by doing so, to the point of being a laughingstock. Not that many of those living in and around Allshire would gossip with his peers about who he was courting, but word would travel. It would not do well for his reputation to court a spinster who grew up in an orphanage, regardless of whom her father might have been. If they married, how much worse would the censure be for him?

The next day, she taught at the orphanage, her favorite day since she was able to teach mathematics rather than one of the fluffy subjects. After a fulfilling day with the children, she headed home for an afternoon free of commitment. This was not a day of rounds.

As she approached the walled courtyard of her cottage, she noticed the gate stood ajar. Oh, abomination! Harry would be waiting for her. She braced herself to see him pacing in front of her door armed with a remark about coincidences.

It had been a relief not to face him alone the past few days. At least telling him of Walter's courtship had not been a terrible mistake. She had not expected Walter to be so public about the courtship. For some reason, she had expected him to do it privately, and so admitting to the rector that the baron was coming to pay court had seemed reckless.

Now that Harry knew, and now that Walter had arrived, as well as her brother, how would the rector behave? Would he try to sabotage Walter's suit? Would he find a way to convince Sebastian he was the better suitor in hopes her brother might have a hand in whom she married?

She suspected she knew his approach. He would try to convince her that Walter's intentions were not honorable, that the baron's goal would be to set her up as his mistress.

She had a giggle thinking of the cottage by the sea Walter might soon own. It would be devilishly naughty of Lilith to tell the rector about the cottage and that she was considering Walter as a protector rather than a betrothed. Of course, she would never say such things. All the same, it gave her a giggle to think of his reaction if she did. It would serve him right.

For shame, Lilith, she scolded herself.

With a malevolent grin, she opened the gate.

Only, it was not Mr. Harry Sands who stood at her door. In fact, no one stood at her door. A pair of black boots and buff buckskins that framed a shapely derrière peeked out from one of the raised beds of her herb garden. The body that went with them was nowhere in sight, buried between greenery and bent over the soil. An abandoned coat and waistcoat rested on the opposite planter.

Not one to take such occasions for granted, she appreciated the sight. Savoring the vision of slender but muscled thighs and admiring the bottom that went with them, she watched him dig about in the dirt as though searching for Atlantis.

Fanning her face ineffectively with her bonnet, she approached.

"Drop your signet ring?" she asked.

Walter sat up so fast he tipped backwards and had to brace himself. "Don't you know it's impolite to startle someone?" He was all smiles under his tricorn.

"Oh, I'm terribly sorry. Have you not heard? Orphans aren't raised with toffish manners," she teased.

"Good thing I'm here, then. I can teach you to behave yourself."

He stood, brushing dirt off his buckskins, a hopeless effort, as the breeches were obviously soiled, a matching patch of mud circling each knee. When he straightened and looked at her, she forgot to breathe. There he was, all tall, masculine man, a bead of sweat trailing down his temple and into a sideburn.

Lilith was at a loss for words. All she could think was how desperately she wanted to kiss this man.

"I see I've dumbfounded you, Lilith. An unusual sight, I know, to find a baron gardening, and not just any baron, but your own Lord Collingwood. Well, admire my handiwork. Tell me if there's a future for me in horticulture." He waved a hand to her garden bed.

There were at least two dozen spots with freshly turned soil, all neatly wedged between her herbs.

When she did not immediately respond, Walter said, "Mr. Turnbow said September is the best time to plant the bulbs. If I've not botched it, they should flower in the spring."

Lilith looked from her bed back to Walter. "You planted bulbs, you say. *Flowering* bulbs?"

"Yes, indeed. He was kind enough to advise that these were the easiest to plant and grow, so no need for a green thumb. There might be hope for me yet. I was supposed to plant them with the pointy end up, wasn't I?"

Lilith could do nothing but laugh. Only once she started, she could not stop. She laughed harder and harder still, bowling over with a hand to her side. By the time she could control the fit of hilarity, she had to wipe tears from the corners of her eyes.

"Oh, Walter. I'm not sure if I should kiss you or scold you."

He frowned. "Good Lord. Choose the former, and I'll plant a dozen more."

She shook her head. "You do realize this is an *herb* garden?"

He stared, his expression blank.

"Ah, well. Mr. Turnbow has been trying to get bulbs into my herbs for years. Cheeky monkey."

"Show me," Walter said, kneeling and smoothing his hands over the soil he had overturned.

There was nothing to do but join him. It was not as though she needed to change, for her dresses were utilitarian, at least for her needs, which included gardening.

Kneeling beside him, her knees sinking into the cool softness of the earth, she touched her hand to a tall, green stalk with purplish flowers. "This is motherwort. It's used during the recovery time after birth. Once this clump finishes flowering, I'll harvest and dry it. And this," she reached for a stalk with yellow flowers, "is yarrow. I use it during the birthing as a handwash and cleanser. There's approximately thirty different herbs in the garden, most versatile."

"I don't suppose tulips and snowdrops count as herbs?"

Smiling, she said, "Not quite. I grow herbs for my midwifery. With the herbs, I can take leaves or blooms or stalks, depending on the plant, and infuse them with tea, sustenance, or warm water. They're medicinal, not ornamental, though quite a few do flower, as you can see." Walter's face was so crestfallen, she covered his dirt-coated hand with her own. "Tulips and snowdrops will be a lovely addition to my herbal bed. I couldn't have asked for a greater gift."

They stared at each other for a long moment, long enough for her to realize their thighs were touching. She sucked in a breath. How could it be so hot at the beginning of autumn? She could feel herself sweat, though she knew it was not from the weather, which offered a crisp breeze despite the bright sun.

If she looked any longer into his fathomless green eyes, she would fall into their depths.

And then she heard a muffled cry.

Looking about the garden, she tried to focus on the sound. It continued, a muted cry, not unlike a hungry baby, but not a baby. She could not explain the sound. A whimper? Lilith furrowed her brows and looked at Walter. He shrugged, though he looked around, as well, obviously hearing the same sound as she. Rising to her feet, she tracked the noise.

"Good heavens," she said, "it's coming from my cottage. You hear it, too? I'm not going mad?"

She glanced over her shoulder. He nodded, looking perplexed, a hand sweeping through his curls, his discarded coat and waistcoat slung over the arm holding his tricorn. A hand to her breast, braced for whatever banshee hid in her cottage, she opened the stable door.

Inching to her, its stomach against the floor, its head bowed, and its tail wagging, was a tri-colored, long-eared puppy. As soon as she gasped at the sight, it stood on wobbly legs and galloped at her, flopping onto her feet and whimpering, knowing at first sight that she must be his new mother.

"Oh. Oh, Walter," she mouthed, unsure if she spoke the words aloud. "What have you done?"

The pup looked up with large brown eyes and gave a woof. How could she resist such a face? Reaching down, she picked up the bundle and nuzzled its neck.

Walter stood behind her just outside the cottage. "The innkeeper bred this lot to train for Sir Gene's hunts. I absconded with one. With permission, of course. He's a fine-looking Foxhound if ever I saw one, though I suppose you'll have to train him to track the scents of herbs rather than foxes."

When she turned to him, the puppy in her arms, she saw only a blurry-edged figure. Why, for goodness' sake, she would tear up over a puppy, she could not say.

Wiping her eyes with the palm of one hand, she said, "Do come in. I'll make tea."

"No, I should take my leave. It wouldn't be proper, not without your brother present."

The puppy pawed at her as she scratched behind his ear. "Have you reverted to insisting I have a chaperone? Come in, Walter. The door will remain open. It always does. And besides, I'm a grown woman."

He hesitated, looking over his shoulder, not at all at ease with the situation. Nevertheless, he entered.

Lilith could not stop herself from admiring him as he set his coat and waistcoat over the top of a chair, wearing only his shirt, the open vee at the neck revealing a dusting of reddish curls. The last time she saw him so undressed, he had been running on the beach. Breathless and blushing, she buried her face against the puppy.

To hide her reddened cheeks, she carried the puppy with her to the kitchen for the wash basin and a breath of air. After a few deep, calming breaths, she brought the bowl out for Walter to wash his hands of dirt. She set it on the table next to her flowers.

"Jasper," she said, sitting in one of the fireside chairs and nestling the puppy on her lap. "I shall name him Jasper after the wise men."

Walter sat opposite her, grinning from ear-to-ear. "You like him? Not too ostentatious? He seems too smitten with you to return him."

"I have no idea what I'm going to do with a puppy, but yes, I like him. Love at first sight. Thank you." Gratitude did not express the torrent of emotions, but it was all she could say.

To express the sentiment to Jasper, she rubbed his neck until his back foot thumped her leg.

"Will you hold him while I make tea?"

"I daresay tea making can't be above my skill set. If I can master gardening, perhaps I can excel in the kitchen, as well. Point me the way, give me instruction, and I'll make the tea, shall I?" He was already on his feet.

"Sit. I'll not have you bumbling about in my kitchen. Making tea is an advanced skill, and you'll only end up over-steeping my leaves." Her tone was light and teasing enough to deepen his smile and twinkle his eyes.

When she handed over Jasper, who whimpered to leave her embrace, she was reminded of when she had placed Freya in his care, their arms overlapping, separated only by new life, and Walter's face full of curious trepidation.

To break the spell, she said, "I'll need to get him a doggy bed. He can't very well be carted around and held by everyone. Oh, heavens, what do puppies eat?"

"Fear not," said Walter, rubbing noses with the pup. "I'll bring all you need. The shops are amazingly accommodating, as is the innkeeper, Mr. Hill."

When she stepped into the kitchen, leaving the boys to fend for themselves in the parlor, she aimed to be as quick as she could about things. She did not fancy wasting quality time with Walter or the new addition to her life standing in a kitchen. Leaning against the cabinetry and drumming her fingers against the countertop, she stared at the kettle, waiting for the water to boil.

What in good heavens was she going to do with a puppy? Or tulips and snowdrops for that matter? Love them, of course. Love them for the heartfelt intention that brought them into her life. Love them for their own loveliness. The real question was what she was going to do with Walter? If only he could be of her world, a farmer or a tradesman in the village. But then, he would not be Walter.

As though summoned by thought, he stepped into the kitchen and leaned a shoulder against the rounded cob doorway, his booted ankles crossing one over the other, Jasper cradled in his arms, sound asleep in puppy bliss.

"We thought you might be lonely," he said.

"I don't believe Jasper was terribly concerned." She eyed the sleeping pup.

"Right. Well. You were taking too long."

"Ha! Now we have the truth. I believe I've sabotaged myself, for a watched kettle never boils." Lilith busied herself by portioning the leaves.

Walter watched her silently, one of his hands scratching Jasper's neck.

"When I was young," he said once she rescued the kettle from the coals, "I would sneak into the kitchen to watch Cook prepare tea or food or desserts. Mrs. Barstad was her name. Waddled when she walked. At the time, I thought it was because she got into the pies. Now, I suspect it was from gout. I loved watching her bake. It fascinated me. I dreamed of becoming a great cook in the King's kitchen. Of course, she'd remind me of my station and that I employ cooks rather than the other way around, but a child's dreams can't be staunched. She retired after my father died, lives in the country with her husband. We have Mrs. Avery now. Seems nice enough. Can't say I've watched her in the kitchen, though."

Lilith listened to him as she prepared the tray. There was something appealing about the image of a russet-haired little boy with angelic curls and fairy green eyes peering over a counter to spy on the cook.

Did puppies eat biscuits? She wondered. She added an extra biscuit to the tray just in case. Tray in hand, she nodded to the parlor and followed behind Walter. Setting it on the footstool between the chairs, she poured them each a cup.

Jasper woke with a yawn, stretch, and tail wag. Nudging Walter's leg, he begged to be let down. The puppy made short work of wobbling his way around to sniff the floor, the chair, the footstool, and Lilith's feet. He did not stay awake long, only long enough to prop his head on her foot and harrumph himself back to slumber.

"What else did you dream?" she asked, curious what heirs to baronies dreamed when they had everything already.

Orphans rarely dreamed. Oh, they did, but dreams were depressing when there was nothing but the harsh reality of life. She was fortunate to have been sent to Mrs. Brighton's orphanage. The alternative would have been a convent or workhouse.

Mrs. Brighton had encouraged dreams, but practical ones, ones that would help the orphans decide a trade they might wish to learn. Even those dreams were outrageous for orphans. Mrs. Brighton, in her brilliant way, made as many of those dreams come true as she could, working with industry tradesmen to set up apprenticeships and more. When some of the girls would toss a fit about dance lessons, knowing full well they would never see the inside of a ballroom, Mrs. Brighton would weave a tale of all the many ways they might attend a village assembly, tales realistic enough that the girls would dance their hearts out.

But what of little boys who had the world in their hands?

Walter stared into his teacup. "You mean, what did I dream aside from being a chef?" Stretching his long legs in front of him and leaning back against the chair, he tapped his saucer in thought. "I don't think I ever stopped dreaming. I dreamt extravagant dreams. Magic carpet rides included. It wasn't until reality intruded that my dreams changed shape. When I reached my majority, I dreamed of a carefree existence. I wanted to win curricle races, travel to more countries than my mates, eat the spiciest food to win a bet, ridiculously dim-witted things that meant nothing. I saw every one of those dreams to fruition."

"And now?"

He pressed his lips together, closing his eyes for a moment. "I stopped dreaming after my father's death. I didn't see the point. All I would have dreamed was to have him back, and that's something no amount of wealth or connection can accomplish. There was nothing I wanted except him."

Lilith set her teacup on the tray and reached a hand to touch his leg. She would have aimed for his arm, but he sat too far away.

With a gentle squeeze of his thigh, she encouraged him to continue.

"For the year or so before he died, he tried to settle me. He wanted to teach me about the barony. Hoped I would marry and set up a nursery. I put him off, thinking I had time. The day he died, I was supposed to have gone with him. I had promised. I was to meet him in his study for a talk with the steward, and then we were going to tour the home farm and call on neighbors. He had the whole day planned for us. Except, I was with my mates and lost track of time. One of the fellows wagered another to a curricle race. I thought I had time, so I lingered to see who would win. It wasn't until it was too late that I learned Papa had given up and left without me."

As he spoke, Lilith's hand crept from his leg to cover her mouth. She understood where this was going. She shook her head slowly.

"It was that dashed race. One of them took a corner too fast, and there was my papa. How was I to dream after that? It was my fault. If I hadn't been with my mates, they wouldn't have tried showing off. If I had gone to the house to meet him, he wouldn't have been on the road."

Lilith watched helplessly as his eyelashes darkened with tears. "Walter, none of that was your fault. They would have raced without you. And if you had gone with your father, you might have been killed too."

"That's not the worst of it," he said, not hearing her. "He died thinking I didn't care enough to show up."

"Oh, Walter. He knew you cared. Of course, he knew."

"Did he?" Walter wiped his cheeks and sniffed. "I'm sorry, Lilith. I don't know where that came from. How dreadfully embarrassing."

"There's nothing for which to be embarrassed. Here, let me refill your cup. Tea makes everything better."

He leaned to offer his cup.

"What happened to the curricle driver?" she asked tentatively.

"Reggie. Lord Reginald Pratt. Youngest son of the Duke of Bidcombe. He dreamed of purchasing a commission, but his father wouldn't allow it. Now he's a recluse. I've not seen him since that day, though I've written to him a thousand times and made attempts to see him."

"He's battling his own demons. Best to leave him in peace," Lilith said, reaching a hand down to pet the sleeping Jasper.

"Lilith, I haven't dreamed for three years. Not until I met you. A light shone into my world when you walked out to the gazebo. I saw before me the woman who would give my life meaning. I'm not a morose person. I haven't spent three years wallowing. It's only...I've been lost. Listless. Unable to envision what I wanted out of life. But then I saw you. Everything fell into place, even the legacy I want to create and leave behind. That's what I dream about, Lilith. You."

Walter could tell his words embarrassed her. She tucked her head and made an exaggerated effort to pick up Jasper and coddle him. In all fairness, he had not meant for those words to tumble out, at least not yet.

He was far from ready to propose. As his mother had said, marriages needed more than love, or however she had phrased it. Being in love with Lilith was not enough. Not only did she need to be as in love with him, she needed to *love* him, and they needed to ensure they could battle against the odds, that she could live in his world, and that they could beat the censure without it tearing them apart. He wanted to propose when he was sure or mostly sure of those things.

As Roddam had pointed out after Sir Gene's dinner engagement, it did not matter if they presented Lilith as his half-sister or his sister, she would be ridiculed for her time at the orphanage. The most cold-hearted of the *beau monde* would find other reasons to belittle her. Her country ways, her rustic accomplishments, the questionable manner of her disappearance. They stood a chance if she would agree to be introduced as legitimate. Without that, they fought a losing battle.

Yes, he wanted her. No, he was not ready to propose.

He watched her play with the puppy. She avoided eye contact. Without warning, she stood and left the room, the puppy prancing after her with poised tail and uncoordinated feet.

Well, dash it all!

This was awkward. He sat in her parlor, twiddling his thumbs and feeling sticky from the gardening. Was this her way to dismiss him after his bold words?

He waited. He ate a biscuit.

He waited longer. He ate another biscuit.

He polished off the plate of biscuits. Just as he was about to rise from the chair to take his leave, she came bouncing back into the room, wearing a wide smile that lit up her features, puppy at her heel.

In her hand, she held a makeshift dog toy. She had wrapped some sort of fabric or yarn or woman's work around what looked like a wooden spoon.

"It's not what a baron's puppy might play with, but it's what mine does," she said, sitting back in the chair and engaging the puppy in a game of tug of war. "I shall have to start collecting sticks when I'm out and about. Dogs like sticks, don't they?"

Walter chuckled. "I believe so. You might've simply tossed rope into the room."

"Oh, goodness. A whole length of rope? Perhaps not. But I'll remember that if I'm desperate and need a toy in a pinch."

He watched the two of them play before attempting conversation again. It was well beyond the polite time for him to leave. Manners dictated he stay no longer than fifteen minutes, never beyond a half hour. But he could not make himself move from the chair. Being with her felt so right.

"At one time, Lilith, you said your dreams had been simple. A puppy, for instance. At Sir Gene's, you talked about what orphans dream and your ability to help people realize their dreams. Have you given any thought to your dream? Tell me to be silent and leave if I'm overstepping."

It was too much to hope she would say she dreamed of him. Did she?

"I've given this some thought," she replied. "I'm uncertain I can put into words what I dream, but I *have* tried to dream since we parted last month."

She wrestled the toy from Jasper, who had all but fallen asleep with it in his mouth. Settling him next to her feet for another puppy snooze, she said,

"It's more of a feeling than a thing. I long for a place to belong. Someplace where I'm respected for what I do, valued, and needed. In some small way, I've found that in my work. I help people, a hands-on kind of help. I dream of doing that indefinitely, if not midwifery, then something similar where I'm helping women and children. It's fulfilling and gives me that sense of belonging."

Walter leaned forward in his chair, resting his forearms on his thighs, which were filthy beyond recognition. His valet would have palpitations when he saw the breeches.

"What if you trained midwives at my foundling hospital? Would that realize the dream?" His vision was for her as much as it was for himself.

"Are you trying to hire me?" she asked with a laugh, her fingers curling around the arms of her chair.

"Not exactly, but would it?"

She thought for a moment before saying, "I don't know. To be honest, I don't think so. Yes, I would enjoy training midwives. I'm doing it now with Miss Tolkey. But I'm not a teacher. I mean, yes, I am. I teach at the orphanage for heaven's sake, but that's not my trade. My skill and heart are in helping women. I would want to be involved with the process, the action, not simply talking about it in theory. That wasn't the answer you were hoping for, was it?"

He smiled but did not answer.

What was he to say? That she could not practice midwifery if she married him? She could do anything that made her happy, if he had anything to say about it, but he did not set the rules for what was acceptable.

There had to be a way to realize her dream *and* marry him. Surely.

"The tea's cold," Lilith said after pouring herself another cup. "It won't take but a moment to reheat the kettle since it should still be warm. You would like more tea, yes?"

Oh, she hoped he did. She knew it was well past time for him to leave, but she wanted to extend his stay. She enjoyed his company. Being with him felt so right.

"I'd love some," he said.

Ensuring Jasper was contently sleeping next to the chair, she carried the tray back to the kitchen.

As she checked the water level in the kettle, she gasped to find Walter standing in the doorway again. Just as he had before, he leaned against the corner, one ankle crossed over the other, this time sans Jasper.

He was virile. Positively virile. He filled the tiny kitchen. His frame may be slim, but he was athletic and tall. Her kitchen felt small and overly warm. Though the corners of his lips were curved upwards in a slight smile, his eyes were far from smiling. The green depths watched her, memorizing her movements, studying her features, his eyelids drooping sleepily. No, not sleepily. Longingly.

"A watched kettle never boils," he said, his voice pitched lower than usual.

However in control of herself she was, her body had yearnings of its own. At the sound of his voice, heat pulsed through her veins, sinking down to

tingling toes, back up unsteady legs, and finally settling in her cheeks with a blush.

In two steps, she was leaning against him, her
palms on his chest. *Kiss me*, she thought. *Kiss me, or
I'll burst.*

Reading her mind, as he often did, he cupped
the back of her head in his palm and tilted his head
to cover her mouth with his. When his lips met hers,
partially open, she inhaled deeply the scent of sweat,
earth, and man, the heady aroma of a gentleman who
had worked in a garden to show his devotion to her.
She ran her hands over his shoulders, combing her
fingers through his curls, the edges of his scalp damp
from sweat. Walter brushed her lips with his, still
sweetened by the cinnamon biscuits.

As quickly as it began, he leaned away from her,
his hand slipping from the back of her head to cup
her cheek. He took a larger step back, freeing himself
from her embrace.

Her heart ached.

"You're exquisite, Lilith. Inside and out, the most
beautiful woman I've ever met." He gazed at her with
adoration. "Don't take another step in my direction,
or I'll have to kiss you again."

She took the step.

With a groan, he wrapped his arms about her
waist and lifted her against him until she stood on
her tip toes. His mouth met hers, open and needy.
Sinfully, her hands roamed his torso to feel the muscles of his arms, the muscles of a Corinthian who
enjoyed sports.

Walter's kiss moved from her lips to the curve
of her face.

In his arms, she felt the belonging for which she dreamed. With him, she was secure, valued, needed. She did not have to prove herself to him or earn his respect. She simply was. He desired her for who she was. Desiring him in return, she wanted them to belong to each other.

She tried to pull him closer to her. He resisted, moving back far enough to create a gap between them, although he continued to kiss her, softly, gently.

He kissed her as a gentleman might after receiving the longed-for acceptance to an offer of marriage, but she wanted more. She began to whimper, unsure what she wanted but knowing she wanted more, knowing she wanted to belong, needed to belong, wanted to belong with him.

His whimpering echoed hers.

As if startled by his own reaction, Walter leaned away again. He looked into her eyes, his green orbs dark. He whimpered again. Leaning back further, he looked down between them and laughed a single *ha*.

Her gaze followed his.

Jasper was upright with his paws on Walter's leg, whimpering for attention. She laughed to realize it had been Jasper whimpering, not Walter.

He took a step back further still to reach down to scoop up the puppy. "I think this pup is far wiser than either of us," he said.

She pressed her hands to her cheeks, the reality of the moment settling into a deep embarrassment. What had come over them? What had come over *her*?

He took one look at the forgotten kettle that never made it to the kitchen grate and shook his head. "As ridiculous as I've thought some rules, I do believe there's something to be said about a courting couple never being left unchaperoned. I can't apologize enough for my behavior. Uncouth of me. And I claim myself to be a gentleman."

He laughed as though making a joke, but she could tell from the redness of his ears and neck that he was as embarrassed as she.

"I'm a grown woman," she defended, "and if I want to kiss my suitor, I will."

Jasper licked Walter's hand as he tried to pet the pup.

"I've no complaints," he said. "Believe me. That said, I don't want to put either of us in a situation where we're forced to make a decision rather than letting it be a choice."

Lilith crossed her arms over her chest. "Nothing will force my decision. Nothing."

Walter stared back at her, frowning.

"Right," he said. "I need to leave, Lilith. And we both know it. Will you have dinner with Roddam and me at the inn tonight?"

She nodded, taking Jasper from him when the puppy tried to wriggle out of his grasp to reach her.

Walter made for the parlor to put on his waistcoat. When he struggled with his coat, Lilith set Jasper on a chair and held Walter's coat for him to slip his arms into one at a time.

"Dash it all!" he said, as she straightened his coat and brushed the dust from the sleeves like a proper valet. "I forgot to tell you. The innkeeper, Mr. Hill, mentioned this morning that the village is to host a fête in our honor."

"*Our* honor?" Lilith said, dismayed.

"Well, 'our' being Roddam and me."

"Ah. Yes, that makes sense," she said in relief.

"There's to be a dance after the festivities. Mr. Hill let it slip that this has been in the works since Roddam sent the missive to book the suites, so nearly a month in the making. Sly of you not to mention it, Lilith."

She had not mentioned it because she had not known about it. That fact surprised her. Why would she have been excluded from the planning? She had not even been invited to join the committee. The stab of exclusion hurt. Not only was this in honor of *her* brother and beau, but it was *her* village hosting the fête and dance.

"Your guilt is in your silence," he said, turning to face her and donning his tricorn. "Save me the best set at the dance?"

She grinned. "It's good you ask now because I'm sure all dances will be reserved before the day ends."

In a swift movement, he leaned in to kiss her cheek then marched out the door.

She followed, closing the bottom door behind him and leaning against it. As she watched him walk through the garden, she spotted two figures paused outside the gate.

Miss Tolkey frowned, her hand on Mr. Sands' arm. Their eyes roved from her to Walter and back again. She thanked her good luck that they had not approached the cottage during the torrid scene in the kitchen, for the kitchen was partially visible from the door. So recklessly stupid of her.

Assuming they had come to pay her a call before the walk to Miss Tolkey's home, Lilith waved to them. They did not wave back.

Before Walter reached the gate, they turned and quickened their strides down the road.

Shrugging, she faced Jasper, who remained seated, staring expectantly back at her. What was she supposed to do with a dog?

He tucked his head between his paws, gazing up at her with round eyes and wagging tail.

Lilith sat in the opposite chair and said, "Well, come on, then."

He leapt to its feet, tail vibrating. She expected he would curl up in her lap and be petted. How gravely she miscalculated. In an awkward tumble, Jasper half jumped and half fell off the chair, bounded over to her, pawed his way up her leg until she lifted him, then pranced circles on her lap, licked her face, gummed her knuckles, and fought the fabric of her dress.

"If we're going to get along, you must learn your place in the world, little one."

She stretched out his paws to encourage him to sit still and be petted. He fought her, gnawing on her fingers and alternately growling at her hands and licking them.

"So, I see you will define your own place in the world. I have much to learn from you, Jasper. Well, go on, then, do whatever you'd like."

Jasper circled in her lap three times, and then flopped on his side and fell asleep.

Obstinate.

Chapter 17

T he coastal weather finally caught up to Walter, bringing with it two days of a torrential down-pour to end all downpours along with a chill that seeped into his bones.

Two wasted days. While he and Roddam had not set a definitive leave date, the plan was not to stay long. Roddam was anxious about leaving Lizbeth and his new baby, even if they were in good hands with Walter's mother and Uncle Cuthbert. Walter had more time on his hands since his family need not return to Devonshire until late autumn, but he could not stay behind and court Lilith unchaperoned, especially when the narrative for visiting was to oversee the progress of the hospital, something Walter had no connection to aside from curiosity.

His hope was for a brief courtship. It needed only be long enough to convince Lilith to take the leap. They could then leave Allshire together. Perhaps a wedding near the castle for all to attend before he took her home to Trelowen. Was it too wistful for him to dream of the wedding? He hoped not.

Ever since the heated moment they had shared, he had thought of little but wedded bliss.

One thing was for certain. He could not be left alone with her. However well he had been able to control himself not to act ungentlemanly aside from a rather passionate kiss, he found that control slipping. Yes, in part, that was due to feeling such a strong desire for Lilith. But it was more than that. No amount of discipline could have prepared him for what it was like to embrace someone he wanted to marry, a woman with whom he hoped to spend his remaining days. The emotion of it was overpowering.

Despite her hesitation to wed, he knew she felt the same, for her expression of her own attraction to him when she kissed him was uninhibited, not in a wanton manner, but with innocent conviction, a woman who knew what she wanted but was afraid to accept it. And what she wanted was to belong. With him.

The trouble was, if she would not draw the line of intimacy, he would have to, though he did not want to. She might have professed nothing would force her into marriage, but he worried their actions would compromise them — that the rector and a villager had been lingering within eyesight of the cottage had not been lost on Walter. One sniff of scandal, and he would be honor-bound to marry her. He did not want her to feel obligated. Either she wanted to marry him, or she did not. How humiliating for her hand to be forced if she did not want him as a husband.

He scoffed. *He* was worried about compromising *her*.

His best laid plans were foiled the second the sun shone again. While he was careful not to be alone with her or be seen again leaving her cottage unaccompanied, three moments of shared intimacy found them.

One such moment occurred under the cypress tree on the edge of Sir Gene's property. The two stood out of sight of her patient's home, concealed by low-hanging branches and foliage, but the brief kiss before parting should not have happened, certainly not in so public a place.

The second kiss happened behind the inn, an even riskier moment when Mr. Hill disappeared into the barn to collect supplies for Jasper. The moment took Walter quite by surprise. Lilith turned to snake her arm about his neck and steal a kiss. Only just in time did she slide back to her place a few feet from him.

The third kiss was in the paddock behind her cottage. Roddam remained indoors, a neglectful chaperone, while Walter and Lilith took Jasper to the back to run free, or rather to wobble free, for his puppy legs bore the unsteady gait of youth.

It would seem they could not be trusted together, alone or chaperoned.

Walter looked forward to the distraction of the fête. Such a place would be far too public for either of them to get into trouble. The fête would bring its own kind of enjoyment, for with it would be the evening dance. He counted down the hours until he could dance with Lilith, something he longed to do.

For the week between the first rainy day and the day of the fête, Walter kept busy with more than just kissing Lilith. A few hours each day, he escorted her about the village or took tea or shared dinner with Roddam and her. The remaining hours of the day were his to do as he wished since she taught during the morning and completed her rounds in the afternoon. His time was spent more frivolously.

Namely rowing, fencing, and tea.

Sir Gene had given Walter permission to use the lake at his discretion. Not a single morning passed when he did not take advantage of the access. His midback burned during the first stretch of rowing. Goodness, he was out of shape.

One afternoon, Carmichael invited him for a bout of fencing. However much he found Carmichael a dull dog, he would not turn down the opportunity to wield a sabre. Had he known such an invitation would include tea with the sisters, he would have declined. During tea, they had invited him to use their given names, Lacy and Lynda. He indulged them but did not reciprocate. Only a single touch of his arm with their slender fingers was enough to pump his blood. With ice, that was.

What had changed since London? He recalled he had enjoyed dancing with them. Until recently, he had not known them to be cruel. But it was more than that. For all their giggles, there was nothing behind their blue eyes. Politeness still required he reserve a set each for the assembly.

It was a good week, all in all, and Walter felt he had made progress in the courtship. All in the village knew by now his attentions were honorable, and she gave him nothing but sunny and flirtatious smiles, a far cry from the Lilith he met in July.

The day before the fête, he was enjoying a quiet moment in the inn's public parlor, savoring the remnants of one of Mrs. Hill's prized pies while reading the paper.

Mr. Sands appeared in the doorway, tugging his forelock in an embarrassingly obsequious manner.

Dash it all.

The man had harassed Roddam the previous morning. Walter had hoped to be spared the bother. The rector was kind enough, but there was something about him that smacked of desperation.

This would teach Walter to sit in the public parlor rather than private dining.

"Lord Collingwood!" the rector exclaimed, ignoring the strategically raised newspaper shielding Walter's face. "What a splendid coincidence I should meet you here."

Coincidence his left foot, thought Walter.

He had never been the type to use a quizzing glass. Not only was his eyesight impeccable, but he disliked the lofty image it afforded the wearer. Now, he wished he had a quizzing glass. Alas.

With a grim smile, Walter folded the newspaper and set it aside, stood, and shook the man's limp hand.

"How do you do, Mr. Sands? Join me? I could have Mrs. Hill bring something over for you. Coffee? Tea?"

"Lord Collingwood, you are kindness personified," he said as he took a seat. "I would not dream of imposing, but since you are so thoughtful to think of my parched throat, it would only be courteous to accept. Tea, please. And do call me Harold. My dearest friends call me Harry, if you'd prefer."

Walter waved over Mrs. Hill, who was all too eager to oblige, even bringing a second pie.

The rector smiled too widely, an affectation that did not reach his eyes. It was a shame the man oozed duplicity, Walter thought, not for the first time. For he could be a good-looking chap otherwise.

When Mrs. Hill brought the fresh pie for Walter and tea for two, she added enough sugar to Mr. Sands' cup to turn the tea into liquid candy. Walter grimaced. From the worshipful gaze she cast the man, he understood the rector enjoyed his tea sweet, and she knew it. His good looks were not lost after all. Or perhaps he charmed women better than he did titled men.

"How do you find our humble parish, my lord?" Mr. Sands asked, leaning back in his seat, two friends sharing a coze.

"It's not unlike the villages around my barony. A great place to escape the hubbub of the city, to be sure." Walter sampled a hearty helping of the pie.

If there was one thing he had learned about Allshire, it was that the villagers were blessed with England's greatest pie maker. Mrs. Hill knew what she was about.

"It is to my understanding that you wish to open an orphanage," said the rector after noisily slurping his tea.

"I do. And possibly a foundling hospital. I've come, as you know, with Roddam to see the progress. Mrs. Copeland's done impressive work."

"Yes, yes, all so interesting." Mr. Sands waved a dismissive hand. "Allow me to be of service. I am the overseer of just such a facility."

Walter spooned another bite of pie, chewing slowly, in no hurry to respond. An exaggerated show-ing of silently drinking his own tea, he leaned back in his chair and crossed one leg over the other.

At length, Walter said, "Thank you for the offer of service, but I've interviewed Mrs. Copeland at length. I feel confident I am well armed for the task and can think of nothing you have to offer that I need."

The rector's smile tightened. "Yes, yes, Mrs. Copeland is a bright woman, but she hasn't the experience I do."

Walter arched a brow.

"My lord, I offer you the cunning intellect of a businessman. Planning, building, staffing, monitoring, etcetera, etcetera, a facility of this size is laborious, not to mention beneath your respected station. A man such as yourself need never sully boots or reputation by associating with the riffraff such a facility can attract. Let the humble people worry of such things. Let a man of God whose reputation cannot be tarnished be the one to do the work on your behalf."

Frowning, Walter asked, "What exactly are you proposing?"

"Instead of spending the exorbitant amount of money it would take to start from the ground up, consider joining your cousin-in-law, the revered Lord Roddam, in his patronage. I would oversee all here, and you would have the honor of knowing you've done right for God's children."

Walter's frown deepened. He took his time to refill his cup, adding only a light splash of milk, no sugar or honey. Temptation had him wanting to drink it black just to make a point.

"However thoughtful your offer, I prefer to be personally involved. I have in mind a location midway between my home and London, enabling me to visit as frequently as I need while providing reasonable access from the city. I can't see the Allshire orphanage providing those benefits." A reasonable answer, he decided. Not unkind. Truthful. Pointed.

"Yes, I can see you're an intelligent man, my lord, far more intelligent than I could ever dream of being, but consider my experience. Sacrificing proximity for quality would ensure your continued happiness in the investment."

"Hmm. So, you believe a facility I design would lack in quality?"

Eyes wide, Mr. Sands answered with a panicked edge to his voice. "Oh, no, no, no, that wasn't what I was suggesting. Merely, I do have experience. Valuable experience. It's unlikely you could find someone to oversee this kind of investment who would be trustworthy. And you must consider trust. I won't be the one to speak ill of my fellow man, but not everyone can be trusted with funds."

"And you're trustworthy?" Walter asked, the voice of innocence.

"Yes, yes, I would ensure your donation is appropriately utilized. You need never worry over accounts or site visits with me on hand." Smug after his appeal, the rector finished his liquid confection.

"It's a pity, then, that I've already entrusted my secretary with the task. He sent word yesterday morning with the details of a purchase I plan to make of a site large enough to accommodate the home I envision. Had you appealed to me sooner, I might have been moved, but alas, the deed is done, or as good as." Walter felt no love lost with the rejection.

"Ah, yes, a great pity." Mr. Sands slumped in his chair, chewing on his defeat.

"It's fortunate for you that Roddam's sister grew up in the orphanage," Walter said.

Feigning ignorance, the rector said, "Fortunate? Why, yes, she has returned in abundance all she received from being accepted into the shelter."

"You mistake my meaning." Walter paused to watch the man's eyebrows inch heavenward. "Had she not been at this orphanage, Lord Roddam would not be a patron." As an aside he added, "Nor would I be here."

"Yes, the Lord works in mysterious ways. He brought our dear Lilith to us," he said with a familiar emphasis to her given name, "in order for His Lordship to discover the joys of patronage. Now that he has seen how well-handled have been his donations, he will undoubtedly wish for me to continue to act on his behalf."

What a vain, arrogant man.

Walter crossed his arms over his chest, signaling the end of the discussion. Mr. Sands either did not understand or chose to ignore the motion.

"Lord Collingwood," he began before a slight pause as he tapped a finger to his mouth. "I'm here as your friend and confidant. Perhaps you want to reconsider my offer. Only a small donation need be made now. When you see how enrichingly satisfying it is to help others, you may consider giving more."

Idly swinging the foot of his crossed leg, Walter asked, "And why should I reconsider your offer when I've already given a polite *no*?"

The man had the audacity to giggle. "It does a man good to know there are those who will safeguard his, er, indiscretions."

Walter sat up, uncrossing his legs and resting his forearm on the table. "I do beg your pardon," he said to the rector.

"With the smallest of donations, my lord, I would be willing to overlook the unsavory use of *my* cottage."

Good Lord!

"Let me make myself clear, Mr. Sands. My intentions towards Lady Lilith are honorable. I don't appreciate your insinuation."

The wretched man's smile widened, contorting his features in a most unbecoming fashion. "Ah, then you do not *know*. I understand." Like a man holding a winning deck of cards, Mr. Sands leaned forward and spread his palms flat on the table. "I speak to you as a friend, you must understand. Beware of deception. Ensure you are not compromised. There are those who would take advantage of your station. I know this all too well. For you see, the position of rector's wife is highly coveted."

Leaning further against the table, his face level with the teacup, Mr. Sands continued *sotto voce*, "I say this only out of concern for you. At one point, our Lilith set her cap for that very honored position. I was, you must understand, already courting someone of my own age and station. And though I love all in my flock, I could never marry someone so, er, *desperate*. I believe her age and circumstances are of consideration."

Walter drummed his fingers against the table, fixing the rector with a steely gaze. "And of what circumstances do you refer?"

"I'm not at liberty to disclose the specifics. However, I invite you, my lord, to consider why she has not moved in with Lord Roddam, as a sister of her supposed station would do. Do not be seduced by her charms, Lord Collingwood. Her history at the orphanage is enough to ruin your family's reputation, but her secrets would cause a far greater scandal. I assumed you knew of her…*situation*." His eyes glinted as he added, "And so, you must understand how easily I misunderstood your visit *alone* to the cottage."

Walter's blood boiling, he breathed in through his nose and out through his mouth to calm the rage. It would do no good to overturn Mr. and Mrs. Hill's table.

Only when he had his temper in check did he speak. "My understanding, Mr. Sands, is that it behooves you to discourage a good match to ensure *Lady* Lilith remains in the parish, considering she is the only reason Lord Roddam is a patron."

"Pride goeth before destruction, and a haughty spirit before a fall, my lord." The rector rose from his chair, his smile welded in place, his hands clasped in prayer. "All in my parish are expected to act with decorum. The cottage, you must understand, is mine, let out of kindness. Dalliance in my cottage will not do."

Pressing his index fingers to his mouth, Sands thought in silence before adding, "I come to you today as a friend. I warn you of a serpent in your garden. That serpent is Adam's first wife. Look to the hidden texts of Genesis, my lord. Adam's first wife was equal, wanton, enchanted. God cast her out, but she returned as the serpent. And her name was *Lilith*.

Heed my warning. Let the next time I come to you still be as a friend. I bid you a good day."

With a slight bow, the rector left Walter in peace.

Walter's fingers continued to drum, his glare boring a hole into the back of the empty chair.

Chapter 18

The morning of the fête, Jasper romped beside Lilith for the short walk to the orphanage, looking up at her adoringly every few steps. His tail wagged, his ears flopped, and his feet stumbled. But he kept pace.

Ah, but the scents of the world! So enticing! So distracting! After a quick glance to Lilith, he leapt in the opposite direction to explore a delectable scent just on the other side of a tree.

With a laugh and shake of her head, Lilith followed the scoundrel.

"Jasper," she called. "Come."

He ignored her, on a determined hunt for the source of the scent.

Scooping him into her arms, she said, "You're unabashedly delinquent."

He awarded the scold with a tail wag and tongue loll. Puppy hoisted to her side, she headed into the orphanage, her first stop the office she shared with Miss Tolkey.

For the past week, Jasper had accompanied her everywhere. Her patients enjoyed his company during the rounds, and the children fawned over him during the lessons. The new game was that the most well-behaved pupil got to hold him. She was not sure how long that trick would last, but so far, the children were vying to be the most well-behaved.

When she entered the office, she was surprised to find Miss Tolkey behind the desk, grading papers. The girl looked up, but instead of greeting Lilith with her customary smile, she jerked her head back to the paper before her, her quill working furiously across the page.

"Good morning," Lilith said, chipper in tone.

For the entirety of the week, she had been feeling inexplicably happy. There was a sudden sense of rightness about her life. She could not explain it aside from Walter. Or Jasper. Or both. Perhaps it was to do with being home, as well, and back to her midwifery, though she could not credit her contentedness to that when she did not feel as at home as she ought.

Something had shifted in the village. Being excluded from the fête planning was a blow to her ego. It was not the first sign of distress. Many of her friends had trouble of late looking her directly in the eye. The unusual part was she was uncertain if the shift happened with her or with them. Had she changed? Was she seeing them for how they had always treated her? Or were they seeing her differently? However it was, she could not credit the parish for her happiness.

Lilith stood in the doorway, Jasper wriggling at her side, he eager to discover new smells, she staring at the top of Miss Tolkey's mousy brown head.

"Good morning, Miss Tolkey," she repeated. "Are you excited for the fête? I could scarce sleep last night for excitement."

Silence was her reply.

Shrugging off the behavior under the assumption her companion did not wish to break her concentration, Lilith set down Jasper so he could waddle his way around the office, smelling every corner and object in sight. She dug through the drawers of her desk for the morning's lesson.

There would not be time for much before the festivities began, and the children would undoubtedly not hold focus, but she had to try. Her plan was to assign them math homework concerning the fête. They would count the numbers of people, pies, wins, and other such figures and use those to help practice their tables.

Unearthing the math lesson and a spare bit of parchment in which to scribble the homework, she set about her task. And then paused.

"If you're not with the children, then who is?" Lilith asked.

Not quite meeting her eyes, Miss Tolkey said, "Mrs. Copeland."

She offered no other explanation.

Fanning a quill feather against her chin, Lilith studied her companion. Had her grandmother taken another turn? Jasper curled up at Lilith's feet, exhausted from all the excitement of new and old smells. She leaned down to scratch his ears then prepared her quill.

Five or more minutes passed before Miss Tolkey spoke up of her own accord. "I'll be taking over Mrs. Willard's care. Mrs. Leland's, as well."

Lilith looked up, wide-eyed, but only the top of the brown head with its perfectly straight part looked back.

"Goodness, but why? Are you ready? You've not yet looked after a patient alone."

Miss Tolkey shrugged, back to her grading.

Lilith said nothing for a stretch. Only last Tuesday, she had tended to Mrs. Leland. The woman had been distracted but kind.

Lilith replaced her quill in its stand. "I think it grand you've made connections. Stay for tea after church, and we'll look over the patient notes. You'll need to know the difficulties Mrs. Willard faced with her first child, and I'll want to discuss all you should watch for with Mrs. Leland since this is her first."

"No, thank you," was all Miss Tolkey said.

Reaching down for Jasper, Lilith hauled him to her bosom and cradled him for a sleepy belly rub. "Is it your grandmother? You seem out of sorts," Lilith said.

"My grandmother is well, thank you. I must decline tea. It wouldn't be proper. Oh, and you needn't walk me to church anymore. The Reverend Sands has agreed to see me to and from church every Sunday."

"That is most kind of him. But tea? Whyever would it be improper?" Lilith swallowed against the lump in her throat. It sank like a stone in her stomach.

"I know all about you," Miss Tolkey said, hushed but harsh tone, her quill's ink forming a dark puddle on the paper. "I saw with my own eyes your *protector* leaving your cottage. Don't fib or deny. I also know you've pressured Harry for marriage. Are you in trouble? Will His Lordship not do right by you? You should've known better. Men such as he don't oft support women such as you. And so, you must guilt a good rector into marriage? You may think

I'm young and innocent, but I'm not blind or stupid, Miss Chambers. You're a wicked woman who's brought sin into a good man's cottage. I'll thank you to leave me be."

Lilith sat, stunned, her jaw slackened, her hand still against Jasper's tummy.

There was no way of knowing what the rector said or what Miss Tolkey saw, for Lilith would not ask. Not that it mattered.

How foolish of her. She could scarcely be angered at the rector since it had been she who had invited the reluctant Walter inside the cottage unchaperoned, assuming that was the incident to which Miss Tolkey referred.

Though she knew it was improper to have invited him in, she did not see why it was cause for accusation. She was a grown woman! Most of the parishioners had visited her cottage at one point or another for tea, conversation, or advice. What was different about Walter? It was not as though she had done anything wrong. Not exactly. Not entirely. And yet Miss Tolkey thought them lovers! That she was his *mistress*! How lowering. He had made it clear to all he was courting her, not employing a mistress. But there it was. One of her dearest friends saw her as a seductress, a woman of loose virtue and low morals.

Then, why would any of them think a baron would court her? She was an orphan. An orphan of questionable lineage. She was nobody.

Rising from her seat, Jasper licking her fingers to encourage more belly rubbing, she left Miss Tolkey alone, closing the door quietly behind her, the lesson remaining forgotten on the desk.

Confused, angry, embarrassed, Lilith marched to the classroom to collect the children for the fête. No longer did she care to give them homework or teach a lesson on their tables. Let them enjoy the day for what it was.

Her hand on the door handle, she paused, inhaling deeply to calm her spirit. Her eyes closed. She would not bring her anger into the room. Opening the door as silently as she could so as not to disturb Mrs. Copeland's teaching, she entered the back of the room and stealthily clicked the door closed behind her.

Only, it was not Mrs. Copeland sitting at the front, though she stood off to one side, observing. It was Walter. Lilith's heart pounded. Miss Tolkey forgotten, Lilith stared at him in amazement.

There he sat in tailored finery, reading. A collection of grubby children gathered about him.

His voice soft, dramatic, every few words paused for dramatic effect, he read, "'As soon as you enter the great door of Guildhall, look up.'"

She recognized the tiny book in his hands, no larger than a thumb, *The Gigantick History of the Two Famous Giants*.

He read with animation, looking from one child to the next between pauses, waggling his eyebrows, and acting altogether like there was nowhere else he would rather be. She ignored the wriggling Jasper. She was struck dumb, immovable. His gaze met hers, and though he did not stop reading, his eyes twinkled a smile of their own.

And she knew.

She loved him.

For some time, she had been *in* love with him, though she could not say for how long. Maybe as far back as when she caught him unawares running along the Embleton beach, or maybe as recently as when she saw him knee-deep in her garden. For however long, she had been in love. But now…Now was different. Her soul sang. Her heart filled. Her eyes teared. She belonged with him.

"Puppy!" came the shout that shattered the moment.

All faces turned, seconds before a storm of children raged towards her, their narrator forgotten, arms stretched for Jasper. She set him down, his tail vibrating. He greeted his fans with a woof.

She hardly noticed. Her eyes, unfocused and blurry, saw only Walter.

Walter escorted Lilith to the village green, her arm tucked under his, Jasper prancing beside them. Mrs. Copeland had agreed to take the orphans to the festival. It was a blessing they were invited to attend. Walter suspected Sir Gene invited Mrs. Copeland after Roddam made such a fuss about being a patron. The man was not unwise. Walter would shake his hand heartily for it since it enabled him to have Lilith to himself. Roddam was not so lucky. The poor man had been accosted earlier in the day by Sir Gene and Lady Graham who insisted he spend the day at their side.

For Walter, the day held promise. Egg-and-spoon races, a needlework contest, archery competitions, strongman competitions, boat races, tug-of-war, three-legged races, and so much more. Walter was to judge the pie contest, though he could not imagine Mrs. Hill would have stiff competition.

Each booth and competition teemed with people. Children ran about the green, leapfrogging, chasing each other, and flying kites. The fête was alive with frivolity.

Despite his surroundings, Walter had eyes only for Lilith. She smiled shyly at him from time to time, wearing one of her less threadbare sprigged muslins, a straw bonnet adorning her head, an aura of bashfulness glowing her cheeks. She had not said anything about his surprise visit to the orphanage. He hoped he had not overstepped by coming to her place of employment.

The children had been welcoming, eager for attention. Never had he thought reading to a group of children would be so satisfying, and yet he could not unsee their bright faces, lit with adoration. One girl had insisted she hold his hand for the whole of the reading. One little boy had picked his nose from start to finish. An older child, an adolescent really, had crossed his arms and rolled his eyes except when Walter was not looking at him, for in those moments, he leaned forward to better hear the story, likely imagining himself touring London as Walter described it. A dark-haired girl had caught his attention straight away. Upon seeing her, Walter imagined Lilith as a frightened girl, ripped from her family and tossed into the fray.

The grown Lilith, needing no adornments or expensive walking dress to enhance her beauty, laughed up at him, pointing to the mud pit prepared for the tug-of-war. It was sheer will that kept him from turning her to face him and kissing her soundly and resolutely in front of all.

Roddam waved them over, at his side Sir Gene, Lady Graham, and the Carmichaels. Lacy and Lynda, he noticed, were affecting ennui, accented with an occasional disdainful glance to the rambunctious children. He shook his head. Such attitudes had no place here. Lilith, he admired, did not disguise her excitement.

"I daresay, this is a splendid idea, Sir Gene," Walter said. "It's time I did something like this for my barony. An annual fête would be a perfect tradition to start, I think."

"The villagers seem to enjoy it," was all Sir Gene said, surveying the festival from behind his quizzing glass.

Lady Graham, burrowed in winter fur, though the day was pleasantly cool rather than frigidly cold, said, "If only it were not so cold. I fear I might take chill. It's a lovely day otherwise."

Lacy, wearing a walking dress far too fine for a fête, twirled a parasol. "We'll pay for this good weather with rain."

"Hear, hear," agreed Sir Gene.

A woof caught the man's attention. He turned his quizzing glass on Jasper. "Is that one of my hunting hounds?"

Before anyone could answer, Roddam interrupted. "The tug-of-war should start soon. I best choose a side."

"I hope you're not serious, old boy." Sir Gene released his glass' ribbon to gape at Roddam. "That's for the laborers. I'll never understand the appeal. Do you not know the losing team will end in the mud?"

"Aye, I do. Best give my strength to the weaker side, then."

"Oh, I see! You're to ensure they win," said the baronet.

Roddam winked at Walter, saying to Sir Gene, "On the contrary. I plan to lose."

The baronet stared at the earl, bewildered.

With a nod to all, Roddam made for the mud pit.

Someone tugged at Walter's hand. He looked down to see the little girl who had insisted they hold hands during the reading. Saucer-eyed, she stared up at him.

"Sophia, isn't it?" he asked, kneeling.

The girl nodded, her hazel eyes brightening to be remembered. Wordlessly, she tugged at a sad kite limp on the ground.

"Let's see if we can fly this, shall we?" he asked.

Clasping her hand in his, he was about to look up at Lilith when he overheard the Carmichael sisters, though overheard implied they spoke quietly, when in fact, they said their peace loudly enough for all in the vicinity to hear.

"It must be a great comfort never needing to choose what to wear," said the voice.

An answering reply tittered. "When you only own two dresses, it must save time deciding. One needn't even employ a lady's maid."

"Can you imagine the ease of preparing for the day? A simple braid, an old rag, and done!"

"Too right. One is tempted to bring back barbaric fashions, complete with club."

With a chorus of giggles behind him, Walter's rage mounted. Enough, he thought. Enough.

Rising to his feet, his hand gripped trustingly by Sophia, he turned to the Carmichaels. His mouth opened, prepared for a cutting remark, when another hand touched his arm ever so gently. A red-tinted world softened at the sight of Lilith's expression. She held his eyes with her own and gave a slight shake of her head and an amused lift at the corners of her mouth.

"Shall we fly a kite?" she asked, breaking eye contact to look at Sophia.

A returning smile on his lips, he reached for Lilith's hand and laced his fingers with hers, audience be dashed. He was going to marry her, even if it ruined him. Let them all see.

A beautiful girl on each hand and a dog at his heels, Walter headed for the green to fly a kite.

Sebastian's team lost the tug-of-war, and the earl had to excuse himself from the festival to wash and change. His parting words, that he hoped to return in time for the boat race, were accompanied by a shake of his muddy boots and a flick of his muddy hair, inadvertently splattering the hem of the Carmichael sisters' dresses, sending them into a fit of vapors and home to change.

Lilith could not remember when she had been happier. Though she was content with her life in Allshire, she could not recall ever being *happy*.

True, the beastly women had made her feel about two feet tall in their attempts to alienate her, but with

Walter by her side and the children gathering around them, she knew she belonged. Not in the village, nor in his world, but with him.

If only they could purchase a little house away from both worlds and live together, unbothered. She was not convinced she could marry him if the continued ridicule by the Carmichaels was a taste of the censure to come.

For now, though, she basked in love.

After enjoying the egg-and-spoon race from the sidelines, Lilith and Walter partnered for the three-legged race. Lilith convinced Jasper to sit between Martin and Sophia.

Walter knelt at her feet and knotted a rope about their legs, casting her an occasional smile, his eyes squinting against the sun behind her, his tricorn useless at that angle. To keep from toppling over while he tugged at the rope, she clasped his shoulder, relishing his warmth in the cool breeze. Her dress was not the best choice for autumn weather, as she could feel the wind bite her limbs with each gust.

Their legs secured together at the ankles, she hooked her arm around his waist. He wrapped an arm about her shoulders. Their competitors rallied. With the crack of the signal, they were off. Walter coordinated their steps.

One, two, one, two.

Her grip tightened around him. Her body leaned into him. The heat of his side warmed and thrilled her.

"We can win this!" Walter said as they took the lead.

Cheers and jeers alternated from the sidelines as partners raced to the finish line. Jasper's bark joined the crowd. A quick glance at their competition, Lilith spotted Mrs. Copeland and Mrs. Elliot not far behind. The milliner and her husband were mere paces away. She could not see the others without turning her head.

"One, two, one, two," Walter chanted.

Then she stumbled two before one. His hand captured her upper arm. They steadied their stance. And off they went again, one, two, one, two. Mrs. Copeland and her sister-in-law took the lead. One, two. Jasper's bark intensified, distraught by his mistress' stumble. Lilith glanced to see Jasper standing on all fours, waiting for the moment to launch himself in for a daring rescue.

Another stumble. She only just caught herself, grappling for Walter to steady her.

And here came Jasper. Walter wrapped his arms around her waist to right them, but Jasper had ideas of his own. He bounded across the green, dodging other couples, sending one pair falling to their fate, eliciting laughter from the sidelines, and launching himself at Lilith and Walter. The puppy grabbed at the rope binding their legs and tugged one way and then the other.

Lilith wobbled, and Walter grasped for her, holding her to him. A tug here. A tug there.

"No, Jasper! Let go!" Lilith insisted, laughing.

She stepped back, entangled her legs with Walter's, and down they tumbled, rolling to one side and taking out another pair of racers. Jasper fought against the rope, oblivious to the chaos. Lilith lay on her back against the cold ground, laughing until her sides hurt. She stared at the blue sky and white clouds, listening to the sideliners applaud the winners, Mrs. Copeland and Mrs. Elliot.

A shadowed face blocked the sky. "Care for a lemonade?" Walter asked, reaching a hand between their linked legs to untie the rope.

Once free, she accepted Walter's hand and was pulled to her feet. Jasper ran circles, a happy puppy to have a rope as his prize for the valiant rescue. All efforts to brush off her dress were wasted. She did not care. However much her sides hurt, she continued to laugh.

Oh, yes, this was the happiest day of her life.

She rested a hand on Walter's arm to head for a refreshment booth. By the time they had lemonade and watched the strongman competition, which eleven-year-old Stephen won, it was time for the pie contest, which Walter agreed to judge.

There were fifteen pies displayed on the table and fifteen anxious bakers looking on as Walter approached.

"Ah, my favorite part of the festival," Walter said, surveying the pies. "How does this work? Do I eat all the pies in one sitting? A hearty challenge, but I'm game."

The women laughed, blushed, and curtsied.

"Only one bite each, or do I at least get a slice?" he enquired.

Mrs. Hill stepped forward, a hand to her bosom. "I've been telling everyone you'll eat the inn out of food soon. Though it's ever so refreshing to know someone of refined taste appreciates my cooking."

"Now, now, Mildred," said an older woman with a mop of red hair under a lacy cap. "Everyone knows my pies are prized. Fit for the King himself." She lifted a pie and waved it before Walter.

He exaggerated an inhale.

With a charming smile, he said, "I may not be worthy of this pie."

The women giggled behind their hands and exchanged glances, besotted with him, despite they were all married with children, most of them happily so. Lilith picked up an exhausted Jasper so he could sleep in her arms before his next bout of playfulness. Knowing he would one day be too big to hold, she treasured the moment.

Though the archery competition was underway, as well as other activities, a small crowd gathered around the booth to watch Walter sample pies and judge their culinary quality. Some were eager for a slice. Others wanted to admire the baron. He tasted each pie with a slow bite, savoring the flavor, closing his eyes in concentration. Each piemaker watched for clues of his favorites.

Lilith stood on the sidelines with the other observers, Jasper snuggled against her bosom.

As Walter moved from one pie to the next, the crowd moved about her to block the view and nudge her farther away. Try as she might to move back to the front with Walter, the crowd blocked her, a walled fortress separating her from him.

The fête had been fun so far. Even the pie judging was fun, especially given how crowd-pleasing Walter made the contest, exaggerating his motions, teasing the onlookers with a wafting of pie aroma.

And yet, on the happiest day of her life, Lilith felt isolated.

Looking about her, she recognized all the faces, her fellow parishioners. She knew them all; yet none of them had been more than cordial to her over the years, some never acknowledging her, others changing their behavior after her brother discovered her. They did not see her as one of them.

A few feet away stood Walter in all his charm, looking too polished in his green silk coat, tan riding breeches, and shiny boots, but somehow still befriending each person with a solitary smile. She glanced down at her dress, her rags. She imagined how she looked in comparison to him. How could he not be embarrassed by her?

Closing her eyes, she tried to envision herself dressed in the finery of the Carmichaels, twirling her own lacy parasol, her hair short, curled, and swept into a chignon. They would see through her, point her out as an imposter. Where did she belong? She did not belong with the crowd around her, though she wanted to and had thought for awhile that she did. She did not belong with the Grahams or the Carmichaels and never would. She was trapped in the middle, isolated.

If she could fit in one world, which? One was full of ridicule, but there would be Walter. The other full of contentment, but there would be no Walter.

Opening her eyes, she watched between broad shoulders and bonnets as Walter offered a slice of pie to a young lady. The lady, daughter of one of the local tenants, was in her early twenties with long eyelashes, pert nose, chestnut brown hair, and petite frame. The girl looked at Walter from beneath sooty lashes, blushing prettily, and looking very much like the kind of person Walter should marry. Lilith blinked away tears. She felt old, frumpy, and forgotten.

And she had missed the announcement of the winner.

Burying her face in Jasper's coat, she wished she could go home. *Ha.* She had no home. Her cottage belonged to the rector.

"Slice of Mrs. Hill's winning pie?" a baritone voice asked.

Lashes wet, she turned her head to peek, her nose pressed against Jasper's neck. Walter stood before her, a pie plate in his hand, all smiles and bright eyes and cologne. With a hand to her elbow, he guided her to an abandoned set of chairs. When she sat, Jasper stirred, stretched, and circled in her lap before falling back to sleep with a huff. Walter held onto the pie plate, two forks tucked under a thumb.

"I have to admit," he said, "I worried the redhead's lemon pie would win. It melted in my mouth. I almost declared her the winner at first bite. Somehow, Mrs. Hill managed to outdo her. The woman's a kitchen sorceress. I'm sure of it."

She sampled a bite. He had not exaggerated. Decadent! It was a rhubarb pie the likes Lilith had never tasted. If she died in this moment, with a bite in her mouth, she would be perfectly content. Her woes of the moment forgotten, she took another bite and moaned.

Walter chuckled, taking a bite for himself. "What do you think of me hosting an annual fête like this?" he asked.

She could see him hosting his own, as much a part of the fun as the villagers, unlike Sir Eugene who watched everything from the other side of his quizzing glass.

"I think you make your father proud," she said.

The corners of his mouth turned down, and he set his fork on the plate.

Jasper nudged her hand, awakened by the scent of food. She shared a bit of pie crust with him.

"He would've loved you," he said. "Above all, he would've loved how happy you make me."

She stared, startled. "Do I?"

"You know you do." His smile returned but softer. "This, today, being with you, as we are now. Nothing could feel more right. Tell me you feel it, too."

Nodding, she said, "I do. I wish we could find a village like this and live in a little cottage on the edge, accepted by all, waving from our chairs in the front garden. No fancy home with servants, no trips to London, no mingling with polite society. Above all, no dinners with aristocrats or the censure that comes with it. Just the two of us, or should I say the three of us to include Jasper, without a worry in the world. Wouldn't it be perfect?"

She smiled wistfully at him, seeing the picture so clearly, wanting so much for it to be true.

His own smile died, the light in his eyes fading. "Lilith. I can't stay here indefinitely. I'm a baron. I already have a home, Trelowen. Your brother may be happy as a recluse, but I couldn't live like that. I have friends. I like dinners. I like dancing. I love London. I want you to come with me for the dinners and the dancing and the glitz and glamor. I can't wait to introduce you to my friends. That's what I wish and what I envision for the future. Us, standing side-by-side in a London ballroom. Us, sitting side-by-side at an annual fête in my barony. If you accept me, you must accept all that comes with me."

With a wan smile, she said, "I know."

Until this moment, the day had been one of Walter's happiest, if not the happiest, though he did have a plethora of fond memories with friends and family. Her words had not ruined the day. At least she saw them together in her vision for the future. But they had struck him rather deeply, a punch to the gut.

It would take time to accustom her to a new way of life, but it was not out of the question that she could learn to be part of the *beau monde*. Once gossip died down about her time at the orphanage, and certainly if Roddam introduced her as his sister, his *full* sister rather than half, she would feel more at home. But she had to want to accustom herself. She had to try at the very least.

As though the moment had not occurred, Lilith scooted Jasper off her lap and stood. With the same sunny smile she had worn all day, she added the plate with the other discarded dishes and returned to grab his hands and pull him upright.

"The boat races will begin soon. Race me to the lake!" Without another word, she lifted the hem of her dress and took off at a run across the green, Jasper at her heels.

What a tease! All he could do was jog after her.

This was the most undignified behavior for a gentleman, he thought in good humor, laughing as he chased her. He was aware a group of children were chasing after him, and that the villagers who were not already downhill at the lake were watching them in reproach.

She raced ahead, her braid bobbing behind her.

The vixen turned at intervals to laugh at him. When she crested the hill and disappeared on the other side, he quickened his steps, cold wind burning his cheeks, his blood pumping, his heart racing. Their visibility to others lost and a sizable gap between them and the stragglers, he raced forward, nearly tumbling down the hill on the other side.

The steepness had slowed her pace. Jasper barked up at him, running back and forth between them with only a few stumbles.

In easy strides, Walter caught up to her, grabbing her by the waist and spinning her. She threw her head back and laughed. Her fists pummeled lightly against his chest as he twirled her to a tree near the bottom of the hill. Angling them behind the trunk in the off chance someone saw them, though as far as he could tell, they were quite alone, he pressed her to the bark and shielded her body with his, his mouth covering hers, open, hungry, tasting of rhubarb.

A hand to the tree next to her head and the other cupping her face, he kissed her with abandon. He loved her with a fierce passion and a deep need. He loved her. So what if people saw? He wanted all the world to know. He loved her and would marry her and spend the rest of his life making her happy.

"Lilith," he breathed, his voice hoarse.

She pushed against him, separating them. "We don't want to miss the boat race," she said in her huskily velvet voice.

Good Lord. She looked thoroughly tumbled, though they had only shared a kiss. Face flushed, braid frizzed, and lips reddened. Exquisite.

For the second time, he had forgotten about Jasper, who tugged at the hem of her dress, hoping for another game of chase. Peeking around the tree, Walter checked for onlookers. Those at the top of the hill had not yet made it this far, and those by the lake were tucked safely around the corner out of sight.

Still, he berated himself. Reckless. Careless. Thoughtless. Caught up in the moment. They had enough of a scandal to battle with her history at the orphanage and questionable lineage. Shaking his head, he offered his arm and walked her sedately to the lake, the puppy following.

It was not as long a walk as he remembered. Soon, they found the crowd gathered about the lake, ready for the entertainment of the boat races. No one paid them any mind other than a few sidelong glances.

Berating accomplished, he now mused at his behavior. Had this been London during the Season, and had she been a young girl like so many he met each year, he never would have acted like this. He would have courted with flowers, drives through the park, tea with her mother and friends, and dances at parties. Never would they have had a private moment together. Never would he have pulled her behind a tree for a salacious kiss. Never would he have gone into her house alone.

What had come over him?

Well, as far as he was concerned, they were as good as betrothed. It was only a matter of a few words and an announcement, and it would be done, giving respectability to their behavior.

They found a spot on the edge of the lake, slightly separated from the crowd. The race was not the type of rowing Walter had imagined. Five boats lined the bank. Five partners climbed into each. Two people per boat, one oar per person.

There was not a dry eye on the bank as the crowd doubled over in peals of laughter watching the partners try to coordinate their oars to reach the other side of the lake where Sir Gene and Lady Graham waited to declare a winner.

Mr. and Mrs. Turnbow managed to make three full circles before synchronizing their rowing. The young lady who worked at the orphanage—was her name Miss Tollkens? Walter could not recall—lost her oar to the lake, leaving Mr. Sands to row with only one oar. One couple went the wrong direction, piloting their boat to the deeper end of the lake. One girl gave up rowing and left the gentleman to finish the race, forfeiting their win.

Had he not been so stuffed from the baking contest, he might have asked Lilith if she wanted to give it a go. He could not recall if he had talked to her about the lake at Trelowen and his love for rowing. Since she loved the ocean, would she equally love the lake? He imagined them rowing together in the mornings, cooling off with a swim, though on a day such as today, the sound of diving into the water gave him chills.

And just as he thought it, one of the boats tipped over, a young man laughing at his partner flailing in the water. From what he could tell, it was a brother and sister pair. They reminded Walter of Roddam and Lilith. What must it have been like to lose a sibling, Roddam by thinking his sister dead, and she by thinking her brother and parents abandoned her? Did she want children someday, maybe a boy and girl of her own? After seeing her with Freya, and now with the children at the orphanage, he knew she would be an amazing mother.

"Have you ever wanted to find your mother?" he blurted out.

She picked up Jasper, who had fallen asleep at her feet.

"No. I didn't know she existed until Sebastian and Lizbeth arrived at my doorstep. My memories of a mother are of Jane Lancaster, the countess, Sebastian's mother. She raised me and is the only mother I've ever known." Her tone was matter of fact.

"But once you learned she existed, didn't you want to find her? Ask her why she left?"

"I know why she left. She was an unmarried woman with a child. She would have been kicked out for her condition, and she wouldn't have been able to find employment, not in that state, much less with a baby. I don't blame her for abandoning me. She had no choice. As a midwife, I see this situation far more than you can imagine, especially with servants of the gentry. Before you think them loose, know that many of them don't have much say in the matter when the unwanted attention is from the lord of the house or his sons. You may not see the tarnish of your world, but I do. I see its underbelly."

Walter rubbed the back of his neck and remained silent as Mr. and Mrs. Turnbow took the win. The crowd applauded their good luck and dispersed. Most were eager to return home to change before the dance, others returned to work.

"It's not that I don't see the tarnish, Lilith. I do, or at least I know of it. I see it from the other side, and while you can help the women, I'm helpless to listen to my peers boast their conquests, fair out their scandals, or hide their secrets until someone exposes them. Is village life any less tarnished? Are the parishioners of Allshire wearing halos?"

"Hardly." Lilith scoffed. "But it's different. Their sins are their own, not what's forced on them by those with wealth and power."

"Do you think, then, that your father used your mother?" Walter was not altogether sure he wanted that question answered.

She shook her head. "I don't think so. There were letters. That's how Sebastian found me. She wrote letters to our father. If they're to be believed, she was in love with him and thought he felt the same."

"Ah."

Yes, he understood that situation well. He knew any number of gentlemen who carried on affairs with their staff, though he had no way of knowing how many were consensual dalliances, how many were love matches, or how many were forced.

"If you could find your mother, would you want to reunite? Family is the most important thing in this world, I believe. Surely, you'd want to meet her."

Oh, why had he asked? He did think family was important, but he did not want to open this door. His whole intention was to find her mother to ensure there would not be a conflict should Roddam introduce his sister as legitimate. The plan was already set in motion, having begun at Sir Gene's dinner. If Lilith wanted a relationship with her mother, it could ruin everything.

No.

No, that was selfish.

He would support the reunion if she wanted it. All it would mean is that they introduce her as the illegitimate sister. And so what if everyone knew he married an illegitimate?

Even as he accepted this, he heaved a sigh of relief when she answered.

"I have no wish to reunite. What purpose would it serve? It would complicate both our lives. She birthed me, yes, but she is not my mother nor my family. Family is comprised of the people who love you and who you love in return, not blood relations. Your world bases itself on bloodline, but it's wrong. Family is about love, not lineage."

She followed the crowd around the lake, everyone heading back to the village.

"I'm surprised you say that, Lilith. If you truly believe that, why do you define yourself by your birth when your family is at the castle, wanting you to be part of their lives?"

She sighed. "I don't define myself that way. It's a fact of life. It's not *who* I am, but it is *what* I am."

"And what of those who love you for who you are?"

She turned to answer, but her eyes lit on something over his shoulder. "'Bastian!" she called out.

Roddam jogged up behind them, having approached from the hill. He clapped Walter on the back then swung around to Lilith's other side, tucking his hand under her elbow since Jasper had already claimed her arm.

"I can't believe I missed the boat race," Roddam said. "Did I at least make it back in time to reserve the first set tonight?" With a quick look to Walter, he added, "Assuming it's not already taken."

"It's yours," Lilith said. "I now have two sets reserved. I won't be a complete wallflower at my first dance."

Though she laughed, Walter was shocked by her words. Her *first* dance? Had Allshire never held a dance, or had she never been invited? He squeezed her hand.

Chapter 19

The door opened to reveal a dashing and dark Sebastian, grinning devilishly with a box in his hand. When Lilith saw Walter standing behind him, she stepped aside to let them into the cottage.

"Ready for the ball, Lil'?" her brother asked, unceremoniously thrusting the box into her hands.

"For over an hour, I've been practicing dance steps. I only hope I don't stomp on toes," Lilith said, eyes riveted on the box.

It was small, rectangular, tied with a ribbon.

"What is this?" she asked, looking from Sebastian to Walter and back again.

"Open it and find out, goose." Sebastian chuckled.

Releasing the ribbon, she lifted the lid and gasped. A sapphire pendant with a solitary diamond lay nestled in the box.

"Oh, 'Bastian. You shouldn't have! I can't accept this." She shook her head, nervous to be holding something so precious.

"Nonsense. Turn around so I can clasp it. If it helps, I'll guilt you into wearing it by saying that if you don't wear it, you will have me in the mopes all evening."

He pulled out the necklace and nodded for her to turn.

"But it must have cost more than I've earned in my life! I can't possibly wear it," she continued to protest, even as he laid the cold gem against her throat and drew the chain around her neck. Gooseflesh covered her arms.

"Don't you know ladies aren't allowed to talk about money?" he responded. "And besides, I have more money than Croesus. What else am I to do with it than adorn the ladies in my life? Now, turn so we can see how it looks."

Lilith reached up to touch the pendant, anxious to be wearing something worth more than her life. The consolation was Walter's expression. He admired her from head to toe with languid, half-lidded eyes of fathomless green. His grin was diabolical, a heady combination with his angelic looks. Her stomach flip-flopped.

"Yes, I think that'll do," Sebastian said, turning to Walter with an arched brow.

She watched Walter swallow, his Adam's apple bobbing.

He licked his lips, the tips of his ears turning ever so slightly pink. "Uh, yes, I believe it will. I mean, uh, no. That is, it's missing something." And then he, too, thrust a box at her.

"This really is too much." Her breathy reply belied her anticipation for another gift.

She never had considered herself materialistic, but then, she had never received gifts before. For all she knew, she did enjoy gifts. The second box was square, tied with an identical ribbon. Making short work of it, she lifted the lid to reveal a matching sapphire bracelet.

Oh!

They had outdone themselves.

She blinked the blur from her sight as Walter clasped the bracelet about her wrist. He smiled an irresistible, knowing smile, one that echoed the beat of her heart. She smiled back.

With such an auspicious start, tonight was to be a grand evening!

Between the fête that morning and now, she had rested, and then prepared a bath. For most of the bath preparation, she had longed for Hannah. By the time she filled the basin, she needed another rest, though it did feel good to have a thorough cleaning, even if the water was icy and made her teeth chatter. Dressing had likewise been a chore, just as it had been for the dinner party.

She wore the blue dress and matching slippers she had purchased with Hazel and attempted another top knot with her hair, though it was far too long for styling. How Hannah had managed, she could not guess. The gloves she owned did not match the dress, but they would have to do. Her shopping adventure with Hazel sprang to mind. The dress alone had been an extravagance. Why could the slippers and gloves not come with the dress? Ah, but no, they charged separately for each item. Madness. Another memory from her outing with Hazel niggled; Hazel discreetly trying to teach Lilith not to pull out pin money — a vulgar act, as no one of quality carried or handled money directly — and winking that all purchases would be billed accordingly to the earl or baron. She also recalled other moments during the outing where, if she were not mistaken, Hazel subtly offered or demonstrated how to look or behave, as though the outing were more than a fun shopping spree between two ladies but also one of instruction. Had Lilith paid more attention, she could have learned a great deal. She was chagrined not to have realized what Hazel was about.

When she looked in the mirror after dressing earlier this evening, she had been pleased. Though she was more handsome than pretty, and though the dress was simple and plain, she knew herself to be looking her best, at least as good as she could without a lady's maid or modiste. Unlike the dress she had worn at the dinner, this dress was high waisted and of the latest fashion. Oh, yes, she was quite pleased with how she looked and vainly hoped Walter agreed.

Standing now before Walter, she flushed to know herself attractive and desired.

Walter was dressed for London, she observed. He wore a formal frock coat this evening, something she had never seen him wear. He was breathtaking. The embroidery, echoed in every piece of his ensemble, including his shoes, was intricate and plentiful, displaying a floral motif, colorful against the black and gold silk brocade. Even the buttons on his waistcoat had embroidered flowers.

Sebastian, too, wore a handsome ensemble, but she had eyes only for Walter this evening.

With a farewell to Jasper, who had to stay home for the evening, much to his disappointment, they left for the inn. Though Sir Eugene had offered to host the dance in his ballroom, the consensus was that the villagers would feel more comfortable in the upstairs assembly rooms of the Black Bull Inn.

The walk was short, but Walter managed to use the time well.

He leaned close to whisper, "You take my breath away."

The irony? His words stole *her* breath. She barely had a chance to regain those breaths before she stepped into the ball and had them stolen all over again.

Oh! She thought, not for the first time in the past half hour.

Never had she been in the upstairs rooms of the inn. Her first thoughts were of the room itself. The sheer size astounded her, the room long and wide with open windows lining the top half of the one-and-a-half-story walls. The chilly air sweeping in from the windows made her shiver. But then she took in the ballroom and was awestruck.

Oh.

Oooh.

Hundreds of candles lit the space, a dazzling display of flickering glitz. Chandeliers glittered, sconces sparkled, candelabras guttered. Promenading about the room, standing before mammoth mirrors, or sitting on settees were the guests, dressed in the finest silks and satins Lilith had ever seen. Their jewels danced in the reflected light. Their feathered headdresses nodded from towering heights.

Her jaw must have hung down to her bosom, for Sebastian asked, "What do you make of it?"

"Oh, 'Bastian. How could you possibly dislike dances? This is divine!"

Though no one looked directly at them, the hush in the room signified all noted their arrival. Sebastian and Walter were, after all, the guests of honor.

Her earlier preening dulled. How had she thought herself looking her best when such glamor filled the room? Touching the sapphire at her wrist, she raised her chin and pulled back her shoulders. She did look her best. Who cared if her dress was shop purchased and snugger around her hips and looser around her bosom than it ought to be when the finer figures of the room wore bespoke dresses custom stitched to their forms? Who cared? She felt pretty in the dress, and that was all that mattered.

Her hand on Sebastian's arm, Walter on her other side, they approached Sir Eugene and Lady Graham with bows and nods.

His quizzing glass raised to a discerning eye, he took in her appearance. "Lovely, lovely, Lady Lilith."

"Thank you, Sir Eugene. I'm honored by the invitation." She afforded a nod to the baronet.

"Sir Gene, my lady, *please*," he said with a stiff lip and slight exasperation.

She repeated his name before exchanging greetings with Lady Graham. At some point, she really would have to better acquaint herself with the rules of etiquette if she were to continue such liaisons, but it would take time. Even now, she was unsure to whom to curtsy and to whom to nod. Out of the corner of her eyes, she watched Sebastian and Walter for cues to see to whom they bowed and to whom they nodded. Living a life as Miss Chambers was far different from living as Lady Lilith, and she was not altogether decided on the latter.

There were more people here than she knew, most landowners from around the parish, not people she encountered in her small world. The few faces she recognized were former patients or the wealthier tenants. She had expected to see more villagers, namely the shopkeepers and farmers. Was that not the point of holding the dance at the inn? For them to attend? There were a few, to be true, along with Harry and Miss Tolkey, who pointedly ignored her, but nowhere near the attendance she expected.

She was out of her element and feeling insignificant. The more she smiled, the more people frowned. Nothing would rain on her first dance, she decided. Her chin raised another fraction of an inch.

Sir Eugene promenaded them around the room for introductions. Each time he said Sebastian's title, his chest puffed, as though the earl were there by his request. Each time he introduced her, he hesitated before saying Lady Lilith. More than a few curious faces assessed her following the introduction, though no one returned her smile. Lilith could not discern if it was that her smile was unwelcomed or if the smile itself was a faux pas.

The Carmichaels stood in one corner, encircled by a group of haughty women, their noses in the air, their mouths grim lines. They refrained from approaching, much to Lilith's relief. How they could look bored in such a stunning setting she could not understand.

Some gentlemen solicited dances, and others found the card room. Though Walter did a round about the room to request a partner for each set, Sebastian promised no one a set except Lilith, and Lilith herself was not asked except by the host. Three sets in the whole of the evening. She was relieved. The last thing she wanted was to make a cake of herself on the dancefloor. The only dancing experience she had was from Mrs. Brighton's lessons. The repertoire at the orphanage had been as limited as the number of partners. More often than not, the girls had to pair with each other, Lilith always leading as the gentleman, more so now that she was the teacher instructing the orphans.

Although guests continued to arrive, the orchestra took its place for the opening set. Sebastian escorted Lilith to the dancefloor, queuing with the other dancers. Walter stood a few people away, partnering a young girl who would have been plain had it not been for the becoming blush rouging her cheeks.

Lilith's pulse raced. *Please, don't step on toes. Don't trip over feet. Don't forget the steps.* She said to herself. Then the music began.

Sir and Lady Graham stepped forward, the other couples following suit. The dance was lively and fun. Less than a quarter of the way through the first dance in the set, Lilith was laughing and enjoying herself immensely. There was little similarity between her dance lessons and the real dance, but at least her feet did not fail her. With Sebastian as her partner, who could do wrong? What she would not give to see him and her sister-in-law dancing together.

Oh, but what a treacherous thought. For that to happen, Sebastian would have to host a ball, which he would likely never do, or she would have to go to London with them. Could she accustom herself to balls? If they were all such as this, she believed she could. There was, after all, little mingling and the pleasure of dancing, or so it seemed thus far. She did not deceive herself into believing all parties consisted of dancing without socializing, but if they did, she could be content in Walter's world, at least so far as the balls were concerned. All her worry that she would be required to dance, and now all she wanted to do was dance every set of the evening.

As the first dance of the set came to an end, and they waited for the next to begin, Sebastian said, "I'm planning a trip to Roddam Hall on the way home. A long detour, granted, but I've business there, and now is as good a time as any. Once I return home, I don't plan to leave again until Parliament returns to session. Care to join me?" Without waiting for an answer, he added, "Collingwood will be joining me."

Lilith's smile slipped at the corners.

Roddam Hall. Her childhood home. The home in which she was raised as Lady Lilith. The home she left behind at the age of eight when she was stripped of all she knew to be dumped on the doorstep of an orphanage.

"I'm not sure I can go back," she answered as the dance began.

This dance had them separate more than together, so conversation paused. Not until the dance brought them together again for a lengthy enough stretch did Sebastian respond.

"It's cathartic, Lil'. I know our experiences at the hall were different, but I've made peace with my time there. You could, as well."

They separated again, conversation stilted. Her opportunity to respond was delayed by an extended set of figures wherein she had to partner with a some-what smelly man with bad teeth.

When the dance brought them together, she said, "I hardly know what would be accomplished by going back. What good would more memories do me?"

At last, the dance ended with another break before the last of the set.

Sebastian took advantage of the moment. "I've no way to know what you'll decide for your life, but the hall is yours if you want it. Say the word, and I'll make it happen."

Her eyebrows raised, her heart in her throat, she said, "Oh, no, I could never! What would I do there? It's far too grand."

"I offer it to you, nonetheless, so you know you have options."

"I wouldn't at all belong, 'Bastian. Imagine me in a grand estate. It's laughable!" she said with an airy laugh.

He tilted his head to study her. "Do you really think you wouldn't belong in an estate? If you truly believe that, then what the devil am I doing here chaperoning you and Collingwood?" He clasped her hands as the next dance began. "Lilith, look deeper inside yourself. You're not a country midwife. You're my mother's daughter. Don't you dare forget it for a minute."

The dance resumed, Lilith unable to form an answer. The words hung between them.

Her mind worked for the remainder of the dance, rationalizing why she should not return. Strangely, she could think of more reasons why she *should*. Though she had scoffed at the onslaught of memories a visit might bring, she did want them. She wanted to remember everything, even the bad. Even her father.

Whether it would make her want to join Walter's world or run screaming, she could not say, but she did want to go back, though not to live. She had her midwifery to return to, of course. The remaining protest she could think of was the backtracking distance to return her to the parish, delaying their arrival to the castle. But then, she realized her brother had no intention of returning her to the parish. Or at least, he hoped she would choose another course.

The dance at an end, Sebastian walked her to the perimeter to join Walter who had already returned his partner to her family. Lilith was short of breath and feeling flushed. Walter was just as bright-eyed. He was in his element. However out of place he looked at the fête, he clearly belonged in the ballroom. His demeanor was at ease, his attire in keeping with those around him, though he remained the best dressed, and his smile revealing his enjoyment. Those who approached him for conversation were met with a flow of topics aimed to set them at ease in the presence of a baron and an earl. All their previous talk of polite conversation made sudden sense.

Her heart swelled to know he wanted her. How easy it would be to say yes. Assuming he still planned to propose. He was at liberty to change his mind. Did she dare say yes? In this present moment, she could not immediately recall why she hesitated in accepting him.

They had no chance in which to exchange words, for the second set was cuing, and Walter went in pursuit of his partner. Sebastian stood by Lilith's side, neither of them engaged for the dance. She found it interesting that no one came up to them to initiate conversation. All had been charmed by Walter, attracted as a moth to a flame, determined to know him and be known by him. No one approached the siblings. Was Sebastian too intimidating? She could count on her fingers the many reasons no one approached her, but it did surprise her no one attempted to befriend Sebastian.

The dancers readied, and before long began their steps to the sound of music. The floor vibrated with their footwork. The music reverberated from the walls. When she first entered the room, it had been chilly from the open windows, but now it was oppressively hot. She longed for a fan.

With a giggle, she reminded herself a fan was entirely practical in the need to keep oneself cool in a heated ballroom, not a toffish fashion accessory. Well, maybe that as well, but she was not becoming a toff after only a single hour at her first ball.

"There you are," said Lady Graham, startling Lilith, who had been looking in the opposite direction. "It's dreadfully hot in here. Shall we withdraw for refreshments?"

Lilith smiled to be included. Perhaps she had been too hasty in thinking she did not belong in his world.

Sebastian nodded them onward, saying he did not wish to intrude on women's conversation. If they had not been in a ballroom, Lilith would have stuck out her tongue. Instead, she walked with Lady Graham to the adjacent room.

"I never attend assemblies," the lady began, "because they're always overly warm. When I host at Arbor House, I have the doors open to the terrace for the cross breeze. This room is horribly designed. I ask you, what good do windows this high do when the cool air circles about the ceiling? Other than threaten to douse the candles."

Unsure how to respond when Lilith thought the ballroom remarkably beautiful, she sipped her lemonade and said nothing. How did Walter go about this whole polite conversation business? If she were to spend any more time in this company, she must learn.

Lady Graham was undaunted by Lilith's silence. Continuing to chatter, she said, "I was asked, of course, to dance this set, as well as the others, but I've had to decline all offers except Gene's. Oh, I know it's bad *ton* to decline, but we *are* in the country, at a village assembly no less, and so I'm allowed to sit out."

Lilith understood the situation without Lady Graham having to explain. "It's unexceptional for you to be fatigued this far along in your condition. Is it only because of the exertion of dancing, or have you been feeling tired at other times, as well? I'll call on you tomorrow for an examination, shall I?"

Indeed, the woman did look worn. Lilith had been so distracted by the ball, she had not paid attention to the shadows under Lady Graham's eyes. How selfish of her not to notice! Though this was the lady's second pregnancy, the first had not been without trials, and that had been precarious given the series of miscarriages she had suffered before finally hiring Lilith as midwife.

Lady Graham grimaced. "How indelicate. This is not the place for such talk. Hush before someone hears you."

Lilith was taken aback. "Your condition is not something to be ashamed of, Lady Graham. I need to know how you're feeling to ensure all is well."

"Never you mind. You've done me a great service, and I'm forever grateful, but you needn't worry about me. Miss Tolpens — or is it Tolknees? I can never remember — is seeing to me now."

The words were a knife to the heart. Had it not been for Lilith, Lady Graham would have in all likelihood lost her twins. That was not a boast but a fact. What had Lilith done that was so wrong? Why was Miss Tolkey taking her patients when the girl had no experience aside from assisting Lilith from time to time as part of her training?

"I fail to understand," was all Lilith could say.

"Don't be modest. You'll be quitting your practice to move in with your family, of course. A lady of your position cannot possibly be employed. And good gracious, no one wants a *lady* as their midwife, least of all the daughter of an earl. Now, let's have no more of this talk. You dance well, Lady Lilith. Who was your instructor?"

Lilith swallowed, her throat burning with unshed tears. "Mrs. Brighton."

"Oh." The lady pronounced the word as though she had tasted a bitter lemon. "I was under the impression your mother might have hired a dance instructor."

"Had I been older, perhaps. I entered the orphanage at eight." Lilith set down her unfinished lemonade, desirous of a return to the ballroom.

"Yes, I see. Let's have no more talk of that unpleasantness either. Oh, look, there's Betsy. If you'll excuse me." And off she walked, leaving Lilith standing alone.

Lilith rubbed her arms, chilled again and feeling conspicuous. As quickly as her slippers could take her, she returned to Sebastian's side, her smile dimmer than it had been when leaving the room.

The young lady danced superbly. It was only a shame about her laugh. Should the Beast of Gévaudan laugh, Walter imagined it would be to the same tune. To ensure their continued enjoyment of the set, Walter changed to more somber topics to discourage laughter. Yes, far more congenial company when she was not amused.

He did his best to give her undivided attention, as he did with each partner, but his eyes, of their own accord, alit on Lilith standing next to Roddam. She glowed with excitement. Her first ball.

He looked forward to taking her to a London ball. The inn's assembly room was stuffy and worn to the point even polish could not resurrect it. Most of those attending wore their Sunday best rather than ball gowns, though there was a fine enough showing of the local gentry to add luster. If she were this starry-eyed at a country assembly, he could only imagine her reaction at a *beau monde* ball. His imagination immediately leapt to the future. Would she object to their hosting a betrothal ball? And simply think of the pleasure of hosting their first event together in London!

When the second set ended, he escorted the young miss back to her family with a bow and words of gratitude for doing him a great honor. During his walk about the perimeter to return to Lilith and her brother, he struggled to recall the girl's name. For that matter, he could not recall with whom he danced the first set. Lilith nestled in every corner of his mind, distracting him from all else.

Roddam gave a nod, and Lilith lit with happiness. Her eyes brightened. Her cheeks flushed. Her smile widened. If he could be greeted in such a way every day, he would be the happiest man in England. Not long ago, she would have greeted him with a frown, straightened posture, and clasped hands, but now, oh, now, by Jove she must seriously be considering accepting him. One did not greet suitors with this much enthusiasm unless there was an anticipated yes to an unasked question.

Had Roddam had a chance to mention the hall? Walter was undecided if he should propose before or after the trip. He would watch for more signs of her inclination first. When sure of her decision, he would ask.

"You're radiant, my dear Lilith," he said, taking his place by her side.

She tutted but the deepening smile gave her away. "Don't be absurd. I'm no competition to the women here."

"Fishing for a compliment? Very well. You're correct in not being competition because you're in a league of your own."

"Good heavens. I was not fishing for a compliment, but you did well enough to have me pink-cheeked for a week," she said, setting her hand on his sleeve.

"Impeccable timing, then, because I do believe the next set is mine."

He wished every set could be his. The trouble was, etiquette dictated only one set could be danced between the same two people. Two sets signified courtship. Three was a scandal. If her sets had not been reserved already, he would reserve a second set.

Their dance was more sedate than the previous two lively ones, which suited Walter well enough. It offered more opportunity for conversation.

How differently she carried herself compared to the other girls. More becoming. More enticing. She was genuine, and in an age of false façades, such a trait was a marked rarity. There was a poise and a natural grace to her movements he had not seen in the previous two dancers. Her expression revealed unadulterated enjoyment. Such an expression would never be seen at a London ball. Some might consider it gauche, but he found it refreshing and alluring, certainly in comparison to the bored frowns of the other women in the room. Their faces said they had seen better dances. Her face said she would cherish every moment.

The dance at an end, he led her back to Roddam.

The rector was buzzing like a midge at Roddam's side. When the clergyman saw them approach, he cast a reproachful glance at Walter, as though scolding a naughty schoolboy, and walked off before they were halfway across the dancefloor.

Why Walter felt guilty, he could not say. The rector was under the impression Lilith was Walter's mistress, but aside from leaving her cottage alone one day, he had done nothing deserving reproach. Well, he had kissed her on more than one occasion, but never within eyesight of others. All his witnessed actions were of honorable courtship. Why the man should think so ill of them, Walter was at a loss to understand.

Aside from the horridly improper conversation the rector and he had shared at the inn, which had included blackmail and veiled threats, the man irritated Walter. Even while ingratiating himself, Mr. Sands maintained an air of superiority as though he thought himself equal, if not better.

To top off the annoyance, Walter noticed that neither he nor Miss Tollbridge, or whatever her name was, spoke to Lilith, obviously cutting her, a move that would not be missed by those present. And what of Miss Turnkey? Was she uncomfortable with Lilith's change in status with an earl as a brother? Or had the Reverend Sands said something to her? Surely not. That would be a new low for the man to stoop to unfounded rumor.

Shrugging it off, he returned Lilith to her brother, conversed for a brief exchange, then sought his next partner of the evening. Though Lilith did not dance this set, she did dance the set after with Sir Gene.

Following a trip to the refreshments, Walter invited her for their second set together. He had waited to ask to give others the opportunity to solicit her hand, as well as to give Lady Graham a chance to introduce her to possible dance partners, all the while worrying he would not get that so-desired second turn. When he asked and found the set available, he was both surprised and relieved.

Throughout their second set together, he wondered why no one had asked her to dance. Could they not see she was stunning this evening? Or was it they knew her as Miss Chambers and could not accept her as Lady Lilith? Whatever the problem, he could not see it. What he could see was their dancing twice together had drawn a fair bit of attention, as he knew it would. A quick glance around the room revealed no one watched them, but he could *feel* them watching as they whispered behind their fans speculation as to why he singled her out.

This would confirm his courtship. With luck, this would elevate Lilith in their eyes. She was not an aged spinster forgotten in a parish orphanage. She was the daughter of an earl and now the sister of an earl, beautiful, eligible, and wanted by a peer. Yes, he was positive this would do wonders for her reputation and their acceptance of her as Lady Lilith.

For the next two sets, he danced with acquaintances of the Carmichaels, two lovely ladies introduced to him by Mr. Carmichael, one being a neighbor of his and the other being the sister of one of his schoolmates. They each led the conversation with him needing to do little more than respond in the affirmative.

His return to Lilith was remarkably different than when he had walked to her after the second dance of the evening. She did not notice his approach. Her eyes were fixed on the wall across the room, her hands hugging her arms. The bright smile drooped. Roddam had gone to fetch beverages, he assumed, for the man was nowhere to be seen. Before he could reach her to ask what was amiss, Sir Gene stopped him. The man babbled, but Walter's attention was fixed on Lilith.

And then he overheard what Lilith must have been hearing.

A group of young ladies, including his next dance partner, was standing not too far from Lilith, talking about her. He assumed they did not realize their voices carried. He strained to focus on the words above Sir Gene's talk about the fast-approaching autumn foxhunt.

"It's all so lowering," said one voice.

"Everyone knows he's an honorable gentleman. If she compromises him, he'll have no choice," said another.

"She's desperate. No one else will have her. I don't care who her brother is, she grew up in an *orphanage*."

"It's disgraceful how she's putting on airs, as if she hasn't been *working*, no better than a servant. He's fortunate he'll be dancing the next set with me. Ethel told me he's been escorting her around town as a favor to the earl, but I wouldn't put it past her to trap him."

"That's not what I heard. I distinctly recall hearing…"

Walter did not hear the rest for he turned to Sir Gene and excused himself. He bypassed Lilith to interrupt the group. They stopped talking as soon as they saw him. Fans and eyelashes fluttered. His dance partner stepped forward and raised her hand for him to take. He did not take it.

"I do beg your pardon," he said to the young lady. "I must excuse myself from our dance."

Without further explanation, he walked away, going straight to Lilith, formally bowing and raising her hand to his lips.

"Would you care to dance, my lady?" he asked.

She nodded, her smile dim.

Roddam returned with lemonade and a joke, unaware how much both were appreciated. As soon as the other couples took their place, Walter saw Lilith to the dancefloor.

He had behaved badly. He knew it. The ladies knew it. By now, the whole room would know it. And he did not care. He refused to stand by and allow them to berate her while she stood on the sidelines, a wallflower at her first ball, ignored by those she had considered friends and acquaintances. He also refused to dance with someone who would speak so ill of someone else, least of all the woman he intended to marry.

Two dances signified courtship. Three dances scandal. May their tongues wag, for he would marry Lilith regardless.

And so, they danced, Lilith none the wiser to the sins of etiquette he had committed.

Chapter 20

Perched on his mistress' lap, Jasper reveled in the ear rub. Lilith scratched heartily all Jasper's favorite spots, bemused by his thumping leg when she got just the right angle and pressure. For the first time since the ball, she was at peace. There was no place cozier or able to bring her solace than her cottage, though Jasper now contributed to that, however independent and somewhat obstinate he could be when she attempted a command.

If she could stay in her cottage and not face the world today, she would be content.

The assembly had begun with so much promise. Her first ball. Glitz and glamor. Walter in all his splendor. Then there was one cold slap in her face after another, all a brutal reminder she did not belong in that world. Walter enjoyed dinners, parties, balls, and the socializing that went along with it all. How could she be with him when she did not want to put herself through such misery? Belittled, insulted, the brunt of gossip. Even Walter's name had been dragged through the mud in association with hers.

The dilemma now was how would she return to her idyllic life without him? She was not sure she could. She certainly did not want to, but neither did she want to be in his world. They could, perhaps, elope to Italy under an alias and start anew. What an absurdly wonderful idea!

With a smile, she hugged Jasper, who was growing out of puppy size far too quickly for her liking.

"Good morning!" Walter called from the other side of the open stable door.

Setting Jasper down, she turned to Walter with as cheerful a smile as she could muster. Her heart thumped a happy rhythm to see him.

His curls were unruly, his smile warm, his eyes bright. How, oh, how was she to sacrifice happiness with him for a life of contentment all to avoid the ridicule and discomfort of his world? But then, it was not only about her. Association with her would bring nothing but scandal to him and his family. She must think of that if nothing else. She must not be selfish.

"For what do I owe this early greeting?" she asked.

"I'll be escorting you to church, of course."

She laughed. "You're much too early! You do realize my cottage is next to the church, don't you?"

"I do. We shall walk at a snail's pace to enjoy each other's company."

"I've not yet had breakfast, I'm afraid. Care to join me?" She opened the bottom stable door to invite him inside.

"Oh, no, you don't. I'll not have you slaving over the kitchen grate for my benefit. A far better idea is to break our fast at the inn where we may be served by the best." He offered his arm. "Not to mention it will lengthen our walk." He waggled his brows.

"You just prefer Mrs. Hill's cooking to mine," she chided, taking his arm after she gave a fond farewell pat to Jasper, who woofed in indignation to be left behind.

Breakfast was far richer than she made for herself most mornings, but she would not deny its superiority. After the meal, they walked to the church where the parishioners were gathering to greet the Reverend Sands. Ordinarily, she would sit with the orphans, but Mrs. Copeland had relieved her of that duty so that she may sit with her brother. Sebastian, however, would not be joining them.

What she did not expect, though she supposed she ought to have been prepared, was that instead of sitting in the back pews, Walter walked her to the front padded pew where they were to sit with the Grahams. Nothing could have been more uncomfortable. After all her mourning over the whispered gossip at the ball, she was to sit alongside the local gentry. Her mouth grim, her chin high, she braced herself.

All eyes turned her way as she walked on Walter's arm down the aisle and took her seat not far from the pulpit. It was not until they sat that she breathed.

A vision haunted a corner of her mind of members of the congregation pointing fingers and demanding they burn the imposter. However ridiculous the notion, she sat rigidly, her shoulders squared, her hands clasped in her lap, her eyes boring a hole in the pulpit.

Not long did they wait before Harry ascended in his vestments and Geneva gown. With a mischievous glint in his eyes and a nod to the congregation, he began with the reading of the banns.

"I publish the banns of marriage between Miss Tabetha Tolkey of the Tolkeys of Allshire and Mr. Harold Sands of the Sands of Wythburn. This is the first time of asking. If any of you know cause or just impediment why these two persons should not be joined together in Holy Matrimony, ye are to declare it."

Lilith's eyes widened, and her jaw slackened. Good heavens!

Miss Tolkey and Harry? She stared, incredulous. When? Why? How? All the times she had seen them together and heard their names paired came flooding back to her. How had she missed it? Oh, she knew how. He had been so busy trying to convince Lilith to marry him for her brother's money she had not thought it possible he had his eyes on anyone else. But why make it official now? Why not continue to try for the grand prize, especially with Lilith's brother in town to help with the convincing?

Well, however it was, it was done. And what a relief. Now, she did not have to worry about him pressing the matter. Perhaps this was one step in their return to an earlier friendship. Given Miss Tolkey's harsh words, Lilith rather doubted that, but friendship would make living in the village easier.

As if sensing her shock, though he could not possibly understand the reason for it, Walter touched a finger to her wrist. With a half-smile, she concentrated on the sermon that had already begun.

Oh, for the love of teapots, she thought. Harry was on about the importance of marriage again. With so much to think about, it was difficult to concentrate on the sermon. Her focus waned. Harry's voice filtered in and out.

How cruel and unfair for them to be of different worlds. If she were prepared to enter his world, or if he were from her world, it could be their banns read. At this point was it that she did not *want* to enter his world because of the censure and ridicule, or was it that she was *afraid* to enter his world because she knew she would embarrass herself and him in the process? There was far more keeping her from a ready acceptance that she desperately wanted to make, but as much as she qualified her hesitation with thoughts of not wanting him and his family to face criticism, ultimately it boiled down to those two points of sheer selfishness. Was it something she did not want or something she feared?

Though a slender gap separated her body from Walter, she felt his heat and smelled his cologne, familiar, reassuring.

"I warn you of the sin of carnality." The rector's voice boomed. "As we talk of the celebration of two souls joining in the holy union of matrimony, let it not be far from our minds those who partake in sin. An important element separates us from them — marriage. It is the element that ensures our place in Heaven while the others are condemned to hell. Let it not be far from our minds for it reminds us to live virtuous lives and shun the sinners."

Lilith snapped to attention. Good grief. What was he on about?

"Deuteronomy 22:20-28 speaks of this. Sins will be discovered. Sinners cannot deceive the Lord. As the book says, should 'the tokens of virginity be not found for the damsel, then they shall bring out the damsel to the door of her father's house, and the men of her city shall stone her with stones that she die: because she hath wrought folly!' The damsel has played 'the whore in her father's house.'" He paused from his recitation, his head bowed. "Let this be a warning to those who deceive and partake in the sins of the flesh."

Lilith tilted her head to one side. This was quite the departure from his typical sermon. She was not at all sure why he would be preaching the sins of premarital relations, but she did not like it, not after Miss Tolkey's accusation of Walter being her protector.

"'If a man find a damsel that is a virgin, which is not betrothed, and lay hold on her, and lie with her, and they be found,' let me encourage them to act honorably before the Lord or face the consequences, for both parties shall be brought first before the city for mortal judgement and then before God for the condemnation of their souls. Men, choose only the most virtuous of women. Women, be only virtuous. Children, obey your parents. Parents, hold fast to your children. As Leviticus 19:29 tells us, 'Do not prostitute thy daughter, to cause her to be a whore; lest the land fall to whoredom, and the land become full of wickedness.' Among us are the souls of sinners, those who have sinned with the flesh without the bond of matrimony."

The more his voice shook the room, the more unnerved Lilith became. It could not be of *her* that he spoke, for she had not sinned nor was it any of his business if she had. And yet there was something disconcerting about the sermon. Short of breath, she clutched the fabric of her dress.

"Lest we forget the fruit of such labor — illegitimacy. Forgive the children among us, for they know not from whence they came. All others who know the sins of their birth are guilty of deceit, for they have not repented the sins of their blood. Until they do, they wear a cloak of lies, doomed to repeat the sins of their mother. And I read to them Deuteronomy 23:2. 'A bastard shall not enter into the congregation of the Lord; even to his tenth generation shall he not enter the congregation of the Lord.'"

The blood drained from her body.

There was no doubt he spoke of her. But why? Why would he say these wretched things?

Her skin felt clammy. Her pulse raced.

If the sermon did not end soon, she may faint or vomit. Only when Walter placed his hand over hers did she realize how badly she was shaking.

How she sat through the remainder of the sermon, she could not say. After the briefest of civilities between Walter and the gentry, he led her outside and to her cottage, neither speaking a word until they reached the door.

What she did not think about was the sidelong glances from those they passed. She especially refused to think about young Harriette, who had been standing next to her new husband, Mr. Isaac Wimple, and had stared at Lilith with the paleness of shock until their eyes met. The girl had looked away, then. She had deliberately averted her eyes from Lilith.

Lilith felt queasy.

When she opened her cottage door, Jasper leapt at her legs. He whimpered, tail wagging. She could do little more than scratch his neck before she turned to Walter and threw herself into his arms. With a slight hesitation, Walter closed the door behind them.

Though her body shook, and her throat burned, she could not bring herself to cry. What would she cry about, after all? It may not have been a veiled attack. No one else may have connected his sermon to her. The reproachful and curious glances were all likely in her imagination.

Walter wrapped his arms around her. Warm, strong, protective arms. This was where she belonged. With him. And yet she did not. She could not be a baroness. Oh, she could not.

Gripping the front of his coat, she lifted her head from his chest to stare into loving eyes. With an assertive tug to pull him firmly against her, she kissed him, a passionate kiss, full of desperation. She wanted him. In neither world did she belong, but in his arms, she felt complete, wanted, and valued. Sliding her arms about his neck, she pressed herself to him, gripping him tightly.

It was he who pulled away, capturing her wrists in his hands and untangling her arms from his neck. Her wrists still encircled by his long fingers, he took a full step back.

"I'll make some tea," he said.

All she could do was nod. He studied her, long and assessing, then kissed the inside of one of her wrists before releasing her hands to go into the kitchen.

Jasper lay with his belly to the floor, his head on his paws, whimpering. She needed to pull herself together. Closing her eyes, she sucked in deep breaths to calm her spirit. She could not let the rector upset her. Feeling slightly better, she sat by the hearth and patted her lap for Jasper to join. His tail thumped all the way over.

When she had a moment to think, it dawned on her that Walter was in her kitchen. Did he even know how to make tea? She thought not. It would hurt his pride if she gave instruction, so she stroked Jasper and continued to steady her breathing.

After far longer than she should have had to wait for tea, Walter returned with the tray. He even poured the tea. Lilith observed in silence, eyebrows raised, the corners of her mouth twitching in good humor.

Taking the saucer and cup from his outstretched hand, she held the teacup to her lips and allowed the steam to encircle her nose before taking her first sip. A bitter, acrid flavor bit her palate. Grimacing was all she could do to keep from spitting it back into the cup. Walter was not so fortunate.

"Blech!" he said with a hearty laugh. "That is the foulest tasting substance I've ever had the misfortune to drink. Well, dash it all. There go my aspirations to be a parlor maid."

She could not help herself. She laughed along with him. Jasper joined in with a baying bark. This was exactly what she needed.

Setting her saucer and cup on the tray, she questioned, "Dare I ask how long you steeped the leaves?"

He stared blankly. "I was supposed to time it?"

"Well, never mind. It was the thought that counts."

He returned his cup alongside hers and leaned back in the chair. He crossed one leg over the other and propped an elbow against the armrest. "I'm sorry, Lilith. I'm certain today was my fault. I should have said something earlier."

Now was her turn to stare blankly.

"The sermon," he explained. "I believe it was directed to me. I think his calling me a sinner was his way of warning me against you. You see, he approached me the other day."

"Harry? He approached you?" Lilith asked, surprised, though she was more surprised that Walter would think the sermon about *him* when it had all too clearly been about *her*.

Nodding, Walter said, "He wished to know my intentions and suspected they were less than honorable."

"He said that to you?"

"Not in so many words. At first, he tried to bribe me with his silence should I be keeping you as my, er, companion, and then he warned me against using his cottage in sin. I was under the impression he believed you would not reveal the circumstances of your birth and that I would want nought to do with you if I knew. He's a weasel, Lilith, and I hope you don't mind my saying so."

She was appalled and horribly embarrassed. This was just like the rector, though, and she resented his interference. Why was everyone trying to push her in one direction or another? Why could they not all leave her to sort things out for herself?

"What a dreadful thing for him to do," she said. "I would never have thought him capable of so distasteful of words or behaviors. When he was first appointed rector, he was all that was good and kind. He seemed truly to care for his parishioners and have an interest in the less fortunate. We were friends. And I confided in him as my spiritual advisor. It wasn't until last year that he changed. After Sebastian found me. After I confessed both my low birth and Sebastian's desire to set me up financially. If it was the greed that changed him or if he'd always been that way, I can't say. I believe it was the greed."

She heaved a breath, her words having tumbled out in a rush.

"I'm sorry to have put you in this position, Walter. You're already receiving censure because of me. This is just a taste of things to come, I'm afraid. You really ought not to have come here. I'm terribly sorry for everything."

Uncrossing his legs, Walter reached over the tea tray and took her hand in his. He held it even when Jasper licked his hand.

"Come with us to Roddam Hall," he implored. "We could be ready on the morrow, if you wish."

Yes, that was exactly what she needed to do. When she returned, all would have settled down. Yes, she would make peace with her past by visiting the hall and return to the village after the dust settled.

Nodding, she gave Walter a half-smile of consent.

Chapter 21

T he carriage bumped and jostled along the tired road. Walter grumbled to himself. Dashed road made a mockery of a well-sprung vehicle.

They approached Roddam Hall from the southwest, its gatehouse not yet in view. He watched her for signs of recognition. What must she be thinking? Was she nervous or excited to see her childhood home? Would it bring back bad memories or good?

The change of scenery, regardless of memories, would surely do her good. The rector's sermon had unsettled them both, and Walter could not very well propose with that muck on her mind. The hall would provide the perfect backdrop to his offer—a preview of her future as lady of the manor and a union between her past and future.

However it came to be, this visit to Roddam Hall was his final opportunity to propose before they would have to part ways, for he would need to collect his family for the return south, and Roddam would need to return to his wife and daughter.

Ah, they had arrived. At last.

Roddam Hall rose before them as they approached the pebbled circle drive. The façade was similar to Trelowen, though different. His home was smaller, more Tudor, with mullioned windows and a pitched roof.

Conversely, Roddam Hall was remarkably grand, if a little worn, Jacobean, the front façade flanked by two canted bays with oriel windows. The roof was flat and hidden by a parapet.

The front door, a hefty and imposing shield of metal nestled under a bow window, opened as the carriage drew near, a handful of staff filing outside to greet them.

Walter searched Lilith's expression for hints to her thoughts. An invisible veil fell before her face, her eyes shuttered, her lips tight, her feelings indiscernible. Roddam, on the other hand, nearly launched himself out of the carriage before it came to a stop and embraced each staff member as if to greet long-lost friends. Walter could not imagine greeting his staff so exuberantly. It was a little awkward to watch, truth be told.

When the carriage rocked to a full stop, Walter ducked out to hand down Lilith after a groom set down the steps. Jasper beat them both by bolting from her lap and across the gravel to sniff all his new friends. Fleetingly, she looked at Walter in what he was sure was panic. Just as quickly, she shrouded her emotions again and stared at the queue of servants.

Her arms hung at her sides, tucked beneath her cloak, her fingers peeking out as her fists strangled the unsuspecting garment.

Walter offered his arm and courage.

Resting a hand on his forearm, she allowed him to lead her to the awaiting group. The staff watched, each with unreadable expressions befitting their station, except for an elderly woman, stooped with age, gripping the arm of a young footman. The woman smiled unabashedly.

Ambling forward, her feet shuffling against the gravel, the woman stretched out her arms and said, "I never thought I'd see you return."

Lilith halted.

Walter cocked an eyebrow at Roddam, who ignored him.

The woman advanced until she embraced Lilith. Since Lilith's hand still rested on Walter's arm, he did not move except to cover her hand with his in silent strength in case she needed it while facing the ghosts of the past.

Releasing Lilith, the woman stood back and looked up. She was a good three heads shorter than Lilith, emphasized by the rounded shoulders.

"You don't remember me. Of course, you wouldn't. You were only a wee babe."

Walter felt Lilith's fingers digging into his arm. She had not moved or spoken.

The woman shook her head. "Mrs. Hunter is my name. You used to sneak into the kitchen with the little master and steal my biscuits. I've wished for your return home, my lady. I couldn't bear not to be here when I heard His Lordship was bringing you."

Lilith released a long breath and said, "I'm afraid I don't remember, Mrs. Hunter, but it's good of you to come."

Roddam stepped forward to help Mrs. Hunter back to the line of staff and introduced everyone to Lilith, who was relaxing more by the minute.

Though there was only a skeleton crew running the estate, a handful of those who served the previous earl had promised to call over the next few days to see their young mistress returned home, those who had not moved for new positions, retired elsewhere, or died. Roddam confessed to having notified and invited each of them individually and personally.

They entered a semi-circular, galleried vestibule and rested while the butler took their hats and cloaks before handing the garments to an awaiting footman. It was good to be inside and out of the cold autumn air.

Roddam leaned against the main staircase, an impressive wooden structure to the left of the entrance with balustrades carved into the shapes of mythical gods and goddesses. "Shall we meet in the Great Hall in two hours for tea? I can show you both around."

Lilith picked up Jasper, who had been running from each servant back to Lilith, and then back to each servant and looping once more to Lilith. "I would dearly like to rest, yes. But first, could we find a bite to eat for Jasper?"

The butler stepped forward. "If you'll follow me, my lady."

And off they went down a long corridor. It did not take Walter long to find his room, courtesy of a nod in the right direction from a footman. Yes, Lilith was right. A nap was in order.

Lilith could not have napped if she tried.

When she brought Jasper to the kitchen for a snack, she met the new cook and had the opportunity to chat with Mrs. Hunter. Jasper met the cook's companion, an ancient sheepdog, blind, scruffy, and spoiled. Jasper fell in love.

Mrs. Hunter's appearance had been shocking. Lilith remembered her, though not at first. It was the sound of her voice she recalled — a sing-song voice, ever so beautifully aged, a Welsh soprano who had been displaced for too long from her home country.

Lilith had sat in the kitchen for far longer than she planned, listening to Mrs. Hunter's tales of the antics Lilith and her brother would get into when His Lordship was away. If Mrs. Hunter was to be believed, the old servants had missed Lilith and mourned her departure as a child, some believing she had died, others claiming they saw men take her. It was not until the longcase clock struck an hour that she excused herself.

Jasper remained in the kitchen. When Lilith called him to her side, he had looked up at her with pleading puppy eyes as though to beg to stay with his new friend. And so, he had.

Though Sebastian had promised a tour, she roamed the halls with her remaining hour, exploring room after room.

The room she had lingered in the longest had been her father's study. As children, she and Sebastian had been forbidden to enter. Now, she sat in the desk chair and closed her eyes. Lilith inhaled as though expecting the smell of pipe smoke lingering after all these years. Instead of her father's resurrection, she sensed Sebastian's presence in every nook and cranny. In all likelihood, he had renovated to remove any reminders of Tobias Lancaster.

Unspeakable horrors had occurred in this very room after she had been sent away. Sebastian had suffered at the hand of their father.

None of the rooms were recognizable, but there was a sort of familiarity about everything. A feeling when walking down a hallway that she had been there before. A waft of some unnamable scent that rushed a flood of memories.

Everywhere she went, the staff called her Lady Lilith. She did not correct them. There was nothing to correct. In this house, she had always been Lady Lilith. She *felt* like Lady Lilith, however absurd that was when she was herself and had not changed other than to step into the hall.

But there was a sense of homecoming she could not describe.

After twenty-five years, she was home. More than once she recalled 'Bastian's offer. This could be her permanent home, not just in memory. The idea excited but frightened her. And what of Walter? She needed more time, time to recall herself, the lady she was raised to become, and she needed to be here to do it. But how? When? Time was not on her side. If she could lengthen their courtship, delay any offer of marriage, she could come home to find herself, prepare herself for a life with him. The trouble was he would return to Devonshire after this. How unfair to ask him to wait. Would they forever be trapped in this cycle of pursuit, courtship, and delay?

When it came time for Sebastian's tour of the hall, her brother did most of the talking, something he did not often do. His first stop was the portrait gallery.

He guided them along the hall, passing the unfamiliar faces of their ancestors.

"At one time," Sebastian said, "I had most of the portraits removed. Namely, I had the portrait of *him* removed." He nodded at the painting to his left. "Since then, I've had them all restored. I refuse to hide from him. Now, I stand before him, unafraid, proud. Seeing his portrait reminds me of how far I've come." Under his breath, he added, "I could never have reached this point without Lizbeth."

The painting was of a fierce man. A young man. He could not have been more than twenty in the painting, if that. His hair was powdered and curled. He stood propped against a statue, a hand tucked in the opening of his coat. His face startled Lilith, for it was not the face she remembered from childhood. He looked, instead, like a young Sebastian. The crinkles around the eyes were not there, and the skin was pale in comparison to Sebastian's darkened, sun-bronzed complexion, and the build was slight. And yet the face was remarkably that of her brother.

She felt Walter before he spoke. His presence wrapped about her as a blanket of courage.

"Oh, I say, Roddam. If you had not said it was your father, I would have thought it was you in fancy dress."

Sebastian grunted. "Any more of that, and you'll be sleeping in the stables, Collingwood." He followed the threat with a chuckle. "And this is our mother," he said, touching the frame next to Tobias' painting.

Lilith gasped when she saw the portrait. Memories, so many memories bubbled and frothed.

The painting was exactly as Lilith remembered her. The countess looked young and fragile with a diamond-shaped face, pale, nearly translucent skin, a V-shaped hairline low on her forehead — a widow's peak, Lilith had heard it referred to by some — and golden-brown ringlets piled high with a bandeau and tumbling around her shoulders. A low-cut gown of gold adorned her slender frame, though it resembled a classic Greek wrap more than a dress.

The woman in the painting did not smile. She stared into the distance, as though looking into a field beyond the painter's shoulder, her eyes sad and searching. Her cheeks were rouged and her eyebrows darkened as though with charcoal. Her eyes were the most striking. They were painted as coal-black orbs.

"It's her eyes," Sebastian whispered, his voice so close to her ear she nearly jumped sideways. "She's remarkably beautiful. This was, I believe, her wedding portrait."

"When I see her here," Lilith said, "I see the same woman of my memories. And yet if I look at the painting as an unbiased observer, I'm struck not only by her youth but her delicacy."

"You won't know this, Lil', but for years, and perhaps still, rumor had it that he killed her. And perhaps he did. But memory is a funny thing. I recall her fatigue. Fainting spells in the parlor, entire afternoons spent in her sitting room, a perpetual tiredness. Do you think he broke her spirit, or was she...delicate?"

Lilith reached a hand to touch the picture frame. Her mother. Not her mother. Her mother in all ways that were the most important.

Walter spoke up from a few paintings away. "Look who I've found!" he exclaimed, waving them over.

With a lingering look at Jane, she followed her brother.

"Well done, Collingwood." Sebastian barked a laugh. "Of all the paintings in this gallery, you've found the one of me in a dress."

"That is *not* a dress," Lilith scolded. "That is a christening gown. You look quite dashing for a babe."

Walter turned to Lilith with a teasing grin. "You're not too shabby either."

Looking back at the painting, she laughed to see she, too, was wearing a christening gown. Although, the more she looked at the painting, the less sure she was which of the babies was Sebastian and which was her, for they were both black-haired and dark-eyed babes in white, frilly gowns.

Jane, looking none too different than the other painting, was seated, gazing down to the babe in her arms. Tobias stood to her right, staring at the painter, a babe seated at his feet. If the observer did not know the truth, this would look quite the happy family portrait, a loving couple with their two bundles of joy newly christened, although later in life than would have been expected, the seated babe around two years in age.

The earls from centuries past were on down the gallery, including their grandparents, Rothchild and Miranda Lancaster, as well as a considerably young Catherine Lancaster before she married the Duke of Annick. Their aunt appeared to be around twelve in the painting. Though Catherine looked haughty, there was a vulnerability about her eyes. Lilith wondered if the now Dowager Duchess of Annick had retained that vulnerability or if the years had steeled her. She supposed she would never find out. From the mouth of the woman's own son and daughter-in-law, Catherine would not acknowledge Lilith as kin.

The painting of Rothchild sent a shiver down her spine. Though he was pictured holding a bible and cross, he looked anything but godly. He looked positively satanic. There was a sinister gleam in his eyes that the painter had captured with bone-chilling skill. While she could not easily forgive her father for abandoning her or abusing Sebastian, she almost felt sorry for Tobias, as well as his sister Catherine, to be raised by such a menacing-looking man.

"Well," Sebastian said as they reached the end of the gallery, "I must leave the two of you until dinner. I've a long-overdue meeting with the steward. I trust you can entertain each other?" With a wag of his brows, he left before either could answer.

"If I didn't know better," Walter said, turning to Lilith, "I would suspect you are both plotting to compromise me into offering for you. It simply won't do. I'll not be outmaneuvered by crafty siblings."

Lilith smirked when he punctuated his sentence with a wolfish grin. "You're too clever for us, Lord Collingwood. We should return to the ballroom before anyone suspects we're up to mischief."

"Too right, my lady." He offered his arm and directed her down the gallery and to the door on the right. The ballroom.

She halted in the doorway and laughed, the sound echoing in the empty room. "You can't be serious," she protested.

"Be careful what you wish for," he said, leading her into the center.

With a bow, he asked, "May I have this dance?"

"Walter! Don't be silly. We're alone, and there's no music."

"Neither of which is important," he replied.

Taking her hand in his, he promenaded her the length of the room. When they reached the end, he turned to face her, placed both hands on her waist, and spun her in circles until her laughter reverberated.

"You're an absurd gentleman, Walter Hobbs. What am I to do without you?" She spoke in jest, but at her words, he stopped in place and frowned.

"Choose not to be without me?" he asked rhetorically.

Her smile faltered, and she stepped out of his embrace.

They had not yet been at the hall for a full day, and already, she was reminded of their time together at the castle. It had been a private world, a magical world, a world in which reality did not intrude. The trouble was, reality would always intrude.

Their time together at the village proved they were an impossible match. Her illegitimacy would be found out. Her time at the orphanage would make her a laughingstock. Her employment as a midwife would be the height of bitter gossip. Their union would be mocked and ridiculed. His family would lose respect. And with it all, she would lose herself. She could *not* be a baroness.

Lilith walked to the windows overlooking an open arcaded porch, her back to Walter.

"I've been thinking of the women at the assembly," he said.

At such a non sequitur, Lilith glanced back at him.

"I've come to the conclusion," he continued, "they envy you."

She scoffed. "Envy me? In what way?"

"Unadorned by jewels and in dresses that have seen too many years, you exceed their beauty. Without guile, you've attracted the attention of a baron. You're the daughter of an earl. You have lived a life free of complications and expectations from polite society. You've found joy in a simple life. You've earned respect through hard work. I could go on, but my point is, how could they not be jealous? With all their accomplishments, jewels, and bespoke dresses, they have nothing to show for their life. They live under constant pressure from their family to find a husband so as not to be a burden. They have nothing of their own, no trade or talent. They don't know their own minds. How could they not be jealous, Lilith?"

"Ridiculous. Those girls couldn't imagine a life without a maid, a life spent in a pokey little cottage, hearing sermons from the back of the church, wearing the label of orphan, scrubbing their own floors, tending their own fires, sewing their own clothes. I work for a living, you know. None of them want my life. They find me deplorable. They may not know of my birth, but it's enough to know how I've spent my life."

"But you have to admit my version is a possibility."

Tutting, she said, "I'll admit no such thing. No one has or ever will envy me."

He swept a hand through his hair then clasped his hands behind his back. "Sometimes, Lilith, we must convince ourselves of other versions of reality or we'll never make our dreams come true. We'll stay rooted in the same muddy hole. I hope you'll open yourself to dreaming while we're here. Shall I return you to the Great Hall?"

Unsure how to respond, she nodded and followed him.

The morning room was best found by way of the
kitchen. This particular route would be uncommon
for masters and guests, but for a puppy parent, it
was a necessity.

Before Lilith joined Sebastian and Walter for
breakfast, she went down to the kitchen to see how
Jasper fared since he begged to stay the night with
his new friend, Milli the sheepdog. Lilith had been
reluctant, worried he would change his mind in the
middle of the night and not be able to find her and
selfishly not wanting to spend an evening away from
him. He won the argument. The cook assured her he
would be fine.

Jasper greeted her with a happy woof but was
otherwise content to break his fast with Milli.

After stealing him for a snuggle, she joined her
brother in the morning room. Walter had not yet
arrived. Saying she was relieved would not be entirely
accurate. She wanted to cherish every moment with
him as though it were their last, but she did not want
to entangle herself any more deeply than she already
had. She could *not* be a baroness no matter how much
she loved him. Her reception at the Graham dinner
and at the assembly had proven that.

The morning room was a Rococo horror, clearly
the work of their grandfather. Though the room was a
pleasing circular shape with arches and tall windows
overlooking a garden, the décor was outrageously

gaudy. An extravagant marble hearth, a too-wide ornamental, gilded frieze of garlands and volutes, and a stucco ceiling of Pan, masquerade masks, and mythological madness overwhelmed the modestly small space.

Sebastian greeted her with a smile before returning to the letter in his hand. His plate, she noticed, was already empty. As early of a riser as she was, it surprised her that her brother awoke even earlier. Selecting a few items from the buffet, she filled a plate with light fare.

She took the seat next to him, unfolded her napkin, and was about to take a bite when Sebastian said, "Eat. I want us to talk before Collingwood joins us."

Oh dear.

After only a few bites, she pushed away her plate. "Well? I can hardly eat now, and I don't wish to feel rushed."

Sebastian studied her with penetrating eyes. She was always under the impression he could read her thoughts straight to the back of her skull.

"Very well." He folded the letter and added it to a stack of others. "But first, coffee."

Building the anticipation, he refilled his cup. She cringed to watch him drink it black. He took precisely three sips before setting it down with a firm clink.

"I spoke with my steward yesterday. He has been on a mission for about a month."

Hands folded over her napkin, she raised her eyebrows. "A mission?"

"What would you say if I told you I've found your birth mother?"

Her heart seized. Oh, she did not want this. No, no, no, she did not want this.

"I would say that I don't want to know anything about her. I've no wish to reunite with a woman who abandoned me for her livelihood. I understand why she did. I don't need an explanation, and there's no reason to rekindle a relationship I never had. Jane was the only mother I knew, and I'd like to keep it that way."

She twisted her napkin around her hands, kneading it, knotting it, untying it.

"Good. I'm glad to hear it. I hated to disappoint you should you want to meet her since she's dead."

He blurted this out so boldly and so matter-of-factly, Lilith dropped the napkin.

"Oh," was all she could say.

Sebastian waited, watching her as though expecting her to sprout wings.

When it was clear she had no intention of saying anything further, though she was dying to ask a million questions about a woman she had only just said she did not wish to meet, he spoke.

"She died within months of leaving you at the hall. Her father was the old coachman, as you know. Before you wonder, he died a few years ago. One could conclude Lily Chambers never intended to abandon you, not until she discovered she was consumptive."

"Oh," Lilith said again.

How different life would have been. How peculiar life was. How strange the stirrings in her heart to know her mother had not abandoned her but had saved her life. She wanted to grieve for a mother she did not know and only moments ago had rejected.

"Why did you try to find her?" she asked.

"I never intended to search for her. As far as I'm concerned, Jane was your mother just as much as she was mine. After speaking with Collingwood, we felt it best to discover her whereabouts. And in light of the findings, I thought you had a right to know."

"Walter?" she asked, incredulous. "After speaking with Walter? Why would you and Walter wish to know her whereabouts?"

"He was worried about potential scandal. You know I want to introduce you to all of society as my sister, my *full blood* and very legitimate sister. He worried there could be impediments to such a plan."

"Ah, I see. He worried I would embroil him in scandal. What did he plan to do if you found her? Pay her for her silence? Why is it men must always meddle? I have relied on myself my entire life. I do not need or want the meddling of men."

She railed at him, though she could not say why.

It was not so shocking, after all, that Walter worried of a scandal. And she was happy to learn the truth of her birth mother.

But she railed at Sebastian, nevertheless.

If people had left well enough alone. If everyone had left her alone to make her own choices. She would — Well. She would make her own choices, that was what.

Not wanting to say more lest she say something she would regret, she excused herself from the table.

The Great Hall was an overly large drawing room of Rococo brilliance. It was not to Walter's taste, but he could appreciate the stucco and marble mastery. The design was not too different than the morning room.

Roddam had explained over breakfast that before his time, the money had gone into the house rather than to pay the workers or staff, which was one of the many reasons he had inherited a nearly bankrupt earldom, along with barren fields and a house in sore disrepair, a fact in seeming contradiction to the splendor of some of the baroque rooms.

Personally, Walter preferred understated décor. Trelowen was certainly that, at least in comparison to Roddam Hall. After hearing the woes of Roddam's inheritance, Walter was even more grateful his father had hired an exceptional steward. Walter knew from his father that had it not been for his mother's dowry, the Collingwood estate would have faced dark times. In addition to paying enormous debts, the dowry had paid for the hire of a new steward.

It was in the Rococo Great Hall that Walter awaited his fate. He was in trouble. When he refreshed and changed after his morning run, he had found only Roddam in the morning room, reading a stack of letters. Roddam warned him of Lilith's upset. Walter was chagrined. All the same, what was done was done, and he could not see that he had done anything terribly wrong. It was not as though he had wanted to arrange their reunion or had wanted to notify her birth mother of Lilith's whereabouts. On the contrary, he had wanted to ensure the woman would never interfere with Lilith's happiness.

Armed with good intentions, he convinced himself she would not be too angry and would even like to stroll the park with him after she had her say.

Poised in a chair by the window, he held a book he was not reading. She would seek him out when she was ready to confront him. He knew her well enough to wager she would. One leg crossed over the other, he swung a foot.

He did not have long to wait. That was, if someone considered staring unseeing at a book for two hours not long to wait. Who was he fooling? It had been nearly three if he did not round down. A wasted morning if ever he knew one. He would have ridden with Roddam about the home farm if he had known she would avoid him this long.

But no, he was not waiting. He was reading. Engrossed in a book. So engrossed, he lost track of time. He peered at the title page. Yes, an engrossing, page-turning encyclopedia. In French. His thumb wedged between page three and four.

When the door to the Great Hall opened and Lilith entered, he rose from his chair and bowed, the book held to his face.

"Ah, there you are," she said in a firm, clipped voice.

She joined him and nodded for him to sit.

Obeying in gentleman politeness, he sat but did not lower his book. He was engrossed, after all.

He turned a page.

Only fleetingly did he glance around it when she cleared her throat. She said nothing, and so, he returned to a careful study of a half-page image detailing decorative niches and pediments.

"You had no right," were her opening words.

Peeking over the top of the book, he was greeted by a furrowed brow, piercing dark eyes, and a grim mouth. It did not take a mind reader to realize she was more upset than he had expected. In hindsight, he knew he had made the wrong decision to enquire after her birth mother. And now, all he wanted to do was grovel for forgiveness. But had it been so terrible to want to help her? No, he had not made a wrong decision; rather, he had gone about that decision incorrectly. He should have spoken with her first.

Walter set the book in his lap and opened his mouth to speak, but she held up a hand.

"It was not your business to find my birth mother. If I had wanted to find her, I would have done so myself."

He started to speak again, and she once more held up a staying hand.

"I *am* pleased now that it is done, as I can put a great many things to rest with the news, but you are *never* to interfere with my life without my permission."

"I never intended to—"

"Don't you dare say you didn't plan to interfere. You did. Intentionally. You set out to save yourself from the scandal of allying with a *bastard*. I think you the worst sort of hypocrite. You've insisted to me on numerous occasions you're not daunted by the possibility of scandal, and yet you've gone behind my back to ensure my past doesn't scandalize you."

Uncrossing his legs, he leaned forward, agitated, desperate to defend himself. This was not at all going how he had expected.

"It was not about me I worried, Lilith. I didn't want *you* haunted by the past."

She laughed harshly. "Liar. What do I care about scandal? It's your family who would suffer. I don't blame you. In all likelihood, I might have done the same thing. But this *is* my life, and you will not make decisions for me."

"This isn't fair," he defended. "I've—"

She cut in. "If you're only interested in me as Lady Lilith, you can leave. Has this all been a game to you? You thought you could land yourself an earl's daughter with a sizable dowry thanks to her brother? Am I so easy a catch to you? The aging spinster no one else wants? If only I would lie to the world that I'm legitimate, you could have money enough to fulfill all your philanthropic dreams while I'm left to rot in a drawing room serving prissy women endless cups of tea and conversation about the weather. Is that it? Are you so similar to Harry Sands?"

"Oh, I say, Lilith. This is—"

"I invited you to Allshire to see *me*. To see my life. To see who I am and what I must contend with in your world. If you've only been interested in the hope I will deny my illegitimacy, you need to leave me be. I've no idea what I will decide, but that decision must be mine, and I will make the one right for me."

Her accusations were devastating. She could not for a minute believe those things, could she? Had the rector led her to believe that of him? Lilith went ever so slightly out of focus. He blinked rapidly, not daring to cry over a trifling misunderstanding. Trouble was, it did not feel so trifling.

"Lilith," he said softly, begging her silently not to interrupt. "If you want me to shout from the rooftops that your grandfather was a coachman, I'll do it. I don't care. And you know I don't care. When the time comes, and it doesn't have to be this minute, but when the time comes for you to choose, I want you to choose without fear. Please, understand, it's *you* I'm thinking of, not me. I know how you're treated.

I've seen it. I don't want you to worry they'll do that in spades. I swear to you on everything I hold dear; I've only thought of you."

She heaved a sigh and slumped against the back of the chair. "I know," she whispered.

They stared at each other for a time. Her face was pale and drawn. He had a world of words, but they all sounded nothing short of begging.

"This has to be my decision, Walter, and by my own making," she said, tucking a loose strand of hair behind her ear. "If I want to enter society as Lady Lilith, then I will find a way to do it. I need you to support whatever choice I make, even if that's to return to Allshire as the humble Miss Chambers. Men have done nothing but meddle. My father, the rector, even my brother, and now you. Everyone has made decisions about my life, forcing me here and forcing me there, never giving me a choice. *I* need to decide where I belong."

Lilith folded her hands in prayer and pressed the tips of her middle fingers to her lips. "I need you to understand, Walter. I need you to understand the battle I'm fighting. I want you to know that this has nothing to do with you or how I feel about you. And it has nothing to do with my illegitimacy. Yes, that complicates matters, but at this point, it does not affect my decision."

He felt a horrid sense of foreboding, as though she had already made her decision and was finding a way to let him down lightly. His fingers curled in a fist so tight, his trimmed nails dug into his palm.

"The trouble is," she said, "I've led an unreliable life, always being uprooted, never knowing my place.

I have spent my adult years fighting to create a place and create reliability. I've worked harder than you can imagine to achieve respectability and make a home for myself. I may not earn much, but what I do earn is from hard work, talent, and personal satisfaction. I could drop everything and move in with Sebastian if I wanted. But that's not the point. The point is how hard I've worked to create a life I love. Choosing to leave that life is frightening beyond words. I would be starting all over."

He was about to interrupt, remind her of some of the ideas they had exchanged, but she continued talking.

"Beyond that, I don't know if I can put myself through the treatment of people like the Carmichaels. At the ball, I stood there with a stiff upper lip because it was the thing to do, but every word was a dagger to my heart. You cannot know what it's like. Everyone loves you. You cannot know what it's like to be publicly ignored or publicly mocked. Have you ever had someone move to the other side of the street to avoid you? I have. These are the things with which I must contend in making my choice."

"Would life with me be so miserable?" he asked, his voice cracking, his fingers aching.

"That's not what I'm saying. What I'm saying is I don't know if I can handle the burdens of your station. If I steel myself enough, it could be possible, but I haven't decided. The instability and unforeseeable frightens me. I…I need more time."

He nodded, hanging his head, not sure if this was the end or the beginning. They still had a couple of days at the hall. He had not yet proposed. There was still time. The news of her mother had been emotional, and his involvement in the search had been a blow. With a bit more time, she would come around. He was not sure what he would do if she did not.

"Do you like your room?" she asked.

He looked up, surprised by the change of topic. A bit of color had been restored to her cheeks, and she tried to smile.

"Good. It's large. Overlooks a topiary garden. Dashed room has a name," he said with a feigned laugh to match her forced smile. "The Zeus Room. Silliest thing I've ever heard."

Her smile almost appeared genuine when she replied. "I'm in the Hera Room."

This time he did laugh. "Are you really? Your brother has quite a sense of humor."

The moment died just as quickly as it began. Walter had a terrible churning in his gut that this was the beginning of the end.

The evening brought rain, a light patter on the window that both relaxed Lilith and kept her from sleep, quite the contradiction.

Nestling under the bedcovers, she shivered and rubbed her feet together for warmth. With the rain came even colder temperatures, the sharp wind finding its way through every window seam. At least she had the benefit of a fire to warm the room. A warming pan had even been tucked in the sheets by a concerned servant before Lilith went to bed.

But it was not the cold that had her chilled. It was contradictions.

Oh, not about the rain, but *other* contradictions. Her dreams for her life.

On one hand, she lived a safe and secure life doing what she loved — helping women who had nowhere else to turn. This was her trade, her talent, her passion.

On the other hand, she wanted to belong somewhere, truly belong, and maybe, if her age was not too far advanced, have a family of her own.

How contradictory, how dichotomous to have to sacrifice one for the other. She could not have both.

Here, everything felt right. The estate, the people, the status, the beau — it all felt right. Frighteningly right. It all felt like *home*. As ecstatic as she should be by this revelation, as much as this should reverse the decision she had already subconsciously made before leaving Allshire, she experienced more fear than comfort. All her searching to find her place of belonging, and all she wanted to do was hide from it.

It was not that she was inadequate for the position of Lady Lilith. That was not her deepest fear. Her fear was the unknown. What frightened her most was not the darkness but the light. She had only ever known darkness.

If she embraced the unknown, made a new life for herself, how long before it was ripped away? She could not belong where she was unwanted. Aristocrats did not want her among their numbers. Society would turn on her, just as it had at the village assembly, just as her father had. Society would shatter her dreams.

And then she would be left with nothing.

Instead of her revelation changing her decision, it solidified it. She wanted to run to her cottage and hide. If she could restore the innocence of life from before her brother discovered her... If she could restore the contentedness and simplicity...

Chapter 22

The mud made soft sucking sounds in protest of Lilith's half-boots. The rain pitter-pattered against her umbrella. The shower from the previous evening continued through the next morning, a light drizzle that annoyed more than ruined plans. She linked arms with Sebastian, who bore the rain against his tricorn and greatcoat in manly stubbornness.

What she had seen so far of the park had brought back more memories than the inside of the house. Outside had been forbidden. As such, she and Sebastian had spent most of their time sneaking outside to frolic in the gardens, stomp through the woods, and roll on the sandy beach.

Her brother had promised a stroll to the coast in the afternoon if the rain stopped. She ardently hoped it stopped by then.

Burrowing into her mantle for warmth, she tightened her grip on the umbrella. The cold bit her knuckles despite gloves. Trailing behind them was Jasper, a muddy, smelly mess of wet and happy dog. He had insisted he join them and would not take no for an answer. Victorious, Jasper dashed here and there to sniff everything in sight.

"We're here," Sebastian said, veering towards a small church. "The rectory is through those trees.

Though I offered the east wing to the steward and his family, he prefers the old rectory. Since it's occupied, it's a good thing we didn't invite our favorite rector, Mr. Sands."

Lilith pinched his arm.

Instead of entering the ancient family church, they walked around the back to the burial plots.

All morning, even through breakfast, she had remained downstairs, talking with the old servants who had come to see her. They came as a group, all eager to see her grown and returned home. There were only seven of them, including Mrs. Hunter. But seven was more than she had imagined would remember her, want to see her, or make the trek to talk with her.

There on a kitchen stool with a handful of servants, sharing stories, though mostly listening, she felt total comfort without needing to prove herself. The feeling was not so different than when she was with Walter. They all hoped she would stay or return soon to live at the hall. Lilith was tempted, but how to do so without refusing Walter? It was beyond selfish to beg for yet more time so she could live at the hall for a few months. All the same, she was tempted by their pleas.

Arm in arm, she and her brother stopped at a wooden cross, rotted by time.

"Here lies Jane Lancaster," Sebastian said, "mother to a brooding devil and an orphan."

Lilith smiled ruefully at him.

Together, they stood, staring at the cross, listening to the rainfall and Jasper's occasional baying bark or snuffle when he found an interesting smell.

How was it she could miss so dearly a woman she had not thought of since childhood? She wondered how she could have forgotten her. Although, that was not entirely true. She had never forgotten her mother. It was not so simple. She had pushed the memories deep inside hoping never to think of them again, those people who must have hated her to send her to an orphanage. How wrong she had been. Since that discovery, she searched for and clung to every memory she could find.

"I want to mark her place with a headstone," Sebastian said. "A memorial statue would not be out of the question."

"Why is there not a headstone?" Lilith glanced around the churchyard.

"Honestly, Lil'? I don't know. Why our father never marked her grave is anyone's guess. He was destitute? He didn't care? He was a boor? He's dead, so let's celebrate her, shall we? A headstone she would like, though nothing too lavish. She never struck me as a lavish person. But what do I know? I was a child. You spent far more time with her than I did."

Lilith patted his arm. "Yes, something simple."

Jasper sloshed his way through the drizzling rain to stand by them.

"'Bastian?" She questioned softly.

"Hmm?" He grunted, his eyes fixed on the wooden cross.

"Although this is a family burial, would you be terribly opposed if we added a memorial for Lily Chambers?"

He leaned back to look at her, as startled by her words as she was by saying them.

It seemed the right thing to do.

Wrapping an arm around her shoulders, he said, "Of course, we can. I'll have the steward order both when I meet with him today. Speaking of which, we should turn back, as he's supposed to meet me at the top of the hour."

They headed back to the hall, his arm still around her shoulders, her umbrella knocking into his hat from time to time. They walked in companionable silence until the house came into view.

Sebastian said, "I've asked Cook to serve me humble pie for causing a rift between you and Collingwood."

Lilith cast him a sidelong glance.

"I should never have searched for your birth mother without your express permission. But since I did, I should have waited until all was settled between the two of you before saying something. Far be it for me to come between you and love. Don't hold my errors in judgement against him. He's a good man. And if I'm not mistaken, he's very much in love with you."

She flushed under the umbrella and turned away from him. "He's a foolish man to think it could ever work between us."

"I was under the impression you were as much in love with him."

"Love has nothing to do with anything," she protested. "Men see the world in black and white. This decision has little to do with love or marriage and all to do with how I live my life. Do you not realize, 'Bastian, it has not yet been a full year since I learned I'm your sister? The life I've known for over twenty years has changed dramatically this year. I've hardly resolved what to do about it all when in comes Baron Charming, charging on his noble steed to sweep me off my feet. Yes, Sebastian, I'm in love with him. I love him deeply. It does not follow, however, that I'm ready to uproot everything I've known."

"A long engagement, perhaps? Ask him to wait? Move in with us or move into Roddam Hall until the Season, then see how you feel? What are you thinking, and how may I help?"

"I need time. I don't want to leave him waiting, though. That seems cruel. What if after all the waiting, I decide I would rather never marry? No, I need to decide soon so I can accept him or let him go. It's only fair to him."

"You know I'll support any choice you make. All I ask is that you not underestimate yourself. I worry your esteem is as caught up in that orphanage as mine was in the ghost of my father. You're remarkable, Lilith. I want you to see that in yourself. Don't let the past hold you back."

She nodded but did not answer.

"Horsey!" squealed the little boy, pulling fistfuls of Walter's hair.

"Neeeeeeeigh," responded Walter, doing his finest horse impression before sipping the world's tastiest and most invisible tea from a teacup.

A little girl with carrot-red ringlets snatched the teacup from him just as it reached his lips.

"No! I need to refill it," she said, turning the teapot upside down to dump invisible tea into his cup.

"Go, horsey! Go!" screamed the boy straddling Walter's neck before kicking at his shoulders to spur the mount.

Walter sat at a child-sized table in the nursery, having tea with three girls of varying ages, the youngest still in nappies and sitting on his knee, shaking an empty cup over his lap — thank heavens for make-believe tea. A boy of about two years thought Walter the perfect horse substitute, while an older brother rode an ancient rocking horse.

The nursery was neither a dusty space nor a renovated space. Walter suspected it looked much like it had the last time Lilith had lived there, though it seemed the maids kept it well dusted and clean.

He was not entirely sure how he got himself into his current mess, but he had no one to blame but himself. The steward had arrived with his children. When the butler saw the steward to the study to await Roddam's return, Walter volunteered to take the children upstairs to play. What had he been thinking?

The youngest, bored with tea, threw the cup to the floor and scooted off his knee to grab a doll. It was in the moment one of her sisters climbed onto Walter's back to ride the horsey with her brother and Walter's submission to crawl on all fours across the floor, ruining a perfectly good pair of breeches, that Lilith chose to open the nursery door.

The look on her face would have been priceless had he not felt every bit as prized an idiot as he looked.

Walter, feeling his face grow warm with embarrassment, tried to stand up, forgetting the children on his back. With a yank of hair, the boy screamed for Walter to go faster, thinking his horse had bucked as part of the ride. And so, Walter galloped faster, or rather crawled at top speed. Lilith watched, her hand held to her mouth, her eyes wide.

Not one of his finer moments.

He traveled a circle about the tea table. When he made his final loop to look up at Lilith, she was gone, the nursery door closed behind her. Had she left from the horror of seeing a gentleman crawling on the floor with children? Had she left because she was still angry with him? Had she been upset that her childhood nursery had been invaded?

"Gooooo!" screeched the boy.

Urging the girl off his back, Walter reached up to pull the boy from around his neck, an action that resulted in a kicking, screaming tantrum. All was forgiven when Walter put him on the horse with the elder brother. He rubbed the back of his neck and stretched. His breeches were wrinkled and stockings scuffed. Could have been worse, he decided, and not bad enough that his valet would resign at the sorry sight of the clothing.

"Baby go sleep," said the toddler holding up a baby doll.

She pointed to a doll bed in the corner.

Walter took the doll and cradled it as though it were real, making the girl smile. "Shall we put baby to sleep?" he asked.

With a nod, she half waddled, half scooted across the floor to the doll bed and patted it. He obeyed like a good nanny. Heaven help the real nannies of the world, especially when they had to contend with five children at once, all under the age of seven.

As he put the baby doll to sleep, the girl rocking the bed with alarming vigor, the nursery door opened again, and in ran a wet Jasper followed by a shaggy sheepdog, and shortly thereafter, the love of his life. The children shouted and squealed and screeched, dropping dolls and horses and teacups to run or waddle over to the dogs. Jasper licked the baby until she fell over giggling. The other children tried to climb onto the skittish sheepdog.

"Now, now, be gentle. Milli is old and blind," Lilith said, kneeling next to the sheepdog. "You must pet her so she knows you're there and then ask her permission. Adding a hug might help your case."

The children, except the youngest, who was busy pulling on Jasper's ears and being licked for her efforts, gathered around Milli and petted and cooed and hugged. It seemed to have done the trick, for the sheepdog lolled her tongue in what might have been mistaken for a dog grin, and let the children climb on her back.

Lilith smiled up at him, looking nearly as relaxed and cheerful as she had when he first arrived in Allshire. He ran a hand through his knotted hair, chagrined at how unruly he must look. Good Lord. Even his cravat was crooked and halfway around his neck.

Walking over, he took one of the child-sized seats at the tea table and sat next to Lilith, grinning at her.

Her smile sly and teasing, she said, "I never thought I would see a proper toff galloping about a room neighing and whinnying."

"It's one of my greatest talents, didn't you know? Wins over the ladies every time."

Lilith threw back her head and laughed.

Yes, this was more like it. He loved when she laughed.

The one in nappies tried to mount Jasper, who was none too sure about that. As Lilith reached for Jasper, Walter scooped the little girl into his arms and flew her about the room, the child dissolving into giggles. It was not until he was on his third trip around the room, when he turned back to see Lilith pulling the eldest girl onto her lap with a book in hand that Walter was struck by the domesticity of the scene — the two of them in a nursery, playing with children who could very well be their own in an alternative reality.

When she looked up at him with tender affection, he almost went down on one knee with a babe in his arms to ask her right then and there. The presence of the children distracted him from the temptation, as did the memory that their most recent discussion had been a quarrel.

It was in this frame of mind that he remained throughout another half hour of play and on through their returning of the children to the departing steward and the dogs back to the kitchen. The rain had stopped, though it could never have been classified as rain, only a light drizzle. Roddam invited them for a cloudy walk to the coast after he changed into something more suitable. For such a destination, Walter, too, needed to change, aside from his scuffed knees being an ever-present embarrassment of dishevelment.

Roddam took the stairs two at a time. Walter was more sluggish, too busy admiring Lilith standing in a shadowed corridor of the vestibule. After a second's hesitation, he approached her.

Simultaneously, they said, "I'm sorry," then chuckled.

As he started to apologize again, she put a finger to his lips. "No, allow me, Walter. I'm sorry for snapping at you yesterday. You didn't deserve such harshness. You did what you felt to be right, and it was a noble gesture, even if I couldn't see it at the time."

He reached up to capture her hand in his, folding it over his heart.

"Don't apologize, Lilith, for speaking your mind. I don't believe in harboring unspoken words. It's how misunderstandings start and hurt feelings lead to deeper pain. I wish every day I had told my father I love him. Don't hold back, Lilith."

He meant the words to bring peace between them after the argument, but her brows furrowed, and her eyes darkened. The longer she frowned, the longer he smiled. He was grasping a thinning thread between them. He could feel it.

Sliding her hand out from under his, she cupped his cheek before kissing him. It was a soft kiss, chaste, a tender pressing of moist lips. She looked into his eyes as she did it. He did not blink or close his eyes. Tentatively, he palmed her waist. As if spurred by his touch, she leaned against him.

Though they stood to one side of the vestibule in a darkened corner, it was too public a place for an embrace. All the same, he gave into the moment. Closing his eyes, his mouth met hers. She twined her arms around his neck.

A door shutting in the distance brought Walter back to reality. They parted, she looking flushed, her eyes bright.

"I've not yet changed," he muttered, self-conscious of the fleeting time before Roddam would return.

She smiled shyly and said, "Hurry back. I want to show you my beach."

Turning on his heel, he raced up the stairs with renewed spirit. It felt rather like yesterday had not happened. She still wanted him. There was still a chance. He rehearsed his proposal all the way back to his chamber.

The storm raged outside the carriage, wind rocking Lilith across the hard seat. The faces of the two men across from her were darkened by the night. Lightning lit only their tricorns and greatcoats. Thunder cracked.

Lilith screamed. The two men did not respond. Their bodies swayed with the carriage. She screamed, her voice hoarse from hours of calling for help. She called for her mother. Where was her mother? Who were these men?

With another clap of thunder, the carriage jolted and slid, slamming Lilith's body against the carriage door, knocking her unconscious.

When she came to, she was in the arms of one of the men, rain blinding her to all but the tip of his hat, outlined with each lightning flash. Kicking her feet and pummeling her fists, she wriggled free, falling to the mud at his feet. Slipping and staggering, she regained balance and set off at a run only to be grabbed by a vise-like fist and dragged against the man.

She flailed, screaming for her mother, screaming for her brother. Where was Sebastian? Why did he not come for her?

A church loomed ahead. Blessed be. She was saved.

The church door opened to a plump woman who ushered her inside. The man released his grip. Lilith hurled herself at the woman, grabbing ahold of her apron for safety.

Smiling down at Lilith, Mrs. Brighton welcomed her home. No, no, this was not home. No, no, no. Lilith turned back to the church door and the rainy night, screaming for her mother and brother. The door slammed, shutting her in darkness.

Scrambling for the door handle, Lilith felt her way down a stone corridor until the cold metal was in her grasp. Wrenching the door open, she ran outside, only it was not a rainy street into which she ran, but her nursery back home.

She was home! Glory be. She was home!

A man, his back to her, stood in the middle of her nursery. He turned.

Walter. Oh, thank the Lord, Walter would know how to find her mother and brother. He would help her. He stood before her, assuring her she was safe.

In his arms, he cradled a baby. Though he did not say so, she knew the baby was hungry. She needed to feed him. Their child? Of course, it was their child! A baby boy. She was home. She was safe.

Smiling, she walked over to Walter and reached for their son.

Walter snatched the baby out of her reach, spitting on her in disgust. His features contorted until the face of her father stared back.

Pointing a gnarled finger, he howled in Walter's voice but with Tobias's face, "Away from my son, devil's spawn!"

She turned to run, but every turn she made, he stood before her, pointing and repeating, "Devil's spawn!"

Over and over the face of her father and the voice of Walter screeched at her. The baby looked up from his swaddling. It was her brother. He pointed a chubby finger and howled, "Devil's spawn!"

Covering her ears with her hands to shut out the howling, she closed her eyes and ran blindly. The nursery door slammed behind her.

Lilith awoke at the clap of thunder, sitting bolt upright, clawing at the bedsheets. Her body shook, her teeth chattering. It took long minutes to remember where she was and to convince herself she was *not* dreaming this time. Another clap of thunder. Pulling the covers up to her chin, she shivered.

Thunder shook the room. Lightning brightened the space. Wind howled.

One deep breath after another, she tried to calm herself. Though she was awake, the groans and creaks of the house frightened her, sounding ever so much like footfalls in the hallway. She pulled her knees to her chest. She did not believe in ghosts. She did not believe the sounds were the footsteps of her father. They were only sounds of the storm. Hugging her knees, she tried to steady her thumping heartbeat.

She was safe. She was home. She was a grown woman. Her father was dead. She did not believe in ghosts.

Walter. She focused on Walter. He was in the Zeus Room in the bachelor wing. Down the corridor, up one flight of stairs. She was safe. Walter was only one corridor and one flight of stairs away.

She remembered, then, as she gulped in breaths and shivered from fear more than cold, she had made her decision. She fell asleep thinking about her decision. The decision had been final and con-fidence-building, but now she was afraid, so very afraid. Terrified. What if she made the wrong choice about her future?

Another clap of thunder, another creak of the floorboards.

She threw off the bedcovers and fled the room, leaving the unlit candle in her wake.

Chapter 23

By the time she reached the Zeus Room, the panic had subsided. The storm had not. Lilith stood outside Walter's bedchamber, staring at the door, caught in limbo. Each time she reached a hand to knock on the door, she stopped herself. What was she doing here?

Fear had taken hold of her moments ago. Fear of abandonment, fear of judgement, fear of solitude, fear of everything. She knew nothing but desperation to be held and loved.

And now?

She had made her decision, though she could not say if it was the right choice. What would going to him now accomplish other than to complicate matters?

It would unite them forever. It would bring unforgettable love to her life. It would replace all negative memories of Roddam Hall with a single, perfect memory. It would be the first moment in her life when she was wanted, loved, and needed. With this action, she could walk boldly to her decision without regrets.

Her eyes closed, the door handle in her hand, she prayed he would not reject her. Hoping the door was not locked, she pushed the handle.

The door gave way.

Her heart in her throat, her breathing shallow, Lilith entered, shutting the door behind her with a decisive click. As her eyes adjusted to the room, darkened by the closed curtains, she heard a stirring before her, though some distance away, a rustle of sheets.

"Who's there? Is something amiss?" Walter asked groggily.

Lilith leaned against the door, her hand still on the handle. She stood in silence, unable to respond. What was she doing here? Walter rustled his way across the bed to the bedside table.

One part of her wanted to open the door and run before he saw it was her. Let him think he had been dreaming. The other part shivered and longed to be held.

He swung his legs to one side of the bed, fumbling to light the candle. She could scarce breathe. Anticipation heightened her senses.

Light arced across the room, momentarily blinding Lilith. She squinted.

"Good Lord. Lilith? Is that you?"

She heard Walter rise from the bed, her eyesight still adjusting.

"What's wrong? Are you unwell? What's happened? Is there a fire? Flooding? A roof cave-in?" His questions tumbled one after the other as he walked to her.

Only when she felt warm hands grip her upper arms did she look up, his outline blocking the candlelight. He had donned a banyan. She blinked, her eyes focusing. The side of his face wore creases from his pillow, his curls on that side flattened. The light behind him cast a halo around his head. Walter. Her angel.

He gave her a gentle shake. "Lilith? What's wrong? You're shivering, and your eyes are red-rimmed. What happened?"

"I...I need you to hold me," she stuttered.

"Pardon?"

When she did not immediately answer, he untied his dressing robe, slipped it off his shoulders, and wrapped it about her instead. The robe was warm from his heat and smelled of him, of that delicious cologne he wore. She burrowed into the banyan.

"Sit. I'll ring for help." He turned to the bell pull.

"No!" she shouted, louder than anticipated, startling them both. "No, I don't need help. I need you."

She stepped further into the room. He crossed his arms over his chest, wearing nothing but a night-shirt that stopped below his knees. His legs and feet were bare.

"Lilith, you look as though you've seen a ghost. You're pale and shaking. Will you sit and tell me what's wrong?"

Seduction was not her forte, it would seem. Not that this had been planned. Oh, she really ought to have made a run for it when she had the chance.

"Please hold me, Walter. I want to be held."

A crease etched between his brows. "I'm not certain that's the best course of action. Allow me to ring for help or escort you back to your room."

She shook her head. "Please hold me," she repeated.

When he did not move, she took a step forward and held out a hand. He stared at it.

Thunder rumbled. Wind whispered from the chimney, the fire in the grate a mere memory from hours earlier.

Squaring her shoulders in determination, she closed the space between them and wrapped her arms around his waist, resting her cheek on his shoulder, her forehead against the side of his neck. She tightened her embrace, breathing in his cologne until his arms came around her and held her.

Neither spoke.

In this moment, there was nothing she wanted more than to be loved by him. She wanted him. She needed him. She feared never seeing him again. She feared facing the rest of her life never having known him.

Lifting her head, she puckered her lips against the side of his neck. At his sharp intake of breath, she kissed his neck again, a slow and sensual trail up to his jaw. No longer did her body shiver, rather it flamed with a hot passion, a need to know the man she loved.

"Lilith," he said, his voice cracking. "You need to return to your room."

Ignoring him, she stepped back to remove the banyan. A shrug of shoulders freed the robe to fall to the floor.

Their eyes met. Twining a hand around his neck, she raked her fingers through his hair and kissed him. Though his lips yielded to hers, his body remained rigid with tension. He would not be so easily persuaded.

"Lilith," he said again. "I need you to return to your room."

Winding his curls about her fingers, she angled her head to kiss him more thoroughly, tasting the sweet evidence of sleep on his lips.

"Lilith," he said, the name muffled against her kiss.

Before he could say more, she sealed his lips with hers and dragged her fingers down his back until he tremored. Gathering a fistful of his nightshirt, she tugged it upwards.

He shuddered a laugh and grabbed her wrist, stepping back and away from her. Frantic, she reached for him, but he grabbed her other wrist, gripping them both securely.

"Tell me you're certain, or I'm taking you back to your room."

He regarded her in the candlelight, his eyes searching hers before sweeping over her to take in the loose tresses of her hair flowing around her shoulders and down her back.

"I want to be with you," she said.

The hesitation that followed was, Lilith thought, only from his making sense of her words, interpreting their meaning as more than she intended, but she would not think on that or say more. What she said she meant.

In a breathtaking movement, he released her wrists and hooked an arm behind her knees, scooping her into his arms and carrying her to the bed. She felt weightless and safe and giddy. He was the most gloriously beautiful man she had ever seen, and he loved her. In no hurry to release her, he angled her in his arms to kiss her eyelids, her nose, and her cheeks.

Rubbing his nose against hers, he whispered, "You rob me of breath, my love. You're beautiful."

He spoke the truth. She knew it. His voice revealed his sincerity.

She could do no more than stutter a sob in reply. Here, in his arms, she found everything she had ever wanted, a place of belonging. She wanted to be a part of him and he a part of her. She wanted them to be one, body and soul, connected, two parts of a whole, so she could never be abandoned again. She wanted to belong.

He watched her sleep. His arm pillowed her head, frizzed hair spilling over her shoulders and onto the actual pillow, tickling his hand, which had gone numb some time ago. Her legs were tangled with his, and one of her hands splayed over his chest, hot and clammy. She had fallen asleep soon after their coupling. He had not.

How could he sleep? He was wide awake, watching her, so in love he could burst.

Her words echoed. *I want to be with you.*

She wanted to be with him. She had made her decision. Despite potential scandal of her birth, gossip of her upbringing, loss of her midwifery and teaching positions, and all other sacrifices, she had chosen to be with him. He wanted to weep with joy. He would do all in his power to ensure she never regretted her decision. He would introduce her to the wives and sisters of his friends, people he knew would accept her and love her. Did she have any friends? He thought not. What she needed was a friend or two to help her navigate polite society.

She stirred, her eyelids fluttering.

As her eyes focused on him, her mouth formed an O of surprise, and then, as though remembering the evening, she blushed and looked altogether beautifully bashful. The candle had not yet burned out, though it had begun to gutter, casting long shadows about the room.

Where they were not touching, the chill of the room crept and tingled, raising gooseflesh over the backs of legs and hips. Everywhere they linked, sweat pooled. He thought briefly of pulling up the covers and drawing the curtains around the bed. But he dared not move. The moment was perfect.

With his free hand, he swept unruly black strands from her face, tucking them behind her ear. She stretched and nuzzled closer, draping an arm over his waist.

"I love you," he said, his tone smiling.

She inched closer, as though trying to crawl inside of him.

Nudging her head into the crook of his neck, she whispered, "And I love you."

Smiling, he drifted to sleep.

After sleeping for an hour, perhaps longer, Walter woke before Lilith. It was strange sleeping next to someone. There was an awareness of not being alone, a vulnerability Walter would not have expected. The sensation was not unpleasant, simply unusual. Never had he slept next to someone.

The air had become chilly, and he had pulled the sheets over them. She was curled on her side, her knees drawn to her bosom, her back pressed to his chest. His arm wrapped around her, their fingers laced.

He would need to wake her soon. Well before dawn, the maid would enter to stoke the fire. Though his valet would not enter the bedchamber, Kory would attend to business in the adjacent dressing room to prepare for Walter's morning ritual. Servants would begin milling about the halls. His time with Lilith was limited. She needed to be in her room well before anyone stirred. Not that he worried about their being compromised so much as he respected her privacy and reputation. There had been enough nose-thumbing at propriety in Allshire. He did not want to validate gossip or have the servants in her childhood home think poorly of her.

It was the change in her breathing that clued him to her wakefulness. She did not move, but her breathing shallowed, and her body tensed. Though he knew she was awake, she gave no indication to him she had awakened, almost as though she were trying to discern if he was asleep. Smiling at the back of her head, he tightened his hold on her, pulling her to him.

Walter nuzzled his nose into her hair until he found her neck. He kissed it. Inhaling the scent of her, he enjoyed the mingling of soap, herbs, and sweat.

"Oh, you're awake?" she asked, turning over to lie on her back, angling her head to face him.

"I am," he said, smiling contentedly. Running the backs of his fingers down her cheek, he said, in case she had forgotten since the first time, "I love you." To seal the matter, he kissed her tenderly.

Though she returned his kiss, she did not return his smile, rather took her bottom lip between her teeth once he had leaned back.

After a lengthy silence, she cupped his cheek and said, "I do love you."

His heart thumping, joy soaring his spirit, he hugged her to him.

"It wouldn't be fair to your family if we wed at Trelowen," he said. "I think we had better wed at Dunstanburgh before departing to Devonshire. I can send the request immediately for the banns to be read. Three weeks, my darling, and we'll be joined." He kissed the tip of her nose. "Although, there is a lovely, albeit unused, chapel here. It wouldn't be too far for the family to come if you'd prefer marrying at the hall. With a bit of polish, it would be perfect."

He propped up his head to better admire her.

She frowned, her eyes widening.

"How ill-mannered of me," he added with a chuckle. "I'm getting ahead of myself. Shall I go down on one knee? This is my first. Forgive my manners."

He sat up, wrapping the bedcovers about him, and positioned himself into a seated kneel.

Pushing herself upright, she drew her knees to her chest, her eyelashes darkening.

He took one of her hands and sandwiched it between his before raising it to his lips. All his practice and preparation of the perfect proposal, and now that the moment had arrived, he could think of only one thing to say.

"Lilith, my love, would you do me the honor of being my wife?"

The elation he felt in this moment was beyond words. It was as though everything in his life had culminated to this point. Everything made perfect sense. He knew the meaning of life and was eager to share it with the world.

In the seconds that ticked by, he imagined the pride and excitement of introducing her to his friends, escorting her to entertainments, hosting parties of their own. His friends would become her friends, and she would find new meaning to life as his baroness.

"No," she said.

Chapter 24

Time stopped.
His smile froze.
The world froze.

He could not move.

"I love you, Walter. I do. But I can't marry you."

Her words came to him through a long tunnel, filtered through ice. He heard but did not comprehend.

"Trelowen, then," he said, finding his voice, resetting the spin of the earth on its axis. "We'll go first to Trelowen."

She shook her head, the black strands, medusa-like, spilling over her shoulders. "You've not heard me. Walter, I cannot marry you. I will not marry you. At least not now. I need time. I need to return home."

"Yes, yes," he said, impatient. "Home. Yes, we'll return home first. You'll want to see your new home at Trelowen."

Lilith moved closer to the edge of the bed, her eyes glistening. "You're not listening. I need to return home to Allshire."

Walter could scarce hear himself think much less hear her words for the pounding of his heart. His head syncopated with its own pounding.

Of all the moments for it to happen, the candle snuffed out. Their world plunged into darkness, the acrid smell of smoke wafting over the bed. Neither moved. Neither spoke. Walter felt his world snuffed with the candle.

Without a word, he climbed off the bed and stalked to the dressing room. Letting the door hit the wall behind it, he rummaged blindly for a pair of breeches, any breeches. He did not care. His eyes had not yet adjusted to the miniscule amount of moonlight sneaking through a crack in the curtains. At least the storm had ended.

Pulling on a pair of riding breeches and struggling to tie and button the odious garment without assistance, he turned back into the room. He was not angry. Not really. He was in a state of shock shaken with denial and topped with humiliation.

And then his shin collided with the edge of an end table that had the audacity to get in his way. He swore he would turn it into firewood.

"Deucing devil from the pits of fire!" he cursed, limping to the chair next to the offending table.

He was not prone to cursing. But then, he was not prone to deflowering maidens, stomping about in the dark, or proposing to the sound of no. With a tender touch, he checked if his shin was wet or sticky with blood. Nothing. But it hurt like the devil. Resting his head in his hands, he stared at the floor. She wanted to return *home*, she had said.

Strangling his hair in his fists, he rose, snatched her nightdress from the floor to set on the edge of the bed, and made for the nightstand to light another candle.

After struggling for longer than he should have, the room blazed with brightness. He blinked before looking over at Lilith. She had not moved. Her knees were hugged to her chest, the sheet covering her for decency. He could not help but notice her cheeks were streaked with tears. The temptation to lean over and kiss them away compelled him to return to the chair by the hearth, putting distance between them.

"Dress," he murmured, staring with unseeing eyes at his breeches.

He heard and saw her out of his periphery, though he did not look up. A flash of white, a rustle of sheets, and a shadow later, she moved to the chair in front of the escritoire.

"My God, Lilith," he said at length. "I never would have lain with you if I had anticipated any other answer than a resounding yes. You're well within your right to reject my proposal, but *we have lain together*. You came to me. And yet you knew. You knew the whole time."

He choked back a sob, pressing a tightened fist to his mouth. He would not be unmanned. Not now of all times. Their blissful union, the honeymoon before the wedding bells, turned sordid.

"I know," she said. "It was wrong of me. It was selfish." She licked her lips and had the courtesy to look ashamed. "I want you, Walter. I do. It's not that I'm saying no, not exactly. I mean, I *am* saying no, but I'm not. It's the life you live that gives me pause. I'm not ready. But I want to be. I need time to prepare. There's much I need to do first."

Her voice was unnervingly controlled. Had she practiced her rejection just as he had practiced his proposal? The thought nauseated him.

She was not finished. "Could we forget you've proposed? Could we simply cherish this moment? I want to remember it as a beautiful moment. I want to remember what we've shared without the tarnish of a quarrel."

Ignoring her, he said, "I offer you more than marriage. You'll have a title, an estate, a house in London, modest wealth, security, a place in society, friends. The contract has already been written with all I offer you, although I've not had the opportunity to share it with you. Allow me to share it as enticement. Any dowry your brother plans to offer will be put into a settlement that is yours and yours alone. And you'll have a jointure should anything happen to me. Will you look at what I've written, what I had planned to bring to my official offer of marriage? I offer you everything."

Lilith sat primly, her feet together, her hands folded, her spine straight. Aside from the nightdress and loose hair, she looked remarkably like when he first met her.

She narrowed her eyes. "If you think I want any of those things, you don't know me at all."

"I don't care if you want them or not. They're yours. They're what I bring to a marriage. If *I'm* not enough for you, maybe these things will be. What else do you want from me? Why am I not good enough?"

"Oh, Walter. You *are*. I *do* want you. But you come with strings attached, expectations, rules, etiquettes....I don't know how to be part of your society. I don't know how to bear a title or how to live in a grand house. Don't you understand? All I know and all I've ever wanted is a simple life, a quiet life wherein I can help people."

He bit his knuckle, driving his teeth deep into the flesh. "London would only be during the

Parliamentary Season. The rest of the year we would be home with ourselves and our friends. Can't you withstand a few months of the year for us to be together?"

"I know you understand this, but I don't think you realize the gravity, how it weighs on my shoulders. I would be sacrificing everything I've built. I'm not some young girl with nothing, desperate to marry so I'm not dependent on my relations. I have a trade. I love what I do. To marry a man of your station means giving up everything and becoming someone I'm not certain how to be. I need time to prepare myself."

He swept his hands through his hair. Why the devil had she bedded him if she knew all along she would reject him? Had he not wooed her well enough?

"I dream of belonging," she said. "I want to be in a place where people know me, where I can be myself, somewhere I never have to worry about being abandoned. For so many years, Allshire has been that place. I've always known where I stand there."

"How could you possibly want to return when they treated you so shabbily? They don't see you for who you are. They don't even know how to see you."

To his surprise, she nodded. "I realize that now. All these years Allshire has been my home. I knew who I was. Now, I'm neither the orphan they thought me nor the Lady Lilith I believe I ought to be. I'm somewhere in between. To accept your offer now is to come to you as this person in between. I need time to settle into the newness of who I am becoming, to fully embrace Lady Lilith. It's the only way we can be together."

It made strange sense to his ears, although all he saw before him was the Lilith he loved. There was not a person caught between two worlds, merely Lilith.

She continued, "Do you realize it has not been a full year since I learned of my parentage, that Sebastian found me? Not even a year. A handful of months only. So much has happened in so short a time. It's too much too fast. You may think me scattered and confused, perhaps a wanton tease, but the truth is I want to say yes, but I can't say yes yet. I need time to prepare myself, really prepare myself. I've been thinking about this so that I might bring to you a proposal of my own. First, I want to return to Allshire and—"

"Oh, Lilith. You can't return. Pandora's box has been opened. You can't restore your old life. They all know your brother is an earl. Some believe you're a lady, others question it, the rest don't know what to think. You can't go back in time and restore that life. You can only move forward. With me. You can have your dream. Think of the orphanage I'm setting up. You wouldn't be sacrificing everything. You can train the midwives, hire teachers, and be part of the administration."

Was he begging? He believed he was.

She stared down at her hands, wringing them, wiping them against her nightdress, folding them, then repeating the process. "I want to return to Allshire not to live but to say goodbye to those dear to me. I must see to my patients who depend on me. They've no one else. They've put their trust in my hands, and I wouldn't feel right to walk away without a backward glance. I want to return and see my current patients to their happy conclusion without taking on anyone new. I can work with Miss Tolkey to prepare her for taking over my position. If this were a matter of stopping by on the way to Devonshire… but it's not. I could need several months to set things to right. After that, I want to prepare myself to be a baroness, for only once I do that can I in good conscience accept your offer."

Walter gaped at her. He thought he understood. She wanted to part ways. Her words sliced at him, ripping the fabric of his being.

He said, "I'll come with you."

She shook her head. "I can't close one part of my life and prepare for another while also playing the role of betrothed or wife or lover. I need to be alone to say farewell to Orphan Lilith and become acquainted with Lady Lilith. And what of your barony? You cannot move to Allshire with me and abandon your home. It was your father's wish for you to know and love the barony. You should be there now, becoming better acquainted with your tenants and employees, learning the accounts. How can you bring a wife to a life you've not built for yourself? Let us take time in our own parts of the world to do what we must before moving forward."

His voice, constricted, was little more than a whisper. "We could do these things together. You could help me with the barony."

"Perhaps. But first, you need to do these things yourself." She paused, made to speak, paused again, then finally said, "While you focus on the barony, I will focus on preparing myself. This has all happened too quickly for me, and for you, as well, I think. I learned of my brother and family a handful of months ago and was only becoming acquainted with it all when I met you. In you swept with offers of love beyond measure. Together we've flamed the fires of that love, and you're leaping to build orphanages and bring home a bride. I believe we both need time apart to sort ourselves. Apart, I can prepare myself and you can, as well, even ask the difficult question if I'm the right bride for you."

"This is a perfectly ridiculous conversation because I'm not looking for a bride. I'm only considering taking one because of *you*. I want *you*."

"I'm not ready to be a baroness no matter how I feel about you. If there's to be any chance between us, I *must* have time to prepare, to better acquaint myself with the etiquette, the manners, the everything. I'm not ready to play the part of aristocrat. You are a shining star who everyone loves. If I'm to be a baroness you'll not resent, if I'm to be more than a shadow in the corner no one likes, I must prepare. I am not a young lady in one of her seasons, accustomed to ballrooms and drawing rooms. I've only known one village and one role. I refuse to embarrass you, your family, or myself. I will accept after I'm confident I can be your baroness in all senses of the word."

Walter refused to accept this. Many young ladies with no aristocratic lineage found themselves with titled gentlemen, yet they did not decline the offer to prepare themselves in advance. They accepted and learned in stride. His thoughts went to his cousins, both country girls who were not trained to be wives of aristocrats, and yet both had slipped seamlessly into their role of wife of nobility.

He argued, "Once I introduce you to my friends and their wives and sisters, you won't be in the shadows. They can help you feel comfortable."

She rubbed her temples. "There's so much I must do to prepare. Have you forgotten about my illegitimacy? I must confront my aunt before I can accept your offer. This isn't something you can do for me. I must do it. I don't know how, but while I'm in Allshire saying my farewells and closing my surgery, I'll be thinking on it. You must understand, Walter, that without resolving Aunt Catherine, all our efforts could be for nothing. You have friends now, but you wouldn't if they learned you married a coachman's granddaughter. Once the scandal spread, you would regret marrying me. This *must* be dealt with before we can marry. Because my brother announces to the world he has a sister does not mean my aunt won't staunch that. She knows the truth and won't acknowledge me. You saw that for yourself. She wouldn't even come to see Freya because I was in residence. Should she speak out, my illegitimacy would be known, and we'll both be ostracized. Any children between us would be tormented as the offspring of a by-blow."

"You're wrong. You're dead wrong. Our children would be legitimate, loved, and protected."

"But not from society's cruelty. You've never received the cut direct. I have. By marrying me now, you and our children would no longer be recognized. We would be pariahs. Love is about putting someone else's happiness before your own. I'm doing that now. I'm putting your happiness first. I'm saving you from scandal and regret. If we rush into this, there will be nothing except scandal and regret."

Lilith shivered. What a fool he was. He rose from the chair, snatched the discarded banyan from the floor and wrapped it about her shoulders. She smiled up at him wistfully. If the situation were different, he would see if he could resurrect the fire. As it was, she could not stay in his room, and he feared their conversation would soon be at an end. She had been thinking about this for some time, he gathered. She had her mind set to do this alone. He could not decide if this was a rejection or a delay. Her words implied a delay, but his heart understood otherwise. She wanted to be away from him, probably to settle back into what she believed would be a simple life in Allshire. Tonight had been her farewell.

As though reading his mind, Lilith said, "I *will* prepare myself, so don't think I'm running away or aiming to return to my old life. I do need to part ways with the old life, say goodbyes, but I have a great deal to do to prepare myself. I cannot tie you to me until I've done that."

"I don't see how being apart puts either of our happiness first," he argued. "That isn't happiness. If you love me as you claim, you'll know my happiness is being with you."

She scoffed. "You're such a starry-eyed dreamer, Walter. Do you think by marrying, all our problems would be resolved, and we would live happily ever after? You're naïve if you believe that. Marriage to me as I am now would ruin your family."

"Marriage doesn't solve problems, but neither does living apart when we ought to be together. I don't believe there'll be a scandal, not with Roddam on our side, not with Annick. A duke's word is a powerful thing, Lilith. If he claims you as his cousin, no one will question it. Your aunt is practically a hermit these days and wouldn't go against the word of her son. And besides, all the *beau monde*, at least those from your mother's time, know you already. Did you know? Your mother brought you and Roddam to London year after year. All saw you. All adored you. And they all wondered what happened to the countess' little girl. No one would question your legitimacy. And if they did, they'd have me to answer to."

She did not reply. Her face was a mask, unreadable, impenetrable. "I'm not explaining myself well. I'm bumbling this. Let me try again. I'm not saying a definitive no. I'm saying…" She took a deep breath. "I'm saying I'm not ready *now*. I'm saying I want to return to Allshire first for a few months to see to my patients, then spend a few more months preparing myself with etiquette lessons and whatever it takes. After that, once I'm ready, I will hope you'll consider renewing your offer. If it were simple, I would say yes or ask you to wait, but I'm uncertain how long this process will take."

"So, you need time," he said. "Then, accept my offer, and we'll have a long engagement. How may I help support you until the wedding?"

"I don't know how long it'll take. A month? A year?" She laughed, a hollow sound. "I can't allow you to throw away your dreams while waiting for me. I don't want to enter a betrothal until I'm ready. I believe it better to say no now and release you of any obligation. You can return home, and so can I. We do what's needed, and then we reunite in the future."

"You're not thinking logically, Lilith. It's not possible to love someone and not want to be with them. It's a contradiction. You can't feel both love and dislike at the same time. It's either one or the other."

"Provoking man," she said with another laugh. "Maybe men can't feel contradictory emotions, but women can. I can. I do love you, but I cannot be part of your world yet. I will do whatever possible to prepare for it because I want more than anything to be with you."

"But if you love someone, you'll stop at nothing to be with them. You'll move heaven and earth." He was begging again.

"Well, then, if you love me, you'll move heaven and earth to understand that I need time. You must let me go, Walter. If you love me, you'll let me go."

He shook his head. "You're still contradicting yourself. You say you hope I'll renew my offer while also saying you want me to let you go."

"It's not a contradiction. If I knew with certainty I could say my farewells and prepare myself in a month's time, then—"

"We have options, Lilith. Far better options than you wandering in the dark scouring for memories. I'm not opposed to a long engagement. Allow us to do this side by side. My mother can do everything to prepare you. You would have no greater instructor on polite society than her. I know you want to return to Allshire for your farewells, but there's nothing there for you, not anymore. I know you want to face your aunt and prepare yourself alone, but it needn't be that way. Come to Devonshire with me so my mother can help prepare you. You shouldn't do this alone. If what you say is true, if you do want to be with me but you're not ready, then let us become ready together."

For the stretch of silence before she spoke, he thought he had persuaded her. Her eyes brightened, and she looked for all the world as though she would accept the offer. It made perfect sense after all. Why prepare apart, coming to him only after she was ready, when they could do this together? He supposed he could accept her wish to be apart if she would simply accept his offer of marriage. They could each resolve their conflicts while being affianced. In this way, there was the security of knowledge they would not be parted, not have a change of heart, always looking to the future. Her hesitancy to accept this made him question her motives. A rejection intended to lessen the hurt? Send him back to Devonshire in hopes he found someone else and forgot about her? His heart thumped wildly.

"I appreciate the offer, Walter," she said at length, "but I cannot accept it. As much as I would love for your mother to be my tutor and for us to do this together, I cannot have you burden yourself with me. What if I can't follow through? What if in my preparations I decide it's too much? What if it takes me five years to feel ready? No. I need time to prepare myself, and I want you to be free in the interim. I *will* come to you, but I need you to live your life until then. If I take too long, and you've changed your mind by then, I'll understand. For now, I need to do this for me, and I need you to let me go."

Desperation frayed his sanity. "I can't."

She exhaled her frustration.

"I can't, and you know I can't. We have no choice now. We've lain together, Lilith. We *must* marry."

"For respectability? I promise I won't brag to my friends," she said sarcastically.

"And the baby?"

She stared at him in wide-eyed horror.

"Don't accuse me of being naïve if you're not going to consider the consequences of what we've done," he said.

She paled. "I did not set out to trap you. I only wanted to be with you. I feared…no, I will not apologize for my actions or make excuses. I cannot think you would use what we shared against me. Is that your intent? Are you proposing out of obligation? For fear of consequences? Willing to let me go but too compromised to do so? Or is it that you're so unwilling to let me go you'll use this to trap me, to force my hand against my will? What is it to be, Lord Collingwood?"

He rose from the chair, closing the distance between them. With hands bracing the arms of her chair, his face inches from hers, he said, "Tell me you don't mean any of that, that you don't think me capable of any of that."

Her face crumbled. Her body shook with noisy sobs.

She took his face into her hands and kissed him, wet cheeks pressed to his, hiccupping lips pursed to his.

"Walter, Walter, Walter," she repeated against his mouth. "I love you. I do. I know you didn't propose out of obligation. I'm so sorry."

She held fast to him, but even as she kissed him and whispered endearments, he knew it was over.

At length, she said, "I promise to tell you if there are consequences. If I'm with child, I'll come to you.

But for now, please, let me go. I *will* find my way back to you, ready for your world. I *do* want to be with you. I know it doesn't make sense to you that I would want to do this with us apart rather than together, but I need to do this alone, and I need you to respect that. I'm not saying no forever. I'm saying no for now. I don't know how else to assure you of my ardor or how to explain my needs, but I promise I will do all in my power to come to you when I'm ready. Can you trust me enough, trust my love for you enough?"

He knelt before her and wrapped his arms around her waist, resting his head against her bosom. She kissed the top of his head.

"Observe, my darling," he said. "I'm moving heaven and earth to let you go because that's what will make you happy."

Chapter 25

J asper huffed in contentment, his mistress dutifully scratching behind his ears while he stretched across her lap, his front paws dangling over her legs. He was growing too fast and far too large to be a lapdog anymore. For as long as she did not care, he did not care.

Today had been a good day. They had played chase in the paddock, his favorite place for exercise, except when she took him for walkies to the river and back. Oh, the scents to explore! Today had been a paddock day. After playing chase, she had hidden treats and bones all around the garden for him to hunt. Too easy. For her amusement, he had circled three times before finding the last bone, although he had known where it was all along.

As contented as he was, he missed Milli. The night sounds scared her, and she had liked him there, protecting her. But how did a pup tell his mistress he would rather be at Roddam Hall where there was more room to run and play, more people to spoil him, and above all, Milli?

With a noisy yawn, he buried his nose between her leg and the side of the chair and fell asleep.

Lilith stretched, feeling sleepy, as well. It had been a good day. She had stayed home with Jasper to complete chores. One of her dresses had needed mending; the laundry needed doing; fresh cakes needed baking; the cottage needed a thorough dusting and scrub, more so now than before given how much Jasper shed. All in all, a good, productive day, without the intrusion of people.

Jasper had desperately wanted to go for a long walk, but it was far too cold, and Lilith had not the chance to hide doggy treasures along the walk for him to discover. Without something to hunt, he was a restless walker. Thankfully, a run in the paddock behind the cottage had sufficed, though calling him in after the fun ended had been a chore. He was willful, stubborn, and easily distracted. And she loved him for those traits.

Days at home were the best. It was Lilith and Jasper against the world. No judgement, no expectations, just peace and quiet.

The return to Allshire had not been unpleasant. Many of her patients welcomed her return. Even the children at the orphanage had run in unruly fashion to greet her.

Not all were so welcoming, though. More people than not were surprised by her return, as though they assumed she had left to live with her brother or to whatever fate. There had been a good share of embarrassment when she first arrived. Some villagers, from friends to acquaintances, averted their eyes when she passed. Others made a point to look notably busy when she approached or were polite but made excuses not to talk long.

She would not say doors slammed in her face, but she would say doors that were already closed remained closed, even when she knew people were at home. It was disconcerting.

Worse, Miss Tolkey, now Mrs. Sands, though Lilith had not been invited to the wedding, pretended she did not exist, which made teaching days arduous. Harry had not come around, and she had not been to church since her return. It was only a matter of time when he would request she move. She expected each day to be the day. After a careful counting of her savings, she believed she had enough to secure lodgings if she could find something available in time. Hopefully it would not come to that. She only needed a little time, after all.

Truthfully, an alarming number of her patients had already transferred to Mrs. Sands' services, though none had been openly critical of Lilith. As predicted by Lady Graham, all local gentry had withdrawn their need for her services.

Lilith was undaunted. If anything, she was more determined to follow the course she had set. This return, after all, was not intended to be permanent. She merely wanted time to set her affairs in order, see to the care of her remaining patients, pay her farewells, and all that was needed before moving to the next step — becoming a lady. That step would be the trickiest. Far easier if she could ease out of her old self, not unlike wearing a favored dress one last time.

Her plan, however, was not as smooth as she had hoped. She had known her return to Allshire would be difficult. What surprised her was the affect to her reputation and the cold reception by former friends and acquaintances. She had expected this part would be the easiest in her journey, a return to the people who knew her, who trusted her, who had put their lives and their babies' lives in her hands, far easier than trying to earn the respect from those in fashionable society. She had thought the known would be safer than the unknown. Return home and prepare for her final farewell, the most challenging aspect being the tearful goodbyes — so easy compared to all that would lie ahead.

She remained confident this was the best decision, but given how many people had not expected her to return, she almost wished she had not. Irresponsible to leave her patients in a lurch, yet a quick break might have proven the better choice. Too late now.

The first week had been unbearable. It started with the heartache of rejecting her chance for something greater, her chance for love and happiness. She wept day in and day out. This metamorphosed into a cycle of self-loathing, for in her attempts to find happiness, she had repeated her mother's sins by giving herself to a man outside the sanctity of marriage. The words of Harry's sermon repeated daily in her head. She had sinned, just as he predicted. She had been a whore in her father's house, just as he predicted. She was a fallen, ruined woman, just as he predicted.

When her monthly courses came during the second week, she wept even harder. All her prayers about unplanned consequences had been answered, and yet she wept. However much of a relief it should have been, she knew only despair. There were no words to explain why she wept, only emptiness. With wordless yearning, she mourned the child she would not have. She had yet to write to Walter with the news. A letter had been started many times, but she could not write the words. What would she say? How were such letters written?

She wished, oh how she wished during those first two weeks that she had said yes. Foolish, foolish woman.

The third week was easier. The passage of time became a balm to her wounds. She hoped Walter felt the same. No matter how many times she tried to explain to him, he had not seemed to understand. He spoke as though their split was forever, that she was softening the blow as she rejected him. Her intention was not to split, merely to bide her time to ready herself, but it had been impossible to explain rationally when in the same breath she could not promise she *could* ready herself. Nor could she promise his feelings would remain steady if she took too long. Undoubtedly, being away from her would have him believing he had made a timely escape. Was he laughing now at the thought of *her* hobnobbing with lords and ladies?

Time and time again, she reminded herself she could not be happy in his world unless she had first fully prepared herself to be a lady.

Though, was she *happy* in this one now?

Filling the Great Chamber with sweltering heat, the fire did nothing to aid Walter's runny nose. He wallowed in misery. Sniveling misery. The latest sneezing fit ended five minutes prior after ten consecutive *achoos*.

He sniveled — miserably — into a handkerchief. Men ought not catch colds. Such conditions were for women with delicate constitutions, not fit and healthy men. Continuing to row on the lake every morning despite frigid winter temperatures was to blame, or so said the physician who had wanted to bleed him dry.

Walter gazed out the multipaned window, surveying the sprawling countryside around Trelowen, the spire of a church peeking above distant trees. He had missed the view. He had also missed his chair, one of his many purchases from his Grand Tour, with its carved and gilded beech and its tapestry of wool and silk. It was French Rococo, the motif of birds and garlands, a complete set with matching wall tapestry and footstool, on which his blanketed feet now propped.

Nestling low into the sunken cushion, he leaned his head against the chairback. An ornamental plaster ceiling stared back at him. With a sniff, he closed his eyes, desiring to see nothing except the back of his eyelids.

This was all her fault.

If she had married him, he would be enjoying his honeymoon rather than suffering from a cold. This chill was her fault. He would not have needed to take out his frustrations on the lake had she been here.

And dash it all, but when was he to be rid of her memory?

He had done all he could since arriving home not to think of her, including telling his solicitor not to breathe another word of that dreaded Colling Orphanage. Though there were not many entertainments in the country during winter, he had made a point to attend them all. His inability to enjoy them was surely her fault, too.

The long journey from Northumberland to Devonshire had given him ample time to think of nothing but her, as had the conversation of his mother, a relentless, chattering interrogation that plagued the drive. His uncle at least had the courtesy not to join in the inquisition, instead turning the conversation at every opportunity to his plans to move north to be near his daughters. What Walter needed now was to purge himself of her.

He hated Lilith for seducing him and knew her promises to be empty. She would have said anything to get out of his bedchamber and escape his petulant groveling. What a loathsome creature she must have thought him. He had begged and bribed, cajoled and threatened. Of course, she would have pandered to him to shut him up. She was an artful seductress, an enchantress.

God help him, but he loved her.

No, he hated her, he reminded himself. He had been a puppet on her string. To the devil with her! Did she think he would wait for months and years for her to decide if he was good enough for her? If she had wanted him, she would have accepted him. The rector had been right about her. Adam's first wife indeed.

Never mind that love making took two willing partners, and that he had wanted to be with her as much as, if not more than, she had wanted to be with him.

No, he was a victim of witchery. A gentleman would not have acted with such impropriety unless bewitched.

After he conquered this blasted cold, he would not sit around and wallow. During the coming Season, he would make a determined effort to find a bride. The girl need only be tolerable. And blonde. Oh, and short. Add youthfully insipid.

At the start of the new year, he would write to Lilith to be sure. Perhaps she would have realized her error in judgment and come running into his arms. Oh, blast.

Achoo.

A new sneezing fit began, disrupting his self-loathing.

Chapter 26

Despite her best efforts to make the most of her remaining time in Allshire, life in the parish did not improve. With each new day and each passing week, fewer doors opened to her and fewer people smiled. People she had known for years averted their eyes when she waved. The few patients she retained failed to answer the door when she went around for their routine checkups. It did not take a genius to realize her reputation was tarnished. No amount of polish would renew the shine.

Unbeknownst to her, the emptiness of her pew at church had been noted.

Speculation was rife.

Mrs. Tilley whispered to Mrs. Owens over their embroidery one afternoon that she suspected Miss Lilith Chambers was outraged by the marriage between her young friend and the rector, for Mrs. Tilley had it on good authority that the midwife had sought with zeal the position of rector's wife. When Mrs. Simmons heard this from Mrs. Owens, she said she had noticed the two women no longer spoke—embittered for being usurped, perhaps?

Mr. Simmons set his wife straight that it was not because of the good Reverend Sands that she stopped attending, but rather her guilt over the sins of the flesh. Mr. Young agreed, for he had seen with his own two eyes Lord Collingwood leaving her cottage on more than one occasion—alone. Mrs. Young concurred and told Mrs. O'Connell about the time she saw them tucked cozily behind a tree in questionable proximity—alone. Had they not danced *three* times at the assembly, asked Mrs. Staple over her tea with Miss Fairweather.

Mrs. Hill let it slip they had breakfasted together at the inn when decent folks were still abed—an unusual occasion, that, for why were they both awake and together so early unless they had not yet parted company from the night before? Mr. Hill defended that he was certain His Lordship was courting her. Mr. Nobles assured him it was a silly notion, for what man of importance would court an orphan of questionable lineage? No, there was havey-cavey business being conducted in the good rector's cottage that would not be tolerated in their respectable village.

Miss Lowell told her mama it was all to be expected, for Lilith was an orphan after all. Mr. Lowell said to Mrs. Lowell it was most peculiar the woman did not go to live with her brother who seemed to take pity on her, though if he thought about it, it was not so peculiar after all. Miss Lowell chimed in to ask why it would not be peculiar when she heard from Miss Carmichael that the brother had introduced her as a *Lady* Lilith.

Oh, yes, speculation was rife.

And life in Allshire became increasingly difficult to bear.

But life had a funny way of nudging a person in unexpected directions, or so Lilith thought when she reflected weeks later. Had she needed to return to Allshire to sort her patients and wish farewells, neither of which were happening as planned, or had she needed to return for an altogether different reason? A reason quite fated it seemed to her. Said Fate knocked one stormy evening.

A bright flash spotlighted her face, waking her from a restless night's sleep. Lilith had been dreaming of serpents in her garden.

Blinking, she tried to adjust her vision to the darkness of night, syncopated by blinding light. A storm raged, raindrops beating a tattoo against the glass. Then she heard an insistent tapping, a tattarrattat easily mistaken for rain, only lower pitched. Straining against the chorus of rain, she listened. There it was again. A knock. Someone was knocking at her door. Good heavens. At this time of night? In the middle of a storm?

Jasper, too, heard the knock, and with his baying bark, catapulted from his bed by the stairs.

Unsure she had the wherewithal to face an emergency, Lilith sat up and lit the candle at her bedside. Her mind raced to think of any parishioners who might be delivering soon. No one came to mind. Had there been an accident? Was there danger of losing a babe? Donning her night robe and slippers, candle in hand, she padded downstairs, Jasper's bay deafening in the small space. Her heart pounded, and her eyes darted to the midwifery bag at the ready by the door. It would take her but a minute to dress if needed.

The knock persisted, urgent and heavy handed.

For a heart-wrenching moment, she wondered if it could be Walter.

Opening the door, Lilith gasped. "Harriette!"

Harriette Wimple, née Ains, stood in the doorway, drenched and shaking, nothing but a thin shawl about her shoulders to protect against the freezing rain. Moving to one side, Lilith ushered the girl inside. Jasper nudged Lilith, trying to sniff the newcomer.

"Back, Jasper. Sit." Lilith pointed to her usual chair.

The rarely obedient Jasper pranced to the chair and heaved a squat on the floor, his tail thumping.

Tending to the immediate took precedence. Lilith set the candle on the table and grabbed the blanket she kept tucked by her fireside chair. She wrapped Harriette with the blanket and rubbed the girl's arms with vigor.

A tear streaked, pale face stared back at her, looking nothing like the vibrant young girl Lilith knew. The cut lip and bruise forming on her cheekbone gave Lilith pause. She stopped rubbing and squeezed the girl into a hug, wet hair soaking part of Lilith's robe.

"Are you here to fetch me? Do I need to dress?" Lilith asked.

The girl shook her head, her body shivering against Lilith's.

Guiding Harriette further into the room, she tucked her into a chair next to the darkened fireplace.

"You've come to see me, then?"

When the girl nodded, Lilith leaned over to tuck her more comfortably into the chair, wrapping the blanket about exposed skin. She took a moment to stoke the embers in the fireplace, adding a log for good measure to resurrect the evening's fire.

"I'll get us some tea," Lilith said, lighting candles to combat the darkness.

While the kettle heated, she shuffled upstairs to find the girl something dry to wear. There was not much to choose from, and the girl was of a much thinner and shorter frame than Lilith, but anything would do to get her out of the wet clothes.

After instructing the girl to change, Lilith returned to the kitchen to sort out the tea and a dog bone. However foolish it might be to spend time making tea, much less to have tea at this time of night, she was no stranger to the sufferings of women, and such sufferings were not bound by time of day, neither was tea. The warmth would do some good, as would the added peppermint. She would have preferred to add chamomile, but the summer's harvest had already been well used. Peppermint would still do the trick to calm her guest.

Harriette had changed into dry clothes and snuggled herself back under the blanket, however damp it must be now, when Lilith carried in the tea tray. There was little in this world, Lilith had found over the years, that was not resolved with a good cuppa. Embracing the silence, aside from the pounding rain and rumbling thunder outside, Lilith poured the tea with a touch of honey. Never underestimate silence or the calming effect of a simple task.

Jasper concurred. He gnawed happily on his bone.

Lilith took one of the girl's hands into her own and encouraged her to drink the tea with the other.

Harriette winced when the cup touched her split lip, but once she tasted the liquid, she closed her eyes and sighed. Not until she finished, and Lilith reached over to pour a fresh cup, did Harriette's lower lip tremble in anticipation of her confession. Lilith nodded encouragingly.

"Do...do you...can you...unmake a baby?" the girl stuttered.

Lilith stared. This was not what she had expected to hear. She had expected, well, she was not certain exactly what she had expected given the various ailments she had tended over the years, not to mention the strangeness of the visit, but she had not expected this.

"Harriette? What happened?" She reached again for the girl's hand, squeezing it.

The girl shook her head and repeated her request. "You must know. Mustn't you? Can you? I...I need to unmake a baby."

Oh, Lilith did know ways. In a pinch, she could even suggest a few herbs. Savin, pennyroyal, rue, argot, among others, all came to mind. Savin was the most popular, but what most women did not realize was they put themselves in as much risk as their unborn child by ingesting such an herb.

Any midwife who had read William Buchan's *Domestic Medicine* would know the risks of willfully terminating a pregnancy. Lilith would never condone such a thing. She had been asked many times for various reasons, but she never assisted. If she could find a way to help the women who found themselves in such a plight, she would, but what Harriette wanted, she would not do.

Instead of answering Harriette's questions, she said, "You wed Mr. Wimple only two months ago. He wants children, yes?"

Tears sprang anew. "I shouldn't have told him. I shouldn't have. But he realized I was increasing too soon. I'm starting to show. We've not been married *that* long. I only told him the truth because I thought he would understand."

Lilith nodded. "Was it he who hit you?"

Hit was an understatement for the look of Harriette's face. Beat would be more apt. New scuffs and scratches Lilith had not seen earlier shown in the firelight, along with an alarming gash to her temple, blood clumping with wet hair.

"No, it was Papa. When I told Isaac, he took me home and told Mama and Papa he refused to live with a sullied woman. He accused them of lying about my virtue. I told Papa the truth, but he…he…I can't go home, Miss Chambers. I can never return home. To either home. He won't have me. They won't have me. They called me…they said…" She choked on a sob, unable to finish.

"How far along are you, Harriette?"

Between sobs, the girl sputtered, "Over four months."

Ah. Yes, Lilith understood. If it had not been so long, Harriette might have convinced Mr. Wimple it was his. Had the wedding night been difficult to explain? Lilith wondered.

"And the baby's father? Does he know? Is he the reason you married Mr. Wimple?" Lilith asked.

Harriette's sobs turned to hiccups. "I…I don't know which one's the father. It was the…the…the Montworth brothers."

Lilith clenched her jaw, knowing exactly what happened, for this was not the first time she had heard that name on the lips of a distraught woman. The Montworth brothers were the sons of Lord

Montworth. His estate was not far from Allshire. The two must be well into their twenties at this point, but she had been birthing their illegitimate children for years, most from young girls like Harriette.

The first time it happened, she had sought the magistrate with Mr. Sands by her side. The problem was the magistrate was a good friend of Lord Montworth and had not seen the problem. Boys will be boys; they need to sow their oats; women lie to compromise titled men. Lilith could list for days the excuses he gave to dismiss the whole sordid affair. Each time it happened, he had grown angrier, not at the Montworth brothers, but at her. How naïve of her, he would say, not to realize what country women were up to, all angling to force good men to marry them, regardless whose babe they carried in their belly. Though she had fought the battle of the Montworth boys for years, she had been unable to do anything to help the women or stop the boys, for they were above the law, the women always to bear the brunt instead.

While Lilith's hatred for the aristocracy originated from how she and the other orphans were treated, her dealings with the magistrate over the Montworths' continued ravishing of the countryside sealed her opinion. They all viewed themselves as being above the rest, better than the rest, above the law. And they were.

It was an opinion she held until quite recently. Her brother and Walter had proven not all aristocrats were bad, but when confronted with this sort of arrogance, how was she to think better of their lot?

Lilith did her best to console Harriette, but it was time for solutions, not pity.

"Do you need a place to stay while Mr. Wimple cools? With time, he should realize the best solution is to raise the baby as his own. No one would be the wiser if the baby arrived a little early." Lilith patted her hand.

"No. I can't go back. I can never go back. He said if I ever came back he'd...he'd...I can't go back."

The girl looked quite frightened, eyes wide, face pale. While she might change her mind, Lilith did not think she would. The girl seemed most serious about never returning.

This would prove problematic. Harriette was his wife, no matter how he felt about her or treated her. If he wanted her back, for whatever reason, he would find her and drag her back. Harriette would have no other place to go and no way of finding work, not without characters, and certainly not if increasing or with a babe in tow. Lilith's heart went out to her, but there was nought she could do.

"He spoke out of anger, Harriette. Once he's cooled, he may feel differently."

"Please, don't say you'll take me back to him. Don't tell him I'm here. I can't go back." Harriette wailed. "But...but I have nowhere to go. What will I do? No one will employ me in this condition."

"Stay here tonight, and tomorrow we'll speak to the Reverend Sands. There must be some place for you to go. He'll know what to do."

Harriette's teacup clattered against the saucer. "No! We couldn't possibly go to him! He knows. He must know. You were there. You heard his sermon.

He as good as condemned me though it wasn't my fault. He said wives found not to be virtuous would be shunned and stoned to death!"

Lilith might have laughed had the situation not been so serious. How many other people had heard the same sermon and thought it about them?

"Your brother's an earl, miss, so maybe he has a little village I could go to and pretend to be a widow. I don't have any money, though. No one will employ a woman with a child, will they? There must be something I could do. You must know a way. I'm not afraid to work. I could be a maid if your brother would employ me. I'll do anything. Please, help me?"

The poor dear's words ran together, hysteric.

"Harriette, you're safe here. Drink your tea. No one will harm you here." Lilith did not answer the girl's questions.

What was she to say? She could not very well foist her on her brother when the censure received would be from the other servants, not from Sebastian.

Harriette sniffled into her cup, an occasional sputtering sob finding its way between sips. "He's an aristocrat, miss. That's what I need. I need someone with persuasion who can help me. He'd know what to do."

The girl was right, Lilith conceded. There was little *she* could do being a tarnished midwife and teacher. Someone with more means and influence could help. Lilith could not see an immediate solution, for even if the girl, as she had said, moved to a village as a widow, she would still need a source of income. But one thing was for certain. Only a person of power could help.

And then Lilith had an idea. An empowering idea. In a flash of lightning through the cottage window, Lilith realized all her decisions, however peculiar, however nonsensical, had led her to this moment, this godsent moment.

She could not bring the Montworth boys or their ilk to justice or save women from scandal, ostracization, or unwanted pregnancies, but perhaps, with a bit of cunning, she could help them find a better life. To be precise, Lilith Chambers could do nothing, but Lady Lilith held the power to help them.

It was time to stop fearing her own potential when there was a greater cause at hand. Was she brave enough to face the unknown before she was ready?

It had been nearly three months since he had last seen Lilith. She should know by now if she were with child. Walter had written to her weeks ago. No answer. He did not want to trap her or force her into a marriage she did not want, but some part of him hoped — no, he would not admit it, even to himself.

After a frigid stroll along the long walk, a picturesque stretch running parallel to the house that offered a view of the front court and from spring to autumn bloomed with blues, purples, and whites, he met up with his gardener. The man thought Walter deranged. Or so Walter suspected. The dead of winter, and he was requesting a new garden.

"And so, you say you've found a place?" Walter asked.

"I have, my lord. The perfect place," said Mr. Holcombe, leading the way past the long walk, through the knot garden, and near the kitchen garden and potager.

When they reached a smallish, raised bed, the gardener waved an arm. "Will this do, do you think?"

"I want it much bigger. The place is perfect, but much bigger. Could we add three more beds?"

Mr. Holcombe scratched his temple. "Will do. You're sure you only want the seeds? Peculiar, like."

"Ah, Mr. Holcombe, don't you see? This will be *my* garden. There's a kind of peace one can find when gardening. I'll sow and tend to these beds myself. I need only advice. I'm a novice, mind."

Shaking his head with a chuckle, clearly amused by his employer's oddity, the gardener said, "A kind of peace, you say? Yes, yes, there is."

It had been a busy winter.

It began with a long talk to his father.

Walter spent nearly an entire day at his father's grave, burrowed in a greatcoat, talking through problems he had not known he suffered. Nothing could erase the disappointment his father must have felt when his only son was showing signs of becoming a wastrel rather than a proud heir. But Walter could make amends and make the memory of his father proud.

He had to *want* to be Lord Collingwood. For so long, he had run from the title. He rejected its future when his papa had been alive, and he rejected its present after his father's death. Accepting it, wanting it, came with responsibilities he could no longer shirk. To his mind, for so long, accepting the responsibilities meant accepting his father's death, something he was not willing to do. No one else could motivate or inspire him to be Lord Collingwood. It was something he had to do for himself. He owed it to his father. He owed it to himself.

And so, it had been a busy winter.

He had reacquainted himself with those living in his barony, from tenants to laborers. He knew most of them, had grown up with many of them, but he did not *know* them. It was time. It was past time. He was getting soft around the middle again from all the biscuits and tea he had taken with neighbors.

Most days were spent similarly. With the lake frozen over, he took to early morning running, followed by mid-morning meetings with his steward to get to know the accounts, including making suggestions of his own under strict advisement. Late mornings were spent breaking his fast with his mother. During the afternoons, he called on villagers to get to know each of them over a cuppa.

He had, truthfully, never had more tea or cake in his life, so by the end of each afternoon, it was a wonder he did not float away on a sea of tea. His cook was threatening to resign since he could scarcely finish dinner. It did not help she always added extra to his plates knowing his healthy appetite.

He fell into a rhythm, a rhythm of contentment. The sentiment was new. For all the years he spent romping and causing mischief with friends, he had never felt this contented.

The busyness of the days kept his thoughts from Lilith. The nights were another matter. Darkness and solitude were the very devil to a heartbroken soul.

Nearly every week, he made the trek to his new property to check the build progress. Though the frost was against them, the workers had made considerable headway. He had a grand scheme. It would not only be an orphanage, school, and foundling hospital, the last of which he decided to do after careful consideration. It would also be an apprenticeship program. The program would connect aspiring pupils with tradesmen and train servants for those interested in working in a house.

Mrs. Brighton and Mrs. Copeland inspired him.

Already, he had called on a fair number of peers who seemed receptive to employing servants from the orphanage. Some greeted his idea with harsh criticism, even disgust, but not all. His offer was to groom servants for the specific household. In this way, he could offer bespoke staff to landowners and employment with pride to dedicated students. There was no way to know if his ideas would work, but they showed promise. Doors did not slam in his face. Far more doors opened than he expected when he first birthed this brainchild during one of his sleepless nights.

Something he had not considered was the unwed mothers. He assumed most of the children in orphanages were sent by lords disposing of their by-blows, relations who could not care for additional children, and solicitors who had no place for a child with deceased parents. But what of mothers like Lily Chambers? Should something not be done to incentivize them to *keep* their baby?

He did not think he would have the means to offer part-time care for children alongside the full-time orphans, or even staff positions for those desperate for work, but he did want to think in those directions. If the women had a place to work or a place for the child to stay, would they not abandon the child? He was hopelessly ignorant about such aspects of the world.

Research had begun. He started by developing a network of employment agencies. Those willing to help such women were few and far between, but he did secure worthwhile connections.

It was all a massive undertaking, one he did not in any way feel qualified to accomplish. And yet he had managed to set the wheels in motion. In only a handful of months, he had accomplished a year's worth of work. During this process, he learned not to underestimate the power of a charming smile, coin, and a title.

His days were long but fulfilling. So busy had he been, he had not attended a winter entertainment in two months.

Would his father be proud? He believed so. Did it make up for disappointing his father? No.

But it was a start.

The only cloud in his sky arrived the morning after meeting with his gardener. A letter. Not just any letter. *The* letter. The long-awaited letter from Lilith.

His hands shook as he opened it. He held it, his eyes closed, afraid to read. What did he want it to say? How would he react if she was with child? And if she was not?

His breathing shallowed.

His heart pounded.

He opened his eyes and stared long at the page.

Walter read the news five times in succession before his tears smeared the ink.

Chapter 27

The *bâton* struck Lilith's knuckles.

"Disgraceful. You have ten thumbs," said the heavily accented Frenchman.

"Have you thought, Monsieur Allaire, that it could be the inferiority of your instruction rather than my fingers?" Lilith asked, her hands suspended over the aged harpsichord.

"*Absurdité. Continuez, s'il vous plaît.*"

Lilith depressed the keys, continuing from where she stopped, mangling Bach in the process.

She never had been good with music, even as a child. As a teacher at the orphanage, she had dreaded lesson days for she could do no justice with the children's musical instruction. Her talent was in mathematics. Could that not be an accomplishment for a lady rather than singing or playing? The recitation of the tables could be impressive in the right company. Or what about performing a complex division problem as a parlor trick? She would be far more entertained by such diversion than listening to someone shame composers.

The lesson ended in time for her etiquette instructor's arrival.

She simultaneously loathed and enjoyed lesson days. Back-to-back instructors, who would not admit the unusualness of teaching an adult what ought to be taught to children, attended her in half-hour intervals to school her in music, dance, deportment, elocution, etiquette, and other such important training she would need as a woman of influence and power.

If she were to step foot into drawing rooms, ballrooms, and parlors, she refused to blunder about like a rusticated orphan, pouring milk when she ought to pour tea, curtsying when she ought to nod, rejecting a dance request when ought to accept, using surnames when she should use titles, remarking on politics when she ought to ask after the weather, and whatever other horrors lurked in the ridiculous rules of fashionable society.

With each day of silliness, she reminded herself it was all for a greater cause. This had been her intention in preparation for entering Walter's world, although she had not expected to begin training so soon, yet now she had an additional reason to become Lady Lilith. This transformation was for the women and children she could help if she used the identity her mother had given her. Not her birth mother, but Jane Lancaster, the only mother she had ever known, the mother who raised Lilith as her own, introduced her to the *beau monde* as her daughter, and prepared her for a world of privilege.

That evening, as Hannah brushed her hair, Lilith asked with bold determination, "How handy are you with shears?"

In the mirror, Lilith saw the lady's maid's eyes widen. "You can't possibly want to cut your hair, my lady."

Though Lilith cringed when Hannah referred to her as *my lady*, she did not correct her.

By ruled measure, Lilith was learning her place and theirs. It pained her to be waited on when she could do things herself, but as she had learned after a long talk with Hannah the day the maid arrived from the castle to Roddam Hall, the staff took great pride in their workmanship, and with it came a set of rules of its own to which she must abide to show respect to her employees. Hannah's calling her by her first name, no matter how friendly they were to each other, was disrespectful on both their parts.

Staring back at Hannah's reflection, Lilith asked, "How short is fashionable?"

"Too short," said the lady's maid, fanning Lilith's hair about her shoulders, then drawing the comb down its length from hairline to tip, which reached proudly to the chair's seat.

"Well, let's not go too short, then. Short enough to be attractively styled. You'll know what to do. Cut it."

Hannah pulled her upper lip between her teeth, a crease forming between her brows. "You'll wake up tomorrow, hate it, and send me back to the castle to be a parlor maid."

Lilith laughed.

Admiring her hair in the mirror, all weighty, fifty feet of it, she said, "I won't hate it. I'll love it. I already do, and you've not cut it yet. Chop it off, Hannah. Just below the shoulders. I want to feel light, free, and unburdened. A new look for the new me."

Heaving a sigh, the girl went for the shears.

Lilith squeezed shut her eyes at the sound of the snip, snip, snip. With each snip, she felt lighter. Why she had not done this sooner, she could not say.

When Hannah finished, Lilith peeked an eye open to see the damage. The result was more startling than expected. She choked back a sob.

Hannah's hands flew to her mouth, misinterpreting her mistress' weeping.

Oh, Lilith loved it. She did. Truly. She saw the memory of the staid Miss Lilith Chambers scattered on the floor around her, a woman who served her well for most of her life, a shield against her true self, a protective armor that had fought through the confines of her orphaned state, enfolded the frightened child abandoned by her family, glanced off the ridicule of the upper classes, and forged a life of respect. That woman was no longer needed. Now, she was Lady Lilith Lancaster, daughter of Tobias and Jane Lancaster, the Earl and Countess of Roddam, sister to the current Earl of Roddam.

And, by Jove, Lady Lilith had fashionably short hair. Well, close to short. Shorter at any rate.

She smiled at Hannah. "Well done. Oh, well done."

By putting aside her selfish stubbornness, she would help women and children across the country. There was much to be done, but it all began with the creation of a lady. As a lady, there was no end to what she could accomplish.

She was not even daunted by a certain aunt she would soon need to contend with, for her Aunt Catherine was the only impediment between her and claiming herself legitimate. She was not daunted because living at Roddam Hall had taught her not to underestimate ingenuity, determination, and aspiration.

There was a sense of home here, a familiarity. She truly felt herself, which was a strange admission.

Leaving Allshire had been difficult, far more difficult than it should have been. Hours she had spent standing in her garden, lovingly touching the stone of the cottage, the dirt where Walter planted the bulbs she would not see bloom, the herbs she would not harvest in the spring. She had wept to leave it all behind. She visited everyone she knew well to wish them farewell, silently assuring them there were no hard feelings for whatever rumors they might have helped spread.

Her last stop before she, Harriette, and Jasper stepped into the carriage Sebastian had sent from Roddam Hall was to the rectory. The Sandses had not known she was leaving, and she was unsure they would receive her. But they did. Grudgingly.

They met her together in the small front parlor of the rectory, both with noses raised and eyes focused somewhere beyond her. When she announced her departure, though she did not admit to where, they had been shocked. Harry said it was for the best since a curate was soon to be appointed, and the cottage would be needed for him. They were delighted about the curate, for Harry would be busy with family duties soon, namely the rearing of his child.

It had been Lilith's turn to be shocked. Miss Tolkey, or rather Mrs. Sands, was already expecting? Not that it should be so surprising, but goodness! Lilith had known couples who spent years waiting for happy news.

On her way out, she thanked him for his kindness and all he had done to aid her over the years. She could have chosen not to call on them. She could have chosen to call on them with reprimands for their unchristian behavior towards her. She could have somehow sought revenge for his unpleasantness. Instead, she shook Harry's hand and smiled, wishing him nothing but happiness. Perhaps her kindness would inspire him, too, to be a better person, the friend she had thought him to be when he first accepted his post.

She foisted her affections on Mrs. Sands, as well, kissing her cheek and wishing her all the happiness in the world. She meant it. Not for a moment did she blame the girl for thinking ill of Lilith when Mrs. Sands was blissfully unaware of the sins of the world. If the girl continued as midwife, she would see far more than she wanted. Lilith hoped the evils of the world would not break the girl's spirit.

It could be argued by some residents that Lilith left because the villagers pushed her out, her and her sinful ways. The truth was far different. She realized her own potential and no longer feared the unknown.

Seeing society's hypocrisy spurred her to face the future and create her own happiness. For so many years, she had hated the gentry and aristocracy alike for their treatment of people, but the villagers had been no different. A parish of God-loving people, and yet they had turned their head at the merest whisper of gossip.

Her hatred had been misplaced. There were good people and not so good people, all mingled together in every class. And in each class, there were people with hearts of gold, people like Walter, people like his mother Hazel, people like the Turnbows and the Brightons. How ashamed she was to remember holding Walter's status against him when it was her own people who had shunned her in the end.

As the carriage jolted forward on its way to Roddam Hall, she had waved to Mrs. Copeland and Mrs. Elliot, the children gathered around them, all waving back tearfully. She had also waved to the milliner and her husband, the innkeepers, the Turnbows, and anyone else she saw in the street. They had all waved back.

It was not easy, though it ought to be. Who would not dream of discovering they could live as aristocracy?

Lilith never dreamed of such a life, at least not after she arrived at the orphanage as a distraught and frightened eight-year-old girl. Such a life was full of burdens, rules, and an ever-present audience, if not from peers, then from servants.

It was not so easy to leave behind one world and enter another, the new world full of more rules than freedoms. She had to accustom herself to living with an audience, for she was never alone, not even when she bathed. Much of her time was not her own either. She now oversaw the hall and all who resided there in addition to spending long hours working on her plan. The worries of before had not subsided, worries of being discovered as an imposter, ridiculed for her humble youth, censured for her years of employment, and ostracized for the path she now chose which would not invite the same sort of scandal as being a midwife, but it was not the sort of endeavor a lady ought to pursue.

To make it all possible, she had to swallow against the nagging voice that she was not worthy and keep herself busy with the preparations for all she had planned.

The most exciting day so far had been the modiste's visit. Her frugal nature and desire not to waste her brother's money had held her back from purchasing all the dresses and accessories some-one of her station would have, but she arranged for the most essential. There was a pulse of energy she had never experienced at being pinned and poked and measured by the modiste and assistants. These were not to be any dresses, after all. These were to be hand-fitted to her frame, designed and sewn for her and her alone.

Not since she was a child had she undergone a fitting. Even the enthusiasm with which she had pur-chased the dress this summer could not compare.

The modiste knew her trade well. Lilith had lim-ited opinion in colors, patterns, fabrics, and styles, leaving all to the expertise of the dressmaker. She did, however, insist all choices be as simple as fash-ion allowed. Wearing a tailor-made dress was one thing, but she refused to be trussed with frills and jewels. The modiste had smiled at this request and flattered Lilith with such statements as assuring Her Ladyship she need no adornments to distract from her handsomeness.

What might have been taken as false flattery was proven true when Lilith surveyed her reflection in an understated day dress that enhanced her smallish bosom in shockingly pleasant ways. Even her too-wide hips appeared enticingly sensual in the cut of the high-waisted dress. No fashion of bygone days. No shop-bought cut. No inferior stitching sewn by Lilith herself. Lilith hugged her arms about her torso and smiled.

What would Walter say when he saw her?

Her smile faded.

She wished she had asked him to wait. She wished she had accepted his offer for them to do this together. But no, her decision had been guided by a higher hand. Had she accepted, Harriette never would have found her at the cottage.

Two months into her time at Roddam Hall, she sat on the icy ground, a blanket between her and the thin layer of snow, staring at Jane Lancaster's grave. Jasper was running amuck in the graveyard, sniffing out every hidden smell buried beneath snow.

"I'm sorry for doubting you," Lilith said. "I should have known you would never have abandoned me. I was nought but a child, alone and confused. Forgive me for thinking ill of you, believing you sent me away. Forgive me for thinking you were angry because I had done wrong. Forgive me for taking so long to return to you. It's been a confusing year. A confusing few decades, really."

She dipped her woolen-clad fingers into the snow, tracing her mother's name.

"You were the only mother I knew. But when I was taken to live somewhere else, I thought you didn't want me. I made the best of my new life until Sebastian found me. It all changed again. Not only did I learn you had died and not been the one to send me away, but that you weren't my birth mother. What was I to do with my memories? Well, I'm here now. I'm becoming the daughter you intended me to be. Family is not about blood but about those who love and support you through thick and thin. Though I was not of your flesh and blood, you loved me as your own. I promise to make you proud."

Jasper pranced through the snow, leaving dog prints in his wake, and came to nuzzle against her on the blanket.

"Isn't it funny, Jasper, how for so long, I thought those who were supposed to love me had abandoned me, when in truth, my birth mother saved my life and would have kept me had she not become ill, and my other mother had no part in sending me away? It was only my father. He was the only one who abandoned me. And yet, the more I think about it, the more I believe he did it to save me, as well. Perhaps he loved me so much he wanted to protect me from himself. I was safe from his wrath. It's funny how nothing is ever what it seems."

She pulled Jasper half on her lap for a hug. Pressing her nose into his fur, she sighed, happy.

"We're going to funnel their love to help others, aren't we? By living the life my mother Jane intended me to live, we'll help people like my birth mother. Oh, I do forgive her for her unmarried passion. I understand now what it is to love but feel inferior. We'll make her proud, too."

The tender moment was lost on Jasper. He whined and struggled against her, wanting to play chase rather than snuggle.

With flushed cheeks and a breathless pant, Lilith chased Jasper through the front door of Roddam Hall, the frosty air biting exposed skin. The pup was generously covered with snow after catching rather than dodging the soft snowballs Lilith had thrown. His lolling tongue denoted his satisfaction with the afternoon.

Racing past the butler to his personal footman—could a dog be said to have a valet? If so, young Frederick held that honor—Jasper led the man to the kitchen, eager for water, a treat, and quality time with Milli.

Lilith, still laughing, proceeded to peel off her wool gloves until the butler fixed her gaze. Ah, yes. Dutifully, she relaxed and allowed him to remove her coat, bonnet, and shawl. How odd it was to have someone remove such articles.

"There's a caller in the Great Hall, m'lady," Mr. Sims said.

"A caller? Who would visit me?" she asked absently.

"A Mrs. Putnam," he said.

The name did not sound familiar, she thought, walking in the direction of the room.

Before she made it far, the butler cleared his throat.

She looked back at him, brows raised, then stepped back to glance in the vestibule mirror. Oh dear. She looked frightful. Her hair was disheveled and her cheeks pink. Looking once more to the butler, she shrugged and laughed.

With a nearly imperceptible shake of his head, Mr. Sims approached. "If you'll allow me, m'lady." And without another word, he reached over to pin up a few of her fallen curls.

Had she been anyone else, Lilith might have kept the caller waiting while she returned to her room so Hannah could change her dress, fix her hair, and lighten her flush. But she was not someone else. She was Lilith. And so, she proceeded straight to the Great Hall to greet her guest. At least the dress was new and ever so lovely.

As soon as Lilith entered the room, the visitor stood, clasping a hand to her bosom.

"It *is* you!" exclaimed the woman.

Lilith stared before joining her by the hearth. The woman did not look familiar. Mid-fifties, fashionably dressed, tufts of silver hair peeking out from under a turquoise turban, a matching winter dress snug around a generous figure. The lady's eyes smiled though her mouth maintained a perpetual pout.

Approaching, Lilith smiled, although she was unsure if smiling was bad etiquette — she would need to consult her instructor.

"You've grown since I last saw you, but I'd know you anywhere, Lady Lilith. No need to look flustered. I wouldn't expect you to remember me. I'm one of your neighbors. Mrs. Angela Putnam."

Stopping herself from curtseying, only just, Lilith nodded in greeting, then turned to stoke the fire.

Oh dear. Not until she reached for the poker did she realize her mistake. With a swift pivot, she ran her hand along the mantel and turned to her guest, posing as though she had intended to stand just so. The fire did not need stoking anyway.

"I'm delighted you've called on me, Mrs. Putnam. Allow me to ring for tea."

As the words slipped out, the door opened, and the butler carried in a tray, anticipating Lilith's hospitality. Taking the opportunity to return to her seat, she waved a hand for Mrs. Putnam to sit.

Once the door closed, she reached for the milk to prepare the cups. Again, she caught herself.

No, no, no.

Tea first, the instructor had taught her. After a lifetime of pouring milk first, this would be a difficult habit to break. As the instructor explained, brittle cups, such as the ones Lilith had owned, cracked if first poured with boiling tea. This was not the case with the finer teacups. A declaration of status and wealth was the pouring of tea first.

Lilith thought it was the silliest thing she had ever heard. While she had not paid attention to her mother's tea pouring habits, she really did believe Jane had poured the milk first. But no matter.

Replacing the milk for tea, she poured the tea first. Mrs. Putnam likely did not care or notice, but Lilith would do this all correctly if it killed her. Her first caller!

"Perhaps you'll better remember my daughters who are about your age," Mrs. Putnam said, accepting graciously her teacup.

Mmm. The warmth of the tea spread through Lilith's limbs. She had not realized how chilled she was from the outdoors.

"Sharon and Sadie. I brought them nearly every time I called on your mother."

Lilith could not recall playing with any children other than her brother, but she supposed she must have. It would have been peculiar if she had not.

Shaking her head, Lilith said, "I'm afraid it's been a terribly long time, Mrs. Putnam. Are they well?"

"Oh, yes. You're a dear for asking after them. Sharon is now Lady Burke, married ten years to the viscount. Sadie is now Mrs. Hamilton. I have six grandchildren between them. My, how time passes!" She chortled.

They took a moment to sample the currant cakes before Mrs. Putnam continued.

"We all thought you had died, I'll have you know."

"We?" Lilith asked.

"The neighbors. We paid a dozen calls to console the widower and bring treats to his two children after Her Ladyship died, but he withdrew from Society. When there were no signs of you, we thought you must have died alongside your mother. There were rumors...." Her words drifted off. "But look at me doing all the talking when I've come to find out about you! I'm the messenger, you see. Everyone is curious. They all hope you will make calls soon, but since you've not done so, here I am. Through snow and cold, I've made it to you. Tell me everything!"

When Mrs. Putnam stopped for breath, Lilith said, "There's not much to tell, I'm afraid. My father sent me to an orphanage where I've lived these past years. Had my brother not come for me, I would never have known my parentage."

With a hand to her bosom, Mrs. Putnam said, "How romantic! The lost daughter returns home. But naturally, he would have sent you away. You would have been a daily reminder of his late wife. You have your mother's eyes, you know."

The lady paused to enjoy a cake but talked between bites.

Lilith listened, in no rush to do the talking. The fewer questions to answer, the better; although, Mrs. Putnam seemed to make her own excuses and explanations for Lilith's departure and return. How differently she acted from those in Allshire. She glossed over the word orphanage as though Lilith had been visiting an aunt instead. A sudden memory struck her of the first time she met Hazel. Had Hazel not been the same? More curious than judgmental?

After all Lilith's misgivings, there appeared a light at the end of her tunnel.

Mrs. Putnam prattled on. "Though it's not for many months, and I've not yet arranged the details or sent invitations, you simply must attend my annual soirée this Season. You'll be quite the sensation."

Lilith looked at her in alarm. "I've not decided on going to London. Thank you for inviting me, though."

"Fiddlesticks. You must go. There's no question. Everyone will be looking for you. It's not every day, after all, ladies resurrect from the dead. I hope you have a sense of humor because I have quite the tale of murder and mayhem to share with you."

Mrs. Putnam carried on for exactly half an hour, sharing with Lilith the many theories neighbors had to explain her disappearance, the darkest rumor being she and her mother had been murdered and buried in the topiary garden. However much the woman laughed, Lilith suspected no one had laughed at the time.

The visit ended well, better than well, in fact, with Lilith promising to call on her and the other neighbors soon. Had *this* been what she feared for the better part of a year? Had *this* been the unknown she sacrificed love, happiness, and belonging to avoid? If she had known taking up the mantle of Lady Lilith would be this smooth…well, she would think about that later.

After seeing the guest out, Mr. Sims turned to Lilith with raised brows. She nodded and swept past him, not missing the twitch of a smile on his lips.

Chapter 28

Early spring arrived. Lilith thought more of Walter each passing day. Did he think of her?

It was inevitable she would see him in London since she had agreed to accompany Lizbeth and Sebastian. She hoped, oh how she hoped he had not taken her request for more time as a rejection. If he had, he could well be courting someone else, betrothed, or even married by the time she reached London. However strong she was in mind and spirit, she could not handle seeing him on the arm of another woman. It was her fault. She had told him not to wait. She had encouraged him to let her go. Despite all her promises of finding him and wanting a renewal of his offer once ready, her words had sounded too much like a rejection for him not to take them that way.

By the time she went to London, it would not have been that many months since they parted, but enough that he could have chosen a different path. How humiliating to declare herself ready for matrimony only to find him elsewhere engaged. The alternative was no less intimidating. What if she arrived in London to find him still available but with no interest in renewing his offer? She had behaved badly the last time they were together, abominably. Worse, she had hurt him unforgivably.

And if he did want her?

She had made the leap of leaving the only home she had known for two decades, a home she had made for herself, to build a new life so that they could be together. Should that fail, she would not lose heart, for she would still have her devotion to helping destitute women. Was all she had done enough to prove to him their time apart had been worth her preparations for life as a baroness? However well she was training herself for a life as a lady, it did not follow she could interact to the extent he would expect, but she was ready to try.

Oh, how she yearned for him.

She dared not anticipate their reunion too much, though. The more eager to see him, the more it would hurt if he rejected her.

Slipping her arm through Lizbeth's, the two ladies walked to the picnic area where Sebastian, Freya, Freya's nurse Mrs. Adams, and Jasper were playing. The sun was bright and the breeze cool, a perfect day for al fresco lounging.

"I've not thanked you, Lizbeth, for coming to Roddam Hall to fetch me," Lilith said, delivering her into Sebastian's capable hands.

"I believe the thanks are owed to you for inviting us for a week before the trek to Lyonn Manor. The caravan to London will be enormous fun with us all together. Even Charlotte looks forward to getting to know you, though I suspect she'll spend more time entertaining us with stories of Austria. It's too early to think of our return trip, but a merrier group it'll be since Papa will be joining us, this time to stay permanently."

Jasper and Freya were newly minted friends, Lilith noticed. Jasper licked Freya into giggles.

It was difficult to believe the baby was already seven months. Lilith had not seen her since early August. When Freya attempted to stand and reach for her auntie, Lilith had been shocked. Not long, and she would be wobble-walking. How had the baby grown so quickly? But of course, seven months was hardly quick.

The excitement of the picnic had been Freya's attempt to join the conversation with an obsessive repeat of "dada" to which Sebastian announced was proof she preferred her papa over her mama. Lizbeth had thrown bread at him until he retracted his words. They had all laughed so heartily, Jasper took to baying.

Mrs. Adams, the nurse, was immensely likable, Lilith discovered. A slim and soft-spoken woman in her mid-forties, she spoke to Freya as though the baby were a tiny adult. The nurse encouraged play as much as structure, something Lilith had done, as well, during her time as a teacher.

Sebastian wrestled Jasper, who was looking more like a horse than a puppy. "You were wise to accept the invitation, Lil'. I would have hated to tie you in the luggage carriage for the entire journey. Don't doubt I would have done it. I need you by my side, as does Lizbeth."

Lilith grinned at Liz, who rubbed her belly, rounded with their second child. That had been another shock. Lizbeth arrived with no need to announce she was increasing. It had been all too visible. The joke of Liz having Catholic twins — two babies born within a year of each other — had not yet worn thin.

Sebastian and Lizbeth were to stay at the hall for a week before heading to Lyonn Manor, where they would stay another week before leaving for London. Lilith's cousin, the Duke of Annick, had expressed some enthusiasm that she would be joining them and taking her place as Lady Lilith.

While she had not yet resolved her approach, she would need to confront her Aunt Catherine while at Lyonn Manor. As the Dowager Duchess of Annick, Catherine lived in the dower house. There would be no avoiding the confrontation. It must be done. And it must be done before they set off for London. The lady had the power to undermine all Lilith's plans.

"I'm afraid," Lilith said, "I will spend more time meeting with employment agencies and those with known philanthropic interests than attending entertainments. I realize it is a necessity to be introduced before I can call on those who might be interested in my endeavors, but I do have a goal, and that does not include prancing about ballrooms."

Sebastian laughed. "And you think we enjoy 'prancing,' as you say? Lizbeth will remain at the townhouse this Season, given her condition, and I'll escort you to the necessary engagements. You need not worry I'll drag you to every party in town."

"We shall get along well then," Lilith joked.

Lilith regaled them with stories of her near blunders when calling on neighbors, as well as the unusualness of everyone being overly kind to her. This had not been her expectation after the chilly reception in Allshire.

"They're only kind to me, I believe, because they recall me as a child," said Lilith. "They would not be so welcoming if I arrived out of the blue, the mystery daughter, or if they knew the truth."

"No, they would not," Sebastian agreed. "It would not stop me from claiming you as my legitimate sister, though. You will always be my sister. I don't give a snap who birthed you."

"Will they be this welcoming in London?" she asked.

Sebastian scratched his chin and thought before answering. "I can't say. Some will. Some won't. Society is made up of high sticklers and gossipmongers, so it's difficult to say the reception we can expect. Those you've met here will help smooth the way. They'll want to introduce you to those they know."

She hoped so. However much her intention was to set in motion a plan for helping others, she did selfishly want to see to her own future. She would not hide in the north afraid of gossip or scandal. She was done hiding. They might judge her for her time at the orphanage, question why her father sent her away, hear rumors of her behavior in Allshire, even discourage her dream for the women's home. Through it all, she would hold her chin high. She would earn respect, just as she had done once before.

Lilith confessed her enjoyment of playing lady of the manor. Never had she thought she would enjoy lording over people, but it was not quite like that. She enjoyed working with the housekeeper to learn the ins and outs of a large house, conspiring with the head gardener, and exchanging ideas with the steward. The feeling she experienced during her first visit, that feeling of being home, had not waned. She was *good* at being the lady of the manor. She genuinely enjoyed it.

"Are you happy here, Lil'?" Sebastian asked, pulling a squealing Freya into his lap. A happier baby Lilith had never seen.

"I do love it. I've seen a different side than the home from my memories. My being here feels right, almost natural, as though I was always supposed to be lady of the manor. For so long, I've sewn my own clothes, cooked my own food, laundered and cleaned on my own...oh the list does go on. I thought I would find myself idle. Indeed not. And it is nothing short of amazing not to have to do those chores."

Jasper rested his head in Lizbeth's lap, a new friend from which to solicit belly and head rubs.

Liz scratched behind his ears. "Will you stay, do you think?"

It was a question Lilith had anticipated their asking but had not sorted how to answer. The question begged for a hint about Walter — would they reunite? Seemed the true, underlying question.

"I don't know, to be honest. I want to stay, but for my plan to work, I believe I need to be closer to London. Roddam Hall is not a convenient location for my future guests, too far north. I would prefer, as well, not to combine my vision with my living quarters. A separation of work and life, as it were."

After raising Freya into the air for a mock toss half a dozen times, Sebastian said, "You're welcome to any of my estates. Unfortunately, the closest estate to London is in Yorkshire. That hardly helps you."

"Does it have to be near London?" Lizbeth asked.

"No." Lilith reached for the forgotten sandwiches, peckish after the walk about the garden. "The benefit of London is ease of travel and proximity to employment agencies. How will the women reach me if I'm in the wilds of Northumberland? They may spend their remaining pocket money to reach London only to find safety is across the country, out of reach."

Sebastian looked at her suspiciously. "Are you ever going to tell us what you're planning? You've been cloak-and-dagger about it."

"Not my intention. I assumed you could read my mind." Lilith laughed. "I want to open a women's home. I shall call it Noach Cottage after Noah's ark. It will be a place of refuge. Women who find themselves in need of a new life will be welcome, no matter the situation. If they have nowhere to turn, they can come to Noach."

"A noble vision, Lilith," said Lizbeth. "Will they all live there under your care? Wouldn't it be overcrowded?"

"The housing is meant to be temporary. The grand vision is rather complex. It will take help from others to see it through. I want to help women relocate with a new identity should they need it, such as what I'm trying to do with Harriette. I also want to help women without characters find work, hence my interest in recruiting the aid of employment agencies who are willing to work with me. Whatever the needs of the women, I want to provide a safe haven to see them through dark times. There will be an interview process before they're admitted to ensure their need is genuine and what I have to offer is what they need."

"Sorry, Freya," Sebastian said to the top of the baby's head. "Your auntie is going to drain me of all my wealth so that you have nothing to inherit."

"Sebastian!" Lizbeth and Lilith exclaimed in unison.

He smiled devilishly.

"I'll have you know," Lilith said in her best school-marm scold, "It will be self-sustainable. All I need are the startup funds, and from there, the women will earn their keep."

"I jest. You're welcome to however much you need," Sebastian said, still grinning.

"Yes, well, I don't wish for much. With luck and determination, I can connect with interested parties who will not only wish to patron Noach Cottage, but also help the women, such as setting them up as a widow in their parish, hiring them as a maid, and so forth. While in residence, the women will learn the necessary skills for survival and work, skills that will help also sustain the cottage. They can learn to garden, to eat what they grow and sell the excess for profit. I needn't pay for a schoolmistress or assistants because the able women can learn that trade while teaching any children present. They can learn to sew and sell their handiwork. They learn to bake and sell the food. I refuse to create something dependent on your funds, 'Bastian. The cottage will run itself."

Sebastian whistled. "Impressive. And you came up with this from a single conversation with Mrs. Wimple?"

"Hardly. I had the initial idea when Harriette came to me, but I've been building on it ever since. I've had several months to mull it over with quill to parchment, including the financial estimates."

"What of Harriette?" Lizbeth asked, rubbing Jasper's belly. His tail thumped in doggy ecstasy.

"While we wait for news from her headmistress application, she's been helping me with the grand plan."

"A headmistress?" Lizbeth echoed. "But she's never taught, has she?"

Lilith knew she was blushing. She could feel her neck and cheek warming. "It was a conveniently timed advertisement," was all she confessed.

"Nearby?" Liz probed.

Lilith cleared her throat and took slow bites of her sandwich.

"Near Devonshire."

"Oh!" Liz covered a hand over her mouth, realization dawning. "Oh, I see. The orphanage?" she pressed hesitantly.

Lilith nodded. "It would seem a certain someone has followed through with his orphanage."

"Yes. It would seem so." Liz looked to Sebastian with a knowing glance.

"Speaking of Collingwood," Sebastian said without the least bit of tact, "What does he think of Noach Cottage?"

Lizbeth cast him another speaking look. It was lost on him. He looked back and forth between the ladies, his brows raised expectantly.

Lizbeth answered first. "He wouldn't know about it, would he?"

"Why the devil not? Didn't you write to tell him?" Sebastian stared at Lilith, his brows furrowing.

Lizbeth again spoke on her behalf. "Darling, not all in the world are as ungenteel as we to write to the opposite gender. She has no reason to write to him."

"You wrote to me well before our engagement. I see nothing ungenteel about it," he protested.

With a sigh of exasperation, Liz turned to Lilith. "You must excuse him. He has no manners."

Lilith stuttered a laugh.

"Very well, then," she finally said. "I confess, I hurt him. Possibly beyond repair. He may never want to see me again, if you must know. He could already be betrothed to someone else. If he *is* willing to see me again, I hardly know if there's a future between us. There's only one thing to do."

They both waited with wide-eyed curiosity.

"I'm going to have to woo him."

"What's this?" Lilith asked her brother.

Aside from Jasper, who was curled at Lilith's feet, his head warming the top of one foot, the siblings were alone in the parlor. Lizbeth wanted to read to Freya in the nursery before Mrs. Adams tucked her into bed.

"Proof you're Jane's daughter," he said.

"We both know that's not true. So, what is this?" she repeated.

Sebastian waved the paper in the air. "Proof you can accept Walter's suit without guilt of illegitimacy."

"Sebastian. Give me the paper. Now. And I did not reject Walter because of that."

An expression of surprise arrested his features. He let the paper fall to his lap, out of her reach.

"Then why the devil did you reject him?"

"It's not your concern, is it?" she replied primly.

He glowered.

Silence stretched.

She huffed. "I did worry how scandal would affect him should Aunt Catherine speak out against me or should the Reverend Sands spread word out of spite. I did worry. But I rejected him because I wasn't courageous enough to face the unknown. Among the many things I feared, criticism was at the top. I experienced censure from the aristocrats in Allshire and knew it would be worse in London and beyond. One taste was quite enough, thank you."

"And now?" he queried, his fingers curling around the parchment.

"I've learned a thing or two about belonging. It's all I've ever wanted. But I've realized instead of waiting for other people to give me a sense of belonging, I must create it for myself. Only I can determine where I belong. I belong with you and Lizbeth. I belong here at Roddam Hall. I'll belong at Noach Cottage. If I have the courage to see it through, I'll belong in Society. I just might belong with Walter, if he'll forgive me for hurting him."

"Brava." Sebastian applauded, his eyes bright with admiration and approval.

As silly as it seemed to want his approval, she did. She wanted him to be proud of her.

Rustling the paper, Sebastian held it up to his face. "Not that you need this, then, but I'll read it to you all the same." With a wink, he read, "'Lilith Lancaster, daughter of Tobias Lancaster and Jane Lancaster, September, 3, 1760 —"

"What *is* that?" Lilith interrupted him, snatching the parchment out of his hands.

She stared at the paper, confused.

"It's your baptismal record."

"Did you forge this?" She pressed the paper to her chest. What, oh, what had her brother done?

Sebastian gave a single *ha*. "That comes from the vicar. It took him far longer than I had hoped to dig through the parish register of the previous vicar. At last, he found the recording of our christening. We were christened together. You would have been, what, two? I was not quite one. I've searched with the help of my man of business for birth records, orphanage records, any records at all to tie you to Lily Chambers or Jane Lancaster. This is all we could find. According to this, and as far as the archbishop would ever be concerned, you are the legitimate daughter of Jane Lancaster."

Lilith studied the paper, speechless.

"Honor Jane by being her daughter, Lilith. Our mother loved you as her own. We are your family. We are the ones who love you. That's what makes someone family, not blood. You've said so yourself. I came here ready for battle. I intended to fight you with my definition of family and how little blood matters, regardless of what law or people believe. I had a pretty speech prepared. It seems I needn't proselytize after all." He paused before adding, "Or do I?"

The paper blurred out of focus. A quick wipe of her hands over her eyes cleared her vision to see her brother smiling warmly at her.

Looking back to the paper, she asked, "And I suppose this one document magically solves all our problems?"

"Not all, but it will staunch anyone who sniffs into your past or spreads rumors. I believe my word will be enough. The word of our cousin will seal your entry into Society."

And so, this was it, she thought. Her ticket to another world. Until recently, it was not a world in which she wanted entrance. Now she had a cause worth fighting for, two if she counted Noach Cottage.

Chapter 29

Sebastian's London house could hardly be called a townhouse when it was located considerably west of the more popular residencies and was too grand even for the denotation of house. It backed up to the Thames with a spacious terrace overlooking the river and was decidedly a mansion. It stretched across a sizable park, iron gates and a gatehouse barring entrance to all those uninvited.

The difference between his London residence and that of the Duke of Annick or even Lord Collingwood was considerable. Although Lilith had not seen Walter's townhouse from the inside, Sebastian had pointed it out none too discreetly on a drive through Mayfair and Hyde Park. She had been to her cousin Drake's London house several times since arriving in London. It was gauche but fashionable. Its proximity to Mayfair made it much smaller in size than Sebastian's, but no less grand. At both Walter's and her cousin's townhouse, there was a noticeable lack of an iron gate. Guests were welcome, invited or uninvited.

Lilith knew her brother preferred a private and reclusive life. Would she? His home seemed so remote.

She had yet to see Walter. She had, however, seen Hazel. There was no mention of Walter during their reunion. A small seed of hope had lain dormant, waiting for Hazel to say *something* about Walter, some indication if he were available and interested in seeing her again. It was not to be had. Hazel praised Lilith's bravery to be introduced, invited her for more than one afternoon of calls, and focused her remaining attention on Lizbeth, who would give birth during the Season. During each minute with Hazel, Lilith had wished she had accepted Walter's offer of tutelage. How fun it would have been. Perhaps it was not too late. Lilith was far from polished, after all.

Being in London was empowering.

She preferred the country. But there was something exhilarating about the energy of London, the hustle and bustle, the fast pace. Meeting new people was even exciting. Lizbeth's sister Charlotte, the Duchess of Annick, took Lilith under her wing and introduced her to key figures within her inner circle, all in preparation for the much more formal introduction to come. Lilith did not find the conversations tedious. Everything was new and *fun*.

While she dared not discuss her plan for the women's home, at least not until she had been more widely accepted and had resolved who would be the philanthropic sort, she did have one patron. The patron in question was not only willing to back the plan with funds, but with resources, ranging from helping re-home destitute women to offering character references for employment. The patron was the most unlikely of people.

Aunt Catherine.

Catherine Mowbrah, the Dowager Duchess of Annick, was a formidable force. Or so Lilith had anticipated. The woman had never spoken of Lilith to Sebastian, although she knew Lilith to be alive and living in Allshire when Sebastian and the rest of the world had believed her dead. The woman had refused to acknowledge Lilith or see Freya since a woman of *natural* birth was staying at the castle.

And yet she was willing to accept Lilith in exchange for being a silent partner to Noach Cottage. Though she would not openly acknowledge Lilith, she agreed not to deny her as her niece. It was as good as, if not better, than Lilith had hoped.

During her visit to Lyonn Manor, Aunt Catherine declined all invitations to dine with them and insisted Lizbeth bring Freya to the dower house, all to avoid Lilith. The time of reckoning arrived the day before they left for London. Procrastination may not have been the best approach, but it took courage to face one's nemesis.

Looking her best, thanks to Hannah, Lilith marched to the dower house. It was farther than she anticipated, two miles west from the main house. Had she known, she would have taken Jasper with her for the walk. As it was, Jasper had been left at the main house with Sebastian to distract him from the absence of his mistress. He did not like to be without her for long.

Her knock was greeted by a dour butler who creaked when he moved. She did not have a card to give him, as he seemed to expect with his out-stretched, gloved hand.

"Will you please inform my aunt that her niece Lilith requests an audience?"

She gave him her haughtiest look. She had been practicing.

So had he, it would seem, for he was unperturbed. "I shall ascertain if Her Grace is at home," he said with a firm click of the door in Lilith's face.

As if he did not know his mistress' whereabouts, she thought with a scoff.

The wait was long enough to be insulting. At least the roses were in bloom. Lilith admired the rose hedges to either side of the portico. They looked newish, as though planted within the last year, but they were thriving admirably. Mr. Turnbow would be awed and have invited the head gardener to tea.

Straightening her dress and running her hands along her torso for the fifteenth time, she waited.

At last, the door opened. The butler peeked out through a thin slat of space. "Her Grace is from home."

Of all the...*harrumph*! Not that Lilith expected a different response, but it was no less irritating.

The butler made to close the door, but Lilith stuck her foot in the doorway with a firm hand pushing the door open, her strength surpassing the aged butler.

"This will not do," said the man, huffing and puffing and reaching out to grab her and escort her off the premises.

Undaunted, Lilith dodged, then darted past him. There was a long gallery stretching from one side to the other. Should she go left or right? From the sounds of the butler's footsteps, she did not have time to second-guess a choice. Turning on her heel, she headed left, opening the first door to an empty room.

"You cannot be here!" shouted the butler, scuttling in her wake.

A quick glance over her shoulder revealed a few footmen had joined the chase. They would be far faster than the butler. As quickly as she could, knowing this may be futile, she flung open door after door, peering in only for a second.

Blast! All empty.

She took the bend in the hall to the west wing.

First room, empty. Second room, empty. Third room...

Lilith jerked to a stop, her hand on the door handle, her eyes riveted on an austere woman rising from a throne-like chair.

In the mere seconds she had to study the woman, she was struck by their resemblance. Aside from the scornful expression, age lines, and silver streaks at the temples, Lilith might have well been looking in the mirror. The experience was shocking.

And then hands were around her arms as the footmen took hold to remove her.

The butler stepped in to close the door. With a bow, he said, "My apologies, Your Grace."

"Leave us," ordered the duchess.

The footmen and butler hesitated.

She arched a single brow.

In renewed haste, the footmen unhanded Lilith. The butler bowed and stepped backwards out of the room, pulling the door closed behind him.

Her shoulders back and her heart in her throat, Lilith took three steps towards her father's sister.

Catherine looked Lilith up and down, assessing. "Well?"

Lilith stared, dumbstruck.

Thumping her gold-handled cane against the rug, Catherine questioned, "You barged in here, so what do you want?"

"I am the daughter of Jane and Tobias Lancaster. I intend to live the life my mother wanted for me, the life of Lady Lilith. I expect you to acknowledge me as your niece." Lilith reminded herself to breathe.

"You are the daughter of a servant. My brother was right to send you to an orphanage."

It was not lost on Lilith that she had not been invited to sit. Clasping her hands before her, she fixed her aunt's glare, refusing to be cowed.

"He was. Perhaps not in the way he did, but he was right to send me. Had I stayed, I would have undoubtedly been treated to similar abuse as my brother. As it happened, I was spared. You know what Sebastian suffered. It was not unlike what your brother suffered at the hand of your father after you left him to marry the duke. You can atone for leaving your brother behind by accepting his daughter, the daughter he took in though he knew me to be illegitimate. He raised me as legitimate. How can you deny his wishes after leaving him behind?"

Catherine's eyes narrowed. "You presume to know a great deal about me."

Lilith did not answer right away. She held her aunt's gaze, willing her words to hit the mark. It had been Lizbeth who told her what little she knew of Catherine, for at one time, the woman had confided in Lizbeth.

When Lilith remained silent, Catherine said, "I suppose you want to masquerade as an earl's daughter so you can secure a good match and live in the lap of luxury, as useless as most wives of the peerage. You're just like your peasant mother, setting her eyes on a prize above her station."

"You're wrong," Lilith said, unflinching. "This has nought to do with me. As Lady Lilith, I can gain the connections needed to open a home that will help displaced and destitute women. Such a home will help those who have no recourse against abusive husbands, no family to turn to should they find themselves ravished and left with child, no means to secure employment without references. Imagine a frightened girl of little more than sixteen, beaten so brutally by her father she would rather die than return home. I can help her."

Catherine's eyes widened. Barely above a whisper, she asked, "How did you know?"

Lilith did not understand the question, but she realized her words affected her aunt. She continued, not wanting to lose momentum.

"They will be safe and trained for a new future. With the connections I make as Lady Lilith, I can find them employment, arrange for new lives, teach them skills to enter the workforce or survive on their own. As the daughter of a servant, I have no influence. As Lady Lilith, I can see this through to fruition."

Her aunt broke eye contact midway through Lilith's speech. Though she returned to her seat, she did not invite Lilith to join her.

Gaze trained to the floor, Catherine asked more to herself than to Lilith, "Why should I help you?"

Boldly, Lilith took a step towards her aunt. "I will do this with or without your consent. I mean no disrespect, but my plan is more important than your opinion. I do ask for your consent. I do not wish to embarrass you, nor do I want you to undermine my efforts by denouncing me. If we work together, imagine what we could accomplish."

A long stare followed. Lilith had the distinct impression her thoughts were being read and her words judged. In the distance, she could hear a clock chime.

"Know this," Catherine said. "I only consent to help you because you have backbone. You are strong willed enough to see this through. Your blood may be dirty, but you've proven yourself a Lancaster. My consent is not without conditions. Sit. I'll ring for tea."

And with those words, Lilith's future was secured.

It was not lost on Lilith that had she gone to her aunt without returning to Allshire or having Harriette knock on her cottage, the outcome would have been different. As it was, her aunt was to patron Noach Cottage.

Lilith no longer feared the *beau monde*. In her heart, she was not illegitimate. No longer would she hide herself. No longer would she be forced into the mud.

"What do you mean the land has been purchased?" Walter demanded.

His secretary, a squat man with thatched brows and a thinning hairline, mopped his forehead. "As I said, I offered a fair price, but the solicitor informed me it had already been sold."

"Double it. Double the offer. I'll sort out the expense later. I *need* that property for the extension, Bromley." Under his breath, Walter muttered, "Who would want uncultivated land with a dilapidated estate in the middle of nowhere?"

"M'lord, I cannot double the offer. Construction has begun."

"*Construction*? It only just sold! What do you mean there's *construction*? Approach the daft bull and offer to buy it from him!"

Walter was beyond enraged. This would foil his plans for the women's home. He had it all planned. In one section of the property, there would be the orphanage and foundling hospital. In the other section, there would be a women's home for those needing shelter until they resolved employment. His vision was still fuzzy on how it would work, but he could sort that out later. For now, he needed the property. Had he known some imbecile would purchase it out from under his nose to build a country home, he would have purchased both lots together. At the time, it had been outrageously priced, and he had not seen the need to spend money for another section when one would do well enough.

Cradling his head in his hands, he stared at the top of his desk.

"I'm sorry, m'lord, but the deal is done. I've begun searching for comparable land and have compiled a list for you to consider." Mr. Bromley moved a piece of parchment into Walter's peripheral.

"I don't want comparable land. I want that land. How am I supposed to ask the women to help at the orphanage and hospital if they have to walk half across Hampshire from one location to the other?"

With a light cough, Mr. Bromley offered, "The plots listed are inexpensive enough to allow the purchase of a conveyance for your, er, guests."

Walter pushed the list back to his secretary. "This is nonsense. I want that property. I want this to be a community. And lest you forget, I would have to spend my time riding from place to place. It'll be time consuming enough making trips from Devonshire to Hampshire, never mind the trips to London." Shaking his head, he asked, "Am I to scrap the women's home, then? Postpone it for now? That might be best. Let me think on it."

"Yes, m'lord." Mr. Bromley shuffled his papers, waiting to be dismissed.

Without looking up, Walter waved a hand. He was not normally so ill mannered, but this business with the property was most unsettling.

To distract himself, he sifted through the stack of invitations. He had arrived early to London to spend time charming employment agencies and meeting with a few peers he thought would be interested enough in his plan to help. The earliness of his arrival had long since passed. The Season was officially underway.

His friends had paid him a few calls to invite him for breakfast at White's or a visit to Tattersall's, but he found his interest had waned and his time monopolized by hiring and meeting the new staff that would ready Colling Orphanage for its grand opening. The foundling hospital was still under construction, but the orphanage would be open for business before the Season ended.

Since he needed to connect with philanthropic peers, he did not avoid all entertainments. He did not even want to avoid entertainments, for they were still dashed good fun. It was only that other things took precedence now. He found joy in his responsibilities. For the first time, he had spoken on an issue of interest at the House of Lords. His father would have been proud.

Later in the month, he would make a trip to the orphanage to ensure all was going well. The new headmistress had arrived, and though she seemed far too young for the position, Mr. Bromley assured him her characters were impeccable. Her delicate condition added to her charm since his whole goal was to help women like her. Her name, Harriette Waters, did not sound familiar, but he swore he knew her from somewhere. Walter had seen her before. For the life of him, he could not put his finger on where.

So distracted, he almost missed an invitation from his cousin Charlotte. She was to host a ball. This would be one entertainment he would not miss. Her parties were always a squeeze.

Ah, that reminded him.

He needed to pay a call to Roddam and Lizbeth. His mother had been there nearly every other day to look in on Lizbeth. Liz's condition had come as a shock to him since it seemed only yesterday when Freya had been born, although nine months was hardly yesterday. He had yet to call on them. He did want to see them. But he had been so terribly busy.

On the fringes of his mind, he wondered if Lilith had come with them. There would be nothing of interest for her in London, but would Lizbeth not want her as a midwife for her second child? His mother had not volunteered information, and he had not queried. The thought of coming face-to-face with Lilith was nothing short of trepidation. What would he say to her?

Chapter 30

Walter hastened his steps, his heels clicking on the cobblestones. He was late. By now, he would have missed the receiving line. He could only hope he would not miss the first set.

This would teach him never to reserve sets in advance.

Miss Pamela was to be his partner. Only one dance had been reserved with her. She was blonde and prim with an enterprising mother. Two days this week, he had taken her for a drive through the park. Two days the week before, he had escorted her to a soirée, and then the opera. Was he courting the girl or merely distracting himself from thoughts of Lilith, testing how it felt to be at someone else's side, perhaps even preparing for the day he realized she would never return to him?

He tried not to compare the two women. It was not easy. Miss Pamela was the antithesis of Lilith and eager to be a baroness. Every time his feelings for Lilith resurfaced, he reminded himself she had rejected him, begged him to let her go. Had she bothered to *try* to prepare herself, as she had promised to do, or had she returned to Allshire and realized how happy she was in that life? How long could he sensibly wait and hope without making a fool of himself? He turned his thoughts back to his dance partner.

When he approached Annick's London house, it was to find a swarm of carriages blocking the road and twice as many partygoers lining the sidewalk. Good. He was not embarrassingly late.

The ride from his orphanage had taken longer than expected. There had been just enough time to bathe and dress before setting off on foot since his mother had taken the carriage, leaving without him since he was late to arrive home.

Making his way through the crowd, a nod, smile, and brief word to everyone as he passed, he mounted the front steps and gave a nod to the butler, who was taking cards one at a time in agonizing slowness. The man spared Walter only a cursory glance, recognizing him as family.

The antechamber was no less full. Several of his mates were standing about, already planning to make a break for the card room. As eager as he was to get inside the ballroom to give his best to his cousin and find Miss Pamela, he could not avoid his friends. As soon as he spotted Everleigh, he did not want to avoid them. Only during the Season did he have a chance to catch up to Everleigh, one of his best Oxford mates, as the fellow lived in the north, not far from Annick.

With a hearty handshake, he greeted his old fencing partner.

"Well met, Evey!" he exclaimed.

"Look who's graced us with his presence," said Everleigh with a jovial glance to his group.

Ah, yes, he had declined most of their invitations. It was not like they would understand. None of them had inherited yet or were not in line to inherit. Mr. Winston Everleigh, eldest son of Viscount Rutherford, was a known gamester and rogue who could not take life seriously if it hit him on the head. No, his friends would not understand he had turned over a new leaf.

"Pardon my absence, fellows," Walter began to say before Everleigh interrupted.

"No need to apologize to us. We know all too well the need to make scarce once the marriage-minded mamas begin to hound. Word has it you're looking for a leg shackle." He waggled his eyebrows.

"Oh, ho ho! Gossip at its finest," Walter protested.

It was beyond fifteen minutes before he could break free, and that was only thanks to their realizing the dancing would begin shortly. They headed for the safety of the card room.

Tugging at his waistcoat and running a hand through his hair, he proceeded into the ballroom. The receiving line had dispersed some time ago and couples were taking to the dance floor. Dash it all! He had not wanted to be this late. He could not even spot Charlotte, Annick, or his mother at quick glance. Plumes of varying heights nodded; sparkling gems reflected the candlelight; cologne overpowered the senses; fine figures reflected in gilded mirrors. A squeeze was putting it mildly. He tried not to think how much he wished Lilith could see this.

"Lord Collingwood!" came a feminine voice behind a group of matrons.

He turned and smiled to see Mrs. Addison, mother to Miss Pamela and three other daughters. Mrs.

Addison, a plump and cheerful woman, waved indiscreetly at him as she bustled over, her daughter in tow.

He greeted them with a bow.

"You've not forgotten you reserved the first set, have you?" Mrs. Addison asked, more scold than question.

She pushed her blushing daughter his direction. If the girl swooned, he would not be surprised.

"It has been foremost on my mind, ma'am." With another bow, he offered his arm to the pink-faced girl. "You're looking quite pretty, Miss Pamela."

She did look pretty. Tight, blonde ringlets framed a heart-shaped face that, he suspected, had been pinched and puckered. She did not strike him as the rouge-wearing type, yet her lips and cheeks were noticeably rosy.

He escorted her onto the dancefloor to join the gathering crowd of dancers. She was at least a full head shorter than him, petite, and exceedingly shy. He liked her. Being her first Season, she would need more town bronze to be comfortable with him. With others, she was social and full of life. Her shyness was reserved for him.

Facing each other in line, they prepared for the first chord to strike.

It was then he tore his eyes away from Miss Pamela to catch sight of Annick leading out his partner.

His heart failed him. Blood drained from his face and limbs.

There, in a shimmering, green ballgown, regally poised, her hair coiled in an intricate knot of raven splendor, was the most beautiful woman of his acquaintance.

Lilith.

For a startling stretch of time, he could not breathe.

Searching his memory, he harnessed the last time he had seen her. Good God. He had lain with that woman! His eyes swept over every curve, enhanced by the bespoke gown.

What the deuce was she doing here?

Before he could turn to his partner and keep from shaming himself by gawking, Lilith turned to face the line of dancers. Their eyes locked.

The morning began in frenzied chaos. Lizbeth went into labor far too early. It was not for another several weeks that the baby was due. Hazel had been summoned to look after Freya since Lilith recruited Mrs. Adams' help. Mr. Trethow had likewise been summoned, along with Charlotte. Sebastian attended the delivery, as he had for his first child.

It all happened much faster than before. It would seem Freya's sibling could not wait to get started in life and was, or so Lilith joked later, already jealous of all the attention big sister was receiving.

At a little before noon, Cuthbert Lancaster, Baron Embleton, gave his first angry cry. He came out screaming, angry at the world for trying to hold him back by a few more weeks. Despite arriving alarmingly early, he was healthy, though on the small side. Lizbeth had fallen asleep almost immediately after delivery, but she did wake long enough to feed her son and for Lilith to feed her herbal broth in turn.

Freya wanted nothing to do with her baby brother, as though she suspected this was the beginning of endless days of stolen attention. She took one look at little Lord Embleton and wailed.

Lilith would not say she envied having two babies less than a year apart, but she did envy with deep tenderness the love her brother and sister-in-law shared. She had found such a love with Walter. Had she accepted him in October, she would not have given him her best and may come to resent him. He had been no more ready than she, still trapped in a cycle of regret over his father. Now, she could bring her all, as could he. But would he have her?

Given the rough and tumble day, Sebastian apologized profusely to Charlotte and Lilith that he would not be attending the ball. Lilith tried to worm out of it, as well, but the family fought her. This ball was in her honor, after all. It was her official introduction to Society. However much she wished to remain at her sister-in-law's bedside, she could not bow out.

It was in Charlotte's boudoir, an hour before they would form the receiving line, that Lilith again tried to bow out, never mind she was dressed and ready. Her nerves betrayed her. She no longer feared the *beau monde*, but she did fear she would suffer an apoplexy of memory and forget everything she had painstakingly trained for over the past several months. What if she stepped on toes? What if she smiled too brightly?

Charlotte patted her hand. "You might not believe this, but I felt the same not so long ago."

"*You?*" Lilith doubted that.

"Yes, *me*," she said. "I was a country girl from Cornwall and had never been east of Exeter. I worried myself silly thinking I would do something gauche."

Lilith tried to imagine the duchess as a country girl. Impossible. Decked in diamonds and emeralds, her auburn hair bejeweled by sparkling gems and piled high, her spine straight with poise, and her nose lifted in hauteur, Charlotte looked born into nobility.

Signaling a maid, Charlotte gave a nod to the wine glasses. In a flurry of movement, the maid produced a wine glass on a gilded platter before Lilith.

"Drink," Charlotte commanded. "It'll help. I promise." The duchess reached for her own glass to swirl and savor. "The more selective you are about your company, the more respected and sought after you'll become. It's easy to choose with whom to converse without cutting anyone. In this way, you can surround yourself with those who share your values." With a reassuring smile to Lilith's worried expression, Charlotte added, "Above all, enjoy yourself. You're family, and no one will question it. Let me worry about the gossipers while you enjoy yourself." She squeezed Lilith's hand. "Chin up. You're marvelous."

Throughout the greeting of guests and early mingling, Lilith stayed at Charlotte's side, suspecting there was more to her hostess than the vain exterior. Though the duchess was not yet one and twenty, she had an innocent kind of maturity. With time and age, Lilith suspected Charlotte would become a truly remarkable woman.

She was a superb hostess, at the very least.

For all Lilith's worrying, she had met enough people since arriving in town to have a set of near-friends surrounding her, including her neighbors from Roddam Hall, most especially the dear Mrs. Putnam, who claimed a special friendship for being the first to call on her.

Even without them, there would have been nothing to fear. Guests were falling over themselves, despite their feigned ennui, to meet her after hearing the circulating rumors during the weeks leading up to the ball. Everyone wanted to meet the long-lost daughter of the fifteenth Earl of Roddam. The gossip caught fire with speculative theories as to why she disappeared, fueled by the older generation with revived rumor that the earl had killed his wife and hidden his daughter not to be reminded of his crime. Lilith knew better, for Jane had always been sickly, but the rumors were too delicious by half.

Her time at the orphanage was not shamed. Instead, they found her a curiosity and vied for a chance to interview her. What was it like to live amongst heathens? How had her brother found her after all those years?

Her dances were reserved before the receiving line dispersed.

It was all overwhelming. It was also relieving. All her fear of ridicule and scandal, and here she was, the toast of the ball. No one even seemed to mind her age.

However awe-inspiring the evening, her eyes searched the crowd for one particular face. Would he come? Did he know she would be here?

Her attempts to focus on conversation failed as her gaze swept the room every few minutes, hoping to spot those beautiful curls and green eyes. It was of him she thought when she chose the ballgown. A foolhardy notion when they had not spoken since early October. But all she could do was think of him. Somehow, she had to win him back.

A Lady Something was nattering at her when her cousin Drake arrived to escort her onto the floor. As she turned a smile to him, she saw over his shoulder the man for whom her heart beat. Walter stepped into the ballroom, his eyes scanning the crowd until they lit on a pretty, young girl in white. His face broadened into a heart-arresting smile. Somewhere in the region behind her eyes, she burned. That smile was not directed at her but someone else.

Unable to look away, she watched him speak to the girl's mama before escorting his partner to the dance floor. Obviously, the set had been reserved.

Lilith was too afraid to ask her cousin if they were courting, or worse betrothed. She did not think she could bear it, and she would not have this evening ruined. What a spectacle that would make if she started crying on the dancefloor! And why should she? She had told him to let her go. She had encouraged him to look about for someone else since she could promise nothing more than to *try* to prepare herself for a life with him. This was her doing. Oh, why had she not asked him to wait? What a coward she had been!

With a nod to Drake, she joined the dancers.

The dance was a dizzying whirl of excitement. However aware of Walter she was, Lilith lost herself to the steps. It would be uncultured for her to laugh, but she wanted to. Drake was an arrogant dancer, performing for her amusement, which made the dance all that more entertaining. Her first introduction to him last summer at the castle had made him seem the worst sort of aristocrat, but now that she knew him, she liked him exceedingly well.

Thankfully, even when separated from him during the dance, she was never paired with Walter.

More than once, her eyes found his. She dared not look away for fear she would seem a coward, a woman pining for a man she had rejected.

When the dance ended, she thought herself relieved of his company. Drake escorted her to Charlotte. But then, before he bowed himself elsewhere, Drake glanced behind him.

"Ah! Look who arrived." Drake turned to Lilith. "Shall we introduce him to the new you?"

There was no question who he meant, of course. Walter stood at the perimeter of the dancefloor, talking animatedly with the girl in white. Oh dear. Lilith would have to come face-to-face with them both. The duke held out his arm for Lilith. Oh dear, oh dear, oh dear. She could not very well say no, could she?

No amount of bracing could prepare her for him to introduce the girl as his affianced bride. She schooled her reaction and bit the inside of her cheek as she approached on her cousin's arm.

Walter turned to them as they drew near. The smile he had reserved for his dance partner turned into a frown when he saw Lilith. He looked embarrassed to see her. Was he ashamed about what they had shared?

Oh, good heavens. Why did she have to recall that now?

And with that thought came a flood of heightened awareness. She could nearly feel the smoothness of his skin beneath her fingertips, though she was some distance away and not touching him. His voice caressed her ears though he had not yet spoken. His familiar cologne wrapped about her. For the love of God, she could even taste his lips. As though testing her reality, she ran the tip of her tongue over her dry lips.

Then they were upon the couple. Drake and Lilith faced Walter and the girl in white.

Drake took the initiative, oblivious to the awkwardness.

"Good to see you, Collingwood. Was worried you wouldn't make it. Allow me to introduce someone you've met before but not met properly. My cousin, Lady Lilith."

Holding her gaze steady, she watched his brows raise in surprise. Walter bowed, then held out a hand for hers.

Please, don't let my hand tremble. She slipped her cold, gloved fingers into his warm ones. If she did not swoon, it would be a shock. She *knew* him. He *knew* her. They had *known* each other. And she had shattered his heart.

"A pleasure, my lady," he said with his all too familiar voice.

Lilith's stomach somersaulted.

He kissed the air above her hand then released it. The mere seconds in which her fingers had been in his palm had felt like a lifeline to unconditional happiness.

Turning to the girl at his side, he said, "Allow me the honor of introducing Miss Pamela."

The girl curtsied. Lilith inclined her head.

He had not said betrothed. But that omission did not guarantee he was not engaged. She heard a faint buzzing in her ears and realized she had been holding her breath.

Drake winked at the girl and said without tact, "Now that you've had a chance around the ring with Collingwood, I do believe it's my cousin's turn. You've saved a set for Collingwood, haven't you?" He turned his eyes to Lilith.

The girl blushed, and Lilith's eyes widened. How embarrassing! If Walter had asked, that would be one thing, but to force them into a dance? She was mortified.

Walter smiled politely. "You read my mind. May I, my lady?"

How no one could hear her gulp, she did not know. "I'm afraid my dances are spoken for, my lord." It was true.

Drake was not to be outmaneuvered. "Give him Seb's dance. Since the old goat won't be here, it's only fair."

"Oh, yes," she said absently with a nervous laugh. "I had quite forgotten. Sebastian's dance. Yes. The third set is yours, my lord."

Walter nodded, then turned to Drake. "Where's Roddam this evening?"

"You've not heard? Blimey. Lizzie surprised him this morning with an heir!"

Walter snapped to attention. "By Jove. I was called from town. Returned barely in time for the ball. Is she well? Is the babe well? Not to speak indelicately, but isn't the news coming *early*?"

Miss Pamela's face could not be redder. Lilith thought of her rather like a child at the grown-up table. But that was unfair to the girl.

Before either Drake or Lilith could answer, Hazel and Charlotte appeared. The conversation continued, but not for long until her next partner sought her for the second set. She had come face-to-face with him and survived. How flushed she must look!

The second dance flew by in a swirl of color. Her partner engaged her in conversation through the whole of it, but she could not recall afterwards what had been said. Her full attention was on the third set to come. Did she dare ask him his relationship with Miss Pamela? That would be rude. But did she dare? How would she know how to proceed if she did not ask?

And suddenly, he was approaching her, his hand held out for hers, ready for his set.

Walter led her to the center with the other dancers. He did not smile. She searched his eyes for answers but found them veiled. With a deep breath, she launched into the dance.

They moved silently, never taking their eyes from each other. Even when separated and paired with others, their eyes remained locked. She tingled with continued awareness of him.

The first dance of the set ended.

"It's remarkably warm, don't you think? Could I tempt you for a walk in the garden?" he asked.

Her heart pounded with such ferocity, she could not hear herself answer, though she must have said yes, for he escorted her to the terrace doors. The London night air was just as muggy as the ballroom, but she was glad to be outside.

The terrace and garden beyond were well lit with colorful lanterns that danced rainbows on the cobbled paths. Both areas were populated with couples. Walter directed her to the garden. They walked in silence, her hand on his sleeve. However short the distance, her mind replayed in vivid detail every moment they had shared since first meeting, every conversation, every glance.

The path took them past other couples, some with chaperones, some without, all with courteous nods in their direction, until they came to a secluded snug surrounded by marble statues. Walter leaned his back against one of the statues and stared at her.

What could she do but stare back?

She had been away from him longer than she had known him, and yet now that she was with him again, she could not imagine how she had survived for so long without him. He was the air she breathed. And how ridiculous was that thought?

Before she could stop herself, the words spilled out. "Am I to wish you happy?"

Even in the dull lantern light, she could see him frown. "Miss Pamela?" he questioned. "I've not yet solicited her hand, if that's what you mean."

Yet.

He had not *yet* solicited her hand.

Lilith's heart landed somewhere at her feet. Was this how he had felt when she rejected him? If so, she did not deserve his forgiveness. But how was she to survive this evening without collapsing into sorrow? No, no, she would not think like this. She refused to think like this. *Yet* meant she had a chance. However slim, she could win his heart.

"You're well, then?" she asked, wishing she could take it back and ask something else. What an inane question. Love was not won with such insipidness.

But how else to broach what she truly needed to ask? Knowing if she would need to court him, earn his trust, or if she simply had to announce she had prepared herself was crucial to moving forward. Or... perhaps there was no turning back for him.

"I am," he answered just as inanely. "And you?" Before she could answer, he added with a sharpness edged by curiosity, "I'm shocked to see you here. I thought you were in Allshire, living a quiet but contented life."

His words came as a surprise. She had assumed he knew, that someone had apprised him of her time at Roddam Hall, that someone at least had told him her whereabouts in London, especially given the time she had spent with Hazel since arriving to town. But then, no one had talked about him to her, either.

"No, I moved to Roddam Hall in autumn. Had it not been for Harriette, I might have stayed longer in Allshire, but she prompted me to make the leap sooner than I anticipated."

He clapped his hands together, startling her. "That's how I know her! From the Allshire church!"

Lilith was confused but only briefly. Blast! In her nervousness, she had let Harriette's name slip. Of course, he would now make the connection between his new headmistress and Lilith. She was glad for the darkness so he could not see her flush.

"You encouraged her to apply, I assume?" he asked. "You know about the orphanage, then?"

"I do, yes. I'm proud of you."

His voice lowered almost to a whisper. "Are you?"

Unsure how to answer without embarrassing herself further, she remained silent.

"How's Jasper?" he asked at length.

She laughed softly. "Spoiled. He has his own valet, if that's not the most absurd thing for a dog to have. You would hardly recognize him. He's the size of a small pony and can no longer fit on my lap, though he's not above trying."

Walter chuckled. He reached a hand to rub the back of his neck. The mannerism was so familiar, her heart ached with longing.

"And Liz is well? Be honest." Under his breath, he added, "I had wondered if you would accompany her. She should not have come in her condition."

"You know how stubborn she can be. And yes, she's well. It would mean the world to her if you called on her in a day or two to meet the babe."

He nodded, his eyes trained on her. "Your dances are reserved," he said.

"Yes, yes, they are."

He laughed awkwardly. "Anyone special you have your eye on? Mr. Kellens is a good-looking chap, I suppose, as far as fellows go."

Who was — oh! Her dance partner for the second set. So distracted by Walter, she had not paid the man any attention, even to the point of forgetting his name. Poor Mr. Kellens. That Walter asked about someone else solidified for her he had indeed taken everything she said that fateful evening as a rejection. Did he believe she would become Lady Lilith for anyone but him, or…was this him hinting it was too late for them? It was time to set aside politeness. She steeled herself.

"Well, now that you ask, someone has caught my eye," she said.

"Ah, yes, I suspected." Walter crossed his arms over his chest and dropped his gaze to the ground. "You've been well received it seems. It's not surprising you have suitors."

"No, you misunderstand. *I* have my eye on *him*. The trouble is I'm not sure he'll have me, to be honest." She wished she could see him better, but the lighting was too poor. Simultaneously, she was glad for the shadows in which to hide.

"He'd be daft not to have you. If you've set your cap at him, all you need is to smile, and he'll be yours."

She bit her bottom lip. This was hopeful indeed!

But then it went terribly wrong.

Pushing himself against the statue, he bowed. "If you'll excuse me, my lady. I wish you the world, but I've no desire to watch you pay court to someone else." He turned to leave.

Oh dear, oh dear.

"Walter, Wait!"

Without thinking, she grabbed his arm.

When he turned, his expression stormy, she reached up to capture his face between her hands. Before he could move away, she kissed him. She met his lips with an open mouth, desperate for him to know how sorry she was for hurting him. All that happened in their absence needed to happen for them to be together, but she was deeply sorry at how she had gone about it.

In her kiss, she poured all the love she had to offer, willing him to accept her and forgive her and love her. At first, he was passive, allowing her to kiss him. Then his hands found her waist, and he pulled her against him in a tight embrace. Wrapped in his arms, she was home.

When they parted, it was a slow release, neither wanting to let go.

"After all your hard work to enter Society, you're going to compromise us both and cause a scandal anyway," he said this with a laugh.

They stepped away from each other but stayed connected by an invisible string, or so it felt to her.

"Just to be clear," he queried, "am I the one you have your eye on, or is there someone else?"

"Of course, it's you. It's always been you and forever will be. But what about Miss Pamela?"

"She's sweet, but I'm not courting her. How can I when I'm in love with you?"

"Oh, Walter." She worried she was to be a watering pot after all. Clearing her throat of the mounting tears, she said, "Well, it's a good thing, then, because we're to be neighbors. It would have been dreadfully awkward otherwise."

"Neighbors? I'm afraid you'll have to explain."

"I purchased the property next to Colling Orphanage. I knew it was a gamble, but the location was divine. The estate is in disrepair, but there's a wonderful row of laborer cottages on the property that will be perfect for what I have planned. It was horribly high priced, but Sebastian's solicitor was able to haggle. Impoverished gents are apparently easy to persuade."

She was rambling. She knew it, but she could not stop herself. Words tumbled out in her excitement. It had been so long since they had last spoken. What she wanted to say was how much she had missed him, how much she wished she had accepted his proposal, how much she wished she had not been a silly ninny. Alas, she rambled about the property instead.

"*You* bought that property?" He was all astonishment. "Why? I had my eye on it! I feel cheated. You snagged it right out from under my nose! What could you possibly want with it?"

With a giggle, Lilith said, "I'm not the least sorry. But before I tell you my plan, I want to ensure you want me for more than my brilliance."

If she did not act now, she would lose her nerve.

Taking his hand in hers, she asked, "Walter Hobbs, would you do me the honor of making me the happiest of women by marrying me?"

The silence that followed set her heart pounding anew. This was too soon. She should have waited. She should have renewed the friendship first. She should have made her apologies. She should have waited for him to renew his proposal instead. This was not how it was done!

"You've made me so proud," she said, filling the silence in hopes of convincing him, "by following through with all your plans. Let me make you proud too. Let me prove to you how fit I am to be a baron's wife, never to embarrass you. I've been training, fulfilling my promise. And I —"

"Lilith," he said, cupping her cheek in his gloved hand. "Oh, Lilith. You needn't persuade me. You were fit to be a baron's wife even in your hand-sewn dresses. You could walk about London in a sack, and you'd still turn my head and make me proud. You have nothing to prove. You're a stunning woman inside and out. I only hope I'm worthy of you."

When she made to speak, he pressed a finger to her lips. "If you're certain you'll have me," he said, "then yes. Yes, I'll marry you. A thousand times over, I'll marry you."

Walter sealed his declaration with a kiss.

Epilogue

The Season ended with a flurry of activity. After accepting Lilith's proposal, however unusual it was for a woman to propose to a man, Walter publicly courted her for two weeks before announcing their betrothal at Mrs. Putnam's soirée, an event that raised the woman's status in Society to near celebrity.

During the courtship, he was seen taking Lilith to the opera, sending her flowers, escorting her to the park alongside the Duke and Duchess of Annick, and walking with her and his mother through the pleasure gardens. He knew how hard she worked to avoid any sniff of scandal, while his own behavior in Allshire had been deplorable. It was a wonder the gossip of that botched courtship had not made it to London drawing rooms. He wanted all above board this time.

After three weeks of banns, an announcement in the paper, and a betrothal ball, Lilith and Walter wed at St. George's in Hanover Square, an event followed by a wedding breakfast in which a hefty number of the *beau monde* was invited and subsequently attended.

Throughout the breakfast, she wove fanciful tales for the guests' amusement of her time at the orphanage and her discovery of her identity. She had whispered to him later that she discovered her identity indeed — a woman capable of any feat. The most remarkable, in his opinion, was that all through the breakfast, she had smiled, and the whole world smiled back.

During their wedding night, a sacred memory to him, she had given a pretty speech before he had swept her into his arms.

With her cropped hair fanning about her shoulders, dressed in a deliciously laced and silken nightdress, she had said to him between sips of wine, "I am proud of who I am, I'll have you know. I owe it to my mother who risked all to raise me as her own. I owe it to my other mother who risked all to birth me, keep me, and then save me before her death. I owe it to my brother who suffered unspeakable horrors because of my supposed death. I owe it to Lizbeth who searched high and low for me to save Sebastian from the depths of despair. I owe it to you for loving me as I am. And I owe it to myself. I *am* happy. Not contented, mind. Happy. Deliriously so. Maybe it's not fashionable to appear happy, but I want the world to know my love for you and my love for life."

He listened with raised brows and a tapping foot, eager to get on with the undressing. There was no doubt in his mind she was happy, though she could not possibly be happier than he.

Ah, but his attention should be on the present, not the past. He stood at Lilith's side under the bright rays of the sun, toasting to the grand opening of both Colling Orphanage and Noach Cottage, the joint effort of Baron and Baroness Collingwood.

Annick raised his arms, twirled his baton dramatically, and cued the symphony. The music had been written by the duke especially for the event.

Only a small crowd was invited to celebrate, making it more special for all in attendance. A few guests came from London, a few more from Devonshire, but most importantly, his entire family attended.

Lizbeth, cradling her son, stood with Hazel and Mr. Trethow, pointing to the soon-to-be foundling hospital.

Roddam walked over, a bright-eyed Freya perched on his hip. Shaking Walter's hand, he said, "Well done, Collingwood. Well done. You're setting a new precedence for the care of society's unwanted. May the world take notice."

Freya, dressed in a fashionable baby bonnet and matching poppy-red dress, clapped her hands in approval.

Walter turned to his wife only to realize she was no longer by his side.

Ah. There, frolicking in the most unladylike manner alongside Jasper, was his wife. With a quick bow to Roddam, he hurried after her. He had the impression he would be romping after her free spirit for the remainder of their lives. The thought had him smiling throughout the opening ceremony.

The next evening, while snuggling in the lord's chamber at Trelowen, he propped himself on an elbow and looked down at her. "Well, my love? How do you like it?" he asked, running his finger down the length of her nose.

"Hmm. Maybe we should do it again so I know to assess it properly."

He threw back his head and laughed. "I meant Tre-lowen, silly goose! How do you like your new home?"

"Oh!" She blushed. "It's perfect. I loved it at first sight. If I had come last year, I would have thought it too grand. After Roddam Hall, this home is the perfect size. And the garden, Walter! Oh, the garden." Leaning her cheek against his chest, she sighed.

"If you're good, I'll let you help me work a quarter of the herb garden."

"If I'm — a quarter! Of all the —" She harrumphed indignantly.

With a kiss to the tip of her nose, he said, "And if your herbs grow faster than mine, I'll reward you with a kiss at the top of the Yew tree."

She huffed, grumbling about unfair advantage that he sowed his herbs earlier in the year.

"I have a better idea," he said. "How about a hon-eymoon to that cottage by the sea?"

"You remembered my dream," she said, nuzzling against him.

Running his fingers through her hair, he con-fessed, "Actually, I was thinking about how much I want to hold you with the backdrop of the ocean."

"Mmm. I like this idea. And Jasper can come?"

Walter nodded, imagining with chagrin the fre-quency with which the spoiled pup would interrupt their intimate moments.

"Now we know what it's like to live happily ever after," he said.

"Happy for now at least," she argued.

"Nonsense. Envision the big picture, my love. It's happy forever because no matter what adversity we face, no matter what disagreement we have, no matter what hardships, we'll have each other and weather the storm together."

She rolled onto her side and wrapped an arm over his shoulder.

"You're right, of course. Happy ever after, then. But first, show me the big picture of how much we belong together."

With a chuckle, he rolled onto his back, pulling her with him.

A Note from the Author

Dear Reader,

Thank you for reading this book. Supporting indie writers who brave self-publishing is important and appreciated. I hope you'll continue reading my novels, as I have many more titles to come. To learn more about the era, traditions, etiquette, and more, consider visiting my research blog, a new post added every one to three months: www.paullettgolden.com/bookresearch.

I humbly request you review this book with an honest opinion in as many venues as possible, be it Goodreads, Amazon, or otherwise.

One way to support writers you've enjoyed reading, indie or otherwise, is to share their work with friends, family, book clubs, etc. Lend books, share books, exchange books, recommend books, and gift books, be it personally, to a library, in a Free Little Library, or to a secondhand bookshop. If you especially enjoyed a writer's book, lend it to someone to read in case they might find a new favorite author in the book you've shared.

Connect with me online:
www.paullettgolden.com
www.facebook.com/paullettgolden
www.instagram.com/paullettgolden
www.twitter.com/paullettgolden

You'll also find me at such places as Goodreads, Bookbub, Amazon's Author Central, and LibraryThing.

All the best,
Paullett Golden

If you enjoyed *The Baron and The Enchantress*, read on for a sneak peek of the next book in The Enchantresses.

The Colonel and The Enchantress

Teaser from 2019 edition

Prologue

1790
Five years ago

S tretching out his legs, Duncan Starrett lay across the picnic blanket, his forearm sinking into the dewy grass beneath. His eyes met those of his love's, wide, walnut brown, framed with black lashes against alabaster skin. For nearly a year he had loved her, yet one look still made his pulse race.

"I want to come with you," she said, brushing silken fingers against his cheek.

"I'll return before you notice I've gone; a decorated hero worthy of your hand."

She pleaded with sorrowful eyes.

"The battlefield is no place for you, Mary. How could I fight for crown and country when worrying about your safety? Not that your family would ever consent for you to follow the drum."

"Oh, Duncan, let's elope! It would be so romantic!" Wistful, she clasped her hands, looked to heaven, and fell back against the blanket with a sigh.

Tree branches danced shadows on her features. His heart beat with quickened pace as he leaned over her, tracing her lips with his fingertips. Leaving her behind would be the most difficult task of his life. His Mary. His love.

"Dream of my return," he said. "We'll attend the best parties, dance until our feet blister, and ride into the sunset on our fastest horses. Once I return, I'll ask your brother for your hand."

She combed her fingers through his hair, sending shivers from scalp to toes. Pulling him to her, she kissed him, a gentle pout of moist lips pursed to his.

"We've lingered too long," he murmured, lost in the depths of her eyes. "Go home before you're missed."

As an ensign in the Light Dragoons, Duncan saw more ballrooms than battlefields, easy to do when there were no battles. He craved the clash of swords and thunder of guns. After a childhood filled with his father's romantic war stories, Duncan longed to experience the scenes for himself: hiking impossible hills, meeting the enemy with sword drawn, wading through rivers, sleeping beneath the stars. In the quiet of the night, he brandished his sabre at the darkness, practicing his moves, striking a dashing pose.

1791. Lieutenant Starrett had yet to see war. Was this his route to heroism? Was he fated to return home, an officer who had never drawn his sword?

Days turned to weeks, weeks to months, months to years.

The French were at war with themselves, launching a revolution against their monarchy. The British Army remained idle, waiting. Waiting for what? An opportune moment to fight? Duncan wanted to fight now. For too long he had waited for action. He recalled the promises made when his father purchased his first commission—the crown would take advantage of France's weakness. When was this grand takeover? His blade was sharp, his gun clean.

1793. Captain Starrett ached with desperation to prove himself. If the dragoons could not bring him to war, perhaps a foot regiment could.

And war he found. Or rather, war found him.

The daring! The glory! The action exhilarated him. He roared into battle, a fierce foe, his heart in his throat, his body tingling with excitement tinged with fear. He fought for his life, for his country, for his father, for Mary. In this moment, he was man. Raw power, passionate and invigorated, victory red.

Arrogant and foolhardy, he thought himself debonair, a real hero.

The elation of battle pulsing through his veins, he wrote to Mary. He could not very well return after wielding his sword only once. He wanted more. He thirsted for more. What was another couple of years after the four he spent waiting? It was not as though he would never return.

1794. Major Starrett dabbed the tender skin of his stomach with a wet cloth. The blade he faced had come too close for comfort. Only now did he realize how close, having sliced through his waistcoat and grazed his skin. The more superficial, the more troubling. He winced with each stroke of the cloth.

However safe at camp he was, the apprehension of more bloodshed pumped a buzz in his ears. The morning would see fighting renewed. His limbs were clammy from the cold sweat all too familiar both post- and pre-battle. Today was both. Tonight, he would dream of holding Mary, inhaling the aroma of her lavender-scented hair, savoring the feel of her velvet skin.

Summer 1794. He trudged with throbbing feet, overwrought muscles, and pounding head, disillusioned by war. Lost were his dreams in a sea of red, bathed in the glow of regimental coats mingled with blood. This was not glamorous. This was not heroic. This was a horror show of vacant stares and flashing steel. No longer did he crave the battlefield with its death and guilt. He was Charon, ferrying sons from their mothers and husbands from their wives.

And yet, he still craved the valor, the camaraderie, the rhythm of the drums, the sounds and smells of gallantry.

Autumn 1794. Lieutenant-Colonel Starrett of the Light Dragoons led his men into battle from atop a stallion. British, Dutch, and Austrian troops launched against the French, a proper invasion of a weakened and ruler-less country. With sabre at the ready, he leaned forward and squeezed his thighs to the hot horseflesh, signaling his mount to charge. The formation was tight, mere inches between cavalry riders. A roar of power erupted as they broke through infantry lines, slashing an opening for the foot regiments.

There was no greater feeling than a horse beneath him, an inseverable bond between beast and man. Only his legs and weight signaled his horse's movements, for his hands wielded weapons of war rather than reins. His horse, Caesar, was an extension of himself.

Boxtel was a fierce and bloody battle, but Duncan was untouchable atop his stallion.

1795. Colonel Starrett shivered. More men had died from exposure than battle, a harsher winter they had not seen. With white clouds for breath, they prepared to defend the frozen waters of the Lower Rhine. The horse pawed the iced earth, ready. He stroked Caesar's neck, his hand trembling.

The enemy lined the opposite bank, muskets aimed, bayonets fixed.

Signaling his regiment, Duncan drew his sabre, the taste of blood on his tongue, the smell of fear in his nostrils. Time slowed. Seconds stretched to infinity between spur and charge.

The cavalry hoofed alongside their field commander, an impenetrable wall of horse muscle and blades. The enemy marched across the frozen water, the Holy Spirit on their side. Duncan's attention funneled. He knew only the hoofbeats of his horse, the song of bullets, and his steady breath.

Steel clanged and men cried as cavalry broke the line at the river bank. A moment of victory before it all went wrong. Another line crossed the river, muskets aimed, bayonets fixed. Another line behind them. And another. His regiment, decimated by the cold, chattered teeth along the river's edge as they watched the endless onslaught of Frenchmen.

Retreat! The cry echoed through the ranks, the survivors running or fighting their way back to safety.

Duncan, his hands wielding weapons in defense, nudged Caesar to about-face. Without further encouragement, the horse turned and retreated, the whole of the allied troops doing likewise.

His one thought—get the men to safety.

A soundless slap to his lower back broke his focus. He looked to either side, expecting to see one of his men. Leaning forward to quicken the pace away from the river, he felt a tightening pressure along his spine, warming as it twisted, a fire poker sinking into his flesh then tugging.

The scorch spread, hot and wet.

As he straightened, slowing his mount, he felt winded, the air knocked out of his lungs. He panicked, struggling to breathe.

Before him, arm outstretched, hovered an ethereal Mary. His Mary. His lady love. Even as he reached out to her, his head swam in a dizzying vortex. Their fingers touched as he slumped against Caesar's neck.

About the Author

Celebrated for her complex characters, realistic conflicts, and sensual portrayal of love, Paullett Golden
writes historical romance for intellectuals. Her novels,
set primarily in Georgian England, challenge the
genre's norm by starring characters loved for their
imperfections and idiosyncrasies. The writing aims
for historical immersion into the social mores and
nuances of Georgian England. Her plots explore
human psyche, mental and physical trauma, and personal convictions. Her stories show love overcoming
adversity. Whatever our self-doubts, *love will out*.

Paullett Golden completed her post-graduate
work at King's College London, studying Classic
British Literature. Her Ph.D. is in Composition and
Rhetoric, her M.A. in British Literature from the

Enlightenment through the Victorian era, and her B.A. in English. Her specializations include creative writing and professional writing. She has served as a University Professor for nearly three decades and is a seasoned keynote speaker, commencement speaker, conference presenter, workshop facilitator, and writing retreat facilitator.

As an ovarian cancer survivor, she makes each day count, enjoying an active lifestyle of Spartan racing, powerlifting, hiking, antique car restoration, drag racing, butterfly gardening, competitive shooting, and gaming. Her greatest writing inspirations, and the reasons she chose to write in the clean historical romance genre, are Jane Austen and Charlotte Brontë.

Connect online
paullettgolden.com
Facebook.com/paullettgolden
Twitter.com/paullettgolden
Instagram.com/paullettgolden